The Rowan Tree
A Novel

Robert W. Fuller

Cover design by Gordan Blazevic.

ISBN: 1481810308
ISBN-13: 978-1481810302

To Claire Sheridan

Man is a creature who makes pictures of himself
And then comes to resemble the picture.
  – Iris Murdoch

CONTENTS

COMMENCEMENT

May, 1990

"Dr. Rowan Ellway ... "

The sound of her voice brought him to his feet. Even after all these years, he knew the invocation by heart: " ... in the name of Jefferson College, and by virtue of the powers vested in me, I confer this degree upon you with all the rights and privileges thereunto appertaining." Easter unfurled the silk-lined velvet hood, raised it over his head, and placed it around his neck.

Her official letter, with its offer of an honorary degree, had reached him two months earlier at the American Embassy in Moscow. Clipped to it was a note, handwritten on cream vellum embossed with the initials ERB. Although the scent was faint, Rowan recognized it as her fragrance. Rubbing his finger back and forth over the raised letters like a blind man, he had read it again and again:

> Dear Rowan,
>
> I do hope you will accept this overdue honor. I look forward to seeing you after all these years. Please drop by the President's House after the ceremony, say around nine.
>
> As ever,
> Easter

BOOK I

EASTER BLUE

PART 1

A SMILING PUBLIC MAN

1970–1972

… the children's eyes
In momentary wonder stare upon
A sixty-year-old smiling public man.
  – William Butler Yeats, *Among School Children*

CHAPTER 1

May, 1970

He let himself into their Upper West Side apartment and listened for Sara. Though no sounds or sights revealed her presence, after five years of married life, Rowan could sense when she was home. As he hung his coat in the hall closet, her muffled voice reached him from the kitchen.

"I'll be right out."

He took his usual spot on the sofa and scanned the room. Orange crates still held their college books, but a Tiffany lamp that Sara had bought to celebrate his move to the dean's office at Columbia hung over a worn easy chair. He took off his shoes and inched his feet across the coffee table, nudging aside a stack of Sara's professional journals to accommodate his long legs.

"Champagne, Mr. President," Sara intoned as she entered the room bearing a tray with two crystal flutes. She was wearing a lime green miniskirt and a T-shirt. She still looked more like the student he'd fallen in love with six years earlier than the chemistry professor she'd become.

"Wow! Mumm's Red Label, and new glasses. You splurged."

A fly-on-the-wall observer would have noticed that Gumby had his rubbery arms wrapped around the neck of the bottle and was clinging to it for dear life. But this did not call for comment from Rowan. The green doll had seen them through their marriage, serving as a kind of mascot or witness. Sara, who'd acquired Gumby in college, orchestrated his appearances: Gumby sitting in the freezer wearing a tiny muffler; Gumby crawling out of the bathroom cabinet ...

"We can afford good champagne now," Sara said, undoing Gumby's grip. By the way, your mother called, gushing. She's so proud—her son, a college president! I'm sure she'll make the most of it with her friends."

"By Christmas she'll be asking when I'm moving to Harvard. Her ambitions know no bounds." He frowned, hesitated, and looked directly at Sara. "Does the bubbly mean you accept the role of Jefferson's first lady?"

She handed him the bottle. "Until the butler arrives, you'll have to do cork service," she said, ignoring his question. As he removed the cork she plopped down at her end of the sofa. Their champagne fizzing, they swiveled to face each other.

Just as their feet were about to meet in the middle, Sara jumped up and ran to the kitchen. "Oh, thank god I haven't burned the pizza," he heard.

She returned with two plates, each holding half of what twenty minutes earlier had been a frozen pepperoni pie. In one flowing movement she settled back into her spot and handed Rowan his half.

He knew from experience that she would answer questions that were hanging between them when she was ready. After delicately biting off the tip of a slice, she asked, "Did you tell the trustees I won't be living on campus?"

"When I mentioned your NYU job, one of the men asked how often you'd be at Jefferson. Before I could answer, another trustee jumped in. She said her husband spends weekdays in Washington and stays in Manhattan on weekends. That seemed to satisfy them."

"My life is none of their business," Sara said emphatically. "You know I support you 100 percent, but they're hiring Dr. Ellway, not me. If they expect me to play hostess they're going to be disappointed."

"They don't see the president's wife serving tea and cookies to students, but ..."

"But, what?"

"Look, I know you'll do Jefferson students more good as a role model teaching at NYU than you would serving tea at Jefferson, but the trustees will be disappointed if you're never around."

8

He reached for one of her feet, still calloused from her ballet days, and began to rub it. "And so will I."

Sara made as if to pull her foot back and bury it between the sofa cushions. "You don't have to do that," she said in what he recognized as a ritual protest. "They're so ugly."

Until her late teens, she had devoted herself to ballet with the same single-minded passion she now brought to chemistry. But by the time she'd left high school it was clear that her knees would not withstand a dance career.

As always, his touch calmed her, but after a few minutes she tucked the foot he'd been rubbing under her free leg, and he slipped his empty hand between the cushions.

"We'll survive this," she said, draining her glass. "Your being off at Jefferson isn't that big a deal. It will make weekends together special."

"You could come out Friday evenings and return late Sunday. It's only an hour's flight to Michigan."

"Sure, but won't you be in New York regularly on business?"

"Yeah, there's a monthly meeting of the Investment Committee. Anyway, you're right, we're not poor anymore, so travel's no problem. They're doubling my Columbia salary, and we get a free house, a mansion actually, plus a cook and a housekeeper."

"Wow! Bring the cook along when you come." Sara hated cooking. She always said that chemistry had all the recipes she could stand in her life. "Is it really a mansion?" she asked him.

"You'll see," Rowan said, wondering if the stately, ivy-covered Georgian manor would prove a drawing card.

"I can't wait to see it." Rowan refilled their glasses, and when they'd drained the bottle he reached for her, and she yielded to his pull.

§§§

Rowan invariably woke up first. When he rose from the rumpled bed the next morning, he glanced down at Sara, still asleep, her long auburn hair spread across the pillow. Wide-set eyes, full cheeks, and a petite nose combined to give her face a pleasing symmetry. But what held his gaze was her earnest look. Even when she was asleep, she always seemed full of purpose. Indeed, what had first caught his eye was the determined way she strode across the Columbia campus. Spotting her at the chemistry building one morning, he contrived to run into her that afternoon at the department's daily tea. Only after they'd begun dating, and she'd told him about her dancing days, did he connect the elegant way she carried herself with her ballet training.

Losing her childhood dream had strengthened her resolve to succeed at science, and she'd clawed her way to the top of a field ruled by men. He was proud of her.

Rowan set out a multivitamin and a glass of orange juice for Sara and was wondering whether toasting the last of the bagels would freshen it when the phone rang. It was Wilfred Knight, the kinetic chairman of Jefferson's Board of Trustees, calling from his command post in a mid-Manhattan skyscraper.

"Your visit to the College is set. We've booked you solid."

"I'm looking forward to getting started."

"Jefferson's due for an overhaul. That's why we chose you. Oh, before I forget, there's one small formality."

"What's that?"

"Barring unforeseen developments, the board expects you to serve at least five years. And, for the record, I must remind you that presidents serve at the pleasure of the board. You understand, I'm sure."

"I understand."

"You wanted to meet some more students. I've arranged a welcoming party at the airport."

"Good," Rowan said, relieved to be done with the formalities.

"Call me when you get back. I want to hear your impressions."

§§§

The call had roused Sara. As she padded down the hall he took the bagel out of the toaster, quickly spread it with cream cheese, and served it to her as she sat down.

Looking skeptical, she washed down the vitamin with a sip of orange juice, stared at the bagel, shifted around in her chair, and looked up at Rowan.

"There's one thing we didn't talk about last night. The clock's ticking, Rowan. If all goes well and I get tenure, then there will only be a few more years for me to get pregnant."

They'd been over this ground many times, not as antagonists but as partners. "That was Knight on the phone. He expects me to serve five years, but after four they won't care if I leave."

"But I'll be almost forty by then."

"Maybe when you're settled at NYU we could get a nanny and manage somehow."

"It's no good raising a baby with Daddy a million miles away."

Rowan was looking into an abyss. He sat down and reached across the table for Sara's hand. "Last night I lay awake thinking about not seeing each other from Monday to Friday ..."

Sara sat up straight. "I've got to be in the lab, or else. Without my career, I'd just be Mrs. Rowan Ellway."

Sara had always dreaded turning into her mother, who'd given up a career in biology to raise a family. If Rowan ever wavered in his support for her career, a holiday dinner with her family was all it took to remind him how the bitterness of unrealized ambition can poison a marriage.

"It's just that, well, it's beginning to hit me what being alone out there is going to be like; all the socializing ... you're so much better at parties than I am."

Rowan loved engaging with people one-on-one, but chitchat made him uncomfortable. At cocktail parties he'd feel that while one part of him made small talk another part was watching from a distance, judging him a phony.

"Oh, they're gonna love you," Sara said, leaning over and kissing his forehead. "Just try to smile more, you're too serious."

"That's the problem with this job. You have to put on a happy face like that 'sixty-year-old smiling public man' in the Yeats poem I showed you. I'd rather be dead than act like that."

11

"If you leave after four years, you'll only be thirty-seven."

"That would leave us enough time to start a family, don't you think?"

"Might be pushing our luck."

"Well, we've been lucky so far, plus you're so healthy and fit."

"There's no evidence that fitness extends fertility," Sara said. "I've looked into it. But what about you? What do you see yourself doing after Jefferson?"

"What concerns me most about this move is that, in just a few years, physics will have passed me by. Nobody's going to want me."

"I'm not worried about you. You've always had plenty of ideas."

§§§

A few days later, cramped into an economy seat, Rowan flew to Jefferson for his début as president-elect. Columbia students had already resorted to force in pressing their demands for a say in University affairs. Jefferson's students had not yet turned their fury on the College itself; his honeymoon at Jefferson could be brief.

Old President Jacoby and his wife had tried to appease Jefferson's students by offering them refreshments in the President's House. When he had refused to address their demands, they had stormed out. The next day the college paper had run an editorial calling for the president's resignation. Mystified and hurt, Jacoby had called Chairman Knight for moral support. But when Knight had asked him how he planned to respond to student complaints, Jacoby's only idea was to hold a teach-in on civility.

As the head of a global foundation, Knight had his finger on the national pulse; this was not the first time Jacoby had turned a tin ear to calls for change, and Knight had had enough. He had little trouble persuading his fellow trustees to offer Jacoby a nice retirement package and seek new leadership for the College. Rowan had learned these details from Knight himself at a lunch in his private dining room at foundation headquarters. Over dessert, Knight asked him the same question he'd asked Jacoby: How would you address student grievances?

Rowan had said they could no longer be treated like kids. They were young adults, and colleges had to recognize it. What's more, when it came to civil rights and women's rights and student rights, the young were on the side of history. It was their elders—professors, administrators, and trustees—who had to change.

He knew that Jefferson was looking for a new president but he wasn't concerned about offending Knight; if the board saw the job as mollifying students, he didn't want it. Rowan's answer evidently had met with Knight's approval because, within the week, he'd been invited to campus to meet with the presidential search committee.

He was aware that in normal times his stint as a dean at Columbia wouldn't have qualified him for a college presidency. Presiding over a campus was a job traditionally given to seasoned older men. But these were not normal times—campuses everywhere were erupting.

During his search committee interview, one thing had come up again and again: While he was teaching physics at Columbia, Rowan had also taught science in a predominately black Harlem high school. Jefferson's white liberals couldn't get enough of it. They seemed to want to believe that, when it came to race, he was a step ahead of them.

For two full days, trustees, administrators, professors, and students had grilled him, not only on race, but on all the hot-button issues of the time: the status of women, dormitory life, educational policy, and governance. At the final committee interview, the chairman led off.

"We've been grilling you all day, Dr. Ellway. Do you have any questions for us?"

"They all boil down to one: Are you serious about reform?" Rowan paused to let this sink in. "When I was a student here fifteen years ago, Jefferson shaped my worldview. But lately, I've thought that the College has become a defender of the status quo. Unless you're serious about reform, I'm not your man. My first act would be to appoint a commission to examine our strengths and weaknesses and draw up proposals for some far-reaching changes."

"You'll get no objections from the board," Knight interjected. Rowan knew that in Knight, he had a formidable ally, but he also knew that many key reforms would require the approval of the faculty.

"But will I get your active support?" Rowan looked directly at the student and faculty delegations. "Reform is not easy and it's not cheap. For example, achieving ethnic diversity at Jefferson will require more counseling and tutoring and more scholarship money, and that means changing our priorities." Several students nodded.

"For starters," Rowan said, glancing at Knight, "I'd expect the board to take special action to increase the College budget for these items for the current fiscal year and for every year thereafter."

The inquisition was over; it was now a courtship. Even before Rowan had left campus, Knight told him that he had conducted a straw poll, and the job was his if he wanted it.

As a dean at Columbia, it had riled him to watch his superiors try to placate students who wanted reforms with nothing but cosmetic fixes. Jefferson seemed eager for fundamental change, and he'd promised himself that if he ever got the chance, he'd take no half-measures. Now, to his astonishment, that chance was his. His doubts about the job dissolved—he wanted it. He phoned Sara to tell her the news. She said she was happy for him. For an instant, he wished she were happy for *them*, but he had long since accepted the reality that he had his passions, and Sara had hers.

CHAPTER 2

"Hello, President Ellway. I'm Easter Blue," she said, offering her hand.

"Hello," he replied. "Thanks for meeting me."

"This is Robin Star ... and Victor Pao," Easter indicated two students a half-step behind her. "We're here to welcome you on behalf of the student body of Jefferson College."

"I appreciate the welcoming party," he said, wondering if her Afro was soft or scratchy to the touch.

"Congratulations on your appointment," Robin said, drawing up to his side. She had red hair and freckles and, like Easter, wore an ankle-length skirt. But there the similarity ended. Easter's skirt was a sophisticated African print that emphasized a voluptuous figure; Robin's was a tie-dyed souvenir of the Summer of Love and gave no hint of curves beneath it.

"You still look like your yearbook photo," Robin gushed.

"We'll take you to the Jefferson Inn," Easter said. "There's a drop-in at the College cafeteria tonight and an open forum in the chapel tomorrow afternoon. Afterward, the Black Caucus is expecting you for dinner."

Victor, who spoke English with a trace of a Chinese accent, insisted on carrying Rowan's bag. As they approached the car, he asked the president-elect, "How does it feel to be back?"

"Ask me in a few days. I expect a lot has changed."

"Not everything, thankfully," Victor said, his formal manner echoing his tie and jacket.

"Are the students as studious as ever?"

"Absolutely," Victor replied with unmistakable pride. Rowan looked sideways at Robin and caught her sarcastic grin.

En route to the inn, Easter steered the conversation deftly as she navigated the country roads. At Jefferson's town limits, Rowan became aware of his mounting anticipation. He'd taken this road into Jefferson scores of times as a student, and now he was returning to campus as president-elect. Suddenly, wailing sirens interrupted his reverie. Police cars were racing toward a swarm of people in front of the administration building on the far side of Jefferson Square. Easter parked the car at the inn, and Robin and Victor hopped out.

"What's going on?" Robin called to a passing cyclist.

"We've taken two Army recruiters hostage."

"I heard this might happen," Robin said. "I don't know about you guys, but my place is over there." Without so much as a backward glance, she raced off toward the campus.

"Robin!" Easter called after her. Exasperated, she turned to Rowan and apologized, trying to be a dutiful hostess.

Rowan, peering through the trees, could just make out the lettering on a huge banner: JEFFERSON FOR PEACE AND JUSTICE, as the sounds of the crowd rose and fell like a howling storm, punctuated by honking horns. His mind was racing; joining a student antiwar protest was no way to make his first appearance, but retreating to the inn wouldn't do either. He had to free himself of his student hosts.

He turned to Easter. "You go ahead. I'll register and then come have a look."

Easter looked relieved. "Are you sure? We were supposed to show you around."

"It seems our agenda has changed."

She flashed him an approving smile and headed toward the mélee, calling over her shoulder, "I'll come for you at six."

Victor had taken Rowan's bag to the inn. Catching up with him, Rowan said, "Don't you want to join the others?"

"Frankly, no, I do not support these demonstrations. My parents came here as refugees from China. College students have no idea what Asian communism is really like."

Victor left Rowan's suitcase in the care of a bellhop and took off. Rowan noticed that he headed away from the fracas. The bellhop, recognizing that in Rowan he had a captive audience, seized the opportunity to denounce the demonstrators.

"Military service used to be a badge of honor. These kids treat us vets like we're the enemy."

Rowan nodded ambiguously and picked up his bag, insisting that he carry it to his room himself. After he changed into a clean shirt, he set out across the square to discover his new life.

Halfway across the green, he mounted the steps of a gazebo for a better view of the demonstration. From his perch he could see dozens of students violently rocking a vehicle bearing an Army insignia. More students locked arms in a larger circle to block the advance of helmeted police brandishing truncheons. Numbering only a dozen, and facing an incensed mob, the police seemed to think better of assaulting them, and retreated. Minutes later he heard tear gas canisters detonating, and saw clouds of smoke waft over the crowd. From his experience at Columbia, he knew to keep his distance. Before long, the uniformed recruiters abandoned their surrounded vehicle and staggered into the protective embrace of the police.

Wandering incognito around the periphery of the battlefield, Rowan could see paramedics in gas masks giving oxygen to students overcome by fumes. He heard the mournful sound of sirens in the distance as he made his way back across Jefferson Square to sanctuary in the inn. Good god, he thought, what have I gotten myself into?

§§§

Precisely at six that evening, the phone rang.

"We're here," Easter said. "Shall I come up and fetch you?"

"No need, I'll be right down."

As he stepped off the elevator a half-dozen students leaped to their feet. He went around the circle shaking hands while, at his side, Easter introduced each one. The group walked across the town square, and into the cafeteria where the smell of greasy food displaced the lingering traces of tear gas. His little posse accompanied him to a large table where students were boisterously rehashing the day. Easter hushed them and introduced Rowan. Robin led

17

off by asking what he thought of the demonstration. All eyes fell on the president-elect.

"I'm not speaking for the College," he began, to an audible sigh of disappointment, "but once I take office I intend to argue my *personal* position that this war is unwise, unjust and unwinnable." He paused to let this sink in. "And that the sooner American troops are withdrawn, the better."

There was a burst of applause from all over the cafeteria. Turning to face the gathering crowd, he said, "I'll elaborate on my views tomorrow at the open forum, but tonight, I'd like to hear what you think." His invitation unleashed a torrent. One after another, students held forth, on co-ed dorms, racial diversity, the draft, town-gown relations, inflexible requirements, and on having no say in College governance. They were so grateful to be heard that there were no more questions.

Rowan would have been there all night if, just before midnight, Easter hadn't climbed up on a chair, waved her hands for quiet, and called out, "Aren't we going to let President Ellway get some sleep? He has a full day tomorrow." Rowan took the opportunity to offer her a supporting hand as she stepped down. Instead of immediately letting go she gave it a tug, and headed for the exit, clearing a path through the throng for the two of them.

Outside, as they made their way toward Jefferson Square, the chapel bell began to sound the hour. Rowan silently counted off nine chimes, then finished the count aloud: "ten, eleven, twelve." Turning to Easter at the stroke of midnight, he asked, "Were you afraid I'd turn into a pumpkin?"

"By this time tomorrow, you may wish you had," she said. "You turned the tables on us tonight, but tomorrow the Black Caucus is going to insist on hearing your views."

"I'll be ready. But enough politics for tonight. Do you mind if I ask you a personal question?"

"Not at all."

"Your plans? Your goals?"

18

The silence that followed made him wonder if he'd over-stepped. Finally, she said, "You mean what do I want to be when I grow up?"

"Something like that."

"Oddly, I've never felt like a kid, even when I was one. Perhaps it's because my father always took me seriously, even when I was little. He's a history professor at the University of Chicago. After I graduate, I want to explore Africa and then specialize in African history, probably at Oxford."

"Any particular focus?"

"As a matter of fact, yes. I want to study the slave trade—how my people got here—and I want to understand not just who bought them but who sold them."

"*That* is an interesting question."

"Why do you think so?"

"Because it's not just a race question, it's a human question."

"I thought you might understand."

They chatted easily as they crossed the square. It was so dark below the canopy of elms that they felt the need to visually confirm each other's presence in the occasional pools of light under the lamp-posts. When they reached the inn, Easter said, "Tomorrow you'll be meeting Bill Stone—he's the Caucus chairman. He's graduating on Sunday. Bill can be a bit ... well, blunt."

"Are you trying to warn me?"

"Maybe."

"Don't worry. To win faculty support, we'll need both militants and moderates."

"Exactly," she replied, extending her hand. He reached out and shook it.

"Good-night, Easter," he said. "Thanks for taking care of me tonight."

"My pleasure," she replied, and turned to cross the dark square. As he watched her form recede, he imagined her as an ally in the battles to come, and he couldn't picture her being on the losing side.

§§§

Rowan awoke to a gray, soggy day and found that the battery in his shaver was dead. Normally, he tried to do something else while he mindlessly ran the Norelco over his face, but with a spare razor he had to monitor the task. He was not one for mirror gazing. He'd weigh himself occasionally, but apart from that, he was indifferent to his appearance. Asked to describe himself, he'd have been hard put to say more than that he had a long face, blue eyes, and light-brown hair that refused to lie flat on one side of his part. He'd recognize himself in photos, but less from his facial image than from remembering the occasion on which the photos had been taken.

The novelty of looking at himself in the mirror brought Sara to mind. She took far more interest in his appearance than he did. He'd barely thought of her since he'd arrived, but now he remembered her advice—that a little humor would ease things with the faculty. None of his limitations had caused him more trouble than what she called his "irony deficiency."

Distracted, he nicked his chin. He rinsed off the reddening suds, dressed quickly, and took the elevator down, blotting his cut with his handkerchief one last time before stepping out into the lobby. Four professors rose as one to welcome him. The group spokesman was Donald Bentley, chairman of the chemistry department and, of particular interest to Rowan, an ex-boyfriend of Sara's from her undergraduate days at MIT. Rowan was pleased to see that Bentley had developed a paunch in the years since college.

"Welcome back to Jefferson, Dr. Ellway," Bentley declaimed. "On behalf of the faculty, I congratulate you on your appointment. We're here to offer you whatever help we can. Shall we get some breakfast?"

Bentley led the way to a private room in the inn, decorated with floral wallpaper from the forties. A lone potted fig tree stood dying in one corner. Set out on a side table was the same fare—watery orange juice, lukewarm coffee, and greasy eggs—that Rowan remembered from the visit he'd made for his interview.

He'd hardly lifted his cup before Bentley turned to finances. "What can you tell us about your fundraising plans? I presume the board informed you that faculty salaries at Jefferson are barely keeping up with the profession."

Rowan resisted an urge to say what he thought of this question. How could a faculty leader go straight to the issue of compensation in turbulent times like these? To hide his annoyance, he put his arms on the table and made himself lean forward, all ears. Bentley was just warming up.

"The grapevine has it that you pried a million dollars for Columbia out of our own board chairman. Correct me if I'm wrong, but I don't believe we've received a nickel from Mr. Knight's foundation. If I may be so bold, Dr. Ellway, what's your secret?"

"It's no mystery. I simply convinced him that we'd deliver on his investment. If you truly believe in an educational project, funders will too."

That triggered a heated discussion of the merits and demerits of several innovative grant proposals the College had in the works. Without taking sides, Rowan let Bentley know that they were the kind of projects he would go to bat for.

Their time up, Bentley escorted him to his next appointment. Anticipating a solicitous query regarding his wife, Rowan beat him to the punch. "Sara sends her regards. She's at NYU, working around the clock on her research."

"Sounds as if she hasn't changed. Do give her my best." Rowan thought he detected compensatory nonchalance in Bentley's manner. Then, adopting a confidential tone, Bentley added, "I wouldn't want to leave you with a false impression, Dr. Ellway. Some of the reforms you've mentioned have already been discussed by the faculty, and I must say we have not found them compelling. On the contrary, for the most part, they are ill-considered, if not irresponsible. My colleagues are reasonable men. We're willing to debate the issues, but in our opinion the College is in pretty good shape. Getting our votes won't be like shaking ripe fruit off a tree."

Rowan wondered what Sara had ever seen in this prig. If Bentley were actually speaking for the faculty, then winning its approval for his plans was going to be much harder than he'd imagined.

§§§

The benefactor of the new library, George Clay, had insisted on giving the president-elect a guided tour of the half-finished building that would bear his name. With Mrs. Clay trailing behind her husband like an obedient dog, Mr. Clay showed Rowan through every room in the monument he was erecting to himself. From the sundeck on its roof, they had a panoramic view of Jefferson's tidy campus. The clouds had lifted and vapor rose from the groomed athletic fields that lay beyond the nearly completed "Mike" Marlborough Men's Gymnasium, named for the trustee who had provided the funds. Presiding at its dedication would be one of Rowan's first ceremonial tasks as president. When he asked if a tour of the building was on his schedule, he was told that Mr. Marlborough had insisted on showing the president-elect through the gym himself, and was making a special trip in from Detroit the following day to do so.

At the center of campus stood a cluster of limestone buildings overgrown with ivy, all dating from the early twentieth century. These included Seeger Chapel, the College Archives, the Administration Building, which held his future office, and a classroom building topped with a patina-covered copper-domed astronomical observatory. Students moved like columns of ants along sidewalks linking the buildings. Rowan recalled the sting of the winter air on his face during his student years as he'd biked along these paths to early morning classes.

Clay Library was being built on a large lawn adjacent to Walker Gymnasium, an architectural gem and home to the basketball team on which Rowan had played in the fifties. Taking his arm, Clay directed his attention to the old gym. "I thought you ought to know that our bequest for the library is contingent on the removal of Walker Gymnasium, which won't be needed with the new gym. Clay Library merits a panoramic setting, I'm sure you agree."

Some of Rowan's happiest hours had been spent in Walker, so Clay's threat to his dear old gym felt like a blow. By the time he freed himself from the dutiful rigors of smiling at Mr. and Mrs. Clay, his face ached.

§§§

As he picked up his room key at the inn, the desk clerk handed Rowan a note, handwritten on cream vellum embossed in maroon with the initials ERB. It read:

> Jefferson's Black Caucus invites you to a barbecue tonight at six o'clock at Sojourner Truth House.

The note smelled faintly of perfume. It was signed "Easter." Below her signature was a postscript.

> P.S. See you at the forum this afternoon. Good luck.

§§§

Rowan arrived early for the open forum at Seeger Chapel and, keeping his head down, managed to go unrecognized at first. Students were streaming into the cavernous chapel from all directions. A dozen black students sporting Afros sat together in the front row. Easter's long neck made it easy to pick her out of the group. A faculty contingent occupied the last few pews. A few rowdies in the balcony called out to their friends below. As Rowan mounted the stairs to the stage, students sitting on the floor directly below the podium recognized him, and one called out, "Go for it, President Ellway." Their good faith touched him, and he promised himself not to fail them.

Most of the student body was there, come to see the man chosen to replace the one they'd hounded from office. Half a dozen placards poked out of the crowd: ABOLISH DORM VISITING

HOURS; US OUT OF VIETNAM; BLACK IS BEAUTIFUL. NO MILITARY AT JEFFERSON was held aloft by a white student wearing a Lenin cap. The banner proclaiming JEFFERSON FOR PEACE AND JUSTICE, tattered and mud-splattered from the previous day's fracas, was draped along one wall. There were microphones in the aisles, and students were lining up behind them.

Rowan detached the mike from the lectern, walked to center stage, and stood gazing out at the upturned faces. He felt like a gladiator entering the Coliseum. With exams behind them, their final protest registered, and graduation imminent, the students were in a festive mood.

He waited for his audience to hush. The noise level fell, then flared again, but slowly died away until a single cough echoed like a shot from a cannon. Into the silence, Rowan said, "Any questions?"

A student in torn jeans and a Capezio T-shirt spoke into a microphone. "There's a rumor that Walker Gym is going to be demolished to make room for the new library. Dance has nowhere else to go. Is the rumor true, and if so, what are you going to do about it?"

"Razing Walker Gym was apparently part of the deal that's bringing Jefferson the Clay Library. I've spent many happy days in Walker and hope to spend many more. At this point, all I can say is that I have a very hard time picturing Walker's demolition."

A boy on the floor below the stage stood up and, without benefit of the mike, hollered loud enough for all to hear, "Can the food in the College cafeteria be improved?"

After pondering the question for as long as he dared, Rowan deadpanned, No.

Raucous laughter exploded. When it subsided, the same student followed up. "You look too young to be a college president. Are you ready for this job?"

"Same answer." The laughter grew friendlier.

When he addressed a crowd, Rowan invariably felt a part of himself detach from the man at the podium and take up a position overhead, calmly observing the scene below. An hour of robust give-and-take flew by before the moderator stepped in. "We have time for one last question. Even though he's not in line, I know that no one will object if I give Professor Rivers the last word."

"Thank you very much," Rivers began solemnly. From the sudden stillness, Rowan knew this was their spokesperson. "Over the last few years, many of us have spoken out on civil rights and the war in Vietnam. I'd like to ask about the role you see for Jefferson—*as a College*—on these *national* issues."

Rowan was not going to duck this one. "We're at a crossroads," he began, "not just our college, but our country as well. There are several areas where the past can no longer serve as a guide to our future. As a College and as a country we're rethinking the relationship between the races, between the sexes, and between elders and the young.

"I think our College's namesake had it right. If, as Thomas Jefferson said, we are all created equal, then why shouldn't our student body and faculty reflect our nation's diversity? Why shouldn't a college education be as available to the poor as it is to the rich, and as hospitable to women as to men? Why shouldn't students have a say in the way they live and the courses they take?

"The whole country is searching for answers. Only once or twice a century do colleges get a chance to set an example for society, and this is one of those times. Before the year is out, I expect Jefferson to have taken a stand that will make us all proud. We've done it before, and with your help, we will do it again."

§§§

He was on his way out of the chapel when Easter appeared. She gave him a lovely smile and a thumbs-up, but before he could respond, a group of students had cornered him.

As she'd done the previous evening, Easter lingered unobtrusively, then picked the right moment to extricate him from the well-wishers. "The president-elect is expected at Sojourner Truth House in ten minutes," she announced. Instantly, the group bowed to Easter's claim, and she stepped in to lead Rowan off to his rendezvous with the Black Caucus.

As they approached Truth House, Rowan sensed that their conversation, which had seemed like play, had become work. Once inside, she showed him to a seat on the long side of a large oak table, and positioned herself in a chair opposite him that had obviously been held for her. On cue, an intense young man at the head of the table, clad in a traditional dashiki, gaveled the meeting to order.

"Welcome to Truth House, Rowan Ellway. My name is Obea Uhuru and I'm the chairman of Jefferson's Black Caucus. It's our custom to put business before pleasure."

Making a mental note of Bill Stone's name change, Rowan nodded his assent, but Obea, who had the peremptory manner of one accustomed to being heard, was already forging ahead.

"Jefferson's student body is 98 percent white, 1 percent black, and 1 percent other minorities. Apart from a token exception, the faculty is all white. What do you intend to do about that?"

Rowan waited for the murmurs of agreement to subside, then said, "Jefferson has about four thousand students, and we've been graduating about ten blacks a year. If the senior class reflected the racial composition of the country, then it would include at least one hundred minority graduates."

"We're not interested in 'minorities'," Obea interjected. "The Asian and Native Americans can take care of themselves. We're here to speak for our black brothers and sisters."

"What about black faculty?" someone yelled from the far end of the table.

"A president can't make faculty appointments, but he can refuse to forward departmental recommendations to the board if the recruitment process hasn't included black candidates ... "

"We proposed that to your predecessor," Easter interrupted, "and we got no response. Zero." Rowan was startled by the force of her comment. She pushed back her chair and rose to her feet. Eyes blazing, she spelled out her case in a tone that commanded the attention of the room.

"Since I arrived, not one new professor has been black. This is unacceptable. Student admissions are only marginally better. Jefferson says that admissions are color-blind, but the numbers say otherwise. You have to understand, Mr. President, that things can't continue like this."

When confronted at Columbia, Rowan had tended to get defensive, but Easter's indignation was passionate and impersonal. Her tone seemed directed at the institution, rather than at him, and he responded with an equanimity that surprised even himself.

"Do you recall your first impression of Jefferson?" he asked. "Take a moment and remember how you felt. Did you come away from your interview certain that you were wanted here? Or, did you detect some ambivalence in Jefferson's approach to you?"

He looked at each person around the table, but didn't wait for anyone to answer. Looking directly into Easter's eyes, he said, "If we go into black high schools and tell students we want them, if we make them know that the welcome awaiting them at Jefferson is a warm and sincere one, and if they understand that to mean that we'll provide them with all the academic, financial, and emotional support they need, we can make Jefferson a mecca for black students."

He took a deep breath, then continued.

"Word will get out, and within a few years we'll have highly qualified black students clamoring to get in, and topnotch black faculty applying for teaching positions. I'll set an example with the administrative appointments I *do* control as president. There will be at least three new black administrators by Christmas. I'll ask the Black Caucus to interview the candidates and give me your views on their suitability. But understand this: I will make the appointments, not anyone else. Instead of lowering standards, which is what the faculty fears, we're going to surprise everyone by raising them. I don't expect to convince you now, but I am absolutely certain we can do this."

From that point on, though there were some expressions of skepticism, and several stories of promises broken, the Black Caucus adopted a wait and see attitude toward the new president.

When Obea declared the business done, they moved to the patio for the barbecue. Obea draped his arm across Easter's shoulders and, smiling proudly, addressed Rowan, "She's pretty persuasive, don't you agree?"

"You make a good team, but I'm not your opponent."

"We're glad to have a sympathetic ear, but we've got to see results."

Over dinner, Rowan learned that Obea had been born and raised in town, and asked him what it had been like growing up in the College's shadow.

"The College was off-limits to us. It was a castle inside a moat."

"Do college students still work in the public schools?" Rowan recalled his own tutoring in the local elementary school, in a program organized by one of his math professors.

"Just a handful. What we really want is access to the gym and pool. They're hardly used during the summer, just when townies most need something to do."

"I'll look into that," Rowan said, jotting a reminder in a notebook he carried in his breast pocket. He then brought up the subject of the status of women at Jefferson. Easter had plenty to say on this subject, and Obea fell silent. Catching a glum expression on his face and mindful that friction between the civil rights and women's movements was good for neither, Rowan suggested they call it a night.

"I have to go to the art library," Easter said to Obea. "I'll drop Dr. Ellway off at the inn."

"Okay," Obea replied, giving Easter a kiss. As she and Rowan left the patio, he called out after her, "See you back here tonight."

"Obea speaks for all of us," Easter said as she ushered Rowan out. "If the College actually hires some black teachers and admits more black students this year, you'll have our support ... across the board."

"I understand. I'm counting on your help."

Under the first lamppost in the square, Easter said, "It's my turn to ask a question ... okay?"

"Fair enough."

"What's your fondest memory of Jefferson?" The timbre of her voice confirmed that they were off-duty.

Before he could reply they were again hidden from each other by night. He ruled out telling her about the weekend he'd spent with his girlfriend in Niagara Falls, but to impress her with an athletic achievement, he'd have to inflate his modest record. As they passed a lamppost, he landed on a vivid memory. "As a sophomore, I cut class to hitchhike to a Van Gogh exhibit in Toledo, Ohio. I'd never cut a class before, and it felt like a mortal sin. I only did it because I looked up to the guy who had asked me to go with him. Tony Radcliffe was a legend at Jefferson. When Viva Zapata came to town, he dressed up as a revolutionary, rented a white horse, and rode it around campus to promote the film. Tony just wouldn't let me say no. I still think of the corner of College Street and Main, where we hitched our first ride, as a leap that changed my life."

"How?"

"Afterward, I stopped playing it safe."

They had reached the inn. Easter said nothing, but looked up at him pensively. Then she asked if she could stop by and see him when she visited campus in July.

"I'll be disappointed if you don't."

"Till July then. Good-night, Dr. Ellway."

"Good-bye, Easter."

When he reached his room above the square, he went to the window. As Easter crossed the first pool of light, he saw her turn and glance over her shoulder toward the inn.

CHAPTER 3

July, 1970

To her colleagues at NYU Sara played down the role, but in truth, being the president's wife, even in absentia, pleased her. Rowan hoped that her fondness for ceremony might yet find an outlet at gala functions which, several times a year, lit up the President's House. Soon after he got the job, Sara had called Buildings and Grounds about redecorating the residence.

For the first time in his life, Rowan questioned his assumption that to spend money on décor was to waste it. He'd been raised by depression-era parents and absorbed their deprecating attitude toward appearance and style. His two sports jackets were threadbare, he owned one pair of brown shoes, and Sara had pronounced his trousers *baggy*. His only criterion for clothing was serviceability, and it had taxed his wife's patience to badger him into buying a new suit for the interviews at Jefferson.

But as the sixties had unfolded, Rowan came to understand that style played a part in political change. The house they were inheriting was dowdy, like the aging couple who'd occupied it since the fifties. He sensed that modernizing its look might, in a small way, help renew the college culture and spirit.

On moving day, Sara accompanied Rowan to the campus. When the College driver turned into the driveway of the President's House, her face lit up.

"Oh, my God," she said, taking Rowan's arm when they stepped out of the car onto the slate path that led to the front porch.

"I tried to tell you," he said, pleased that she was impressed.

Sara darted off to explore the house, and he headed for the kitchen to see what was in the fridge. To his delight, there was a steaming casserole on the counter.

"I thought you might want lunch," a voice said. He turned around and saw a short, round-faced woman in a bright apron.

"My name is Margaret," she said in a strong clear voice. "I've cooked for the last two presidents." Her tone made it clear that she owned the kitchen.

"Hello, Margaret. I'm Rowan. Sara is upstairs checking things out. As soon as she's had a look, we'd love to have some of your casserole. It looks delicious."

"It's chicken with broccoli. Hope you like it. Shall I set two places in the dining room?" Margaret asked.

"Right there, in the breakfast nook, is good." Rowan pointed to a cozy little alcove flooded with sunlight. He knew instantly it would become his favorite spot in this mausoleum. "I'll get my wife."

The breakfast nook looked out on a long sloping backyard. The casserole was as good as it looked, and Rowan was about to serve himself a second helping when Margaret came up to them.

"You might want to save some room for dessert," she said, setting a bowl of warm peach cobbler on the table. "There's ice cream too."

"It's a masterpiece!" Sara said. "Good thing I won't be around too much; I'd put on weight."

When Margaret withdrew, Sara said, "It's all very regal. I had no idea."

"So you like it?"

"The house has possibilities, but as I suspected, the décor is atrocious. The head of Buildings and Grounds is meeting me here at two."

"Don't break the bank."

"It looks like 1952 in here. Wait till you see what I have in mind."

§§§

A few days later, when Sara left for New York Rowan found himself alone in the mansion except for Margaret's daily comings and goings, weekly visits by a housekeeper, and a seemingly endless parade of craftsmen following through on Sara's plans.

From day one he began dropping in on people—faculty, deans, dorm counselors, groundskeepers, librarians, janitors, cooks, secretaries, coaches, even the men who stoked the College's cavernous coal furnace. To his surprise, many of the people he visited wanted to tell him their secrets. All varieties of personal confessions, skeletons in the closet, tips on the stock market—even scandalous gossip—were pressed on him. Every time he agreed to do something, he made an entry in his breast-pocket notebook, and as soon as he got back to the office he set about fulfilling those promises that required his personal involvement, delegating the others.

During the interview process, Rowan had met Steve Hobson, a young English professor renowned on campus for his course in modern poetry. Hobson had a burly, athletic build, and his rhetorical skill had won him the respect of his faculty peers. Soon after Rowan had arrived, he'd asked Hobson to gather his colleagues for informal discussions over lunch; Hobson was concerned that, by Thanksgiving, Jefferson's antiquated policies might trigger more student protests.

Toward the end of the first lunch, Rowan brought up his plan to establish a commission to review every aspect of College life. A lively older professor with white hair and mischievous eyes seized the opportunity to give him a quick course in the psychology of leadership.

"The faculty is never going to do anything but talk unless there's constant, hands-on leadership. That means chairing your own commission, Mr. President."

"You think so?"

"Even though the faculty holds the legislative authority, that doesn't mean you lack power. Your power lies in what we psychologists call 'transference'—the deference that comes from people mistaking the incumbent for the office. But be warned: it only takes one misstep to break the spell."

"You mean a faux pas … or a political mistake?"

"Anything that makes them see you as merely human, like themselves."

"Well, I am human. We all are."

"Hide it as long as you can. Because, once you disappoint them, they'll blame you not only for your mistake, but also for their loss of enchantment. From then on, things will go downhill."

§§§

Chairman Knight had urged Rowan to pay a courtesy call on John Rideout, a Washington-based attorney and singularly influential College trustee. He'd made his reputation by defending the foreign service officers Senator McCarthy had targeted during the Red Scare. Mr. Clay's call for the demolition of Walker Gym gave Rowan all the reason he needed to consult Rideout, and in early August he found himself in Rideout's sumptuous office, not far from the White House, gazing down at Pennsylvania Avenue.

Rideout began by commending Rowan for his "willingness to bear the burden of service," essentially making it sound as if he were a mere water-carrier, whereas Rowan saw his presidency as an opportunity to make change. Rideout ended his pep talk by asking how he could help.

"I got a call this week from George Clay. He wants to know when we're going to demolish the old gym. He wants my personal guarantee before he'll release the second half of his four-million-dollar bequest for the new library."

Before Rowan could go any further, Rideout exploded. "Jesus, I warned Jacoby about that. That library is Clay's monument to himself, and he'd have given the money regardless. I'll be damned if I'll see Walker Gym sacrificed to that fool's vanity." He paused, reached for a cigar, and passed the humidor to Rowan.

"Like one?"

Rowan eyed the torpedo-sized cigars, recalled a coughing fit induced by a much smaller one he'd once tried, and declined. Rideout then set about lighting up. His jaw was so large that the cigar all but disappeared in his maw. He leaned back in his leather swivel chair, put his shiny black shoes up on the mahogany desk and, taking a puff, calmly inquired, "Tell me, what do the kids think of our old gym?"

"It's home to the dance program now, plus intramural sports."

"And the faculty?"

"Everyone loves the place."

"Okay, here's the plan." Rideout then gave Rowan a lesson in power politics, ending with a jovial, "We've gotta let Clay rape us, but don't worry, we'll give him a good dose of the clap."

§§§

As Easter walked into his office, she struck him as prettier than before. He got up from his desk chair and went around to greet her.

"I hope you're getting some rest this summer," she said, offering her hand. "Things are going to heat up fast once we're all back."

"I'll be ready. Would you like some tea?" On a table behind his desk Rowan kept an electric kettle, a teapot, and several large tins of loose black tea.

"I'd love some."

"What are you doing here on campus? The place is empty."

"Oh, lots of things," Easter replied vaguely. He surmised that she'd come to see Obea.

Rowan poured the tea—amber, earthy, and strong—and suggested she drink it like the British, with a little milk. Noting her plans to study in England after graduation, Easter took his advice.

"Something's just come up and I need your help," Rowan said.

Easter nodded attentively and leaned forward, clearly pleased to be asked.

"You know that Mr. Clay is insisting we tear down Walker."

"That is *so* stupid. Bill—I mean Obea—is up in arms. He says there's no room for intramural sports in the varsity gym."

"Easter, I've been wondering if a little demonstration of affection for Walker Gym could be organized, with media coverage, to persuade Mr. Clay to reconsider. What do you think?"

Easter leaned back and, with a smile that grew broader as she took in his meaning, said "Now *this* could be interesting. Obea was on the football team. He could get the jocks involved."

"Do you know faculty who would participate?"

"Professor Cowper is interested in Jefferson's architectural heritage. He's my honors advisor. I'll sound him out. I can keep your name out of it."

"Yes, that would be best." He thanked her and, jotting his home number on his card, gave it to her, saying, "Call me anytime."

As she stood to leave, he asked, "You're not going to change *your* name, are you?"

"Obea thinks changing 'Easter' to an African name would make a statement."

"What statement?"

"That I'm proud of my roots."

"But 'Easter Blue' already makes a statement. 'Easter' stands for rebirth. And in the French tricolor, 'Blue' stands for *Liberté*. Hard to top that."

"True. Plus, changing my name would upset my parents …"

"Were you born on an Easter Sunday?"

"Yes, but my birthday hasn't fallen on Easter since. It will again some year, far down the road, when I'm old and gray, and…"

"And ready for rebirth," Rowan finished her sentence.

§§§

The following evening was hot and humid. Rowan was in the kitchen when the phone rang.

"Hello, Dr. Ellway?"

"Hi, Easter." He knew her voice instantly.

"I talked to Professor Cowper about the gym and he's going to lead a procession of professors around the building in full academic regalia! And Obea and I had *no* trouble recruiting students."

"When will it happen?"

"The first Friday after school starts. My friends on the paper will make sure TV cameras are there. This demonstration won't go unnoticed, I promise."

"Just don't blow me out of the water. I'll need my political capital later."

"I won't let it get out of hand."

"While it's happening, I'll be with Clay, watching it on TV and asking him to back down."

"This is fun," Easter said. Then, turning serious, "It's apt to be the only demonstration that is … fun, I mean."

"I want to talk to you about what comes next. Are you here for the weekend?"

"I'm leaving first thing tomorrow."

"Do you have time this evening?"

"Sure. Give me half an hour."

§§§

Easter arrived at about eight o'clock wearing a short red halter dress that revealed smooth mocha-colored shoulders. He showed her through the house to the back terrace that looked down a deep lush yard ringed by lilacs and rhododendrons. When they sat down, Rowan told her he intended to appoint four faculty, four students and several deans to a commission on Jefferson's future that he would chair himself.

"Which faculty members? Which students?"

"Steve Hobson has identified some open-minded faculty. I'm hoping you'll help me with the student appointments and serve on the commission yourself."

"Oh! I'd be honored."

He excused himself to get the iced tea and returned holding two tall glasses dripping beads of condensation. As he handed her a glass, she asked, "Is this where you cool off in the evening?"

"When it's this hot I go to the College pool."

"Doesn't it close at six?"

"One of my perks is a master key to the College. That includes the pool. When I was a student you had to swim two laps to graduate."

"Whatever was the point of that?"

"Probably a holdover from the days when colleges aimed to educate—pardon the expression—'the whole man,' body, mind and spirit."

"Sounds rather nineteenth century."

"Well, it terrified my friend Huey Scott. Today, he's Princeton's only black professor. As a student here he ran the fastest quarter mile in the state but he couldn't swim a stroke. I taught him to dog-paddle, and swam along with him so he could meet the requirement and graduate."

"He must be your secret weapon for finding black faculty!"

"That's why I mentioned him." Despite Huey's show of optimism with the Black Caucus, Rowan knew it would be hard to recruit black professors. There still weren't that many candidates, and Ivy League universities could offer higher salaries than a college like Jefferson. If Huey Scott couldn't help him find some black faculty, he didn't know where else he could turn. "I've talked to him and he's already scouting for us," Rowan concluded optimistically.

Easter's smile brought him back. "Do you swim?" he asked.

"My father taught me in the University of Chicago pool. Going there made me feel special, but also guilty. I never once saw another black kid in that pool."

"That reminds me of Obea's idea to open the pool to the town kids. We're going to do that."

"I'm supposed to be at his place now. Would you like to come tell him yourself?"

"Why not? I'll grab my trunks and we can all take a dip afterward."

§§§

Swimming in the College pool made Rowan feel like a student again. He could still perform his old feat of doing two laps underwater, and he was pleased to see relief on Easter's face when he completed the round trip and surfaced in front of her. Obea did not seem impressed.

As if to match his exploit, Easter climbed the diving tower; she stood poised on the board for a moment, concentrating, and he stopped breathing as her svelte body arched through the air in a swan dive.

"Easter and I have been together from the day she got here," Obea announced as she swam to the ladder. "I scare 'em and she charms 'em. A princess, don't you think?"

"Good cop, bad cop?" Rowan ignored the question.

"Exactly. Without Malcolm X, King wouldn't have been effective."

"I take your point, but I don't think scare tactics are what's needed now."

"Lasting change is the objective," Easter added, hanging onto the side of the pool with one hand while she treaded water. She climbed out and sat between them.

Cool for the first time all day, they sat dangling their legs in the water. Rowan was struck by the contrast between the straggly brown hair clinging to his forehead like a damp mop and the tight black curls that crowned their heads.

"Easter and I have been brainstorming how to save the old gym," Obea offered.

"The coalition we're putting together will be a first for Jefferson," Easter continued, directing her remarks to Rowan. "Athletes and artists for Walker Gym."

After driving them back to Obea's apartment, Rowan's mind returned to the image of Easter soaring through the air in her crimson swimsuit. As if to blot it out, he turned on the car radio. "Intense fighting near Da Nang has resulted in heavy American and Vietcong casualties. After evacuation of the wounded, the area was subjected to saturation bombing by a squadron of B-52s." Rowan followed the war closely, but tonight it seemed almost peripheral.

§§§

In bed, he had just turned off the light when the phone rang.

"I thought you were going to call me," Sara said. "Are you coming tomorrow? I tried you earlier and got no answer."

"Sorry, it's later than I realized. I took a dip in the College pool. Yes, I'll be there by four."

"I've missed you. Let's take a walk in Riverside Park."

"Sure, plus dinner and a movie."

"That sounds great."

Rowan closed his eyes. The heat was oppressive, and he threw off the sheet. Although the swim had left him pleasantly fatigued, it was a long time before he fell asleep.

CHAPTER 4

Fall, 1970

The banner headline in *The Jeffersonian* read: "Walker Stands! Clay Crumbles." Below was a photograph of Professor Cowper in his academic gown standing defiantly in the path of a bulldozer bearing down on Walker Gym.

Everything had gone as Rowan had hoped. Speaking from Walker's steps the next day, Clay explained that in proposing Walker's demolition, he was merely carrying out President Jacoby's wishes. "I'm as happy to see it spared as you are," he declared, receiving a roar of approval from the crowd, which prompted him to announce an additional donation to renovate the gym to accommodate the dance program.

Standing alongside Clay, Rowan raised the benefactor's hand as if he had won a prizefight, but at his first opportunity the president slipped away.

He had just gotten back to his office when Easter appeared at the door. He greeted her with a "bravo" and round of applause, and she reciprocated with a dramatic curtsey. Her controlled delight was so captivating it made Rowan forget the distasteful charade he'd just been through with Clay. At the podium, when Clay placed the blame on President Jacoby, Rowan had felt sheepish for not setting the record straight. Then again, what would that have accomplished? Now Clay, by dangling a further gift, would keep Rowan on a leash. This is what I'm being paid for, he thought.

§§§

Rowan pored over a printout of the College's budget until midnight, trying every so often to reach Sara at their apartment in New York. They had planned a quiet weekend at Jefferson, and he still didn't know when she would arrive.

On his fifth attempt, she answered.

"It's working! My chem experiment! Everything's falling into place. There's nothing more exciting than discovering something no one else knows."

"Telling the world about it, perhaps?"

"That's good too, but there's an exquisite moment when you're the only person in the world who's in on the secret."

"You sound like you just came in the door. I bet you haven't had a bite all day."

"Not since breakfast. Hang on while I grab something."

He pictured her trim figure, thick auburn hair pulled back in a ponytail, and he wished he were there.

"Here I am," she said, her mouth full. "We're low on food. Nothing but canned tuna and ketchup."

"Then what are you eating?"

"A dead cookie."

"We'll get you some decent food this weekend. Margaret asked me your favorites. When does your plane get in tomorrow?"

"You know, Rowan ... the redecoration seems to be proceeding without me, and I've just now got my apparatus running. I really want to be in the lab. I'm sorry, but ... would you be terribly upset if I didn't come out this weekend?"

He folded and unfolded a corner of the printout before answering.

"Sara, you haven't been here since moving day. I've been looking forward to spending the weekend together."

"You could come tomorrow and stay through Monday morning," she suggested. "We'd have two nights."

There was no use forcing the point. Time together mattered more than where they spent it. "I'll have my secretary Chloë push back my Monday appointments. Congratulations on your experiment. Now order in a pizza before you keel over. I'll take you out for a proper dinner tomorrow."

§§§

To save money, Rowan had proposed that Jefferson's traditional Inauguration ceremony be scaled back and folded into a regular all-College assembly. So, toward the end of October, he turned his attention to his inaugural address, still a week away, but he soon realized that a constant stream of calls and visitors made it impossible for him to concentrate in his office. Even his house felt public. He asked Chloë if there was a vacant, secluded space somewhere where he could work without interruption and she suggested a little-used room on the top floor of the College Archives, a small building on campus.

Chloë had it furnished with a desk, sofa, and phone, and Rowan added an electric kettle, a small refrigerator, and a pillow and quilt for the sofa. He tacked prints on the walls, and on his desk, placed his favorite memento—an ivory polar bear carved from walrus tusk, which he'd inherited from his grandfather. For as long as he served as Jefferson's president, this room in the Archives was to be his sanctuary.

§§§

On Inauguration Day, Sara sat in the front row with the wives of Jefferson's other senior administrators and gracefully played the role of the president's wife. Since June, they'd managed to spend only a dozen or so days together, and Rowan was relieved and grateful that she'd made it to the ceremony. Wilfred Knight, surrounded by his fellow trustees, formally dubbed Rowan B. Ellway President of Jefferson College, and charged him with the safekeeping of the College Scepter and with upholding Jefferson's hallowed traditions.

His acceptance speech outlined an ambitious agenda, including greater ethnic diversity, more women faculty, the abolition of residential visiting hours, more freedom for students to take courses of their own choosing, and a voice in College governance for all stakeholders in College affairs. Rowan believed that much of the recent strife in academia could have been avoided if the traditional governors of colleges and universities—trustees, administrators, and faculty—were routinely exposed to the viewpoints of student and staff representatives, and included their input in decision making.

The students listened attentively and, heartened that someone was at last addressing their concerns, gave the speech a standing ovation. Rowan came away feeling buoyed and optimistic, but when at last he and Sara were alone that evening he was taken aback by her lack of enthusiasm.

"You know, I'm seeing things differently now that I'm teaching. Unless students at Jefferson are considerably more mature than the ones at NYU, they won't be able to handle all that responsibility."

"Telling them what to do makes them rebellious, not responsible," Rowan countered. Increasingly, talking college politics with Sara felt like sparring with his own faculty. She wouldn't let the matter drop.

"It seems to me that just as I'm trying to climb the academic ladder, you're trying to tear it down."

"Nothing that happens at Jefferson will have the slightest effect on NYU," Rowan protested. "Your colleagues can't possibly be interested in what we're doing."

"You'd be surprised. They read *The Chronicle of Higher Education*, and it's covering Jefferson. Are you feeding them stuff?"

"The PR office may well be," Rowan admitted. "We do want to get our story out."

"Well, it affects me. Every time Jefferson's in the press, I'm on the hot seat."

Rowan looked at her hard, stifling a surge of anger that he realized came from feeling trapped by the situation their conflicting agendas had put him in. "I understand," he finally said wearily. "You're tenure track, and you'll need your colleagues' votes. What do you want me to do?"

"Please, just dial it down a bit. I'm afraid that if they see you as an opponent, they'll see me that way too."

November, 1970

The Commission on Jefferson's Future met every Wednesday at four. When there were disagreements along student-faculty lines, Easter often stepped in to mediate. Once, when conflict loomed between Rowan and a professor over creating an interdisciplinary program in the arts, Easter finessed the matter by suggesting that it be referred to a subcommittee, one that included her, but neither Rowan nor the professor. Rowan, noting her adroitness, raised no objection, and a confrontation was avoided.

After Commission meetings, Rowan's route to the President's House coincided with Easter's to Sojourner Truth House, and they soon established a pattern of leaving together and reviewing the day's work as they strolled home.

One Wednesday evening, near the spot where their paths diverged, Easter said, "Today, I had the feeling that you were somewhere else."

"I've heard most of these arguments before. Yeah, my mind was wandering."

"Where to?"

"I've been reading *Doctor Zhivago*. Today I was daydreaming about the Trans-Siberian Railway."

"That sounds exciting. I'd like to see Siberia someday."

Winter hadn't come to Michigan yet, but the harsh November wind was cold on his face. For an instant he pictured them together in a compartment on a Russian train, a steaming samovar, tea for two. He quickly changed the subject.

"Where will you be for Thanksgiving?"

"In Chicago with my folks. And you?"

"New York."

"I'll miss our walks. I look forward to our talks ... after the meetings."

"I enjoy them, too." His breath froze, and vanished in the space between them.

"Have you noticed that our initials have the same three letters?" Easter said.

Where was she going with this? he wondered. "Yes, I noticed the 'ERB' on your card. Mathematicians call that a 'permutation.'"

"What's the 'B' stand for in Rowan B. Ellway?"

"I was afraid you'd ask; my middle name makes me feel like a kid on the school bus. We teased each other about that."

"C'mon," Easter said, poking his arm.

"Okay, but don't laugh. The 'B' is for Bartolomeo."

"So you have Italian ancestry?" To his surprise, she hadn't even smiled.

"It was my Italian grandfather's name. I secretly like it, but I never use it."

"And where does 'Rowan' come from? It sounds dashing to me."

"That was my Scottish grandfather's name, after the rowan tree. It's related to the hawthorn and has white flowers and red berries. Pasternak sees rowanberries as drops of blood, metaphorically."

"Red and white, and I'm Blue," Easter mused. "The French tricolor, again, and the American flag for that matter."

"So, what does your 'R' stand for?"

"'Rakiya.' It's African. My father is proud of our African heritage, and he tucked the name in there hoping I would be too. It worked. I wish you could meet him."

"Perhaps next year, when you graduate. He teaches history at the University of Chicago, right?"

"You remembered."

"Of course."

"I'm very proud of him. He had it so much tougher than we do today. His father was a sharecropper, and his father's father was a slave ... until the Emancipation. That's as far back as we can trace our family."

"I have a feeling you're going to do your ancestors proud. You know, that's how the Chinese see it—your accomplishments bring glory not to your descendants, but to your ancestors, in recognition of the fact that it was their sacrifices that put you in a position to do what you do."

They had reached the spot where they parted ways. "Happy Thanksgiving, Bartolomeo," she said.

Rowan had to repress an impulse to give her a hug. Flustered, all he could manage was, "You, too." He regretted his lame response.

§§§

Word spread at Jefferson that something was brewing, and nervous faculty told their colleagues at other colleges. Articles in Jefferson's student newspaper were predicting Armageddon. Among the letters to the editor was one from Donald Bentley, announcing weekly brown-bag lunches for "faculty interested in clarifying Jefferson's historic mission as a traditional liberal arts College." When Rowan read it, he faced the facts: Sides were being drawn for the battle to come.

The buzz emanating from Jefferson attracted national media. The *New York Times* ran a story on educational change that featured Jefferson's plans, and CBS News invited Rowan to be on a televised panel about the reforms sweeping American campuses. Though the timing meant he'd have to fly back that same evening to keep a commitment to chair an all-college forum the following morning, he didn't have to think about it; it was a great chance to represent Jefferson on national TV.

Rowan left for New York the day before the broadcast and met Sara for an early dinner at their favorite French restaurant. Excited by the prospect of his first appearance on TV, he told her about a new program that Jefferson was initiating which would enable students to design interdisciplinary majors.

During the meal Sara said, "I'm sorry I won't be able to watch the broadcast. I have to attend a party hosted by the chairman of the chemistry department. It won't look good if I skip it."

Rowan nodded. He knew that junior faculty had to show the flag at social events or risk the consequences, but he was disappointed.

"Hey, I'll ask the department chair to turn the show on during cocktails. He keeps asking to meet you; I think he's got his eye on administration. Can I tell him you'll see him next time you're in town?"

"Stoking his ambitions doesn't sound like fun."

"C'mon Rowan, I need this guy's support. It won't hurt you to talk to him."

§§§

As he opened the door to the President's House, the phone was ringing. It was too early for Sara to be calling.

"Hi, Rowan, Steve Hobson. Just wanted to say 'well done.'"

"I wasn't too blunt?" Rowan asked, hoping to draw Hobson out.

"Straight, I'd call it. The other panelists came off mealy-mouthed. Ironic detachment just doesn't cut it in times like these. You stole the show."

Hobson was always supportive, but what made Steve different, what had won Rowan's respect and trust, was the specific nature of his assurances, plus the occasional criticism. Rowan thanked him for calling and settled down in front of the TV to await Sara's call.

The phone kept ringing. Wilfred Knight was full of superlatives; a trustee with media experience offered a less-than-flattering critique of his TV persona—"Speak faster, lighten up" was the gist of it. The dean of the College thought the national exposure would make Jefferson's faculty more likely to follow their new president's lead.

"What about 'a prophet has no honor in his own land'?" Rowan asked.

"We're going to repeal that one this time around," the dean replied.

It was getting late and he realized Sara couldn't have gotten through, so he called her.

In the afterglow of the show, Rowan was feeling optimistic. "The phone has been tied up," he said. He was grinning. "Everyone seems to have something to say about the show."

"My colleagues were watching," Sara said.

"So, what did you think?"

"You looked great on TV, Rowan. I was happy for you, it's just that what you said … well, it led to a big argument at the party."

"Ouch. But I guess I'm not surprised."

"It put me in an awkward position."

"I couldn't get by with platitudes. If your colleagues were more—"

"It's not that simple," Sara cut in. "I have to live with these guys."

There was an awkward silence, then Sara asked, "Does your faculty back these changes?"

"Some of them agree with your colleagues. But there's a lot of support for reform, especially among the junior faculty. The vote will be close."

He was relieved when Sara dropped the subject to remind him that they were spending Thanksgiving with her parents on Long Island.

Then Rowan paced, stopping to gaze out the rear window down the frozen moonlit yard. Though he tried not to, he often took Sara's solicitousness toward her colleagues as a lack of support for him. With a shiver, he turned away and climbed the stairs to the second floor. As he was undressing, the phone rang again.

"Hi. Hope I'm not calling too late, but I knew you were up ... your line's been busy."

"Hi, Easter. Yes, the phone's been ringing."

"Everyone watched. You made us proud."

"Thanks. I'm glad it's over."

"See you tomorrow?"

"Yes, at the commission meeting, and afterward?"

"Afterward, too. Good night, Dr. Ellway."

"Good night, Easter. Hey, wait. Since I call you Easter, you should call me Rowan."

"Oh, I'd like that." He could tell she was smiling. "Rowan," she said, as if testing his first name on her tongue. "Yes, that sounds good. Sweet dreams, Rowan.""

CHAPTER 5

Rowan had cleared his calendar for Thanksgiving week so he could give his full attention to the dedication of the Mike Marlborough Men's Gymnasium. Marlborough and his wife were coming in Monday for a banquet with alumni and current athletes. He still looked fit and dashing, like the athlete he'd been in his college days. His wife looked like a former model. Tuesday was the ceremony, with ribbon-cutting, speeches, and competitive sporting events.

All was routine, except for one thing, and handling that one thing had obsessed Rowan for days.

At the recommendation of the athletic director, and in response to a petition signed by more than two-thirds of the student body, Rowan had given the go-ahead to dividing the locker room of the new gym into separate but equal parts—half for men, half for women. As long as women's athletics lacked a comparable facility, Marlborough Gym would be equally available to everyone.

Women students and faculty had long lobbied for a new women's gym to replace the dilapidated one that had housed women's athletics for as long as anyone could remember. A proposal to take over Walker Gym when the men abandoned it for Marlborough had been rejected in what proved to be a short-sighted bid to force the trustees to build a gym for women as up-to-date as Marlborough.

The division of the locker room had been accomplished prior to the gym's dedication by the simple device of adding a wall down the middle. By the time Marlborough arrived on campus for the big event, male and female students were using the facility in equal numbers. He was outraged to discover that men and women were showering on opposite sides of a single room divided by what he saw as a breach of the blueprint he had approved.

But the pressure of events left Marlborough no chance to lodge a meaningful protest. The repurposing of the gym was a fait accompli, and to resist it would have spoiled the greatest day in his philanthropic life. Before long, Marlborough was swept up in ceremonies celebrating his largesse.

The next day, however, he dropped by Rowan's office. Giving full voice to his displeasure, he added ominously that the president's highhandedness had prompted him to question his philanthropic priorities.

Rowan's suggestion that he consider another grant to fund a separate but equal gym for women was met with a sneer.

§§§

Rowan and Sara spent a leisurely Thanksgiving holiday with her parents. It proved to be a respite from the tension between them over the reforms, and Rowan returned to Jefferson with his vitality restored. To wrap up before the Christmas break, the Commission on Jefferson's Future decided to meet every day in December beginning at four in the afternoon and running into the evening.

One evening, their work ran late, and it was ten o'clock before he and Easter began their walk across the empty campus. Christmas lights winked at them through the bare branches of the trees on Jefferson Square. It was snowing lightly and Rowan offered Easter his scarf.

She took it, thanked him, and covered her head the way Muslim women do. Then she said pensively, "There's something on my mind, Rowan. I don't know ..."

"Try me."

"Something's changing."

"Oh? How so?"

"It has to do with Obea. He took me under his wing freshman year. I saw him as a mentor, but he saw me as his woman. That was okay with me ... then."

"And?"

"Well, he graduated six months ago and he's still in town."

"He probably stayed for you."

A snowflake fell on Easter's nose. She rubbed the spot.

"I can't respect a guy who just hangs around waiting for me."

"He's still a political force in the College, and in town."

"I know, but once I graduate, I'm out of here. I'm applying for a Fulbright, and if I get it I'll spend the summer in Africa before I go to Oxford."

"You'll get it. Is Obea planning to go with you?"

"I don't know what he expects, but I want to do this by myself. He makes fun of my work on women's rights, says it's for white girls."

"That's short-sighted."

"He was against opening the new gym to women. We had a big fight about it. Why can't I care about women's issues? Or Native Americans'? Or Siberian tigers' for that matter!"

Rowan laughed, fantasizing that her mention of Siberia meant she wanted to take the Trans-Siberian Railway, possibly with him.

"Sometimes I feel guilty for not identifying more exclusively with blacks," Easter continued, "like Obea does. Freshman year, he really opened my eyes to the importance of backing up black pride with black power."

"He's right, of course."

"But that's exactly why I want to see the women students support the women faculty. There are lots of us and very few of them, but together we'd have real power. Obea is against black women putting energy into the women's movement. He says overcoming racism is the number one priority. I don't disagree with that, but I see the two movements as complementary, not opposed."

Easter took a breath and, as Rowan was silent, she continued.

"In grade school, teachers used me as a poster-child, and now Obea wants to do the same thing. At first I went along, but I can't anymore. Sometimes I feel like I don't quite belong anywhere, and at the same time that I belong everywhere. Does that make any sense?"

"Complete sense."

The wind blew cold and Easter moved closer to Rowan until their shoulders brushed. "I know I've had it easier than most of the blacks here, growing up in a professional family. I've been trying to persuade Obea to go to law school."

"He'd make a good lawyer. I'd be glad to recommend him."

"He'd see that as an attempt to get rid of him."

They were approaching the spot where their paths usually diverged. They stopped and faced each other.

"Thanks for listening," Easter said.

"Anytime."

Easter suddenly reached up and brushed the snow from Rowan's hair. Caught off guard, he took her hand and, squeezing it, slowly lowered it to her side.

"Till next time," she said.

"Next time."

He hadn't gone far when he heard her call his name, then she was running back to him. "Your scarf, I almost forgot," she said breathlessly.

"Keep it if you like."

Easter lowered her eyes.

"I'd love to," she said through a veil of softly falling snow.

§§§

The following evening Rowan ate his dinner, as usual, in the nook off the kitchen. Afterward, he stretched his legs along the bench and leaned back against a large pillow. The fallen snow outside his window reminded him of Zhivago's snowbound sojourn with Lara in the dacha at Varykino. His thoughts were interrupted by the shadowy emergence of a human shape crossing the lawn toward the house. From the silhouette, long before he could see a face, he knew it was Easter. She hurried up the stone steps to the terrace where, in the heat of summer, they'd sipped iced tea.

He opened the back door and invited her into the warm bright kitchen. She was wearing his scarf. He tried to help her off with her coat, but her arm got stuck and he fumbled awkwardly.

"Would you like some coffee?" he asked, indicating the pot.

"No, thanks. I wouldn't have just come without calling but ... "

"No, it's fine. Here, have a seat."

"My mother just called and I've got to go home right away. My dad had been having chest pains, and his doctor put him in the hospital for observation. My mom wants me there. I wanted to see you before I left."

Someone pounding on the front door made them freeze.

"Stay put," Rowan said, jumping to his feet. "I'll see who it is." When he opened the door, a dozen student carolers launched into "Good King Wenceslas." Relieved that his visitors didn't expect to be asked in, he stood in the open doorway shivering, and trying to look appreciative.

"Joy to the World" echoed through the yard as the singers trundled off. When he went back to the kitchen he found Easter gazing out the window at the snow-covered yard. Her melancholy filled him with a powerful urge to wrap his arms around her, but he asked, "How long will you be gone?"

"Just till Monday. I'll miss the next commission meeting."

"Oh, don't worry about that." Rowan playfully took hold of the two ends of her scarf as if to prevent her from leaving, and quickly let go. "Thanks for coming over."

They smiled their good-byes and he watched as she crossed the yard. Just before she disappeared through the hole in the hedge she turned and waved good-night.

He sat down in the breakfast nook and the smile on his face froze. My god, what was happening to him? He was married to a woman he respected, admired, and loved. He held a position where even a hint of scandal could be disastrous. He was getting closer to Easter than he should, but every time he tried to distance himself, he ended up doing the opposite. He felt his back break out in a cold sweat.

Before heading upstairs he phoned Sara to suggest that they get tickets for the New York City Ballet performance of Balanchine's *Nutcracker* during the holidays.

§§§

Once he was back in New York for Christmas, he and Sara settled into their familiar routine. On an impulse, they invited their Columbia friends to an impromptu dinner party, and spent the afternoon preparing for it. While Sara dusted and vacuumed, Rowan went shopping for the ingredients of the one dish he knew he could produce without a hitch—pasta alla puttanesca. He also bought the makings for a green salad and picked up some vanilla ice cream and frozen strawberries for dessert. To make sure the party of eight would not run out of wine, he picked up five bottles of cheap Chianti, the same label they'd served when they lived on an assistant professor's salary. He wanted this party to be like the ones they'd had when they were all starting out.

With the salad made and the sauce simmering on the stove, he went to look for Sara. The living room was immaculate; he found her on her hands and knees scrubbing the grout around the bathtub with a toothbrush.

"What are you doing? No one's going to inspect the tiles." They'd had conversations like this before. Although neither was unhappy with their division of household chores, Rowan believed Sara spent too much time striving for unattainable perfection.

"Women notice these things."

"Our friends won't."

"I hate mildew. You worry about the food."

"There's nothing more to do, and I can't sit while you work. Come on, the house looks fabulous. Let's go for a walk."

"I'll relax once this is done. Read the paper. I'll be out in a few minutes."

§§§

Not until he brought out dessert did his guests ask about his new job. With the mention of reform, his former colleagues either turned serious and skeptical or breezy and superficial. As at Jefferson, the conservatives were full of questions but didn't want them answered, and the liberals were full of answers and didn't want them questioned.

Rowan tried to steer the conversation back, to rekindle old friendships, but a subtle change had crept into his relationships. He detected in his former colleagues that same curious blend of deference and dismissiveness he was shown by the faculty at Jefferson. What was it about his new job, about the title *president,* that seemed to distort things? He didn't feel any different. He didn't see the job as putting him above others. Rather, the longer he did it, the more it seemed like a detour that was separating him from the world of ideas. Not a few times, he'd recalled trustee Rideout's take on the job as carrying water, but his old friends saw his attempts to dispel the glamour of the role as false modesty.

"Come on, Rowan," said George, a recently-tenured associate professor of physics at Columbia. The brown turtleneck sweater he wore seemed to accentuate his habitually stooped posture. "Once you've grown accustomed to the salary and the perks, you'll be hooked. And before long, the Ivy League will come calling. You're on the gravy train, man. I've never seen anyone get off voluntarily. Just look at Karp."

Karp was the former Chairman of the physics department who'd hired both Rowan and George. A recent Nobel Prize for work he'd done as a young man had put him in the running for several university presidencies, and he'd just resigned to accept one of them.

"His wife is thrilled about the mansion they're getting," George's rail-thin girlfriend interjected.

"If I know Karp," Rowan said, "he'll pay no attention to what the students want. Within a few years they'll be barricading his office."

"I can't see why anyone would give up physics for administration," remarked John, a young mathematical physicist with eyes as quick and blue as Rowan's. "Holding students' hands and massaging faculty egos must get old very fast. Why'd you do it, Rowan? Not for a mansion, I'm sure."

"I thought I could help put things right."

"Like how?"

"Well, for example, I think students are better served when faculty are not always telling them what courses they must take."

"If you don't come back soon, there'll be no return," John continued. "Physics is moving on. I think the department would still take you, but … "

"I've got to finish what I started," Rowan interjected. "Besides, I'm already obsolete in physics—with two years in the dean's office, and now this, that part of my life is over."

"We're going to miss you," John said.

"But he's not going to miss us," George countered. "He's already making twice what we are, and the sky's the limit."

Rowan took George's third person reference to him as an excuse to clear the table. From the kitchen he could hear Sara questioning George about how he'd won tenure at Columbia, and soliciting his advice on how she could do so at NYU. As Rowan added her empty plate to the stack in his hands, she didn't look at him.

"There are always more bodies than there are tenured slots," George said, "and it's often impossible to tell whose research is going to pay off. So the senior professors ask themselves: Can I live with this person for the next twenty years?"

"That's just what I'm afraid of," Sara said. "It's not going to be easy winning them over, especially if they see me as an extension of Rowan."

"I would have thought that was an asset," John chimed in.

"He's more liberal than the chemists at NYU," said Sara.

Rowan, who'd returned to clear away the salad bowl, said, "So I'm in the enemy camp, huh?"

When no one responded, he went to load the dishwasher. From the remove of the kitchen he felt like an alien, eavesdropping. He'd always seen professors as otherworldly in their commitment to truth and excellence, but now he began to see them as any other professionals, as members of a guild. For the first time he sensed that this tour of duty as an administrator would not only mark the end of his days as a physicist but, eventually, his exit from academia.

Later that evening when the guests had gone and he and Sara were alone, he tried to explain the nostalgia he'd felt for the times when their parties were gatherings of peers.

Sara admitted to some of the same regrets, but ended up insisting that the change was simply part of growing up. "It's not just 'Love and Learning' anymore," she said. "The name of this game is 'Careers.'"

Rowan's heart wasn't in this game, never had been. He was glad they'd be spending the coming week away from friends and relatives, cross-country skiing in the Berkshires. A cabin with its own well and a propane generator had been in Rowan's family for more than a century and, throughout their marriage, had provided them periodic respites. No one would bother them there. At Rowan's insistence, the cabin didn't even have a phone.

§§§

This year he took Lawrence Durrell's *Alexandria Quartet* to the country but found no solace in its complex tale of illicit love. While he read, Sara graded chemistry exams and prepared her lectures for the spring term. For her, this wasn't a chore. She loved teaching.

"Walk me through your typical day," Sara said one evening. They were sitting at opposite ends of an overstuffed, hand-me-down sofa that Rowan had hauled to the cabin when he was a graduate student. They leaned against its arms, facing each other, their feet touching. "I have no idea how you spend your time."

Rowan reached for her left foot, pulled off the wool sock, and began rubbing it.

"My workday begins at seven in the morning and usually runs till ten at night. Over breakfast, I often meet with individual faculty and staff, or with trustees or donors, but I get up several hours earlier and have tea by myself in the nook off the kitchen. Without that time alone, I'd go nuts. By eight, I'm in my office, and at nine there's a staff meeting. After that, I have appointments with faculty, students, administrators. Lunch is usually with a departmental chair or dean."

"It sounds monotonous. Evenings?"

"I'm often invited to dinner by a faculty member or by students to their dorm. Afterward, I go back to the office. It's like that every day, even weekends. When I don't call it's because I'm sucked dry. Sometimes I hear myself saying something I've said a dozen times before, and it's like hearing myself on tape."

"Are you thinking of leaving?"

"I promised the board five years," Rowan said weakly.

Sara dragged herself up from the sofa and announced that she was going to bed. Rowan lingered uneasily for a while, then put on his parka and stepped outside to look at the stars.

§§§

They spent New Year's Day back in the City, walking in a frost-covered Riverside Park, attending a concert in Carnegie Hall, and dining at the Russian Tea Room. Over dinner he extracted a promise from her to visit Jefferson more often. He was proud of Sara, his ambitious, successful wife. By the end of the evening he felt bravely optimistic about their commuting marriage.

§§§

When Rowan returned to Jefferson he passed the first days of the new year in solitude. With no students, the campus felt like a ghost town. From his office window he could see across the flat landscape to the barren trees on the horizon. In their summer greenery, they'd looked happy, but now, raising their naked arms, they seemed sad.

Once, through his window, he saw Obea leading a group of children across Jefferson Square toward the new gym. Easter had told him that he was working for the county's Social Services Agency and had petitioned the college to open the gym to town youth during vacation breaks as it had done in the summer. From his unseen perch, Rowan felt a wave of sympathy for this driven young man.

Easter was in Washington pursuing her honor's research at the Library of Congress, and he was relieved that she wasn't around. He had an appointment in Washington the following week, but had decided not to mention it to her.

His reverie was interrupted by a buzz on the intercom.

"You have a call from Easter Blue," Chloë announced.

"I just called to say Happy New Year," she said cheerily. After he asked her about her father's health, he steered the conversation to the reforms the committee was working on. As they neared the end of the call, Easter said, "It's awfully dreary here. Just work, work, work … all day in the library. I miss our talks."

"Look, the U. S. Commissioner of Education has asked me to brief him on our reforms. I'll be in Washington next week." He immediately regretted saying it.

"Oh?"

"Would you like to come along when I meet him?"

"I'd love to."

Why had he told her? So much for his good intentions.

"Your presence could work to Jefferson's advantage," Rowan continued. "The combination of a white college president and a black student leader would get his attention."

"When are you getting in?"

"9:30 Wednesday morning at National. The meeting's at eleven. Afterward, I'm off to New York."

"I'll pick you up. I'm staying with a girlfriend who lets me use her car."

"I could take a taxi and just meet you at the commissioner's office."

"I'd like to rehearse during the drive into town."

§§§

Easter was waiting for him when he got off the plane. She was wearing a dark green wool suit over a creamy silk blouse, and with her black leather attaché case she looked every bit the young professional.

They approached each other without touching—a handshake seemed too formal, a hug too intimate. As they walked to the parking lot a voice called out, "Hi there, Rowan. What are you doing here?"

It was John Rideout, the trustee whose advice he'd sought about the threat to Walker Gym.

Caught off guard, Rowan managed a Hi, John, then babbled "I'm on my way to see the commissioner of education. This is Easter Blue, a student working with us on the reform commission."

"Good to meet you, Miss Blue. Good luck, you two. Gotta run."

Rowan tried to hide his discomfort at running into a trustee, though he sensed that Easter had noticed.

Their meeting ran far beyond its allotted half-hour. By the time they left his office, the over-worked commissioner, who'd given up the teaching he loved to manage an unresponsive government bureaucracy, had remembered why he'd once deemed the classroom a noble calling.

§§§

It was an unusually warm winter day and they strolled along the Mall toward the Washington Monument, rehashing the meeting.

"How about some lunch?" Rowan asked.

"I'd love some, and I know a good café a few blocks away."

After sharing a tuna-melt, they took alternate bites of a strawberry shortcake. Then, Easter brought up Obea, concluding, "I wrote him last week that I'd rather just be friends."

"How'd he take it?" With his fork, he guided a bruised strawberry to the side of his plate.

"He phoned and asked if I was with someone else. It's not going to be easy for him, but I know it's the right thing for me. I can't be what he wants. I won't be … " Her voice trailed off and she looked away. Rowan leaned across the table and gently touched her hand. He thought he noticed a slight bronzing of her neck and wondered if it could be a blush. Better not to know, he thought.

§§§

Before he left Washington for his weekend with Sara, Rowan called Chloë to see if anything had come up that required his attention. She said that Mike Marlborough had phoned, insisting on seeing him. When she explained that the president was in Washington, Marlborough replied, "Then tell your boss that I expect to see him at eleven o'clock tomorrow morning in his office." Chloë added that Marlborough had rebuffed her attempt to schedule the meeting for the following week, and had refused to say what was on his mind.

Rowan called Sara and explained that instead of getting in Friday night, he'd arrive Saturday afternoon. "I shouldn't stand up the College's biggest donor, at least not the first time he commands my presence. Chloë says Marlborough is very worked up."

"Couldn't you just phone him?"

"Not at this point. He's already en route and can't be reached. I'm really sorry about this Sara, but it gives you Saturday in the lab, and we'll still have two nights."

§§§

One aspect of his job that Rowan had not anticipated was that he often became privy to information that ought to have remained private. The latest incident of this kind, and by far the most serious to date, had arisen before he'd left for Washington in the form of a phone call from a bail bondsman. He was inquiring about an officer in the admissions office, George Harvey. He'd been taken into custody, along with all the other patrons of a gay bar in Detroit, and had given Jefferson College as his employer.

Rowan had assured the bondsman that Harvey was an employee in good standing, and received the bondsman's assurances that he would be released on bail within the hour.

Only minutes before arriving at his office Saturday morning did Rowan connect this incident with Marlborough, and why he'd insisted on their meeting.

After the barest of pleasantries, Marlborough asked him if he'd gotten wind of the arrest of a college employee in Detroit.

"My understanding is that Mr. Harvey is free on bail."

"That's all very nice, but what I want to know is, why you haven't fired the faggot?"

"Innocent until proven guilty."

"Admissions officers are Jefferson's face to the world," Marlborough continued. "We certainly can't have a queer filling up the College with homosexuals."

Rowan avoided a direct reply by asking Marlborough how he'd come by his information.

"I have my sources."

Marlborough was a VIP in Detroit, known as a fervent Jefferson alumnus, and Rowan surmised that he'd been tipped off by someone in the police department. In an attempt to calm him and avoid making any promises, Rowan told him that he'd consult with the College attorney and be in touch early in the following week.

"This is not a legal question," Marlborough responded heatedly. "It's about Jefferson's image. Having women in the gym is bad enough, but I draw the line at catering to pansies. I expect you to take the appropriate action over the weekend."

"I'll get back to you as soon as possible," Rowan said, rising from behind his desk and leading Marlborough toward the door. "I understand your feelings, but I have to tell you that I regard dismissal as a penalty of last resort and, from what I know, Harvey's detention by the Detroit police does not rise to that level."

"I made this trip to give you fair warning, Mr. Ellway. If he's not gone by Monday, I will have no choice but to bring the matter to the attention of my fellow trustees."

Rowan understood that this was Marlborough's way of threatening his job, and countered with, "I'll be consulting with the board myself, Mr. Marlborough. You'll hear from me shortly."

As soon as Marlborough had gone, he asked Chloë to book him on the next flight to New York, and left immediately to keep his date with Sara.

§§§

"Well, out with it. What did Mr. Mike want?" Sara asked as he took off his coat. One of her hats covered his usual hook in the hall closet. Their apartment smelled musty and unlived-in. She poured them some wine; he took his usual place on the sofa and recounted the Harvey story.

"Marlborough played football for Jefferson, graduated in the fifties, and went on to make a fortune in the tire business. There's no doubt that he's a very influential trustee, but his clout is based on money, not the respect of the other board members."

"Wasn't he pissed off when you opened his gym to women?"

"Yes, but he was virtually alone on that one. When no one would join him, he shut up."

"You probably made an enemy then and there. What are you going to do about his ultimatum?"

"I thought about it on the plane. I'm going to inform chairman Wilfred Knight, and John Rideout, the trustee who advised me on Clay's threat to the old gym, that I will not fire Harvey. If the board agrees with Marlborough, they're going to have to fire me first, then remove Harvey themselves."

"Are you sure you want to be that confrontational?"

"Marlborough will be sounding out trustees this weekend, trying to round up enough support to force the issue. He's utterly determined, and he's made it a test of wills. I don't see any other way to back him down."

"How do you feel about this, apart from the test of wills? I mean, I understand that a president can't let individual board members order him around, but what do you think of Marlborough's concern about a gay admissions officer?"

"I think straights have treated gays like whites have treated blacks. We've assumed we're superior, and it's got to stop."

"Same with women," Sara added.

"Exactly. I'm not innocent myself, but now I'm in a position to refuse to go along with this kind of thing. If the board disagrees, they can take this job and shove it."

"Don't get too self-righteous, Rowan. Just stand firm. By the way, how'd it go in Washington?"

"The Commissioner seemed impressed with our plans. By the time I left, he was looking for a way to give the College a grant so he could take credit for what we're doing." Rowan noticed that he'd omitted any mention of Easter.

"What was he interested in, specifically?"

"Cost containment, productivity, and broader participation in governance. Our goal is to not turn applicants away on financial grounds any more than we would because of race or religion."

"Or, homosexuality."

"Or, that," Rowan agreed. "No discrimination other than that based on academic promise and performance."

"It's going to take time to bring everyone along," Sara noted.

Rowan couldn't express these ideas without getting excited, and as he elaborated on his plans, his enthusiasm grew.

"You know, Sara, the only reason I ever got into administration was to do something about this. 'All men are created equal' doesn't mean a thing if it doesn't mean equal access to quality education."

"You've got history on your side," Sara said. She pointed to the Tiffany lamp hanging over the easy chair. Their mascot was dangling from the shade. "Gumby seems to approve of what you're doing," she said.

"Good. I couldn't deal with his rejection. I'm sorry if I sometimes get carried away, Sara."

For as long as he'd been conscious of such things, Rowan's sympathies had been with the underdog. Recently, he'd caught himself getting short with a conservative faculty member, and now he was preaching to Sara.

"Where does your passion come from? You didn't have a deprived childhood."

"True, but I remember lots of kids who did, kids I grew up with, like Arlene."

"You never mentioned her. Who's Arlene?"

"In second grade I had a teacher who started each day by inspecting our fingernails. There were poor kids in the class, kids like Arlene, from families who worked the dirt farms that used to dot New Jersey. She wore the same faded red dress to school every day, and she spoke in a whisper. She was so tiny and frail, I wondered how she made it up the steps of the school bus. One morning, her nails were dirty, and the teacher told her to go to the hall and stay there until they were clean."

"Is that it?"

After he pushed back the lump in his throat, Rowan said, "I remember wondering how Arlene could clean her nails in the hall, with no soap or water. Later, on our way out for recess we saw her slumped against the wall, her hands over her face. She peeked at me through her fingers. The image of her huddled there—helpless and humiliated—haunts me."

As she got up to go to the kitchen, Sara said, "Maybe I missed something, but that doesn't quite seem to explain *your* passion."

No, it doesn't, Rowan thought. What *was* the source of his concern? he wondered.

CHAPTER 6

In February, when Dr. Noel Ford, one of Jefferson's more illustrious graduates, visited the campus, Rowan took the opportunity to reach out to the leading faculty opponent of reform. He arranged a tour of the new Science Center for Ford, now a top official in NASA and a potential Jefferson trustee, and invited Professor Bentley to accompany them. Bentley had accepted with such relish it had made him uneasy, and he saw his mistake the moment he heard Bentley characterizing the new admissions strategy to Dr. Ford as "quotas in disguise."

Rowan was about to jump into the argument when they joined a biology lab in progress. Across the room he saw Easter peering through a microscope, a male student standing alongside her with his hand on her shoulder. Feeling an involuntary wave of jealousy, he turned away, and the muffled sounds of Bentley importuning their distinguished guest brought him back to reality.

Once again, Rowan wondered what Sara could ever have seen in this pompous defender of the status quo. He stepped toward Dr. Ford and addressed him without so much as a glance at Bentley.

"Dr. Ford, you came to Jefferson on a full scholarship. The reforms we're considering are designed to open Jefferson to people, *independent of their means*—people like you were then."

"Surely, Dr. Bentley," Ford said, "the faculty shares the president's concern about the high cost of a Jefferson education."

"Of course," Bentley agreed, "but most of the cost increases arise from economic factors beyond our control. The faculty shares my conviction that we should find solutions by enlarging the College's endowment. Fundraising is the primary responsibility of the president, not policy reform, which is the prerogative of the faculty."

Bentley looked at Rowan. So did Ford.

"I learned at Columbia that the best way to raise funds is to raise a standard. When funders see that we stand for something worthy—like making college more accessible to deserving students--money will follow."

"Sounds a lot like our situation at NASA," Ford said. "Unless we make Americans proud, Congress cuts our budget. But tell me, Dr. Ellway, what kind of reforms could reduce costs without also eroding quality?"

"Exactly!" Bentley chimed in. "Preserving quality—that's my point."

"The commission is exploring more productive uses of College resources. For starters, the campus is idle for one-third of the year. I'll put our detailed proposals in the mail to you, Dr. Ford. We'd welcome your critique."

Turning to Bentley, Rowan explained that their guest had an appointment with one of his former math professors. When he and Bentley were alone, he said, "I was surprised that you chose to air our disagreements. His appointment to the board would strengthen the College."

"There's more at stake than an appointment to the board. I've given my life to Jefferson. I don't intend to stand by while you destroy it."

"You have every right to your views, but why are you trying to alienate Ford?"

"Because I don't want anyone on the board who supports the changes you're proposing."

"You mean who supports *me*."

"You don't care about the college," Bentley said, moving off. "The faculty sees you as a Boy Wonder who's using Jefferson as a steppingstone to something bigger."

§§§

In March, under pressure from a group of alumni to establish an exchange program with Hebrew University, Rowan agreed to lead a delegation to Jerusalem during Easter week. Aware of Sara's Jewish heritage, the alumni had made a point of inviting her, all expenses paid, but in the end, and despite her parents' and Rowan's urgings, she felt she had to decline on the grounds that her absence from the lab would hurt her prospects.

On the day of the trip, Rowan got to his office well before the College car arrived to take him to the airport. There was a letter in his in-basket from Noel Ford, declining appointment to Jefferson's Board. Damn, Rowan swore to his empty office, convinced that Bentley had scared him off.

"What's the matter?" Looking up, he saw Easter peering through his open doorway. He put all thoughts of Bentley, Ford, and Jefferson College on hold.

"I came to see you off, and I brought you something." She handed him a small box wrapped in maroon velvet cloth and tied with silver ribbon. "Open it on the plane."

Rowan felt uncomfortable about receiving a gift from Easter, and at a loss for what to say, asked, "May I open it now?"

"Only if you promise not to say a word."

"Okay." He unwrapped the box.

In it there was a miniature glass replica of an Easter lily. "So you won't forget me," Easter offered, looking up at him. A surge of affection made him reach for her hands and pull her toward him. Wrapping his arms around her, he held her tightly, and it took every last bit of his will not to kiss her. Taking a step back, he picked up his suitcase with his free hand and, cradling the lily in the other, left the office without saying a word.

§§§

Although he was assigned a middle seat, he was relieved that it was between strangers, so he wouldn't have to chat with anyone in the delegation. Thinking about Easter, wondering what would've happened if he'd kissed her, he was glad to be at thirty thousand feet, safely away from her. That close call, his arguments with Sara, and the repetitiousness of his job, made him wish he could just keep on flying around the world forever.

After the group checked in to the American Colony Hotel, he threw himself into the work and joined his colleagues on tours to Jewish, Christian, and Muslim religious sites.

§§§

By the time Rowan returned to Jefferson he'd convinced himself that he could maintain a proper distance from Easter. They would be friends, but nothing more. If Sara couldn't or wouldn't come out for weekends, he'd go to New York.

He was unpacking from his trip when the phone rang. He immediately recognized Easter's voice,

"My father's had a heart attack. I'm packing to go home."

"By train?"

"Yes. There's one in an hour."

The train to Chicago stopped in a city not far from Jefferson. "I'll take you to the station. I'll pull into the parking lot behind Truth House in five minutes."

Easter came out as he drove up. She threw her bag in the back seat and they sped off.

"My mother phoned to tell me that a janitor had found my father on the floor in his office. He's still unconscious. The doctors aren't saying anything."

"Your being there will help him recover."

"You think you know your parents, but when something like this happens, you realize you don't. If he were to die, all I'd have are some photos and a few stories. My children would never know him."

Rowan reached across and put his hand on her shoulder. She cupped it with hers, and stared out the window.

At the station he waited while she bought a ticket, then walked her to the westbound platform.

"I'll stay as long as I have to. I can work on my thesis at home."

The train pulled into the station and a conductor stepped off to board the waiting passengers. Easter lingered until the last minute. As she turned to go, Rowan embraced her. She clung to him, and he buried his chin in her hair.

The whistle blew. She mounted the steps, and the conductor slammed the door behind her. Standing at the top of the steps, Easter looked down at Rowan. He gestured to her to lower the window. She leaned out, and he craned his neck upward. Just as the train lurched into motion, he took her face in his hands and kissed her on the lips. He watched her as it gathered speed and carried her away.

On his way home, he almost rear-ended a car at a stop sign. When he walked in the house, the phone was ringing.

"Hi. I hope you weren't asleep."

"Hi, Sara. What's up?"

"I'm in San Francisco, remember? At the American Chemical Society conference. I tried you earlier, but you were out. I want to hear about Israel while it's still fresh in your mind. Where were you anyway? There was no answer in your office either."

"I must have been in the shower."

"How was your trip?"

"Great, we're going to be exchanging a dozen students with Hebrew University." Rowan pulled at a tangled coil in the phone cord while he waited for her to continue.

"Rowan, I miss you. I'm starting to worry."

"About what?"

"About us, about our marriage."

Rowan's heart sped up. A wave of guilt overcame him. He mumbled, "What brings this on?"

"I feel bad that I missed the Israel trip. It's just, oh, I don't know. We're together so little. And when we are, we can't escape our jobs. We need a real vacation. Alaska, perhaps. You've always wanted to go there. I could get away right after the year-end departmental party."

"When is that?"

"The day after graduation."

"That sounds good. Then, without thinking, he added, "Sara, I don't know how long I can carry on like this. On my own, I mean."

He could almost hear Sara revving up, and braced himself for her response. "Are you blaming me for not living there?"

"No, I don't blame you."

"I'm the one who's suggesting a vacation."

Why had he said anything? Before he could reply, she went on.

"Remember, it was you who left New York, not me. We both had perfectly good jobs here."

"I'm sorry, Sara. I don't want to argue. I never expected you to give up your career for mine. It gets lonely here, that's all."

After they had hung up, Rowan remembered that Sara was giving a paper at the conference. For years, he'd followed every step in her career; now, he'd even forgotten to ask her about her presentation.

§§§

On graduation day, sunlight flooded the solarium off Rowan's bedroom. Still in bed, he spent a few minutes gazing out the window at the elms overhanging the house. Soon he would get up, shower, and put on the suit that Sara had insisted he buy the year before. Same suit, different man. In a few days he'd be in New York, and they'd fly to Juneau for a cruise along the Alaskan coast that Sara had booked.

From Chicago, Easter had reported that her father was slowly regaining his strength. Always the conscientious student, she had arranged with her professors to carry on with her studies at home so she could continue to visit him daily.

§§§

After collectively pronouncing them "Bachelors of Arts with all the rights and privileges thereunto appertaining," the president traditionally presented each senior with a diploma. This time, the procession took more than an hour, and by the time it was halfway through, Rowan was on automatic. When one student celebrated his degree with a back-flip off the stage, Rowan took a moment to scan the cheering audience. There was Easter, looking regal and self-possessed. She wore a red sundress with thin straps tied in bows over her bare shoulders. Smiling, she raised four fingers and gestured toward the administration building.

After the last student had clowned his way across the platform and Rowan had greeted hundreds of parents at the reception, he slipped away to meet her.

She was waiting for him in the lobby outside his office. With a quick glance around, they rushed into each others' arms. He encircled her waist and lifted her off her feet, pressing her body against his. This time he kissed her long and hard and full on the lips.

She had the presence of mind to pull him into his office and lock the door. Arms still encircling her tight, he lifted her onto the edge of his desk so she sat facing him. Her eyes locked on his, she reached up to the bow on her left shoulder and gave it a tug, not to untie it, but to suggest he do so. She was presenting herself to him— as a gift to be unwrapped—and her desire heightened his own.

He moved between her knees and released the bow, then reached for the other and gave it a gentle tug. The dress fell from her shoulders to reveal full, bare breasts, and in the next moment he was covering them with kisses. His hands moved up her long thighs and found that she wore nothing under her dress. He could barely breathe as she deftly unbuttoned his shirt. Then he stood back for the instant it took him to shed his pants. She wrapped her legs tightly around his waist as he slipped into her.

After a year of sexual tension, consummation was swift and unrestrained. As they untangled their bodies they laughed in relief, now that the ambiguity they'd lived with was over.

"I wasn't prepared for this," he said. "I couldn't stop myself."

"Don't worry, I took precautions," Easter said, reading his mind.

Then she said, "You're the first man who ever took the trouble to get to know me. Thank you for … for finding me."

§§§

Later, with darkness covering their exit, they crept out and drove back to the train station. In the car they talked about the graduation ceremony and her father's condition, but not about what had happened between them.

Rowan drove home feeling a mixture of elation and dread. They'd been lucky this time. He promised himself there wouldn't be another.

CHAPTER 7

The day after graduation, Rowan flew to New York. As his cab splashed through a puddle on the Upper West Side, he recalled a windy, rainy afternoon, early in their relationship, when Sara had shared her umbrella with him on their way to a local pub. The memory made him sad.

Nostalgia fed his hope that somehow he could put things right.

§§§

"Hi," Sara called to him from the bathroom when he came through the door. She sashayed into the living room and struck a pose. For a moment Rowan was speechless.

"Your ponytail—it's gone." Then he noticed what she was wearing. "How come you're all dressed up?"

In a black velvet Chanel suit, new to him, she looked cut out for success, at once alluring and imposing.

"I told you, remember? The department party. There's just time for you to change."

"Oh, no, Sara, I'm exhausted. That's the last thing I want to do."

"You can't back out now. Everyone's expecting you. Besides, I want to show you off."

"To the same guys who hated me on TV?"

"I'm sure they won't mention it. If anyone does, you can change the subject."

"It's just that I was hoping to get a break from academic politics," he said wearily.

"Listen, tomorrow we'll be on a plane to Alaska and, once we're aboard ship, we'll have nothing to do but rest."

"Okay. I'll put on my smiling face."

The chairman of Sara's department greeted them at the door and showed them into his spacious Greenwich Village apartment. The punctuality of chemists, which Rowan traced to the exacting nature of their work, meant the party was in full swing a mere ten minutes after the appointed hour of eight. Handing their coats to an aproned maid, the chairman himself saw to their drinks. Then he led them to a small group of men and introduced Rowan as "The President of Jefferson College and our Sara's husband."

Rowan knew this scene by heart: the Harris tweed jackets with leather elbow patches, the "you-can't-touch-me" bravado that came with tenure, a defensive undercurrent in those who hadn't measured up, and, no mistaking it, the barely-concealed hostility toward administrators like himself.

After a few minutes of pleasantries, a fortyish, goateed professor brought up Rowan's TV appearance. Sara looked at Rowan over the rim of her wineglass with an apologetic smile and a silent plea not to rise to the bait. The professor wanted to know if Jefferson had found it possible to recruit more women and black faculty without lowering standards. Rowan framed his response in non-confrontational language, hoping he'd soon be able to retreat to the company of the chemists' wives and not have to talk shop.

"Recruiting first-rate minority faculty isn't easy. There still aren't many black students in the graduate schools, but that problem will ease with time. We anticipate African Americans making up about 10 percent of our undergraduate body within three years."

Who could possibly object to that? Rowan thought, accepting an hors d'oeuvre from a server.

"Of course we too have considered affirmative action," another professor said. "It sounds good at first, but isn't it really just reverse discrimination—against whites and Asians?"

Rowan couldn't ignore that. "What we're trying to do at Jefferson is compensate for a century of de facto discrimination that has denied admission to African Americans."

"How long is that going to take?"

"A generation or so," Rowan replied. Noting a faint smear of cocktail sauce on his inquisitor's chin, he used his napkin to remove any possible traces from his own.

"Frankly, I don't find your argument convincing. Discrimination against one race cannot be ended by discriminating against another. We'd welcome more blacks, but we want them to get here as we all did—strictly on merit."

"That's our long-range goal too" Rowan continued, "but I don't see any blacks in this room, and Sara is the only woman in your department, so 'strictly-on-merit' doesn't seem to be working."

"Isn't the solution to improve secondary and primary education?" another professor proposed.

"That's part of the solution, for sure, but we've also got to address the present emergency. If we continue to shut blacks out of the professions, this country is going to come apart."

A thirty-something man blurted out, "I'd feel better if our department were more proactive." Rowan wished there were more like him at Jefferson. But the young man's colleagues greeted his show of support for Rowan with pained silence. Rowan expected the department chairman, who had yet to say a word, to speak for them all, but one of his lieutenants moved in to quash any further defection.

"Frankly, my concern with compensatory programs is the students themselves. Whenever you use people as guinea pigs, you run the risk of doing more harm than good."

The young man who had dared to challenge his seniors looked despairingly to Rowan for help.

"We intend to see that the experiment succeeds," Rowan said. "An essential part of our strategy is remedial work, tutoring, counseling—whatever it takes to make up for inadequate preparation. Frankly," Rowan locked eyes with the man who had just "franklied" him—"fear of doing more harm than good is usually just an excuse for standing pat."

"Oh, really," said a short professor with tortoise-shell glasses, his voice oozing disdain. "We think you're downplaying the danger of grade inflation. Won't the pressure to lower standards be irresistible?"

Rowan felt himself losing patience.

"Tell me," he addressed the short professor, "don't you think women and blacks deserve role models, too? Like the ones we men have always had?" With a sweep of his arm, he drew a circle around the group of men.

"The solitary woman professor at MIT was an inspiration to me," Sara volunteered. "I'll never forget … "

"Yes, of course," the professor cut in, "but doubtless she had *earned* her rank, as have you, Sara. Role models can serve no purpose if they're tainted by suspicions of favoritism."

In contrast to Rowan's burgeoning intensity, the professor's tone was perfectly modulated as he wrapped up his case. "Let me assure you, Dr. Ellway, our department has given this a great deal of thought. Some of us fought hard to get rid of Jewish quotas in the postwar years. I'd be less than honest if I didn't tell you that I find your arguments for affirmative action specious at best and disingenuous at worst."

Rowan, who stood a head taller than the professor who had just spoken, looked down at him, meeting the challenge. "You seem to be saying that I'm either an idiot or a hypocrite. Would you care to rephrase your remark?"

He wanted to hammer this smug little man through the floor and into the apartment below, but instead, he simply leaned slightly toward him. As a buzz rose from the group, a distraught Sara grabbed Rowan and, mumbling apologies over her shoulder, dragged him toward the adjacent room. He'd had enough, and let himself be led away.

"How could you?" she hissed when they were alone. "I'll never live this down. Never."

Staring at her now, Rowan saw not the elegant self-assured woman he'd arrived with, but a harpy. Her eyes looked smaller and closer together, her nose sharper.

"There's more at stake here than image. That guy was insulting and wrong, and you know it."

"Do I? Do I really? You're so busy sounding off, you don't know what I think anymore."

"What *do* you think? I'd like to know."

"We'll discuss it at home."

"That's where I'm going now. Are you coming?"

"I've got to try to patch things up. We'll talk in the morning."

"I'll be up." He left without a word to anyone except the maid.

Once away from the party, walking alone through near-empty streets, he had the sense that he and Sara were on separate halves of an ice floe that had split in two, and were ineluctably drifting apart. All his life he'd had a vague sense of being an outsider. Now he felt like one in his own marriage.

§§§

Around midnight, Rowan heard Sara's key in the lock. He looked up from the TV as she came into the room. She didn't sit down with him on the sofa, but took her stand at the window.

"How'd it go?" Rowan asked.

"They're still arguing. Are you pleased?"

"If it makes them think, yes."

"What's come over you, Rowan?"

"My views haven't changed."

"But you have. You're a different person. You were always impatient, but now you're belligerent, even reckless."

"I thought I was rather patient with them, actually, until your colleague insulted me. And besides, what's wrong with a little passion when it comes to justice?"

"It divides people, that's what. You just made things worse."

"Look, Sara, I come here to get away from academic politics, and you make me spend my first night home with those Neanderthals."

"Those 'Neanderthals' are my colleagues. I needed your support and you embarrassed me."

"You don't support me either, not where it matters. You haven't spent a weekend at Jefferson all semester."

"Don't give me that." Sara threw her keys down on the table, turned her back on him, and went to the kitchen. Rowan got up and followed her.

"You've always known how important my career is to me," Sara said as he slumped on a chair at the kitchen table. "And there's no time for us when I go to Jefferson anyway. No, the question is why you're never here. Maybe you think I'm a Neanderthal too."

When Rowan didn't speak up immediately, she added, "Well, I guess you do. Really, Rowan, why don't you come home more often?" She crossed her arms and took a step back. "Have you got a chick on the side? Is that it?"

Rowan looked up. His face told her what he could not.

"Oh, my God," she said, backing up until she was against the refrigerator. She could read him and he knew it.

"No, wait, Sara. Please come sit down."

Sara didn't budge. "Tell me. Are you having an affair?"

"Not exactly."

"What's that supposed to mean?"

"I don't know how to say this."

"Say what?"

"You're right, Sara, I *am* a different person."

"Answer my question."

"Okay. I've formed an attachment."

"An attachment? You mean to a woman?"

"Yes."

"Who is she?"

"She's a student. We've been working together for almost a year. It started as a friendship, and gradually it has become something more."

"What do you mean 'something more'? You can't be sleeping with a student. That's unthinkable!"

"Yes, well, I suppose, but I don't think of her as a student."

"So you have slept with her?"

This was the question Rowan had dreaded. Without looking up, he said, "Once."

"Oh, no, you bastard. I thought I could trust you."

"I'm sorry, Sara." Rowan stood as if to go to her.

"Have you lost your reason? Don't you know that even *the appearance* of involvement with a student would get you fired?"

"I know."

"You don't know anything." For an instant, Rowan imagined that he saw hurt on Sara's face, that she might break down. If she had, he might have found a way to her. But tears were not for Sara. She'd always maintained that she hadn't cried since she was seventeen, when she learned she didn't have the knees for dance.

Then she jolted him with a question he didn't anticipate: "Are you in love with her?"

"I love you. No one will ever know about this."

"Bullshit. You're an open book."

"We're in a lot of the same meetings. People are accustomed to seeing us together."

"What's her name?"

"Easter."

"That's an odd name. Easter what? Egg?"

"Easter Blue."

She rolled her eyes and sat down on the other side of the table. She stared at him.

"You're losing it, Rowan, losing it completely. You're not the man I married."

"I've been trying to figure out what's happening to me, to us. All I can think of is that, well, you and I, we have no private life together ... to balance the public lives we live apart. There are so many times at Jefferson when I feel I'm just playing a role, impersonating myself."

"Gee, Rowan, excuse me if I don't feel for you. You have to end it, that's all. I won't live with this. Don't be here in the morning." Turning her back on him, she walked down the hallway to their bedroom.

"I'm so sorry, Sara," he called after her as she slammed the door. He heard the lock click. His suitcase was still in the front hall where he'd dropped it that afternoon. He picked it up and headed out to find a room for the night.

He waited until nine the next morning before he called Sara. Either she was not answering or she was out. Then he thought of trying her at her lab. She answered on the first ring.

"Can we talk?"

"Not until you've told 'Miss Egg' that it's over," she said sarcastically.

Rowan took the first flight back to Jefferson.

§§§

For three days he didn't let Easter know that he'd come back early, intending to end the affair.

If it were only her exotic beauty, he knew he could easily have given her up. But he loved Easter for more than her swan's neck, her full lips, her sensuality. She took him to places in himself he couldn't get to alone. Together, they were working something out—and yes, it had something to do with race, but it was more than that. He felt real with Easter.

Their relationship, which he knew others would see in terms of rank, was for him beyond rank. Easter was his closest ally in the battle of his life. She was no "chick on the side."

§§§

Late in the evening of his third day back he phoned Sara.

"Would you agree to a 'leave of absence'?" he asked.

"Does that mean you're going to keep seeing her?" Sara said.

"I don't know."

"Well, unless you give her up, it's over for us. Ruin your life if you want to, Rowan, but I can't let you take me down with you."

Rowan could think of nothing more to say. Was this how the conversation that had defined their marriage would end?

§§§

Without students, the campus was quiet. The leisurely atmosphere that had settled over the College after graduation gave Rowan and Steve Hobson plenty of time for racquetball.

During a water break, Steve caught Rowan off guard.

"I think that girl likes you."

"Who?"

84

"You know who, Easter Blue. I see you together a lot."

"What makes you think she likes me?"

"The way she looks at you."

Rowan wiped his face on his sleeve and took a swig of water, but said nothing. Finally, he gave Steve a helpless shrug and changed the subject. "Are we still on for Saturday?"

Though he wasn't willing to discuss his feelings for Easter, Rowan did confide in Steve about his growing distaste for administration.

"I'm not cut out for it," he said as they left the gym. "I hate repeating myself."

"You're just what Jefferson needs right now. Without your pushing them, the faculty would just dither. But, if I may give a word of advice, it wouldn't hurt to do a bit more schmoozing. The faculty has got to feel that you respect them."

"All I know is that the minute this job is done, I'm going to drop out of sight."

Steve, who taught modern poetry, said, "You remind me of Emily Dickinson's 'Somebody-Nobody' poem. Do you know it?"

"No."

"It goes like this:

How dreary to be somebody!
How public like a frog
To tell your name the livelong day
To an admiring bog!"

Rowan thought for a while, then said, "Yes, public life makes me feel like a frog ... croaking the same refrain over and over."

"I don't remember the first verse exactly, but it's about being a 'nobody'," Steve said. "Look it up."

That night Rowan searched his anthologies until he found it. As he read Dickinson's lines, he felt a kinship with this solitary, prescient woman.

I'm nobody! Who are you?
Are you nobody, too?
Then there's a pair of us—don't tell!
They'd banish us, you know.

How odd that, at the moment, he was a somebody to others and a nobody to himself.

CHAPTER 8

By early June, Easter was free. She offered to meet him anywhere. They agreed on a three-day weekend in the nation's capital. By noon the following Friday, Rowan had checked into the Rosewood Inn with a dozen red roses under his arm. After a shower, he paced the room nervously waiting for Easter's call. He put the flowers in a vase on the bedside table, turned down the spread and plumped the pillows. A few minutes later he decided the undressed bed looked presumptuous and remade it.

He heard her footsteps in the hall and opened the door just as she was about to knock. She dropped her bag and flew into his arms.

"You've been traveling for hours. Are you tired?"

"No, but I do want to freshen up."

Easter peeked into the bathroom.

"Hmmm, nice. I think I'll have a bath."

Rowan took their lack of small talk as a sign of their ease with each other. She disappeared into the bathroom, but left the door ajar. While she drew her bath, Rowan took half the roses out of the glass, plucked the petals and scattered them on the bed.

"How about a back rub?" she called out from the tub.

"At your service."

The tub was a vintage piece, standing off the floor on claw feet. Easter lay submerged in bubbles, her dark shoulders rising above the milky suds, her Afro speckled with foam. He took off his shirt, knelt behind her, and dipped his hands in the water to warm them before he touched her shoulders. She leaned forward, and slowly he traced the curve of her spine down to her narrow waist. He kissed the nape of her neck and rubbed it with his soapy palm.

Then he took her head in both hands and lowered it back onto a towel he'd placed over the rim of the tub. He worked little circles, starting on her temples and then down along her high, round cheeks. He continued to her chin and down her graceful neck to her collarbones.

He reached under her arms and slid her up toward him, exposing her back. He cupped her shoulders and gently moved his hands down over her breasts, again and again, lightly brushing her rising nipples. She closed her eyes and relaxed into his touch.

He moved to the side of the tub and perched on its edge to face her. She looked up, her head tilted demurely to one side. He slowly traced her mouth with his thumb and kissed her lips, first lightly, and then deeply, her familiar taste flavored slightly with suds. Taking her hands in his, he gently drew her up, and she rose like Venus out of the foam that slid down her body. He stared at her gleaming, naked beauty.

She stepped out of the tub, turned to face him, and methodically unbuckled his belt. Rowan pushed his trousers to the floor. She led the way to the bed and lay down among the rose petals.

"I feel like a Hindu princess," she said, pulling him down.

As he kissed her he felt her opening to him. Locked together they rocked back and forth in each others' arms, the dance picking up speed and force until the space between them seemed to vanish in a breathless spasm of pleasure.

They lay in each others' arms for some time.

Nibbling her earlobe, he whispered, "What does the lady desire?"

"Tea for two would be grand." Easter made a "T" by placing the forefinger of her right hand across that of her left, and then, in quick succession, raising four fingers with one hand and two with the other. "T-4-2," she said, spelling it out for him.

"I get it, I get it," Rowan said with a groan.

Twenty minutes later Rowan answered the room-service knock and took the silver tray from the waiter in the hall. As he and Easter sipped tea, they planned what they would do if they were ever recognized in public.

The chance airport encounter with trustee John Rideout had been a warning. Their cover story would be that they had run into each other on the street and were catching up on College politics. They even rehearsed inviting their discoverer to join them for coffee. After a decent interval, Rowan would excuse himself as if to keep an appointment, and they'd meet back at the hotel within the hour.

Their light-hearted scheming led to a playful tussle that quickly escalated into athletic lovemaking. Easter was a strong woman, and she relished her physical power. While Rowan lay flat on his back, she straddled him, taking him into her, deeper and deeper with each plunge. Her throaty moans were the sweetest music he'd ever heard.

Afterward, they lay back, exhausted and happy. Rowan draped a sheet over their nakedness and listened to her breathing as she drifted off.

§§§

It was mid-afternoon when they woke up. Rowan had reserved a car, and suggested a trip to the shore.

"When I was little, my parents used to take me to the beach in Maryland," he told her. "One time, we went out in a rowboat, and the motion made me sick. My mother told me to stop whining or get out. I couldn't imagine anything worse than that boat, so I leaped over the side. She grabbed my hand, but trailed me in the water alongside the boat until I promised to behave if she pulled me back in."

"Your ma didn't mess around."

"It was hard to please her, but when we did she'd show her love by baking pies."

"Pie equals love?"

"That was the equation. Would you like to drive out to Chesapeake Bay?"

"Can we get there by sunset?"

"Easily. It's midsummer. It'll be light till nine."

"I can just see you leaping out of that boat."

"Crazy, huh?"

"Not really. You take risks. I'm more cautious."

"Less foolhardy, perhaps?"

"No, your lack of fear is what I love about you."

§§§

After a dinner of crab at an inn overlooking Chesapeake Bay they wandered out on the sandy beach, walked half a mile along the shore, and lay down under the darkening sky. It was a balmy summer's night. Easter rested her head on Rowan's arm.

At dinner they'd noticed inquiring stares. This kind of attention was new to Rowan, and he met it with smiles that masked a steely determination to protect her from slight or embarrassment. Just five years earlier, restaurants like this had still displayed "Whites Only" signs.

As they headed back to the car, reflected moonlight glimmered on the breaking waves. "How about staying right here tonight?" Rowan suggested. "Could you manage without your stuff?"

"Sure. I'm a camper. I noticed on the map that we're not far from Chincoteague Island. One of my favorite books was *Misty of Chincoteague* … you know, about the wild horses. Let's stop there tomorrow."

They walked over to the registration desk together, where Rowan asked the clerk for a double room.

The clerk's eyes nervously flicked back and forth between them. "I'll have to check," he mumbled, and hurried off through a swinging door into a back room. When he didn't reappear, Rowan began to worry, and Easter picked up on his thoughts.

"Maryland is the South," she said. "They might give us trouble."

"There are laws against discrimination in lodging …"

"Rowan, I remember waiting in the car as my father was turned away from one motel after another. I learned from him when to fight and when to walk away. If there's a problem, let me handle it."

"We'll handle it together," he replied, as the clerk returned with an older man.

"I am the manager. It is our policy to provide rooms only to married couples. I must ask you for proof that you are legally married."

"Do you require such proof from every couple?" Rowan asked calmly.

"We reserve the right to do so."

"And when do you exercise that right?"

"That's our business." The manager wasn't going to back down.

Easter took Rowan's hand below the counter and then spoke. "There's a federal law against racial discrimination. My uncle holds a senior position in the Office of Civil Rights, U. S. Department of Justice. We shall be lodging a complaint against you. Good night."

With that, still clutching Rowan's hand, she turned and headed out the door. As soon as they were in the car, Rowan said, "You amaze me, but we don't have his name and address."

"It was a bluff. I don't intend to follow through. What's the use?"

"Then I will. Wait here a minute," and he jumped out of the car and headed back to the inn, returning moments later with a brochure.

"I'll report this," he said as he got in the car.

"Thanks, but if it made the news, it could give us away."

"Oops, forgot about that. Well, maybe your threat will make him think twice."

"Nothing changes bigots like that except a big fine."

"Let's drive toward Chincoteague and try a motel."

"All right, but I'm staying in the car till you've booked the room."

Wanting to avoid another incident, Rowan did as she suggested. Once they were safely in the room, he wanted to talk about what had happened, but Easter lay down on the bed and said, "Come lie with me."

"What's the matter?" Rowan asked. He was agitated and it was hard for him to be still.

"It brings back memories of arguments my parents had in these situations. When my father was insulted he could get quite belligerent. Sometimes, when my mother tried to calm him down, he'd turn on her."

"What happened?"

"She'd go silent, I'd start crying, and in the morning he'd apologize."

Rowan put an arm around her. They lay still for a while. She was the first to speak.

"You know what I came away with?"

"What?"

"When you attack someone's dignity, you just embarrass yourself."

§§§

After Chincoteague, they stopped at the spot where, in 1607, English settlers had established a colony at Jamestown, initially with help from the natives, but later over their dead bodies. A sign proclaiming that Jamestown was also where the first African slaves had disembarked moved Easter to volunteer that her grandmother was the product of a black slave and a native American woman. Rowan observed that this meant her ancestors had arrived in the New World thousands of years before his.

Resting after their long drive back to the Rosewood Inn, they were content to read the Sunday papers, order meals from room service, and make love.

Before they parted they worked out a few rules for protecting their dangerous liaison. In public, they would be friendly but formal; neither of them would share their secret with a single soul; if ever confronted, they'd both deny everything.

A last rule was proposed by Easter. "When we do get together, let's make love first and talk later, okay?"

"How come?"

"We talked for almost a year before we made love; we've paid our dues."

"I like that. From now on, love before politics."

CHAPTER 9

With students gone and many faculty away for the summer, Rowan tried to imagine life beyond Jefferson. After spending the day in his office—dressed in jeans unless he had a meeting with a donor or trustee—he'd return to the President's House and watch the nightly news while he ate the dinner Margaret always left warming in the oven.

TV coverage of the war in Vietnam made him recall Tolstoy's Pierre wandering through the battlefield at Borodino during the Napoleonic war. He imagined that actually seeing the Vietnam war would change him, as it had Tolstoy's protagonist. He wanted to experience what Pierre had. Maybe he could find a way to go there the following summer, he thought.

Easter's father had bought her a dark-green secondhand Citroën for the trip between her family home in Chicago and Jefferson College. She visited Jefferson every other week.

She would call Rowan before she left the house but, at Rowan's insistence, they would rendezvous at little motels a safe distance from campus.

The rest of the time, they went about their work. Easter made up the biology labs she'd missed in the spring semester, and consulted with Professor Cowper about her honors thesis. From nine to five, Rowan struggled to stay ahead of the endless demands of his office. When he could no longer stand being cooped up he'd suggest a walk to his next visitor, and hold their meeting while they strolled across the campus.

Since he was in high school, friends had sought Rowan out for personal advice and help with their problems. The office he now held seemed to only increase these requests. A psychology professor asked him to find a job for his troubled son; Margaret lingered one evening while he consumed the meal she'd prepared and asked his advice about her teenage daughter, who'd dropped out of high school. The variety of personal problems that were brought to him was dizzying. Dealing with them was sometimes wearing, but it was also a welcome respite from the sameness of the political issues that claimed most of his time.

He traced his role as counselor to a change that had come over him at thirteen. He still remembered exactly where he was standing when he realized that you could just go on asking *why?* forever. At first, the absence of absolute moral answers made him feel unmoored and alone. But as his new perspective took hold, it loosened the grip old certainties had had on him, and he became curiously nonjudgmental about others' predicaments.

Detachment failed him, however, when he tried to see himself as he saw others. He had misgivings about his love affair with Easter, yet now, strangely, she was the one thing in his life that made him feel alive. Somewhere he'd heard the soul likened to a pilot light on a gas stove. This job was depriving his soul of oxygen, slowly dowsing the flame; losing Easter would snuff it altogether. Jefferson College owned his public self; he wouldn't let it take possession of his private one as well. His relationship with Easter was all that saved him from becoming a "smiling public man."

Through the grapevine he'd heard that quite a few students were having affairs with faculty members, but a president having an affair with a student?—that was, as Sara said, unthinkable. If anyone had even so much as suspected it, a little detective work could easily have exposed the truth. But the crazy audacity of it was probably what precluded such suspicion. At worst, their relationship might be interpreted as a harmless flirtation.

Their secret was safe with Sara. Rowan knew she felt too keenly that their fates were linked to give him away.

§§§

When Easter phoned one evening to ask if she could stop by the house, Rowan hesitated, unwilling to take the risk of her being seen there.

Noting his pause, she added, "To drop something off. I'll just hand it to you from the car and be on my way."

"Maybe I'm getting paranoid. What is it, anyway?"

"You'll see. I'm due at Professor Cowper's shortly, so it'll be quick."

To preempt her honk Rowan loitered in the front yard until she drove up. He went around the Citroën to the driver's side and, without a word, she presented him with a pie.

"Pumpkin pie?"

"Sweet potato. I've seen references to it in slave stories, and decided to try my hand. Pie equals love, remember?"

"If you make me pies, I'll be *your* slave."

§§§

After she'd driven off, as Rowan reached the front porch, an unfamiliar car pulled into the driveway. To his amazement, out stepped Sara.

"Hi there," she called to a gaping Rowan.

"What are you doing here?" he stammered, trying to hide the pie.

"We'll talk in the house," she said, slamming the car door.

Inside, she began, "Was that your girlfriend? How sweet of her to bring dessert." Rowan, who reacted viscerally to sarcasm, strode to the kitchen and stuck the pie in the back of the fridge.

"Would you like a drink?" he asked.

"Some wine, if that's all right with you."

Rowan pulled a bottle of wine from the rack, uncorked it, and poured them each a half-glass.

"You didn't tell me she's black."

"What if she is?"

"It surprised me, that's all. Men in midlife crisis usually fall for blonde cheerleaders."

"I don't think this is a midlife crisis."

"What is it then?"

"A partnership. We share the same goals. We work together. We became close."

"Is this where you have your trysts?" Sara asked, pointing upward. "In *our* bedroom?"

"No," Rowan said firmly. Hoping to mollify her, he added, "Never."

"How chivalrous! Listen, Rowan, I've come to settle this. Every paper in the country will cover this story when it comes out, and believe me, *it will come out*. Don't you see the danger—to Jefferson, to yourself, to me?"

"What exactly do you want?"

"How long has this been going on?"

"Since graduation."

"You must be out of your mind."

"No one knows except you, and no one else is ever going to find out."

"Doesn't the College have rules against exploiting students?"

"She's a consenting adult."

"She's just a college girl. I'll bet she's pleased with herself, bedding the president."

"You can't have it both ways. Victims don't gloat."

Losing her composure, Sara yelled, "You've got to give her up … while you can."

Rowan knew this was going nowhere and, looking for a way out, asked her if she planned to stay the night.

"Absolutely not. I'm sure she's been in every bed. I came to let you know I'm filing for divorce."

Sara had been pacing around the room, but now she sat down and faced him. "I'm thirty-seven. I want a child, and here you are chasing a babe. It's disgusting."

Rowan put his hand on her shoulder. He hated failing her and hated himself for letting it happen. She pushed his hand away and got up. "Don't touch me," she shouted, and stormed out the front door. He watched helplessly as her car sped away. She had left just in time to catch the last plane to New York. It occurred to him that no matter how upset Sara was, she never lost track of time.

§§§

The next time they met, Rowan asked Easter what she thought people would say if their relationship were known.

"I'm sure a lot of girls would be jealous," Easter said. "I've heard them talk. They see your wife's absence as giving them a chance."

"You know, don't you, that a lot of the men around here have imagined making love to you. If they found out about us they'd feel jealous of me for having done what they'd like to do, and at the same time guilty about their desires. They'd try to resolve this conflict by making an example of me."

When Easter just sighed, Rowan went on, "People imagine all sorts of connections, but only rarely do they find a way to each other. Now that we have, it seems inevitable—but only to us. To everyone else it would seem unnatural and immoral. A year ago, it seemed impossible to me."

CHAPTER 10

September, 1971

From the steps of the new library, Rowan looked out on the throng assembled for the dedication. About half the faculty had turned out. A half-dozen trustees were seated on the dais with him and the benefactors, George and Adele Clay. Mike Marlborough had informed Chloë that he would not be attending.

After praising the generosity of the donors, Rowan turned the microphone over to George Clay, and feigned attentiveness while he solemnly invoked the virtues of labor and learning. A year of ceremonies had made Rowan allergic to ritualized speechmaking, and whenever he found himself attending to platitudes—his own or others'—he felt like he was wasting his life.

As Clay droned on, Rowan's thoughts turned to the upcoming faculty vote on the reform package, and he reminded himself to check with Easter about student support. No sooner did he picture her in his mind than he saw her standing alone off to one side of the audience. Easter was what made George Clay and his kind endurable.

§§§

Rowan had quickly come to appreciate Easter's adage of love before politics. With Sara, physical intimacy had grown out of verbal intimacy; after a perfunctory kiss on the cheek they had typically talked through whatever was on their minds, and only gradually warmed up to the possibility of sex. With Easter it was the other way around: love first, talk later. He suspected that Easter's rule was one reason they never quarreled.

They'd agreed to meet in the snack bar after the ceremony to work out a strategy for the looming showdown over the package of educational reforms.

"I'd guess that one-third of the faculty backs the commission's proposals," Rowan began, "and about the same number are against us. Most of the uncommitted are simply waiting to see which way the senior members of their departments will go. Only a handful are genuine independents, but if we present them with sound arguments we can win them over. That's my main job. There are two others—one for me, and one for you."

"What?"

"I think of them as the outside job and the inside job. The outside job is to build enthusiasm for the proposals beyond Jefferson. *Newsweek* is doing a story on American colleges, and a reporter called about spending a few days on campus to get our story. I've also signed up for another round of speeches to alumni on the East Coast. I'll urge graduates to write their favorite professors and ask them to support the commission's proposals."

"And the 'inside job'?"

"That's yours—getting students to ask their professors to vote for change."

"I'll reconvene the group that saved the gym. If you know which faculty are undecided, we'll go after them one at a time. If we have to bake them cookies, or take them flowers, to get their votes, that's what we'll do. Anything short of sleeping with them."

"Ah ha! At last she reveals why she seduced the president!"

"Anything for the cause," Easter said with a grin.

"Seriously, if I can get the alumni to weigh in and together we can change five votes, we'll win."

"We shall overcome," Easter chanted.

§§§

He was surprised when Chloë buzzed him on the intercom and said, "President Ellway, Easter Blue would like to see you for a few minutes." Now that he saw so much of Easter she seldom came to his office.

"Hello, President Ellway," Easter said in a voice he realized was for Chloë's benefit. With the door shut behind her, she took a seat and explained, "I've got an official request, so I thought I'd raise it formally. I know you'll say no, if that's the right answer."

"Let me guess," Rowan said cheerily. "You need a recommendation for the Fulbright." Meeting Easter in his office took him back to their innocent days.

"Nope. I've already lined up the support I need for that. Besides, wouldn't that put you in an awkward position, knowing each other as we do?" Easter gave him a coy look.

"Actually, I've come to see you about funding for the trip Professor Hale is leading to Africa over Thanksgiving. It will cost about a thousand dollars per person, and there are ten of us going. Apparently he's still several thousand short. I suggested he ask you for help, and he told me you'd already pledged five thousand from your contingency fund. Some of his pledges haven't come through, and he's embarrassed to ask for more."

As Easter spoke, Rowan could see how much she had matured. She'd always been clear and direct; now she was developing the calm self-assurance required of a successful leader. He wished he had her patience.

"That reminds me," Rowan said. "I need to get a letter off to the president of the university in Dakar about accommodations for the group. As for the money, let me phone my friend Huey and see if he knows someone whose heart and wallet this might open."

Over the intercom Rowan asked Chloë to put in a call to Huey Scott at Princeton. In less than a minute she had Scott on the line. Rowan explained the situation and then sat back and listened, glancing occasionally at Easter.

When he hung up he said, "*That* was a surprise. Right off, Scott said he'd find us the money—no problem. He mentioned a few likely contributors and offered to prime the pump with the honorarium he's receiving for a speech at Notre Dame next week. I'll let Hale know he's got the funds he needs. He admires Scott, so he'll take his support as a vote of confidence."

"That's terrific, but it didn't take him ten minutes to say that. You were awfully quiet."

"You'd never guess what he told me. He said I'll soon be hearing from an Ivy League university about interviewing for its presidency. He's got to mean Princeton. I know they're headhunting, and Scott is on the search committee."

"That's wonderful!"

"He said they've been checking into my credentials for months ... and that they'll be expecting me to bring Sara along for the interview."

"What's she got to do with it?"

Huey's news had sent Rowan's mind racing. For a few moments, he'd imagined making his mother proud with an Ivy League presidency. He'd forgotten his estrangement from Sara and his exasperation with public life, until Easter's question brought him to his senses.

"Of course, the whole idea is preposterous ... on several counts."

"Because of me?"

"Well, first off, I don't even like administration. Of course, if they found out about us, I'd instantly be scratched."

"What are you going to tell your friend?"

"That I can't be a candidate, that I'm committed to Jefferson. When I tell him that Sara and I have split, he'll stop trying to change my mind."

"My friends wonder why I don't date," Easter said. "It's not easy ... coming across as if I have no love life when actually I'm so happy." Her wistfulness touched Rowan.

"I had a homosexual friend at Columbia who worked in the dean's office. He had to hide his relationship from his coworkers so the higher-ups wouldn't get wind of it. Now I know what it's like to be in the closet."

§§§

When they met off campus that evening, Easter said, "I was upset this morning. You noticed."

"After you left, I realized the strain this is putting you under."

"That's not it. It was the mention of your wife. I'd put her out of my mind, but she exists. Even though she's in New York, I feel her presence."

"I felt you withdraw. I can't help wondering if this is worth it to you."

"How can you ask that?" she said, reaching for his hand. "The problem is that we exist only in private."

"But is it enough—a closet relationship?"

"If it weren't, I wouldn't be here. You must never doubt me, Rowan. I'm a one-man woman and you're my man." Her voice broke as she finished.

"So long as you're a student we can't be together, but that's not forever."

"Eight more months and I graduate," Easter said, pulling herself together.

Rowan closed his eyes and exhaled. "This has been a tough day. Something came up this afternoon."

Without naming names, Rowan described an incident a dean had brought to his attention. A student was accusing a professor of suggesting that he'd write her a better recommendation for graduate school if she'd sleep with him.

To his surprise Easter interrupted him. "I don't know who the girl is, but the professor's got to be Philpot. I've heard things about him ever since I got here and I'm glad someone's finally nailed the bastard."

"I called him in and confronted him with the charge. At first he maintained that the student had proposed the deal. But faced with hearings, he turned contrite, swore it would never happen again."

"Without public exposure, how can you be sure?"

"I can't. But the student refuses to go public. I told Philpot that we'll have his job if there's a recurrence, and I relieved him of his chairmanship."

"I'd want his head."

"Without public testimony from the woman, tenure would protect him, but it made me think about *our* relationship. *We* know there's a difference, but no one else would see it as we do. Your friends, for example—what would they think?"

"That it's cool."

"And Obea, what would he say?"

"He'd be jealous, even though he's got a new girlfriend. He's against black women dating white men under any circumstances. If Philpot was messing with a sister, Obea would make his life miserable."

Easter stood up. "But if Philpot laid a hand on me, I'd knock him into next Sunday," she said with relish. Rowan had the impression that she wished Philpot had given her the chance.

"Well, you could, because you're strong and self-confident. But many students would be intimidated."

Rowan paced the room, feeling more vulnerable to Easter than ever before. "This has got me thinking, Easter. I can't help wondering how you see me, how my position affects you. Would you feel the same way if I weren't president?"

She walked over to him and took his hand. "Mostly I just see you as a man, but every once in a while I see you as president, like this morning in your office, or when I see you in a suit. It's not *why* I love you. I wouldn't love just anyone who was president, and I'd love you even if you weren't."

"Are you sure?"

"I'm sure, but I don't deny that status is part of a man's appeal—like looks are part of a woman's."

"Sad, but true."

"Look, it's more likely I'd love you as a nobody than you'd love me if I were forty."

"I hope I get the chance to prove you wrong," Rowan said with a smile. "Why do you think love goes where it shouldn't?"

"'The heart has its reasons, of which reason knows nothing,'" Easter quoted Pascal.

"John Keats would agree."

"How so?"

"He trusted in 'the holiness of the heart's affections.'"

§§§

104

By the end of October, copies of the Commission's report were in every mailbox on campus. If the faculty adopted its principal recommendations, Jefferson College would become proactive in diversifying its student body and faculty, granting students more say in their curricular choices, and broadening the participation in governance to all constituencies.

To generate outside support for increasing minority enrollment and giving students a voice in educational policy, Rowan made a seemingly endless series of speeches to alumni groups. After one of them, he phoned Sara at her office, and she accepted his invitation to meet for coffee in the Village. Although they hadn't been face to face since the summer, she seemed to have accepted the new reality. He wondered if time had mellowed her, or if she were seeing someone else.

§§§

Sara arrived wearing eye makeup and a short, stylish red dress. As a graduate student, she'd had little regard for fashion. Now she was wearing the chic kind of outfit she used to scoff at.

"You look right out of *Vogue*," Rowan said.

"Different roles, different rags."

"What's your role now?"

"Woman-on-the-way-up is half of it. The men who run the department treat me better if I dress well."

"What's the other half?"

"Dating. Nice clothes enlarge the pool of candidates—like affirmative action," she quipped. "But in the lab, I'm the old me."

"I miss the ponytail."

"That's history. *You're* looking as fit as ever."

"Racquetball."

"It must help to have a girlfriend."

"I don't want to go into it, Sara, but yes, it helps. And yourself?"

"I'm seeing a professor in the classics department." Sara caught herself. "Hey, that's none of your business." She reached across the table and gave his arm a pat.

"That's true," he said, relieved to hear she was dating. "I was the one who drifted away."

Sara looked at him. "I should have known you would, left on your own. You tried to tell me, but I was too wrapped up in my career to hear you. I wasn't myself ... the last time we saw each other."

It never took Sara long to find her footing, he thought.

"Obviously, you've managed to keep everything quiet ... so far."

"She's mature. We're discreet," Rowan said, eager to get off the subject.

"I know I sound like a broken record, but you know what will happen if you're found out." She paused. "You still care what people think, don't you?"

"I still care," Rowan said wearily, "but not in the same way." He drew a breath. "I'm a bad actor, Sara. The job was fun for a while, but I don't know how much longer I can carry on. In the last week, I've explained the reforms to six alumni groups in six different cities. And I think half the faculty hates me."

"No!" Sara said. "They might think you're too impatient, but they wouldn't hate you for that."

"They think I'm using Jefferson as a steppingstone to the next job. At least Bentley does."

"Administration doesn't suit you, and Bentley's an ass."

"I feel bound to stay five years."

"Tell them you made a mistake."

"I feel I have to finish what I started."

"Well, before you bring the house down on my head as well as your own, I want to finalize the divorce. Not in anger, Rowan, just to limit collateral damage."

"I'll pay for the attorney," Rowan offered. It was the least he could do.

"I'd like to stay friends, Rowan, if you're willing. If you need a place to stay in the City, well, you're still paying the rent on our apartment. I'm hardly ever there."

Walking Sara back to her office Rowan felt a slight lifting of his guilt. At the entrance to her building she hesitated between offering her hand or giving him a hug, but then opened her arms and gave him a tight brief hug. This brave woman was once my wife, he thought. Just before she disappeared into the crowd Sara called out after him, "Happy birthday, Rowan." That weekend he'd turn thirty-five.

§§§

An envelope marked Personal and Confidential, in Easter's handwriting, was the first thing he saw on his desk. A birthday card contained a note.

> Follow these instructions: Go to the intersection of College and Main. In the northwest corner you will find the object of your quest. Happy Birthday. Love, Easter.
>
> P. S. Meet me at 8 tonight in our usual place.

Without looking at the rest of his mail he did as instructed. He was amazed that Easter remembered. He'd only mentioned it once, the day they met, more than a year and a half ago.

Exactly where he and Tony Radcliffe had stood with their thumbs out en route to the Van Gogh exhibit was a hand-painted sign on a stake. Rowan parked the car and got out.

> *This historical marker*
> *commemorates the spot where*
> *Rowan B. Ellway*
> *took the leap.*
> *May the Patron Saint of Explorers*
> *watch over him on all his ventures.*

§§§

He found her waiting for him with a little round cake.

"You remembered."

"It was when you told me about not playing it safe that I fell for you. You're an explorer. I admire that."

107

Rowan sat alongside her on the edge of the bed. "I've compared that journey to this one. I landed on my feet with Tony."

"We will, too. Make a wish."

"I wish we could walk out of here and just keep on going." He took a quick breath and blew out the candle.

"You've almost accomplished what you came for. By Thanksgiving, we'll have the votes we need."

"I envy your trip to Africa. Perhaps we can go together sometime."

"Impossible. In Africa, a black woman in the company of a white man is taken for a whore."

"You're kidding."

"Unfortunately, no. Tourists pick up the local girls. Traveling together in Africa would be humiliating for me."

Rowan swiped some frosting off the cake with his finger. "Would you like to go away together over Christmas break?"

"I'd love to. But not where we have to hide."

"We'd be anonymous in Paris."

"Paris! I've always wanted to go there."

"I'll arrange it while you're gone. Just save the week after Christmas."

"I will, yes, I will."

CHAPTER 11

Rowan booked their Paris trip at a travel agency in New York. Easter would fly into New York from Chicago the day after Christmas, and they'd go on to Paris together.

He also reserved a room in his favorite hotel in Montparnasse near the Luxembourg Gardens. What a privilege, participating in Easter's *education sentimentale*. Or was it the other way around? Was she the tutor, he the novice? The fact that the question even occurred to him was a measure of her mystery. There was something elusive about her, something private and inscrutable.

"And what name shall I put on the other ticket?"

The agent's question brought him to attention. When he answered, he felt as if he were giving up the name of a coconspirator. As he walked through lower Manhattan, tickets in hand, he began to question the wisdom of this trip. What if someone spotted them in Paris? But he wouldn't back out now. He wanted this as much as she did. It would be the first time since their drive to the Maryland shore that they'd spent more than half a day together.

§§§

Shortly before Easter was due back, Rowan received a letter she'd mailed from Dakar near the end of her stay.

> Dear Rowan,
>
> I love Senegal. I'm planning a return trip next summer. Our first day we made the trip to Gorée Island, a speck of land in the Atlantic just a few miles from Dakar. Gorée was the last thing African slaves saw before they were shipped to the New World.
>
> It was eerie, walking the pretty lanes of Gorée under bougainvillea and wrought-iron lamps, imagining my ancestors being packed onto

slave ships. Our guide called Gorée the "African Auschwitz."

A university lecturer named François Merle told me that the library still has the original mercantile records of the slave traders. Some from the 17th century. When he asked why Western scholars had shown no interest in them, I asked if I could see them. He ended up inviting me to spend Saturday at his country estate. His mother is Senegalese, his father was French, and he has homes in both Dakar and Paris.

I know you're wondering what happened, so let me set your mind at rest. Yes, he made a pass (I have to admit I found it flattering), but no, I did not sleep with him. I told him what I told you: I'm a one-man woman, and he accepted that like a gentleman. He offered to get me access to the archival records when I return next summer.

Love always,
Easter

§§§

Paris has long provided taboo-breaking couples an escape from the closet. After rehearsing their cover story on the off-chance that they might be recognized by someone with Jefferson connections, they went about in public like any other couple. They attended the ballet *Giselle* at the Palais Garnier, and Bizet's *Pearl Fishers* at the Opéra-Comique. Easter was delighted that the French shared her fascination with African art, and they spent several afternoons gallery-hopping on the Left Bank.

One afternoon, after a walk along the Seine ending at Notre Dame, they warmed up over café au lait in a little bar in the Latin Quarter. After they'd both noticed an older woman kissing an obviously younger man at a nearby table, Easter whispered in Rowan's ear, "I can't imagine what she sees in him. I've always been drawn to *older* men."

§§§

The next morning Rowan suggested a trip to the Rodin Museum. He loved the eroticism of Rodin's figures, and as they wandered among the exquisite marble sculptures he could sense that she too found them arousing.

Later, back in their room, he set about opening her eyes to that beauty by undressing her and, as he removed each article of clothing, kissing what it concealed.

Afterwards, Easter seemed subdued. When he asked her if she was all right, she said, "I missed having you inside me."

Paris's legendary embrace of lovers gradually relaxed all their inhibitions—in bed and on the streets. Below the Eiffel Tower, a street photographer hawking Polaroids cajoled them into buying souvenir photos of themselves. They posed as the lovers they were, arms around each other. Huddled over the developing prints, they marveled as their ghostly images rose into sharp relief.

At a final dinner on New Year's Eve in a cozy Montmartre restaurant, the waiter delivered a bottle of Beaujolais Nouveau to their table, compliments of an anonymous patron. Only when an elderly Frenchman passed their table on his way to the door did he reveal himself with an approving nod. It was the first time anyone had acknowledged them as a couple.

§§§

On his return to Jefferson, Rowan began drafting a speech that he'd deliver to an all-College assembly in Seeger Chapel on the eve of the faculty vote. He'd met personally with undecided faculty, and Easter's troop of student lobbyists followed up. He made a list of anything that might boost their chances of winning support for the program and assigned every item on the list to someone. As the showdown approached, he felt like an orchestra leader who knows the musicians could perform the piece without him, but nonetheless

111

continues to wave his arms lest they lose confidence, put down their instruments, and wander off.

He was in his office polishing his speech when Easter burst in waving a telegram.

"Rowan, I got it! The Fulbright!"

"Wonderful! I knew you would. You've earned it."

"Will you come see me in Oxford?"

"Of course."

When they sat down, he told her what he knew of Oxford, and she described her ideal flat: a sitting room with an electric fireplace, a second room large enough to hold an antique featherbed, and a small kitchen where she would cook roast beef and Yorkshire pudding when he visited.

CHAPTER 12

From a solitary chair at center stage, Rowan watched the crowd settle into the pews. After a few minutes he walked to the podium, detached the microphone and stood looking out until all eyes were on him and the room was utterly still. He acknowledged a few friends with a nod but couldn't spot Easter.

"Two years ago Jefferson College was in turmoil. Standing in this very spot I realized that you were serious about reform, and we've been working together since then to bring it about.

"The changes we've proposed are fundamental, not cosmetic. Everyone in the Jefferson community will be affected.

"Our predecessors helped open people's eyes to the immorality of segregation by race and by gender. The proposals we're making—to recognize students as adults, to create a multiracial Jefferson, and to achieve parity for women—give new meaning to our namesake's proposition that 'All are created equal.'

"In addition, we're proposing a new and equally far-reaching commitment. These reforms will make access to Jefferson College independent of class as well as race, religion, and gender. It will not be easy to reach this goal, but we're asking the College to embrace it.

"Colleges like Jefferson hold special places in our hearts because they change us in ways no other institutions do. Over the four years you spend here, there's a transmission of mind, from teacher to student, that marks the birth of your adult selves. It is your teachers, the faculty of Jefferson College, who embody its cultural traditions, and who pass them on to future generations. And it is to these custodians of our ideals that we must look for leadership in times of crisis. I know we can count on Jefferson's faculty to reassert the College's historic role as a leader in educational innovation, excellence, and equal opportunity."

Here Rowan paused to add weight to what he was about to say.

"I know that some of you think I see Jefferson merely as a steppingstone."

He searched their faces. Every eye returned his gaze.

"I'd be lying if I said I wanted to spend the rest of my life here. These days a typical college president lasts about as long as an undergraduate, and that seems long enough to me." He waited for a ripple of laughter to subside.

"But as long as these initiatives are tied to my presidency, speculation about my ambitions clouds the real issues. If you choose to go forward, I want you to do it for yourselves. From this moment on, this plan is yours, not mine. I want the faculty to be able to endorse the proposals without endorsing me as president.

"Accordingly, I propose to separate the College's future from my own. Next week, after the faculty has rendered its verdict on the new direction embodied in the commission's report, I shall call for two votes of confidence—one from the student body and one from the faculty. Lacking the support of either constituency, I will resign."

He stood silently for a few seconds. He felt that a weight had been lifted from him, that his job was done. As he turned to leave, he saw Easter off to one side. With a beautiful smile, she flashed him a thumbs-up.

§§§

A week after Rowan's speech, the faculty, by a slim majority, adopted most of the commission's core proposals. The most controversial of them—to cap costs, which would have required changes in the College calendar—was handled in the time-honored way: It was referred to a committee for further study.

The Jeffersonian heralded the reforms on diversity, electives, and governance, and ran an editorial praising the termination of the College's practice of surrogate parenthood: "At last the dormitory rooms we pay for are really *ours*. It's about time the faculty admitted that it has no right to impose its Victorian-era morality on us. Even the U. S. Constitution now gives us the vote."

Rowan could only marvel at how fast sexual mores had changed. As a student, he and his then-girlfriend would have been summarily expelled if the dean had learned of their love life. Now, Jefferson was setting up coed dorms, and *Life* Magazine was sending a photojournalist to get the story.

A few days after the faculty vote and before the double referenda on his presidency, Rowan left for New York to wait out the returns that would determine his future at Jefferson. He'd instructed the administrative staff to do nothing to influence the outcome.

Though the votes of confidence had seemed like a good idea at the time, he soon realized that a narrow victory in either constituency would actually be worse than a defeat. He needed two landslide victories or one outright rejection to be free—either to forge ahead with a mandate or return to private life.

There was never any doubt about the student vote. The reforms met virtually all their demands, and they were relieved and grateful. Though the media depicted students as enjoying sit-ins and demonstrations, the vast majority were eager to focus on their careers. Once their grievances were addressed, student activism petered out almost overnight.

The faculty referendum was another matter. The more Rowan thought about post-commission politics, the more he realized he'd given the faculty a way to cripple him. A thin victory would spare him the immediate humiliation of outright rejection, but it would consign him to a role he couldn't tolerate much longer—fundraiser in chief.

When the provost called to congratulate him on getting 95 percent of the student vote and splitting the faculty down the middle, he realized that he had indeed been snared in a trap of his own making.

§§§

With two weeks remaining in the spring term, Rowan found himself office-bound, keeping appointments from dawn till dusk with potential funders, faculty leaving town for the summer or on sabbatical, and seniors just wishing to say good-bye.

He was caught off guard when a delegation from a new campus organization, the Gay and Lesbian Alliance, stopped by to invite him and Sara to what they were advertising as the first openly gay dance on an American campus.

Rowan's attitude toward gays had long been live and let live, and although he'd had gay friends, they'd been the exception in the straight circles in which he and Sara had moved. At a gay dance, the ratio would be reversed, and the thought made him uncomfortable.

Not willing to say no to the students, and not enthusiastic about attending, he wondered if Sara's unavailability might provide a gracious way out.

"Sara's based in New York. I doubt she can make it on such short notice."

"No problem," said the group's leader. "It's you we need."

"Why, if I may ask?

"To legitimize us in the eyes of the College."

"To do for us what you routinely do for other groups," said a member of the delegation. "Show your support. Take a public stand. Give us the College's blessing."

"I see," Rowan said. "I'm not much of a dancer, but ... okay, I'll come."

"It begins at eight and should be in full swing by nine."

"I'll be there. But please don't expect me to dance."

"It's a deal," said their leader. "Things haven't been easy for us here."

"Not anywhere," someone chimed in.

"We're hoping it gets better for us at Jefferson after this. We appreciate your support more than we can say."

§§§

Just before midnight on the eve of graduation, Rowan and Easter met outside the Archives. Rowan unlocked the door and, side-by-side, they climbed the stairs to the room where he'd written the most important speeches of his presidency.

Tomorrow, Easter's status would change from student to alumna. Her parents would arrive in the morning and, immediately after the traditional post-graduation reception at the President's House they would drive her to Chicago. The following day she would leave for Senegal and a summer of travel in Africa before taking up her Fulbright at Oxford in the fall.

Not making love on campus wasn't the only rule they broke that night. Reversing their pattern of 'love first, talk later,' they surrendered to the finality of the occasion and talked late into the night.

"I hope you're not going to give that Senegalese playboy another chance," Rowan said, only half-joking. "That's not why you're going back to Dakar, is it?—to see the dashing Monsieur François Merle?"

"C'mon, Rowan. Dakar is the only place that has the records I need for my research. And Monsieur Merle has access. I'll stay in the university dorms for a week or so, then move on to Ghana and Nigeria. I expect letters from you at every American Express office on my route."

"They'll be waiting for you."

"And anyway, 'Monsieur François Merle'"—she pronounced his name in an exaggerated French accent—"isn't a playboy."

"What is he then?"

"A gentleman who likes me, that's all. You're not jealous, are you?"

"Of course I am. Has he been in touch?"

"In response to my follow-up, he confirmed his offer to get me into the archives. Don't worry about him, Rowan."

"Okay, I won't." He paused to consider whether he should tell her about the invitation he'd received from the Gay and Lesbian Alliance, and decided he should. After he'd recounted his meeting with the delegation, and admitted his ambivalence over the invitation, Easter said, "This won't be the first time you've stuck your neck out, but I have to admit that just this once I'm glad we're not a couple."

Her confession brought laughter which eased Rowan's qualms. When it had subsided, Easter added, "But, Rowan, I want

117

you to know that I'm proud of you for everything you've done. We got most of what we wanted in the faculty vote. Jefferson will never be the same."

After a long pause, Rowan said, "So, what's next?"

"Tomorrow you meet my folks."

"I've looked forward to that, but now that it's about to happen, I'm nervous."

"Sooner or later they'll have to know about us. When I was living at home, I worried that they might catch on, but now I don't care."

"How about we tell them a year from now? We can post-date everything."

"Like how?"

"Oh, we could say that on a visit to Oxford I called to say hello. We began corresponding and one thing led to another. It's better that our love life appear a few years younger than it actually is."

She took his hand and continued, "If you do leave Jefferson while I'm at Oxford, we can take a flat there. You can read and write, and we'll travel during my breaks."

The tremor in her voice told him that she was already feeling their separation. Study and travel were exactly what he yearned for—and he couldn't imagine anywhere he'd rather call home than a flat in Oxford.

"You know, Emily Dickinson was right. I feel like public life has turned me into a frog. When I do leave this job, I'll need time to find myself."

When, deep into the night, they ran out of talk and made love, it was tinged with melancholy. He kissed her on both cheeks and on the top of her head. She gave Rowan a good-bye hug and then turned away to hide her tears.

He listened as her footsteps receded down the stone stairs. When the outside door snapped shut, he peered through the screen of ivy covering the window and saw her disappear, then reappear as she passed beneath each of the lamps on the path leading across the dark, empty campus

CHAPTER 13

Easter's letter from Senegal arrived shortly after she'd left Jefferson. On her first day in Dakar she had made a return trip to Gorée Island. She included this vignette:

> As we pulled away from Gorée for the trip
> back to Dakar, boys were diving off the ship
> for coins passengers tossed into the sea.
>
> After a day spent contemplating the horrors of
> Gorée's dungeons and slave ships, I wanted to
> be alone. I wandered to the rear of the ship
> and watched as the island shrunk in the dis-
> tance. I noticed a man looking out to sea, and
> when he turned to face me, I could see that
> Gorée had affected him deeply. He reminded
> me of you, and I sensed that he wanted to
> speak to me. With a drawn smile in my direc-
> tion, he shrugged, almost apologetically. I
> wanted to tell him it wasn't his fault, but I
> couldn't speak.
>
> I felt him watching as I made my way down
> the gangway, but when I turned to wave good-
> bye he had vanished.

§§§

On the same day that he received Easter's letter, the local paper published a front-page story headlined PRESIDENT ELLWAY AT-TENDS GAY DANCE. A photo showed the chairman of the Gay and Lesbian Alliance with his arm draped across Rowan's shoulder.

Lucky I don't dance, Rowan thought. When he arrived at his office, Chloë told him that the phone had been ringing since she got in, and there were already a dozen calls to return: reporters from national papers, Jefferson faculty, leaders of various gay organizations, and a handful of trustees. At the top of the list was Mike Marlborough.

Rowan decided to return the calls in reverse order. He'd gauge the temperature before subjecting himself to Marlborough's invective.

The faculty members on the list were all supportive. One of them had attended the dance himself and said he'd never felt he quite belonged at Jefferson until he saw Rowan in attendance.

The journalists covering the story for national newspapers were mainly interested in the fight that had broken out between townies and students after the dance. Rowan had been home asleep by that time and could add nothing except that he'd heard from campus police that only a few young men had been involved, and they'd faded into the night when the police arrived.

The trustees were another matter. Only one of them, John Rideout, saw Rowan's gesture as upholding Jefferson's tradition of welcoming the marginalized. Several trustees felt that Jefferson should issue a statement to make it clear that the College was not endorsing the gay movement. Mr. Clay urged that Rowan revoke the Alliance's charter. Finally, when he'd returned all the calls except Marlborough's, he asked Chloë to get him on the line.

"Before you tell me your views, you should know that it's a principle of mine, and one for which Jefferson College has long stood, that there is no alternative to equal dignity for everyone in the Jefferson community. As long as I'm president that commitment includes minorities, women, gays, the disabled, and other marginalized groups struggling to find their voices."

"Do-gooders like you understand just one thing," Marlborough replied. "Votes. I didn't have quite enough last time, but now you've given me what I need."

"I look forward to the board debating this."

"There will be no debate. I've got the votes to override your few supporters, and to fire you."

"Then why are we talking?" Rowan said, and hung up. He looked out the window and thought, *This could be it*. Then he asked Chloë to call Rideout.

When he got Rideout on the line, he asked, "Is it true, John? Marlborough says he has the votes."

"He might, but from what I can tell it's not a foregone conclusion. I'm calling around to find out if he's bluffing."

"I'd be surprised if a majority of the trustees share his homophobia."

"That's the nucleus of Marlborough's faction, but there are others who, for reasons of their own, may side with him."

"Who? What reasons?"

"Some board members think you were the right medicine two years ago, but that you're simply not what Jefferson needs going forward."

"And that is?"

"A healer; a great fundraiser."

"Fundraising isn't my strong suit," Rowan admitted.

"Others think you're too radical. For them it's not just the gay thing, it's everything else you've stood for."

"And you, John? What do you think?"

"I think you've been just what the doctor ordered. Fortunately for the College, you've gotten things done quickly—too quickly for the incrementalists, but quickly enough to have put Jefferson back on the map before you'd worn out your welcome. I'd find you a job in the firm, even without a law degree, but I don't think it's what you want."

"No, it's not, not now. If you told me I was through at Jefferson I don't know if I'd protest or celebrate."

"I have a suggestion, Rowan. Want to hear it?"

"Sure."

"Why not use the ambiguous vote in the faculty referendum as a pretext to resign? If you'd rather stay and fight, I think Chairman Knight and I could put together a slim majority of trustees in your favor. But you'd be on thin ice. Your hands would be tied. You've already done 90 percent of all you'd ever be able to do. By resigning now, before the board meets, you'd remain in charge of your destiny."

§§§

121

Rowan composed a short letter of resignation, effective immediately, and asked Chloë to send it to the public relations office for wide release.

Steve Hobson stopped by while Rowan was packing the few personal things he kept in his office. He simply said, "I guess it's not worth your while to carry on in the face of such tepid support on our part."

"Yes," Rowan responded, "but your personal support has meant a lot to me. I'll be in touch."

His clothes and books would be sent after him. The car, furniture, most of what he'd used during the last two years, belonged to the College.

He didn't want to tell Easter what had happened until he was in New York.

§§§

Rowan hadn't set foot in their New York apartment for more than a year, but he hadn't forgotten Sara's saying he could use it. The last he'd heard of their divorce was that her attorney had filed the papers.

When he landed at LaGuardia late that evening, he dialed their old home number. Sara had said she was seldom there, so he wasn't surprised when there was no answer. He still had the key. He decided to take a cab to the Upper West Side, then try the number again.

He called from a bar a few blocks from the apartment—still no answer. He ordered a double Jack Daniel's, then another, and tried the number for the last time on his way out.

Surely she wouldn't mind if he just let himself in; after all, he *was* still paying the rent. He took the elevator to the seventh floor, rang the bell, and knocked. Still no answer. When he tentatively put his key in the latch, it fit and turned, but the door didn't click open as it always had.

The entrance to the apartment stood at the end of an L-shaped corridor. Exhausted and miserable, thinking no one would see him if he sat down in the hall, he slumped against the wall and promptly fell asleep.

"What are you doing here?"

He woke with a start to find Sara staring down at him. For an instant, looking at her face, it was as if the Jefferson chapter of his life had not happened.

"Let's go in and I'll explain," he replied hoarsely as he came to his senses. He felt sick. "What time is it?"

"Late. How long have you been here?" she asked.

"Since nine. I don't feel so good."

She opened the door and took his coat. "Have a seat. I'll get you some water. Are you hungry?"

"Some Alka-Seltzer would be good. I've got an awful headache."

He took his old seat on the sofa. "I'm through at Jefferson."

"What happened?"

"It makes no sense to carry on with the support of just half the faculty, and a gang of trustees gunning for me. I'm done there. I've resigned."

"Did it come out—the girl?"

"No, no one knows about that."

"What's happened to her?"

"She's in Africa. She doesn't know that I've left." He looked up at Sara. "I tried the lock."

"I added a dead bolt. With you gone, I didn't feel safe."

She left for a moment and came back with a fizzing drink, then sat down at her end of the sofa. "What will you do now?" she asked softly.

"I don't know." A knot was forming in the pit of his stomach.

"You could base yourself here for a while."

"Wouldn't that be awkward ... what with your Latin professor?"

"We've cooled it. He doesn't want children. There was no point."

It jolted Rowan to hear her speak of having a child with someone else. He'd always assumed that *they* would have one. That dream had collapsed along with all the others. He glanced at her, and the sadness in her face made him feel his own despair.

He hadn't intended this. He hadn't planned any of it. All of it had just happened. He had an otherworldly sense of seeing himself from above, like a sea bird looking down on a man adrift on the ocean, at the mercy of its currents.

He couldn't speak. He knew if he tried to, he would break down, and he couldn't break down. He never had. He began rocking back and forth involuntarily, trying to swallow the lump that was rising in his chest.

"Rowan, what's wrong?"

The lump was taking on a life of its own, moving into his throat, suffocating him. His body contracted, loosing a muffled, choking sob. He fought to compose himself, glanced at Sara, then broke down. One sob followed another. Sara was dumbstruck. He didn't deserve her comfort and she didn't offer any.

Wave after wave of sadness washed over him—every rebuff he'd suffered at Jefferson, the humiliation of failure, the loss of people he loved.

Defenseless, he collapsed into the sofa's embrace, his hands covering his face, his tears dropping on the cushions. Sara still didn't move, but her eyes shone with compassion. She gingerly reached over to him and pulled one of his hands away from his face, cupping it in hers.

"Stay here."

"Okay, I'll stay for a day or two," he managed. "Just till I figure out what to do."

"Drink up," she gestured at the glass. "Then get some sleep. Things will seem better in the morning."

§§§

He woke up twelve hours later, disoriented. Then, in a quick series of images, it all came back: Mike Marlborough, John Rideout, the flight from Jefferson, alone in the hall, Sara. He got up and went to the kitchen. Propped against their old teapot was Gumby, holding a note:

> R – Teaching this afternoon. There's a bagel
> for you in the cookie jar. See you at six. – S

Where would he go? Easter didn't want him in Africa, and he couldn't ask her to change her plans. Jesus, he suddenly realized, she still didn't know.

He found her number and placed the call with the international operator. A man answered, and summoned her.

"Easter, I've resigned."

"What?"

"I've left Jefferson."

"Why? Where are you now?"

"I'm in New York, at my old place. I'll explain everything in a letter. It has nothing to do with you, with us."

"Are you with Sara?"

"I got in late and she let me crash here."

When Easter didn't respond, he said, "You're not staying with François, are you?"

"I'm in the University dorms, but I'm using his phone. I'm leaving for Accra in a few days."

He hesitated before speaking. "I could join you there … now that I'm free." As soon as he spoke, he regretted it.

"It just won't work, Rowan. This is Africa. But we could meet in Oxford."

Rowan had seen this coming. He could hang on or let go. If they were to have a future, he'd have to let go for now. He could barely get the words out.

"No, Easter. This is your chance. I'll see you in Oxford in the fall."

"Rowan … " her voice faltered. When she collected herself she said, "Will you be all right?"

"Don't worry about me. Expect a letter at the Amex in Accra."

"So long for now, Rowan. I love you."

"I love you, Easter."

He felt empty, numb. In the bedroom closet, he found some worn blue jeans and a pair of old tennis shoes. He'd pick up a few things in the City and head to his cabin in the Berkshires. He dressed, took the elevator to the lobby, and stepped out into a light summer rain.

PART 2

THE HOLINESS OF THE HEART'S AFFECTIONS

1990–1992

I am certain of nothing but
the holiness of the heart's affections.
– John Keats

CHAPTER 14

May, 1990

It was dark when Rowan left the inn. Two decades had passed, but he still knew the way to the President's House. Instead of going around to the front of the mansion, he took his old shortcut through the lush backyard to the kitchen door.

As he came across the grass Easter rose from a chair on the terrace and waved. Her Afro had yielded to a stylish cut, but at forty she still had the intelligent face and graceful figure of the beautiful young woman he had loved two decades before.

Still several paces away, he paused, trying to gauge the temperature of her welcome. He had no idea why, after years of silence, she had arranged this meeting.

"How are you, Easter?"

She held out her arms to him. "It's so good to see you again, Rowan. You haven't changed."

They embraced politely, then he took a step back and looked at her.

"Neither have you," he said.

"Oh, yes I have. This job takes a toll, but you know that. Have a seat. I'll get some iced tea."

Rowan recalled sitting beside her on this same terrace when the house had been his.

"I have a surprise," she announced, and set a tray down on the table.

"Sweet potato pie!" The last time he'd eaten any, she had baked it.

Easter smiled as she took a seat.

"So, you haven't forgotten," he said. To mask his anxiety he asked about her family.

"Well, Adam begins at Princeton this fall. He's spending the summer with his dad," she said, methodically slicing the pie, and as they ate it she told him how much she'd liked his acceptance speech that morning, adding, "Apart from what I read in the papers, all I really know about your life is that you and Sara had a daughter."

"Yes, six months after you disappeared, Sara and I got together … briefly. For most of our daughter Marisol's childhood, we passed her back and forth between us, but when I was posted to Moscow she came along to study at the Bolshoi's ballet school."

Ignoring the pointed reference to herself, Easter said, "She must be a very good dancer."

Rowan nodded, but before he could press Easter further, she asked, "Does she speak Russian?"

"A lot better than I do. Dancers don't get interpreters like diplomats do, but she's picked up a lot from her friends."

As he continued to fill in the blanks for her, making small talk got harder and harder. (Yes, the Russian winters were severe. No, they weren't homesick.) Finally, he stopped talking, shifted in his chair to face her straight on, leaned forward, and asked his former lover the question that had been on his mind for eighteen years.

"Easter, what happened? I tried every address you left me—first in Africa and then at Oxford."

Easter's self-possession had always been one of the things he loved about her. He watched her take a long sip of iced tea, sensing that she was withdrawing, and fought the urge to grab her by the shoulders and shake the truth from her. Say *something*, he wanted to shout—anything. At last she spoke, her voice cheerless and flat.

"A few days after you reached me in Dakar with the news that you'd resigned, I called your flat in New York. Sara answered. She accused me of destroying your career and trying to ruin her marriage. She told me to get out of your lives. I thought you'd gone back to her."

"How could you think that? You knew I loved you."

"I couldn't reach you. Anywhere. I didn't know what to think."

"Why didn't you write me?"

"I did." Her voice was rising.

"Well, I never got anything."

"Oh." Easter sank back in her chair. "Maybe Sara intercepted my letters."

"That's possible, but when I tried calling you again, whoever picked up said you'd left Dakar with François."

Easter stared at him, then closed her eyes. "Rowan … " She paused, then abruptly stood up. "It's hot out here. Let's go inside. Thanks to your successor, the house is air-conditioned. The faculty cites that as his principal accomplishment." She smiled, adding, "After all the changes you brought, I think they were thankful for a breather."

Rowan knew she would continue when she was ready, and used the lull to regain his composure. As Easter put the dishes in the sink, he said, "When the alumni magazine announced your deanship at Harvard, I figured it was only a matter of time before you were offered this job. How do you like public life?"

"Oh, I love my job, but it's a lot harder to get anything done these days. Today's students aren't as passionate as my generation. Remember how I pushed you on black faculty?"

Rowan, still a bit defensive about promises he'd been unable to keep, said "I did what I could. I think there were at least a half-dozen black professors by the time I left."

"You got a lot of things started, Rowan."

"I know, but without you, it all would have been impossible."

Easter led him to the living room. The brightly patterned sofa and chairs that Sara had bought for the house in 1970 had been replaced with the neutral creams and beiges of the nineties. Passing the fireplace, he paused at the mantel to study a framed photograph of a handsome young man in a basketball uniform. It was easy to see his resemblance to his mother. Deep brown eyes, jet-black curls, broad cheekbones, and a gentle half-smile, as if he were trying to look serious and couldn't quite pull it off. He had strong hands and broad shoulders, the lean body of an athlete.

"This must be your son. Nice-looking boy."

"Adam turned seventeen this spring. It's going to be lonely here with him away at college." He thought he heard her voice break, then was startled to see tears in her eyes.

"Easter, what is it? You can tell me."

"François and I separated a year ago ... when I took this job."

"I didn't know."

"For years, things were fine between us. François had connections in Dakar and got me access to the archives of the slave trade. I built my career on that research." She took a deep breath. She was trembling, and Rowan started to reach for her but caught himself.

"This is my life now, my job and my son." She glanced at the photograph, then led Rowan to easy chairs at the other end of the room.

Sensing that a door had closed, he asked, "So, what happened with François?"

"He's never been comfortable in the States. Gradually, he began spending more time in Paris with his business."

"What does he do?"

"He exports produce from his estate in Senegal to France and the EU. He's bi-national, but most at home in Paris."

"And not fond of America?"

"He thinks we're obsessed with race."

Rowan nodded.

"If I'd gone to Paris with him, we'd still be together, but I couldn't turn this job down. My whole life led to it."

"When you were a student, I used to imagine you'd be president some day."

"It was an education, hanging out with you."

They talked until the chapel bell chimed midnight. Rowan took down her e-mail address and promised to write from Moscow. She gave him a hug at the door, and he could feel her eyes following him as he moved through the circle of light emanating from the porch.

At the inn, the young night clerk politely inquired if Rowan knew Jefferson.

"Yes, I've been here before."

"Oh well, you know all about us then," the clerk added, handing Rowan his room key.

As he stepped away from the desk, memories of Jefferson flooded Rowan's mind. In his room he took a chair looking out on the town square, removed his shoes, and mused, *Yes, I've been here before; I know all about it.*

§§§

American Embassy Compound, Moscow

June, 1990

Most American Embassy personnel were housed in a walled compound that included the stately but aging Embassy itself and scores of modern, serviceable apartments of the sort found in any modern city. Though Moscow and New York bore little resemblance to each other, the apartment he shared with Marisol while working as an Expert Advisor at the U.S. Embassy was not significantly different from the one they kept in New York.

Rowan rose from his desk and walked to the open window. The midnight sky was suffused with the white light of northern summers, and below, a boisterous group of teenagers passed in the street bordering the compound.

Since he'd received the honorary doctorate from Easter at Jefferson's commencement, not a day had passed without his replaying their conversation in the President's House. He'd spent hours reconstructing the sequence of missed communications and false assumptions. It was both understandable and forgivable that Easter, misled by Sara into believing she and Rowan had reconciled, would look to someone like François Merle, first for solace and later for support. A man of independent means, Merle could afford to be wherever Easter's studies and career took her.

He wondered if Easter's pregnancy had precipitated the marriage. It hadn't felt right to probe, but whether she'd married for herself or the sake of the child mattered to him.

He had accepted the honorary degree from the College hoping to make peace with her and her abrupt disappearance from his life, but seeing her again had produced the opposite effect.

His thoughts were interrupted by the highpitched voice of a woman speaking English with a Russian accent in the street below. Russian women were now increasingly seen in the company of American men. The end of the cold war had coincided with the collapse of the Soviet police state, and the combination was a potent aphrodisiac for cold warriors on both sides.

After seventy years of oppression, Russians were aching to let loose, and their naïve euphoria brought to Rowan's mind an image of kids running to the candy store after school, only to find their pockets empty.

Rowan, whose desk at the Embassy was littered with envelopes labeled Top Secret, used an empty one for a photo of Easter he'd clipped from *The Jeffersonian*. Examining it yet again, he sat down and wrote her an e-mail.

> Dear Easter,
>
> I'm back in Moscow where your afternoon sun
> is lighting our midnight sky. Seeing you after
> all this time has been disorienting. I want us to
> meet again to prove it wasn't a dream. Marisol
> will be auditioning for Juilliard this fall and I
> expect to accompany her to the States.
>
> Rowan

Rowan sent the message and shut down his computer, wondering how different his life might be now if e-mail had existed back in 1971. No use thinking like that, he reminded himself. He slipped Easter's photo back into the envelope and went to bed, but couldn't sleep. What would his daughter Marisol think of this woman from his past? Had seeing Easter been the end of something old or the beginning of something new?

§§§

The next morning, he opened Easter's reply.

> Dear Rowan,
>
> Do let me know when you'll be in the States.
> As you know, this job often takes me to the
> East Coast, so meeting you would be no prob-
> lem.
>
> For the record, I want to say that you
> shouldn't blame yourself for anything, unless it
> was for loving me in the first place. And in
> that I was your willing accomplice, from first
> to last. Although public opinion would con-
> demn us—as a matter of fact, the faculty here
> is considering legislation that would make such
> relationships cause for termination—it was ex-
> actly what I wanted.
>
> As ever,
> Easter
>
> P.S. I remember you took a trip to Israel when
> you were president. College business is also
> giving me the chance to travel. I'll be visiting
> our London study-abroad program in late July.

Rowan printed her e-mail and put it in the envelope that held her photo. Her postscript had sparked an idea.

§§§

To avoid competing for their one bathroom, Rowan made a point of getting up before his daughter. "I'll be back in time for your performance Friday night," he called to Marisol through the closed door. He'd be away for three days, inspecting a nuclear lab in Novosibirsk.

"I don't like it when you're gone," she complained, joining him now at the tiny kitchen table. "There's nothing to do at night, and TV here sucks."

"I'd take you along if you didn't have class."

"Why do you have to go?" she whined.

"Work." From habits deeply ingrained, Rowan never divulged anything about his disarmament work. His one word explanation—*work*—was the full extent of his description of what he did, to his daughter—to anyone.

"Is *she* going with you?"

"You know my Russian's no good. Without Katya, I'd be lost."

"I don't trust her, Dad. She's like all those Russian girls—they'll do anything to get to America." Like her mother, Sara, Marisol was alert to peoples' motives.

Rowan was less judgmental; his own motives often seemed unfathomable, so why should others' be any simpler? Though the possibility had occurred to him that Katya was playing him, he gave it no credence. "Katya's different," he told Marisol. "She intends to be part of the new Russia."

"Just watch out, okay? Anyway, she's too young for you."

"How young is too young, in your opinion?"

"Well, you're fiftythree, right? Forty-something would be okay, but Katya's not even thirty. The Russians laugh at Westerners with Russian babes. Really, Dad, it's kind of embarrassing." Again, Marisol's concern with appearances reminded him of Sara. But weren't all teenagers embarrassed by their parents? He winced inwardly but didn't defend himself.

Katya had entered his world almost a year earlier. When he arrived in Moscow, everyone on the negotiating team had been assigned a personal interpreter. Katya—short for Ekaterina—was a classic Russian beauty with the fair skin, blue eyes, and hazel hair that he associated with northern peoples who lived a large part of the year in the dark.

For months, he'd watched her rebuff men who'd attempted to flirt with her, and he had taken care to suppress any sign that he might have a personal interest in her. From nine to five, or more often from nine to nine—twelve-hour workdays were commonplace—he never once saw her diverge from attending to the business at hand.

Then, one evening, after a seemingly endless banquet at Spaso House, the Ambassador's private residence, as he drifted away from the other guests, she had followed him. It was after midnight, and he had been hoping he could manage to slip out before the party officially ended. He confessed to her that parties like this were not how he liked to spend his evenings and, to his surprise, she smiled and asked, "Do you miss your family?"

"Marisol, my seventeen-year-old, *is* my family. She's here studying at the Moscow Ballet Academy."

For the first time, Katya dropped her professional manner. Reaching out and touching his arm she smiled and said, "Oh, I love ballet. All Russians do. It's in our blood."

They talked until the party ended, and he offered her a lift home. When they arrived at her address she invited him up to her flat, gave him Russian tea and chocolates, and then, as if it was the most natural thing in the world, took him to bed. After months of loneliness, the attentions of a pretty young woman had been more than welcome.

§§§

"Dad, have you seen my dance bag?" Marisol called out.

"Look in the bathroom. Hurry or you'll miss the bus. Catch up on your homework while I'm gone. After your show Friday, I'll take you to the Metropole."

She kissed him good-bye and raced out the door, her long strawberry blonde hair flying, her dance bag trailing from her shoulder. Even when she was running she moved like a dancer, feet turned out, toes striking the ground before her heels.

Apart from her knees, which showed no signs of the misalignment that had forced her mother to give up ballet, Marisol had inherited from Sara many of the traits of a born dancer—a supple diminutive frame, grace, and musicality. Technically, she had good turn-out, strong feet, and she was fearless on stage. As a child, she'd always moved faster, jumped higher, and turned better than her peers. At seventeen, it was too early to know if she'd be a star, but it was safe to say that she was a prodigy.

Marisol knew that it was a rare privilege for an American dancer to study in Russia. When the authoritarian style of Russian ballet instruction had gotten on her nerves, she'd often had to remind herself how lucky she was. If getting to the top required deference and obedience, so be it.

During their year-long stint in Moscow, she had grown from a teenager into a young woman. Although he would soon lose any real control over what she did, he wasn't worried. Recklessness was not in her nature. If anything, he was concerned that she too readily put the demands of her art above her personal needs.

§§§

Flying between Moscow and Novosibirsk was like flying coast-to-coast across the United States, yet it was only halfway across the Soviet Union. Cramming it into three days was grueling, but he didn't like leaving Marisol on her own longer than that.

A summer storm dampened their first day in Siberia, and a tight schedule kept them going from morning till midnight. As he suspected, the nuclear lab was state-of-the-art. Over lavish meals, Soviet scientists made it clear that they were the beneficiaries of premium salaries, housing, and health care, and unlike ordinary citizens, they had access to Western goods. So much for communism's "classless" society, Rowan thought.

Marisol was not the only one who worried about Katya's motives. While Rowan was in Novosibirsk, a CIA operative on the Ambassador's staff had noticed that he and Katya shared a hotel room. He had pulled Rowan aside and asked him point blank if she was anything more to him than an interpreter.

Liaisons with Russians, while not exactly illegal, were officially discouraged. By now the Ambassador would have been alerted to the fact that Rowan was fraternizing with a Russian woman. The general assumption was that all Russians who had anything to do with the Embassy were working undercover for the KGB. Everyone knew that the KGB required them to file weekly reports on the Americans they dealt with, but that didn't make them spies, at least not the kind who stole state secrets.

Rowan had long maintained that the quality of American intelligence would improve if every CIA spook had a Russian girlfriend. Besides, as he told the CIA operative, he'd learned far more about Russia from Katya than she'd learned about America from him. A sheepish look from the CIA man signaled his agreement.

§§§

Back from Novosibirsk, Rowan had the Embassy car take him straight from the airport to the Bolshoi theater for the student performance. From years of watching young dancers, he'd acquired an eye for budding talent, and he could see that Marisol's technical skills were exceptional. The audience confirmed his judgment with the rhythmic applause Russians use to acknowledge a favorite.

Marisol was elated by the applause she'd received from the discriminating Russian audience, and Rowan whisked her off to a celebratory supper at the Metropole. On the way she told him that she'd had a call from Sara, who had good news. MIT had offered her a tenured professorship, and she'd accepted. She would be relocating her research—and life—to Boston. Rowan was glad to hear that her hard work had paid off and she now had an "alma mater," a very distinguished one to boot.

He waited till Marisol had gone to bed to go to his computer. He reread Easter's e-mail and composed a reply.

> Dear Easter,
>
> Moscow is only a short hop from London.
> Would you consider adding a stop-over here? I
> can't leave Moscow right now, but I would
> love to show you this beautiful city. If you
> need an official reason, it could be to explore
> the possibility of a student exchange with the
> University of Moscow.

Bribery is becoming a way of life in Russia. In that spirit, let me offer you two incentives: I'll set up an appointment for you with the rector of Moscow U and, in exchange for some mascara, my interpreter will gladly accompany you to your meeting and translate your every word into perfect Russian.

Yours,
Rowan

CHAPTER 15

Through a glass wall, Rowan could see Easter running the gauntlet of Soviet customs. At last she emerged, looking exasperated and bewildered. He called to her over the hubbub and waved to let her know he was waiting. Even from a distance he could see that Soviet officialdom had not made a favorable first impression on her.

Taking her bag with one hand and her arm with the other, he guided her past the ambush of cabdrivers and across the parking lot to the waiting Embassy car.

Once inside, she said, "In America, we'd call that racism." Even ruffled, she kept her cool.

"Those guys are holdovers from the Evil Empire. Hey, it's so good to see you. You look terrific!"

"I can't believe I'm here."

"What hotel did Intourist put you in?"

"The National."

"The National is perfect for a first visit. It's at the heart of Moscow, near the Bolshoi. Let's get you checked in and then I'll show you Red Square."

Driving into the city Rowan pointed out the monument of Hedgehogs— tank barriers welded from three girders of steel— that marked the limit of the German advance on the capital during World War II. He'd never passed these stark reminders of Soviet indomitability without a surge of reverence for the Red Army.

"So close," he said. "Three years later Soviet troops took Berlin. Everyone you meet here lost a relative in the war. These people have known suffering unimaginable to most Americans."

"Maybe not to my people. African Americans and Russians have suffering in common."

As they approached Moscow, Easter's presence at his side made him aware of an emptiness that had dogged him since they had lost touch twenty years earlier.

When the taxi reached the hotel, he paid the driver and waited in the lobby while Easter was shown to her room. He kept a close watch on the elevator as if somehow she might come down, get past him, and disappear.

The doors parted and she edged past a group of Russians competing to board. In the seconds it took her to pick him out of the crowd, he caught a glimpse of the girl he'd known decades before. But the minute she caught sight of him, she became the self-assured woman who, barely two months earlier, had received him as the president of Jefferson College. Now it was his turn to play host.

"This place is surreal," she whispered. "What's with those hall monitors?"

"Ah, the nosy, ever-present *dezhoornayas*. There's one on each floor. Their job is to keep track of the room keys, but really it's to keep track of the guests. Welcome to the USSR."

Rowan led her through an underground passageway to Red Square, his favorite place in Moscow. Strolling across the infinite mosaic of smooth black cobblestones, he pointed out the queue of tourists protruding from the doorway of a red-and-black granite mausoleum, waiting for a glimpse of its embalmed occupant.

"Lenin's tomb," he explained.

"Is it worth a visit?"

"From the outside, yes. From inside, no. Madame Tussaud's waxes are far better."

The russet brick walls and yellow ochre buildings of the Kremlin towered above them. At the far end of Red Square stood the iconic St. Basil's Cathedral, and they set out to get a closer look at its colorful faceted cupolas and golden onion-shaped domes.

"This place has seen plenty of history, and it may soon see more. For months there've been rumors of a coup."

"Against Gorbachev?"

"The communist hardliners think he's selling out to the West." He turned to her and, with a gallant bow, added, "Never fear Madame President. The Embassy will evacuate you at the first hint of trouble."

"How about a photo of yourself in Red Square?" Rowan suggested, pulling a camera out of his pocket."

"Okay."

He snapped the picture. "I'll send it to you via the diplomatic pouch. Are you tired? We could go back to the hotel for tea and go over tomorrow's meeting with the rector."

Easter agreed. As they retraced their steps, he glanced at her and said, "Marisol and I would like to take you to the Bolshoi tomorrow night. They're performing *Giselle*."

"Oh, I'd love that. We saw it in Paris, remember? A story of impossible love."

"I've seen it many times since, and I keep hoping for a happy ending."

After a lingering silence that ended in a quick exchange of glances, Easter said, "I'm looking forward to meeting your daughter."

"I think you'll like each other, though at first she's usually a bit reserved around women in my company. She knows nothing about you … or us. How would you like me to introduce you?"

"As an old friend? President of your old college?"

"That sounds good."

§§§

The meeting at Moscow University went smoothly with Katya interpreting. At Rowan's suggestion, Easter invited the rector to visit Jefferson College, all expenses paid, and from that point on he agreed to her every wish.

"You and she make a good team," commented Katya after they'd dropped Easter back at her hotel.

"We had plenty of practice twenty years ago," Rowan explained as the car sped through Moscow to the American Embassy.

"You've known her that long?"

"When I was president of Jefferson College, she was a student. It was a time of social revolution in America and we were on the same side. She presented the award I got in May. I told you about it."

"Not about her. Not that she's a black. The rector and his staff were shocked. You didn't notice? We don't expect to see them in positions of authority."

No longer surprised by Russian attitudes on race, he said simply, "America used to be like that but things are changing."

"You know, Rowan, when I interpret for you I usually feel I'm part of a team. But around her, I felt invisible. And later in the car it was like I didn't exist. She seems like your wife."

"Katya, Easter and I have known each other a long time, that's all." He didn't want to explain his long-ago relationship with her, and hoped Katya would let the matter drop.

"I wish you weren't taking her to the ballet tonight."

"You *were* invited."

"You *knew* I couldn't go, Rowan. I told you we're celebrating Papa's birthday at the dacha."

§§§

Easter was scheduled to spend three days in Moscow. College business behind her, they passed the rest of the first day sightseeing. The historical high point was Lenin's apartment in the Kremlin. They were sobered by the fact that orders resulting in millions of deaths had been issued from this room. As he left her at the National that evening, Rowan proposed spending their final day together in a park on the outskirts of the city.

Easter was waiting outside the hotel when he arrived in the Embassy car, and Rowan gave the Russian driver their destination—Fili Park, a forested area along the banks of the Moscow River.

When the driver had parked, Rowan got a picnic basket out of the trunk, and he and Easter set off into the forest, leaving the driver reading *Pravda*.

"This place feels a thousand years old," she said as she caught her first glimpse of the Moscow River snaking back toward the capital. "Like a primeval forest." She took in the scene, then turned to him. "Marisol is a beautiful girl, but you know that. While we were watching the ballet together, I pictured her up on that stage. Did she say anything about me?"

"She's curious about you."

"What did you tell her?"

"That we knew each other way back when. That we had worked together."

"Go on … ."

"She asked about your son."

"What did you say?"

"Nothing, really. You haven't told me anything about him."

When she didn't respond, he added, "I remember one thing. She thought you were 'cool.'"

"What made her think that?"

"Probably your reaction to the ballet. She could tell you were moved by Giselle's loyalty to Albrecht."

"That's true."

Rowan knew her well enough to sense her fleeting embarrassment. As if to acknowledge it, she reached over and touched him on the forearm. Then, she said, "Here, let me help," and took the thermos he was carrying from under his arm.

They wandered along the Moscow River before settling down under a shade tree on the embankment, where they watched couples stroll along both riverbanks. A young man in a dilapidated boat rowed against the current, going nowhere.

Rowan spread a blanket on the grass and opened the basket, pulling out a loaf of dark bread, a small crock of butter, a jar of caviar, two pieces of apple pie obtained at the Embassy commissary, a bunch of red grapes, and a chilled bottle of the sweet fizzy white wine that passes for champagne in Russia.

He uncorked the wine, filled two glasses, and handed one to her.

"How do you say 'cheers' in Russian?" she asked.

"*Za vasheh zdahrov-yeh*," Rowan intoned. "It's one of the first things you learn here."

"*Za vashas da-rovia*," she pronounced tentatively.

"Sounds good to me," he said. She repeated her new toast as they clinked glasses.

They chatted about the river scene and then about the changes that had come over Jefferson during the past two decades. Shortly before Easter took office, Steve Hobson had left to head a poetry program in California. Donald Bentley, though nearing retirement and no longer chair of the chemistry department, was still an influential voice among the faculty. And Obea Uhuru, who'd reverted to his given name of William Stone during his first year of law school at the University of Chicago, was now a high-profile civil rights attorney in Chicago, and angling for a seat on Jefferson's Board of Trustees."

Rowan couldn't find a graceful segue, so he just blurted it out: "How are things with François?"

"As you know, we're separated."

"Yes, but tell me something about his background, about your relationship. I always wondered why you married ... so quickly."

Easter gave him an inscrutable look—whether apologetic or defiant, he couldn't tell. She explained that when World War II broke out, François's father was a French admiral stationed at the colonial naval base in Dakar. His mother, who still divided her time between Paris and Dakar, was the sister of Senegal's poet-president, Léopold Senghor.

"François doesn't identify as white *or* black. I noticed this the first time I met him. He's your classic cosmopolitan, at home everywhere. A human being first and an African European second."

"A world citizen. I've met a few of them here. Has he been a good father?"

"Devoted. Adam idolizes him. Temperamentally, they're very much alike—self-possessed, imperturbable, confident."

"That he got from his mother."

"I think it comes from social breeding, not biology. Both sides of François's family go way back."

Rowan, in an attempt to show that he wasn't entirely ignorant of things African, said "I've heard of Senghor."

"You heard of him from me!" she said, tossing a grape at him. "He was all the rage in the sixties as the philosopher of *Negritude*. I was reading him my senior year at Jefferson."

"Oh, that's right."

"The point is that François's family ties gave him access to the upper echelons of both French and Senegalese society. Adam is the heir to the Merle family holdings in both France and Senegal."

"So he's French?"

"No, actually he was born in America. I went home to Chicago to be with my mom for the birth."

"I hope you worked 'Blue' into his name somehow. Your family name is too good not to pass on." He'd always loved her name, and wanted her to know.

"François and I had quite some discussion about that," she said with a sigh.

"And?"

"We finally settled on 'Adam Merle-Blue,' on the grounds that a hyphenated last name would work in either America or France and connect him to both families. In practice, Americans often drop the hyphen and omit the 'Merle,' as if it were a middle name."

"What is Monsieur Adam Blue doing this summer?"

"He spent two weeks in Paris with François and his grandma." Easter dug a family photo out of her purse and showed it to Rowan. "This was taken on the front steps of their town house on Place des Vosges. Then he and François spent a month at the family estate near Dakar."

"I'd like to meet Adam. Didn't you say he'll be at Princeton this fall? Perhaps next time I'm in New York we could all have dinner."

"When are you coming to the States?"

"As soon as we initial the treaty. Next year sometime."

Easter leaned back on her elbows and looked up at the leafy canopy overhead. The hypnotic clunk-whoosh of the oars of a passing rowboat drew their attention to the river. Rowan refilled their glasses with the Russian champagne.

"Santé," Easter said.

"*Cheers.*"

Easter took a slow sip. "This is the worst champagne I've ever tasted," she said, screwing up her face.

"It's probably made from the same rotten apples you see in the stores here," Rowan explained, relieving her of her glass. "I bet they served better stuff at that White House dinner you attended a few weeks ago. I noticed your name on the guest list in *The New York Times.*"

"I made that list as the wife of a prominent French businessman. It was a state dinner for the president of France, and François was invited. It was the only thing we've done together since I took the job at Jefferson."

"You know, Easter, after you make a name for yourself at Jefferson, the Ivy League is going to come courting."

"Not if our story ever comes out. *The* issue on American campuses now is sexual harassment. I think I told you that there's a committee at Jefferson drafting a code of sexual conduct for faculty, staff, and students."

"A sex code? I thought we'd seen the last of those."

"They're back with a vengeance. The hard-liners want to forbid all sexual contact between students and staff. A few professors who married students are arguing that colleges have no business regulating the love lives of consenting adults. A group in the middle is advocating a compromise forbidding sexual relationships between students and anyone in a position of authority over them. You know, like a student in a professor's class, or, to pick a purely hypothetical example, between a student and the president."

"Imagine that!"

"So, if I support the proposals, I'm a hypocrite, and if I don't, I'm a libertine. In the current climate, the truth about us would be a career-killer."

"I'd have thought it was ancient history."

"Rowan, you're out of touch. I'd be through."

"Even at liberal Jefferson?"

"It's still puritanical, at least compared to France. I'd be hopelessly compromised. I'd have to leave."

"I've come to believe that our relationship was what kept me going. Public life was suffocating me, and getting out when I did was a deliverance."

Then, rising to his feet, he said, "We'd better go. You'll need a little time at the hotel before you go to the airport." Reaching down for her two hands he pulled her to her feet, and for an instant they brushed against each other. She appeared a bit flustered, and he tried to cover his nervousness by bending down to collect their things.

"Russians would scoff at my calling this a forest," he said as they returned to the car. "It's the best I could do for a day trip. The Trans-Siberian railway passes through thousands of miles of birch and larch trees—that's a *real* forest."

"So, you did take the Trans-Siberian? I remember your talking about it."

"Yes, a few years after I left Jefferson, I boarded the train in Moscow and rode all the way to the Sea of Japan. I don't know anyplace with brighter stars than Siberia. I thought of you out there."

As they strolled through the sprawling park she slipped her arm through his.

"Rowan?"

"Yes?"

"I'm curious about how you and Sara got back together."

"We didn't get back together, apart from the one night when Marisol was conceived. The day after our last conversation I went to my cabin in the Berkshires. I stayed there while I tried to find you, but gave up when I learned you were married. At my lowest, I went to New York to interview for a job. Sara offered to put me up for the night, and it just happened."

"Were you upset about her pregnancy?"

"Not a bit. I felt it was her due. She'd wanted a child for years, and somehow the baby helped me atone for what I'd done."

"Didn't you want to raise Marisol with her?"

"Not together. I got my own apartment in the city, and as it turned out, Marisol usually spent weekdays with me and weekends with Sara. Actually, I think I was a better father to her single than I would have been married. I love having her with me here in Moscow."

"And your work—how did you end up in Russia?"

"During Sara's pregnancy I finally went to Vietnam—as an ordinary citizen on a tourist visa—and got a first-hand look at war."

"I remember your wanting to do that. How did it affect you?"

"Imagine standing over a dying Vietcong prisoner who's chained to his bed and covered with flies feeding off his open wounds. He looks up at you, pleading for help with his eyes." The memory made Rowan's throat tighten. "The image still haunts me."

"How did you get involved in disarmament?"

"My physics background gave me a technical understanding of nuclear weapons, and I studied arms control at the Brookings Institution. While I was crossing Russia on the Trans-Siberian, I developed a deep regard for the Russians. They've survived unspeakable horrors, and they did more to defeat the Nazis than any other nation. I came to feel that the cold war was a historical mistake, and that if some of us began acting as if it were over, it might help to end it. Here I am, still trying."

"I wouldn't have expected to find you back in public life."

"This job looks public, but it's really not. The important stuff is done behind the scenes. Off the record, American and Russian scientists see things pretty much the same way. We all understand that nuclear war is mutual suicide. The challenge is persuading the politicians, who have to either pander to their constituents or bring them along. A politician's job is more like a college president's than people realize."

§§§

On the way back to her hotel, Rowan offered to take Easter to the airport but she declined, having previously arranged to share a taxi with an American couple on the same flight.

"A farewell drink?" Rowan suggested.

"Not champagne!" she said, quickly adding, "Some red wine would be nice. I'll check out while you order."

There was a bar off the lobby. He chose a dimly-lit booth and ordered two glasses of the best red available—Bulgarian. When she returned, instead of taking the seat opposite him, she sat next to him.

Emboldened by the touch of her arm and thigh, he asked the question that had been on his mind all day.

"You told me that you and François are separated. Are you seeing anyone else?"

"I have many good friends, some at the College, more in New York. But there's no one special. My life is my job and my son."

"That's what you said at Jefferson."

"There's something missing, I know."

"Any regrets?"

"I've asked myself that. I don't regret the sacrifices I've made for my career, but I can't say I feel whole."

Rowan reached for her hand. It felt soft and responsive and familiar.

"Easter, our taxi is waiting." An American woman was calling to her from the doorway. "We'll start loading the luggage."

She stood up, and Rowan walked her outside. When they embraced, decades seemed to melt away

CHAPTER 16

The American Ambassador wanted to keep the negotiations going right through Christmas, but the leader of the Soviet delegation could not oblige him. Religion was again becoming a force in Russian society. To placate the Orthodox Christians on his team, the ambassador declared the first ten days of 1991 a holiday, as it traditionally was before communism.

When Rowan reported this to Katya, she proposed they spend a week in her parents' cabin twenty miles north of Moscow. Ever since reading *Doctor Zhivago*, he'd dreamed of living in a Russian dacha. Katya's parents, like many of the Soviet *nomenclatura*, spent January at a Black Sea resort, so both their car and their country dacha were available. The last obstacle evaporated when Marisol accepted an invitation to spend the week at a classmate's home in Tula, south of Moscow.

Before Easter came back into his life, Rowan had almost succeeded in convincing himself that what he felt for Katya was love. High cheekbones gave her heart-shaped face an aristocratic look; he was also drawn to her old Russian soul, and he found the mellifluous sound of her native tongue, while quite incomprehensible, curiously soothing.

For a while Katya's youthful abandon had made him feel young. He didn't dare take her to his apartment in the Embassy complex for fear that the sounds she made during their lovemaking would bring Embassy guards who would hammer down his door with their rifle butts and burst in on them. With a shout, Katya would have repelled the intruders, all the while urging him on, as she had done when a hotel maid walked in on them in Novosibirsk.

On the way to the cabin, he glanced at Katya in the driver's seat, piloting her parents' beloved old Chaika around the potholes on the country road. In the language of photography, Ekaterina was Easter's negative.

The dacha itself consisted of three small rooms—living room, kitchen, and bedroom—and the only heat came from an open fire in the stone hearth. Cold running water was available in the kitchen, and an outhouse stood a hundred paces from the back door.

At this time of year there were few hours of natural light. They used them to hike, and gather the wood they burned in the hearth, and pinecones for the samovar to boil water for their tea. Russian tea was awful, dusty stuff compared to the stash of Fortnum and Mason Royal Blend he kept in his Embassy apartment, but in this winter paradise its inadequacy was easy to overlook.

They spent most of their time reading. Rowan, who had left his technical work at home, tried to understand what Russians loved so much about Mikhail Bulgakov's *The Master and Margarita*. Katya read Danielle Steele novels to work on her English.

§§§

Rowan, back at his residence in the Embassy compound, with no prospect of seeing Easter again anytime soon, stayed in touch with her by e-mail. At the end of one of her messages, he was surprised to find an open invitation:

> Dear Rowan,
>
> Aren't diplomats called home for consultations now and then? As you know, the president of Jefferson College can always find something to do in the nation's capital.
>
> Easter

He replied immediately.

Dear Easter,

I wish it were sooner, but I won't be back in the States till the end of March—over the Easter holiday. I don't know where they'll put me up, so if you're free, let's meet at noon on Easter Sunday at the Jefferson Memorial.

Yours,
Rowan

§§§

In Washington, the undersecretary of state confirmed what Rowan's superiors in Moscow had already told him. In the next round of arms talks, they wanted him to head up the negotiations on land-based intercontinental missiles. The talks would focus on making the "deep cuts" that Presidents Reagan and Bush had agreed on with Gorbachev.

But there was a condition. Rowan's promotion was contingent on avoiding personal contacts with Russian citizens. In other words, no Katya. She would be discreetly transferred to another ministry, and it was unlikely he'd ever see her again.

"Too much is at stake to risk embarrassment," the undersecretary explained. "Their guys in Washington are operating under the same constraints. That's where the policy originates. It's tit-for-tat," he concluded, breaking into a lewd smile that suggested he'd used this pun before.

"When would the assignment begin?" Rowan asked.

"This fall, with the start of the next round. But, as you've been told, the CIA and the NSC won't sign off on you if you're sleeping with the enemy."

"I'll have to think it over."

"Look, Rowan, our girls may not be quite the linguists the Russians are, but they're just as good in the sack."

"Do you speak from personal experience?"

155

His question erased the leer from the face of the Undersecretary, who summarily returned to business.

"May I tell the secretary that you've accepted our offer?"

"As I said, I'll think it over."

"Think fast."

§§§

On Easter Sunday, Rowan reached the Jefferson Memorial well before noon. He'd bought a new shirt for the occasion and had his shoes shined at the hotel. He circled the monument on foot, gradually spiraling inward toward the statue under the cupola. He'd always admired Thomas Jefferson, yet as he sat in the shadow of his statuary likeness, he wondered again how Jefferson had reconciled "All men are created equal" with his ownership of slaves. But he also took delight in the idea that the father of American democracy was also the father of some of Sally Hemings's children. Jefferson's secret love life jibed with Easter's belief that love runs ahead of politics.

A woman waving from the distance caught his eye. A wide-brimmed straw hat hid her hair and forehead, but he recognized her graceful walk. A forest-green ribbon trimmed Easter's bonnet, and as she got closer she peered up expectantly from under the brim.

He met her halfway. From behind his back he produced a bouquet of yellow tulips and presented them with a flourish. She accepted the flowers with a smile and a hug. The touch of her hair against his cheek inspired him to lift her a fraction of an inch, but he immediately leaned forward so her toes regained the ground.

"I'm glad to see you," he said, modulating his voice to compensate for the forwardness of his hug.

He suggested they look for the café where, twenty years earlier, they'd had lunch after their meeting with the commissioner of education.

"I bet it's still there," she said. "Nothing much changes in this town but the man in the White House."

§§§

Except for the addition of an espresso bar, the café was as Rowan recalled it. When they were seated, he said, "The hat transforms you into a portrait of yourself."

"It's not too old-fashioned?"

"It's perfect. 'Easter in her Easter Bonnet'—that's how I'd title a painting of you."

She met his gaze for an instant and then looked down at her menu. For a moment, past and present fused, and he wondered if he detected a hint of a blush on her neck.

As if to steady herself, she filled the momentary silence. "I dropped Adam off at Princeton yesterday. Instead of spending spring break in Florida, he visited me at Jefferson. Unusual for a young man, don't you think?"

The waiter interrupted to take their orders. Without glancing at the menu, he ordered soup and a sandwich. She questioned the waiter about several items and finally settled on *salade Niçoise*.

"How long will you be here?" she asked

"Just long enough to get my instructions. The negotiations are at a critical point. I leave on a military plane tonight."

"Oh, I was going to suggest we go to the Hirshhorn Sculpture Garden tomorrow."

"I would have loved that."

"It's just as well. There are so many Jefferson alumni in this town, I'm still nervous about someone seeing us together."

"We could always resort to our old ruse." Easter didn't pursue it; instead, she asked about Marisol's plans.

"Marisol just spent a few days with Sara in Boston. Tomorrow she's visiting her old teachers at the School of American Ballet in New York, and then she returns to Moscow on a commercial flight." He paused, looked directly at Easter, and said, "The State Department has formally offered me a lead role in the arms talks in Moscow, but I'm thinking of turning it down."

"Why?"

"The promotion would mean more status but less substance. And I'd have to prolong my tour."

He scrutinized her face, hoping to read her reaction.

After a beat, he asked, "What do you think?"

"I have no right to an opinion."

He tried again. "I'm leaning toward returning to the States. For one thing, Marisol wants to be in New York next year."

"So, what's holding you back? Katya?" Her eyes flashed as she spoke Katya's name. It was the sign he'd been waiting for, and he spoke from the heart.

"Katya's been a comfort to me, but *she's* not the love of my life."

From the softening of her face, Rowan understood why she'd wanted to see him—and he had answered her question. As they left the restaurant, she gripped his arm tightly.

CHAPTER 17

Katya waved as Rowan passed through the diplomatic channel at customs. Halfway to the Embassy, she proposed they stop off at her place. He knew what she had in mind.

She was so impatient to have sex, she said he should bathe afterward, but Rowan, coming off an all-nighter on the plane, insisted. Sitting in Katya's stained tub, with the hand-held shower delivering a thin stream of rust-colored water to his back, he tried to soap himself with his one free hand. He wondered how a nation with plumbing like this could field nuclear missiles.

"Aren't you finished yet?" Katya called through the door.

"Almost."

"I'm coming in," she announced, and before he could get up she was standing naked in the tub and lowering herself down onto him.

"I can't stand it when you're away, Rowan," she cooed, handing him a towel. "Will you take me next time?"

"Could you get a visa?"

"If you'd help me."

"There would be no problem on the American side, but your government is stingy with exit visas."

"But do you *want* to take me? Where there's a will, there's a way—isn't that what you say? I've wanted to go to America ever since I was little."

"I'd love for you to see America someday. Come on. Get dressed. I brought you some things."

Katya squealed like a birthday girl as she lifted one treasure after another from the shopping bag—mascara, shampoo, pantyhose, raspberry jam, cocoa, maple syrup. She plugged in her samovar and cut slices of dark sour bread, the staple of every Russian household. As she spread jam on the bread he told her about his new job.

"You'd be Valentin Zelikov's opposite," she pointed out, clearly impressed. "That's prestige."

"Yes, a front man."

"We'd be invited to formal functions. I'd have to get some new clothes."

"You know I hate parties."

"Wouldn't the position give you more power?"

"Not really. I'd be a mouthpiece. The political decisions in these talks are driven by technical realities. I actually have more influence where I am, behind the scenes, shaping the negotiations by providing both sides with objective analysis."

Rowan had never put it so clearly, even to himself. He was most useful marshaling the facts and defusing the paranoia that, on both sides, had driven the arms race for decades. In fact, during the last few months, as he'd seen most of his proposals adopted, he'd begun to dream of returning to the life he loved—writing and research.

He'd decided not to tell Katya about the undersecretary's sole condition—that to move up he must drop her. Since he was leaning toward turning the promotion down, Katya need not know.

§§§

Rowan was listening for the sound of Marisol's footsteps on the paved approach to their apartment and, opening the front door just as she was about to knock, he gave her a welcome-home hug.

"Hi, Dad. I smell coffee. Is there some for me?"

"Since when did you start drinking coffee, world traveler?" he asked, pouring her a cup.

"Once you get used to it, it's not so bad."

Sitting with her as she chattered away, he felt content. It pleased him that she still shared her life with him. He hoped it wasn't simply because she had no one else to talk to. He'd always tried to listen and ask questions without passing judgment. He dealt with the Russians in the same way. Rather than set himself against the other party, his style was to expand options. Most of the time, in a context of expanded choices, problems resolved themselves, whether they were the concerns of a teenager or matters of state.

"Tell me about New York," he said, passing a package of her favorite cookies.

"Goody!" she said, taking one. Rowan saw her mentally adding up the calories, and watched her place a second cookie next to her mug, then deliberately return the box to his side of the table, out of reach and beyond temptation.

"I've got to get back there, Dad. New York is the dance capital of the world, not Moscow. The dancing is more dramatic and theatrical here—and I've learned a lot and I'm stronger—but the Russians can't train you to do contemporary repertoire."

"So, how'd it go at the School of American Ballet?"

"Actually, it was an audition."

"What?"

"And I nailed it! The ballet mistress said that one year in Moscow was a good thing, but two would be too much."

"Are you telling me that you've been asked to join the New York City Ballet?"

"Yes!" Marisol was grinning. Rowan had never seen his daughter so happy.

"Why didn't you tell me right off? Congratulations!" He stood and gave her another hug. "We'll have to celebrate. Have you told your mom?"

"I phoned her from Kennedy airport."

"You've done her proud, Marisol. How is she anyway?"

"Busy as always," Marisol said absently. She broke off a piece of cookie and popped it into her mouth. "What about you, Dad? Will you be ready to leave by fall?"

Rowan sat back down. He couldn't answer that question, not yet, and couldn't even tell when he might be able to.

"I don't know, Marisol."

"Hmm. Well, how was your trip? Did you see anyone I know in Washington?"

"As a matter of fact, I did. I saw Easter Blue."

"That's great, Dad, I liked her." Then, after a beat, "I'm glad you're seeing her."

"Marisol, we're just friends."

He saw a dubious smirk appear over the rim of her coffee cup.

"Look, Dad, I've seen you two together. It's obvious there's something between you."

"It's not what you think."

"It wouldn't upset me if it was. I'm a grown-up, you know. She's so much nicer than Katya, and not too young for you either." She sank into the sofa and reached for the remote.

"She's got a husband, Marisol."

"And a son, right?"

"Aren't you the inquisitor. Yes, his name is Adam."

"How old is he?"

"About your age."

"What's he like?"

"He's a freshman at Princeton and he plays basketball."

"Is that everything?"

"His father is rich. Now, give me that remote and go to bed. How about a walk in the morning?"

§§§

Rowan sat up for a long time. If he *were* having an affair with Easter, admitting it to his daughter would be easy, compared to explaining their actual history.

And what about moving back to the States? His desire to step back, reflect, and write was growing daily. Perhaps he could try to get a teaching job at one of New York City's universities, but without a book to his name, his chances were slim. A book. Yes, he could do that: a book about disarmament. And he could write it in New York.

§§§

Marisol held Rowan to his promise of a walk. When they reached the Moscow River, she made her move.

"You've never kept secrets from me."

"That's true."

"I just want to know if you and Easter are a couple."

"Whatever gave you that idea? I told you she's married."

"Everyone gets divorced these days."

"That may be," Rowan said with a sigh.

"I'm sorry, Dad. It's really none of my business."

"That's right. It's not. There's nothing between us."

"Was there ever?"

Rowan had never lied to Marisol; he didn't know how. "It was so long ago, Marisol, I can hardly remember," he said, trying not to sound defensive.

"When you were married to Mom?" He knew she'd already guessed the truth, so why deny it?

"It's ancient history."

"Like, when you were president of Jefferson?"

He stopped and leaned against one of the trees lining the path. "Just about that ancient."

"What was she, a student?"

When Rowan didn't say otherwise, she stared at him.

"Wouldn't that be sexual harassment?"

"Not if it's what both people want."

"Is that why you and Mom split?"

"It's part of it."

"Why didn't you and Easter get married?"

"She graduated and went off to Africa. I resigned and went back to New York. We lost touch. A few months later, your mom and I got together again, for a while."

"That's when you had me?"

"Yes, Marisol. Two wonderful things came of my leaving Jefferson—I got out of public life and you were born."

"What happened to Easter?"

Rowan resumed walking. "She married a man in Africa. Life doesn't always have a Hollywood ending."

"So, how did you and Easter get back together?"

"I told you, we're not together. We saw each other for the first time in decades last summer … when I got the honorary degree at Jefferson."

"You didn't see her for twenty years?"

"After Jefferson, we went our separate ways."

"That's not like you, Dad. You keep in touch with people you've known."

They returned to the Embassy in silence.

§§§

The following weekend, while strolling through Gorky Park, Rowan told Katya that he was going to turn down the promotion. He waited to break the news until they were seated on a park bench.

"This means I'll be returning to the States," he concluded.

"When?"

"After this round of the talks, probably in the fall."

Katya stood up and seated herself across Rowan's knees, facing him.

"Will you take me with you?" she asked, brushing his hair off his forehead. He was ready for her question.

"Do you want to visit, or do you want a job there?"

"I want to live with you."

"With Marisol at home that just won't work."

"Why not?"

"It just won't. I know my daughter."

She tugged on his sleeve, but he avoided her stare. Touching him on the cheek, she pressed, "Rowan, don't you love me?"

"I'd like for you to see America," he said, turning to meet her gaze. "But the three of us living together—that's impossible."

"Well then, we could do as now. You live with Marisol, I live separate."

"Katya, I have to be honest with you. I've loved our time together. Moscow would have been barren without you. But I *am* too old for you. We want different things. What's worked for us in

Moscow won't work in the States. It's best we recognize that now and remain friends."

He watched her intently, expecting an outburst. To his relief, she was calm and deliberate. She got up, took a few steps back, and standing before him announced, "I want to go to business school. There's no future in interpreting. Russians are all learning English."

"Business school! That takes years, and a lot of money. I thought you wanted to help build the new Russia."

"Russia needs business, American-type business. With my English, I could do well."

"I'm sure you could." He imagined Katya ending up as one of Russia's new millionaires.

"We don't have to marry, Rowan, if I go to America."

"Your problem will be getting permission to leave Russia."

"My father can get exit visa. Student visa is my problem. If you sponsor me, I can stay in America while I get a degree."

"What would that involve?"

"Soviet universities are free, but yours cost dollars. I was hoping you could help me a little, while I study."

Only then did Rowan understand what she wanted of him. She wanted a ticket to America and financial support—exactly what he would soon be providing for Marisol.

"What are you thinking?" she said, putting her arms around his neck.

"I'm thinking I can already barely afford to pay for Marisol."

She backed away, a hurt look on her face.

"I thought you loved me."

He felt like the fool who, to prove he isn't one, has to make a fool of himself. He told her Marisol was expecting him for supper and he had to go. To ease his exit, he promised Katya to think about her proposal.

§§§

165

April 20, 1991

Dear Rowan,

Forgive me for not writing sooner. Sexual politics are boiling over here. I'm being pressured to spell out my personal position, and that puts me in a bind.

You asked for news of Adam. Now that basketball season is over he has more time for academics. Everyone talks about his athletic success as if I should be so proud, and I am. But to me sports is a pastime, not a career. His math professors say he's got talent. I'm hoping that after college he'll put basketball away and make his living with his mind.

What's happening with you?

As ever,
Easter

§§§

April 21, 1991

Dear Easter,

Big news! Marisol will be joining the corps of New York City Ballet. I've decided to leave my position this fall and come home with her. A literary agent in NY thinks he can get me an advance for a book on nuclear arms control.

I hope we'll see more of each other once I'm back. Until then, I remain virtually yours,
Rowan

P.S. I'd love to talk to Adam about his dual talents, both dear to my heart.

§§§

Rowan left his Embassy office and walked the short distance to his apartment in the compound. Katya had kept up the pressure on him, and he sensed the showdown might come that evening at the Embassy's spring party.

There had been times during his sojourn in Moscow when he'd actually considered bringing Katya back to America. He felt indebted to her for turning what could have been a miserable posting into a love affair he would never forget. The trust and affection he'd come to feel for his Russian colleagues had been deepened by knowing her. Love shapes politics far more profoundly than most people realize, he mused. He wanted Katya to have her dream; he just didn't want to go into debt to pay for it, let alone find himself in the company of men who kept a mistress.

Through the open door of his apartment, he saw that it was already crammed with Marisol's ballet friends—slim lithe bodies, elongated necks, shoulders back, feet turned out. The girls, who normally wore their hair in buns, were wearing it loose around their shoulders.

Marisol took him by the arm and introduced him to everyone. They all knew a bit of English, but only a few could sustain a conversation. Good thing too, he thought, because otherwise Marisol would never have learned Russian.

He recognized one of the young men as the dancer who had partnered Marisol in the school recital. He was surprised that this fellow, who appeared so formidable on stage, was only a few inches taller than his daughter, and did not appear very muscular. He asked him how he could lift her so effortlessly.

"Marisol is feather. I only help lift, hold position a moment, then put her down softly. The trick is timing."

"Don't let him fool you, Dad," Marisol said. "Boris is incredibly strong."

Boris glowed, put his arm around Marisol's shoulder, and smiled at her. She slid her arm around his waist.

Just then Katya appeared in the doorway, a wine glass in her hand. Rowan wasn't expecting her until after Marisol and her friends had left for the Bolshoi.

"Rowan," she called across the room. "Come on. The party's out here in the courtyard." Walking over to him, she took his hand and pulled him toward the door.

Marisol made a face and turned her back on Katya. Rowan, with an apologetic glance in Marisol's direction, allowed himself to be led off. He could feel the dancers' eyes on his back as he retreated. Once safely out of sight he turned to Katya and said pointedly, "I invited you for later."

"The other interpreters are already here. Why didn't you tell me it started at five?" She'd already had a few drinks, and tried to cajole him into a party mood. When that didn't work, she tried a different approach.

"One of the new men asked if he could call me."

"What did you say?"

"Look, Rowan, I'm not interested in anyone else. I want to go to America with you. You can take me if you want."

Katya was right, but an affair in Moscow with a beautiful young woman was one thing; putting her through business school in the United States was another.

What had settled the matter, though, was Easter. Since seeing her in Washington, his heart had been telling him that if he couldn't live with her, he would rather live alone.

With his leaving Moscow, he'd hoped his relationship with Katya would end amicably. He didn't blame her for pursuing her American dream. She'd simply placed her bet on the wrong man.

"No, Katya, I'm sorry. I won't be taking you to America."

She looked disappointed, but not defeated. He'd seen her down before and knew that when she ran into an obstacle it rarely took her long to find a way around it.

CHAPTER 18

The weather was lovely in August, and Rowan began most days with a jog along the Moscow River. Although running through the city drew scowls from the natives, he kept at it, not only to fend off middle-age flabbiness, but to clear his head for the demanding meetings that followed. This morning, as he reached the river's embankment he waved to a solitary old woman he'd often seen sweeping the sidewalk. Instead of smiling as she usually did, she was shouting something to him, gesticulating wildly. He stopped and walked back to find out what she was trying to tell him.

"Gorbachev," she was saying, "Gorbachev." Then, in an unmistakable gesture, she drew her forefinger across her neck. The fear in her eyes triggered a wave of dread in Rowan; it started in his chest and shot through his limbs. He turned on his heel, raced to his flat, and switched on the TV.

What he saw on the screen was the Russian setting for a crisis—classical music, a vase of flowers against a black drape, and in the foreground, the red Soviet flag with its hammer and sickle. His cold war vigilance had only recently begun to dissipate. Now, in fear, his adrenaline surging, he grabbed the phone and called his immediate superior. The line was busy.

He was imagining possible scenarios when a commotion in the courtyard drew him outside. Rumors were flying—Gorby's gone, maybe dead, maybe under arrest, definitely not in charge. The KGB is asserting control. The coup leaders are about to address the nation. The American ambassador was speaking over the public address system, telling Embassy officers and staff not to panic, reminding them that they had diplomatic immunity. Stalin had even repatriated German diplomats after Hitler invaded in 1941, he added, hoping to reassure everyone, but achieving the opposite.

Rumors spread through the compound: *Columns of tanks are approaching Moscow. The military is divided. Communications with the outside world are severed. Civil war could break out.*

He ran back to his apartment, looked in Marisol's room, and was relieved to find her asleep. On TV, the flag and flowers had given way to nervous old apparatchiks seated side by side like crows on a wire, croaking that Gorbachev was "under our protection," and calling for calm.

He called the home number of his counterpart on the Russian negotiating team; surely Dmitri would know what was going on. He picked up on the first ring. Rowan skipped a preamble.

"What does this mean, Dimitri?"

"Get out if you can," he shot back. "If the hard-liners win, I'll be accused of conspiring to disarm the Soviet Union and arrested as a traitor. I could be in the Lubyanka by nightfall. You could be charged with spying and be stuck here for months, years. If I could get my family out, I'd go myself."

Rowan's first thought was that he might be able to get Marisol out of the country if they moved fast enough. He woke her and explained what was happening.

"Put what you can in a carry-on bag. I'm going to get you on a plane."

"What about you, Dad? I won't go without you."

"I'll be fine. I've got diplomatic immunity. But if you don't go now you could be stuck here with me for a long time."

"But ... ".

"No *buts* this time, girl!" He dialed the Embassy travel office.

"If there are any flights out of the country, anything at all, going anywhere, east or west, book a seat for Marisol Ellway. Call me back the moment you have something."

The wait seemed interminable, but it was only a few minutes before the phone rang.

"Okay," Rowan said to the caller, "We're on our way."

To Marisol, he said, "Lufthansa has a flight to Frankfurt in an hour. They're holding a seat for you. We're leaving now."

She'd never seen her father in military mode before, but she quickly fell into synch. Tossing her essentials into a duffel bag—dance shoes and leotards, blue jeans, T-shirts, underwear, cosmetics, and her diary—she was ready before he was.

"I'll bring everything else in a few weeks," he told his daughter. Just before they left he grabbed a package of German sausages from the fridge. Nothing brought bigger smiles to Russian faces than bratwurst.

At the sight of Rowan waving two sausages over his head, a Moscow cabby executed a tight U-turn and screeched to a stop in front of them. Giving him one of the sausages and shouting "Sheremetyevo Aeroport," Rowan then passed another one before his eyes, along with a ten-dollar bill. As they climbed in, he told her to tell the driver in Russian that they had to make the trip in twenty minutes—half the usual time.

Darting through traffic, the cab reached a crowd gathering at the "White House," the Russian Federation's monumental parliament building. A half-dozen tanks were forming a defensive barricade around the entrance. People had climbed onto the tanks and were addressing the crowd with bullhorns.

Pointing to a large man with a shock of white hair standing on a tank, the driver slowed down and yelled out, "Yeltsin!" Rowan tossed a third sausage onto the seat next to him.

Moments later they came face to face with a column of tanks advancing on the city and blocking the route to all traffic. Rowan pointed to the sidewalk, slapped another ten-dollar bill on the seat by the driver, and with a sweeping gesture, told him to bypass the blockade. The driver pocketed the bill and steered his taxi over the curb onto the sidewalk. A hundred yards along, he reached a street corner and turned off the sidewalk into an alley that led away from the main road.

Twenty seven minutes later, after a wild ride on back roads, the cab pulled up to the departure terminal. Leaving the last of the sausages on the front seat, Rowan took Marisol by the hand and together they ran to the Lufthansa ticket counter. There, as if nothing were out of the ordinary, an agent assigned her a seat and told her to proceed immediately through passport control to the departure gate.

"I'll arrange for a consular official to meet your flight in Frankfurt and put you on a plane to Boston," Rowan said. "I'll let your mom know you're on your way."

The gravity of the situation finally struck Marisol; she burst into tears and clung to her father. Comforting her, he said, "They can't touch me. But Marisol … " Rowan hesitated.

A Lufthansa agent yelled at Marisol to proceed to the gate.

"What is it, Dad?"

He grabbed her shoulders and said, "Marisol, if you don't hear from me by the end of the week, call Jefferson College and let Easter Blue know what's happened."

"Sure, Dad, no problem."

"Okay, then. Now go. Run."

A tide of fleeing passengers carried her away from him and she disappeared into the labyrinth of passport control.

Standing at curbside outside the airport a few minutes later, he watched as a lone jet powered its way into the sky and wheeled westward, taking his daughter to safety.

§§§

It was two days before Rowan could get a call through to Sara's place in Boston.

"Marisol, it's me."

Before he could say more she yelled back, "Dad, are you all right?"

"Everything's fine. You've probably heard. Gorby's been released."

"Then you're coming home?"

"As soon as the negotiations are back on track. Shouldn't be more than a few weeks. I may have overreacted, rushing you off like that."

"Very dramatic, Dad. I'll never forget that cab ride."

"My Russian colleagues were amazed that the coup just fizzled."

"I'm going to New York tomorrow. I'll have the apartment stocked by the time you get here. Come home soon, Dad."

"I will. And Marisol, don't bother about that call to Jefferson. When I get back, I'll explain everything."

By the time Rowan left Moscow two weeks later, Katya's disappointment had been assuaged by the attentions of a young American scientist new to the negotiating team. Rowan anticipated that within a year she would be living in the States with her new beau, studying investment banking.

§§§

Rowan set off on foot through Riverside Park, overlooking the Hudson River, to meet his daughter for lunch.

In the aftermath of the attempted coup he'd moved his daughter and himself from one great city to another. She was now exactly where she wanted to be, and he was beginning his history of the Strategic Arms Limitation Treaty (SALT). A modest book advance from the publisher and a research grant from The Brookings Institution would pay the rent while he wrote it. He'd cover the rest of their expenses with honoraria from his talks on arms control. The weather was beautiful, the leaves were turning, and from his vantage point, the Hudson looked as pristine as it did in nineteenth-century paintings.

Easter hadn't been to New York since he'd returned, and although they spoke regularly by phone, he was beginning to wonder if she was avoiding him. New York was full of Jefferson alumni, and Rowan surmised that she might not want to be seen with him, particularly in light of the continuing sex code debate at Jefferson.

He had to admit that, while Easter was not unromantic, she'd never allowed matters of the heart to blur her vision. She insisted that love preceded politics, but when it came to her own life she invariably put her career before romance. "My life does not revolve around love," she'd said on more than one occasion. Was she staying away from him out of propriety or indifference? He had to find out.

When he got back to the apartment, he sent her an e-mail.

September 16, 1991

Dear Easter,

What separated us twenty years ago was a tragic series of miscues, not deliberate choice. I can't stop wondering if we couldn't give our story a different ending.

I love you, Easter. I want to see you. If you're not coming to New York soon, I'll come out there. No one need ever know I've come and gone.

As ever,
Rowan

§§§

September 17, 1991

Dear Rowan,

I've thought about this, endlessly. I want to meet as much as you do, but I'd lose all credibility if our story became known at Jefferson.

Try to understand. The debate on the campus sex code is coming to a head, and it puts me in a terrible bind.

Love,
Easter

P.S. I will be in New York early next month for a meeting. We'll talk then.

§§§

Strolling through Central Park with Easter reminded Rowan of the day they'd spent together in Moscow's Fili Park.

"How's Marisol?" she asked.

"She's dancing at Lincoln Center tonight. We're both hoping you can come."

"Does she realize I'm still married?"

174

"Are you?"

"The divorce will be final later this month."

"She thinks we're having an affair."

"Teenagers have such wild imaginations."

She hadn't flinched, but he saw the trace of a smile on her lips.

"I'd love to see her dance, but ..." she trailed off.

"Easter, you and Marisol live in separate universes. There's no risk."

"You're right. I think I'm getting paranoid."

§§§

After the performance, when they entered Marisol's dressing room, Easter presented her with a bright bouquet of mums. She had danced Balanchine's *Serenade* and, even as just a member of the corps, she had drawn the eye.

"You were flying out there," Rowan said.

"Thanks, Dad, and thank *you* for the flowers," she said to Easter. As she was catching her breath, sweat ran down her bare back.

Rowan took a half-step back, glad to see them together. It was only the second time the two most important women in his life had met, and he was relieved that they were at ease with each other. Then he heard Marisol say something he hadn't expected.

"Dad tells me you have a son my age at Princeton. Next time you're in New York I'll get you both comps."

Friends and admirers suddenly flooded the crowded room, clamoring for Marisol's attention, and in the crush, her offer was left hanging.

Taking Rowan's arm and edging them toward the door, Easter shouted over the commotion, "Wonderful to see you," then led Rowan through the crowd and onto the street.

"You didn't respond to her offer," Rowan said.

"I don't know about bringing them together."

"So, what's the problem?"

"Your Marisol is just the kind of girl Adam would like. It would be a bit awkward for us, don't you think?"

§§§

A few weeks later in one of their late-night phone calls, Easter reported that her divorce was official. She added that, since his mother's death, François had been sole owner of the family estate outside Dakar as well as the town house in Paris. By mutual consent, neither she nor François had made any claims against the other's assets or income.

"Are you glad it's settled?"

"The truth is, I'd been thinking about this for a long time."

"Why, exactly? You haven't told me."

"I was never in love with François. Our marriage was always amicable, but hardly passionate. As I did tell you, he was a wonderful father to Adam. I'll always love him for that. But with Adam at college, and me in the Midwest, it made sense for us to go our separate ways."

"Why didn't you file for divorce sooner?"

"I could never bring myself to act. I was afraid it might cost Adam his patrimony."

"You mean if François remarried and had another child?"

"Yes, but my fears were groundless. Along with the divorce, François revised his will, making Adam the sole inheritor of the properties in Paris and Senegal."

"Easter, you're free. The past is the past. The question is where we go from here."

"I know," she said softly.

"When's your next trip to New York?"

"Next month, as usual."

"How would you feel if I came out to Jefferson for a quick visit?"

"I want that too, but I'm—"

Rowan interrupted, saying, "I'd arrive on the last plane from New York and slip into your car like a ghost. We used to be good at this, remember? Name a day."

He heard her thumbing through her datebook.

"Friday?"

"I'll send the details by e-mail."

"I'll pull up to the curb at Arrivals."

"In the green Citroën?" he joked.

"In a green BMW," she said with an apologetic chuckle, and he wondered how he'd made it through two decades without her.

§§§

Rowan had booked a room at a hotel near the airport, so he was surprised when Easter insisted on driving to the College.

"The campus is empty at this hour," she said. "I want you to see it."

He recalled their drive to campus when he was president-elect in 1970. Jefferson Square had been the scene of a riot that day, but tonight it was stone quiet. As she drove past the square he felt like a time-traveler.

In his thirties Rowan would never have imagined that twenty years later he'd find Easter more attractive than ever, but her beauty had grown with the years. Her high cheekbones, once hidden by the roundness of youth, were now pronounced. Her soulful eyes had deepened, their intelligence marked by tiny lines that appeared when she smiled. He reached over and stroked the nape of her neck. She leaned into his touch.

Her route took them past the President's House and Sojourner Truth House—still home to a contingent of black students. He spotted Walker Gymnasium standing next to Clay Library.

"There's something I want to show you," she said, pulling into the parking lot behind the administration building.

"Come," she said, stepping out of the car and leading him toward the Archives. She swiftly unlocked the door and they stepped inside like two shadows vanishing into a cave. Closing the door behind them, she said, "When I got here, your hideaway was a storage room. I had it remodeled. Come."

Following her up the stairs, he noted the sway of her hips. He imagined placing his hands on her waist as he used to, but restrained himself.

At the top of the stairs she opened the door. The room had been transformed into a cozy apartment of understated elegance.

She took his hand and showed him around. "I use it for important guests—trustees, donors, and the like."

"And ex-presidents?"

She smiled. At the far end of the room an efficiency kitchen had been installed. She opened the refrigerator door, and he was surprised to see a demi of champagne. An arched doorway led to a small bedroom with bath.

"What do you think?" she asked.

"Very nice."

She walked to the window and Rowan followed. She closed the curtains. Rowan put his arm around her shoulder, and she turned to face him. She put her arms around his neck and looked up with her characteristic blend of boldness and reserve. He bent down and touched his forehead to hers. She made herself taller by standing on her toes, and offered him her lips.

Rowan met her passion with a hunger of his own, heightened by years of longing. Their lovemaking, tender yet explosive, connected past and present. Afterward, they lay back, side by side, as if only a week had passed since they'd been together.

Finally, she looked at him with mock seriousness, poked him in the ribs with her forefinger, and said, "So, tell me. Would you still love me without the title?"

"Touché," he said, returning her jab. "But are you willing to be seen with me in public?"

"Once the sex code is off the table, absolutely."

"There's no hurry. We know how to wait. And we know how to hide."

They lay still for a while. Then he said, "Easter, you've met my daughter but I still haven't met your son. Marisol wants to meet him too. How about bringing him to a ballet? We could all go out to supper after."

"That would be nice, but Adam is so busy I hardly ever see him myself."

"Tell him one of the ballerinas has invited him. That'll get his attention."

"He's never shown any interest in dance."

"I'll bet he hasn't seen the pros. Great athletes appreciate each other. I've heard Marisol compare basketball to ballet."

"Look, Rowan, it's risky enough—us seeing each other right now. I don't want to tempt fate by appearing in public as if we're one big happy family. You and Marisol can watch Adam on TV. Princeton's going to be playing in the National Invitational Tournament Tip-Off next month."

She spoke with a finality that told Rowan to drop it.

CHAPTER 19

In the world of ballet, Christmas means one thing—*The Nutcracker.* To a ballet company, Tchaikovsky's perennial masterpiece, performed to full houses of children and their parents throughout December, is the difference between solvency and bankruptcy. Veteran dancers dread it, but they do their duty, knowing that *The Nutcracker* pays the rent. For novices, the Christmas classic is a rite of passage and the portal to a dance career. Getting a coveted solo in *The Nutcracker* nourishes the dream of someday dancing the leads in story ballets like *Giselle, Swan Lake, Sleeping Beauty,* and *Romeo and Juliet.* So, when the artistic director asked Marisol to learn the soloist's part in the Arabian divertissement—in addition to her corps roles as a Snowflake and a Flower—she was ecstatic.

From her first dance recital at the age of eight, Rowan had not missed one of her dance milestones, but he would this time, and he and she had both made their peace with his absence. Long before she had been given the soloist's role he'd been planning to spend that week at his cabin in the Berkshires. He had told her that he wouldn't be alone, and was relieved that she hadn't asked him for details.

While he prepared to leave for the cabin, he tuned the TV to college basketball. Only in the final minutes of close games did professional players match the intensity of college play. Even before Easter's suggestion, he'd watched Princeton's games whenever they were broadcast. This season, the Tigers were making their best showing since the Bill Bradley years, and Adam was part of the reason why.

His eyes were glued to the TV when Marisol came in. "Have a seat," he said.

"Aren't you supposed to be on your way?"

"I want to catch the end of this game."

"Who's playing?"

"Princeton and Yale. These kids are so much better than we were. The Princeton girls could have beaten the team I played on at Jefferson."

"*Women,* Dad."

Rowan heard the announcer mention Adam's name and turned up the volume: *"That kid has professional potential. The word at Princeton is that he's also a serious student. Not surprising, I guess, because his mother is the president of Jefferson College."*

"Jefferson? He must be your Easter's son."

"Yes, he is."

Suddenly the camera zoomed in on a handsome young face, mocha in color like Easter's, but the eyes were deeper, and the brow more dramatic. His mouth was set in determination. Even without a smile his dimples were evident.

"By the way, Marisol, before I go ...."

"He's a good-looking dude," she said distractedly, still staring at the TV.

"Who?"

"Adam Blue. Who do you think?"

"Marisol ... ?"

"Yeah, Dad."

"You know I won't be on my own over the holidays."

"Yeah, you told me," she said, not looking up from the game.

"I'll be there with Easter Blue. You met her in Moscow. We're going together."

Suddenly, he had her full attention. She kept her eyes on his for some time, then began to smile. "Okay. I like her, Dad. I'm happy for you."

Just then Adam stole the ball and dribbled the length of the court for an easy dunk. "Cool," Marisol said. "If he weren't so tall he would've made a good dancer. Ellie's dating one of his teammates."

Rowan had known Marisol's friend Ellie since their childhood. Her full name was Eleanor Liang Stewart, "Ellie," for short. "Liang" was Ellie's only link to her Chinese birth parents, but when she was in her teens and tried to find them, the name had proved too common for her to be able to track them down. Her adoptive parents, the Stewarts, were Americans who, while working as Christian missionaries in Hong Kong in the seventies, had adopted her as an infant and brought her back to New York City, where she grew up. The two girls had met in a ballet class at age six and advanced through the ranks together.

"I hate to leave before it's over," Rowan said, "but if I don't go now I'll be late picking Easter up at LaGuardia."

He leaned down and kissed Marisol on the top of her head. Her eyes were still glued to the TV. Adam had the ball at the top of the key and, while looking at a teammate in the corner, hit a free man under the basket.

§§§

When Marisol heard that Princeton would be playing in New York later that week, she asked Ellie to snag an extra ticket from her boyfriend. Now, instead of tracking a tiny image on a TV screen, she was so close to Adam she could actually see the sweat dripping off his face.

Princeton was sitting on a six-point lead with five minutes to go. Madison Square Garden, overrun by Princeton students and alumni, was in a state of near-pandemonium. Adam took the inbound pass and dribbled across center court. From Marisol's seat just a few rows behind the Princeton bench, she could feel his intensity, and when he drove to the basket and put the game away with a dunk it was obvious that the crowd worshipped him.

When the game ended moments later, Ellie led Marisol to the spot where the players and their dates would gather. Marisol recognized him coming through the crowd, on his arm a pretty brunette in an ankle-length leather coat. Ben Steinsaltz, the team's leading scorer and a junior to Adam's sophomore, suggested they walk the few blocks to the Princeton Club, and when they stopped for a traffic light, Marisol pulled even with Adam.

"I believe our parents know each other," she said, looking up at him. "My father was president of Jefferson College in the seventies."

"Really? Have you met her ... my mother?"

The light turned green and they stepped off the curb. Marisol noticed that Adam shortened his stride to keep pace with her.

"Yes, last year in Moscow. She had business at the university and my dad and I took her to see *Giselle* at the Bolshoi."

"No kidding!"

"I liked her, and she loved the ballet."

"How does your dad know her?"

"They met when he was president and she was a student a million years ago."

"Oh, that explains it."

Not all of it, Marisol thought. Rowan hadn't asked her to keep his holiday plans secret, but the experience of living with divorced parents, each dating new people, had long since made discretion second nature to her.

At the Princeton Club, Adam placed himself between Marisol and his date, and they were hardly seated when he continued where he'd left off.

"So, what were you doing in Moscow?"

"My dad works on disarmament. While he was at the Embassy in Moscow, I studied at the Moscow Ballet Academy."

"What was that like? I mean, compared to America."

"In America, ballet is just frosting on the cake. To the Russians, it's life and death."

She was surprised by Adam's interest in dance. He continued asking her questions; then his date began to fidget. Before long, she got up to go to the ladies room.

Marisol seized the moment.

"You seem interested in ballet. Would you like to see *The Nutcracker?*"

"Are you in it?"

"I have a solo in the second act."

"Cool, I'd love to."

"December 30th at eight o'clock. I'll leave a comp for you at will call."

The fact that she would appear as more than just a Snowflake had given Marisol the confidence to invite Adam to *The Nutcracker*. As she'd be a soloist, he'd actually be able to identify her as an individual.

After the performance, he greeted her at the stage door.

"That was awesome!" he exclaimed. Vaguely aware of his lapse into cliché, he sputtered another: "You were incredible!"

Marisol came to his rescue with, "The solo was a first for me. As Snowflakes we're all identical; even my dad has trouble picking me out of the corps."

They were still standing at the stage door. "I'm starving," she said. "After the show, we always go out to eat. I'll take you to our hangout."

Only a few of Marisol's friends had reached the restaurant when she and Adam arrived. She accepted their compliments but waved her way past them to a private booth in the rear.

"I know it's a little late for breakfast," she said, "but I'm dying for a spinach and mushroom omelet."

"You've earned whatever you want. I know ballet is really hard, and … "

"And … " Marisol coaxed.

"And, you were wonderful." This time he did not hide his feelings.

"Thanks. What are you having?"

"A double cheeseburger."

"That's the difference between basketball and ballet. *You* can eat anything you want."

After their food arrived, several dancers stopped by to exchange compliments, among them Sasha, a Leningrad-trained principal dancer with the American Ballet Theatre. When he saw Marisol, he bent down and kissed her full on the lips. Then he said something to her in Russian, and with a flourish, addressed the circle of dancers in English. "This girl has 'star' written all over her. I tell you, her name will someday be known throughout the ballet world."

Marisol squirmed; she didn't like being singled out, especially in front of other dancers. She hushed Sasha and stared down at her omelet.

Later, on the sidewalk, Adam asked her what Sasha had said in Russian.

"He said I belonged at ABT. That's the other ballet company at Lincoln Center, where he's a big deal."

"What's wrong with your company?"

"Nothing. Nothing at all. Its repertoire is more Balanchine, like contemporary. ABT specializes in the classical story ballets. Sasha's a theatrical dancer. I'm good at the technical stuff, but drama has been my weakness. That's what I hoped to learn in Russia."

"Did it help? I thought you were very convincing."

"Yeah, I think the Moscow school helped some, but I still have a ways to go."

"Is that all Sasha wanted?"

"He wanted me to go to a party with him later tonight," Marisol said dismissively.

When Adam was silent, she added, "Dating someone like Sasha can give your career a boost. There's a chance he'd put in a word to the powers that be."

"What did you say to him?"

"That I was with you."

"Oh."

"Tell me what you really thought of the ballet."

"It was like a fairy story. I'm having trouble seeing you as a real person."

"Oh, if you could feel my aches and pains you'd know I'm real. So is everyone on stage. We wipe out more often than people ever know."

"That's hard to believe. Your male partners made me feel like a clod."

"All the dancers have at least ten years of training, some of the principals twice that. I've been studying ballet since I was eight."

"I'm so glad you invited me," Adam said, earnestly enough that Marisol believed he meant it.

"I'm glad," Marisol said, concealing her delight.

"Hey, I've got to go," Adam said, glancing at his watch. "The last train for Princeton leaves in a half-hour."

"My dad's away for the holidays. You could crash at our place." She was not normally so forward.

"You're sure he wouldn't mind?"

"Positive. It's no problem, and I promise not to attack you."

"In that case, forget it," Adam said, grinning broadly. "No, seriously, it would be great. I was dreading the ride back this late."

As he walked Marisol home Adam told her he was leaving for Paris on New Year's Day to visit his father. "I'd already be there if it weren't for the NIT games."

"What does your dad do in Paris?"

"He imports produce from our farm in Senegal. He's hoping I'll take over the business."

"Is that what you want?"

"I don't know what I want. I like basketball, and the coach thinks I might be able to play professionally, but I don't think I could put up with all the travel and hoopla and crap."

§§§

In the apartment Marisol, made a pot of tea. It felt odd to be there with a man who was not her father.

"So, do you think I should date Sasha?" she asked. She knew that she was fishing, but couldn't stop herself.

"The Russian guy? Well, he certainly seems to like you."

"We've gone out for coffee a few times—it gives me a chance to practice my Russian. He's always bugging me for a date, and he won't take *no* for an answer."

"You're not interested in him?"

"Not in that way."

"What's wrong with him?"

"I dated a Russian in Moscow and I didn't like how he treated me. Sasha reminds me of him. He acts like he's God's gift, that I should be grateful for his attention. Plus, he's a star, and I'm, you know, the third Snowflake from the left."

"He thinks you'll be a star."

"Moving up is very rare. I know several girls who thought Sasha would help them."

"What happened?"

"He slept with them a few times and dumped them."

"I have teammates who do stuff like that."

"I'll bet you've broken a few hearts."

"The first year I was on the team it was new and glamorous. Hard to pass up."

"And now?"

Adam shifted in his chair. "I like to think I've grown up. The truth is I'd rather be alone, plus I don't have time. I'm serious about math."

"Math?"

"It's beautiful and all-consuming—like ballet."

It was getting late, so she showed Adam to Rowan's room. When he wondered aloud if her father would mind, she said friends had crashed there before and he was used to it. She got fresh sheets, and they made the bed together.

"Don't expect to see me before eleven," Marisol said. "Finally, a break! After New Year's, we get a week before rehearsals for the new season, but tomorrow's the first free day I've had in months. We could have brunch before you go. I'll be on vacation."

"Sounds good. And thanks for letting me crash."

§§§

When, late the next morning, Marisol heard Adam showering, she hurried to the kitchen and put the kettle on. By the time he appeared she was pouring coffee.

"This is just to get us going. I know a good place for breakfast near the theater."

They walked west toward the Hudson River and headed south through Riverside Park. As they cut over to Lincoln Center they were drawn to the fountain at the heart of the plaza. Their shadows turned it into a sundial, and Adam was explaining how it worked when Marisol squeezed his arm and nodded toward the figure striding across the plaza. It was Sasha.

She pulled Adam down beside her onto the low black-marble ledge ringing the fountain and slid her arm around his waist, snuggling up to him. "Just play along," she whispered.

"Sorry to interrupt," Sasha said, peering down at Marisol. Adam slowly rose to his feet, dwarfing him.

"Oh, hello Sasha. You know Adam."

"Yes, we met last night," he said, taking a step back. "Aren't you taking company class?" He extended his hand to her in the courtly manner of a *danseur noble.*

"Not today," she said, ignoring his hand. He took the hint and ambled off, then broke into a trot when he spotted another dancer on her way to the studio.

Adam offered Marisol his hand; she took it, and rose to her feet. "What was that about?" he asked.

"Maybe he'll leave me alone now," she said shyly. "Did you mind?"

"Not at all." He was still holding her hand, and when he realized it he let it go, and pulled a small camera out of his coat pocket.

"Hey, what's this? You just happen to have a camera with you?"

"Always. It's a hobby of mine. I want a picture of you at the fountain." As Marisol primped, he dropped back two strides, pivoted, knelt, and pressed the shutter.

A gust of wind lifted Marisol's hair, strawberry blonde hair that in the bright sunlight looked almost auburn, like her mother's. "Wait, give me another second!" she said, smoothing her hair again. "I'm a mess." But her radiant face told a different story. She was joyous. At that moment, she felt more alive than she had on stage the night before.

Adam snapped two more photos, put the camera away, and said, "It's New Year's Eve. How'd you like to come to a party in Princeton?"

CHAPTER 20

New Year's Eve, 1991

They caught the five o'clock train from Penn Station and transferred at Princeton Junction to a two-car shuttle—known to locals as the Dinky—that deposited them on the Princeton campus. As the Dinky crossed a trestle above Lake Carnegie, Adam focused his camera on a four-man crew below, propelling a scull through the gray drizzle. He snapped the image just as the oars reached full extension.

"'Water Beetle'," Adam said, pointing to the narrow craft darting across the lake. "I like to put titles on the photos."

"And the shots at Lincoln Center?"

"I'll need to see the prints, but perhaps 'Green-eyed Girl' and 'Fountain Strawberry.'"

"You took three."

"Maybe I'll think of another title when we know each other better."

A few minutes later, the Dinky pulled into Princeton. At the landing, the conductor took Marisol's arm as she stepped off the train.

"Thanks, Charlie," Adam said, joining her on the platform. As if he'd anticipated their meeting, the conductor looked from Adam to Marisol, and said firmly, "Every ending is a beginning." Charlie was famous for oracular pronouncements, and this one was typical. It left Marisol wondering if it applied simply to the year that was ending, or might hold a deeper meaning for her.

Out of earshot, Adam explained that the conductor was a legendary figure in Princeton, beloved for safely and discreetly ushering countless inebriated undergraduates into taxis after they returned from carousing in the city. Locals recognized him as their sage ferryman, and among themselves referred to him as Siddhartha. "After the hero of Herman Hesse's novel," he added.

"I know. Just because I'm a dancer doesn't mean I'm an airhead."

"Sorry, I didn't mean … "

"It's okay, Adam. Most of my friends have no time for Siddhartha or anything else outside of dance. I only know because my dad gave me the book for my birthday."

"And when was that?"

"August."

As they crossed the campus, Adam assumed the role of tour guide.

"Woodrow Wilson was Princeton's president before moving on to the White House," he said, pointing to the house where Wilson had lived. Opposite was old Fine Hall, former home to many of the century's most illustrious mathematicians and physicists.

"Einstein worked there. His law of gravitation is inscribed in a stained-glass window."

§§§

At the party, a steady stream of students congratulated Adam on his tournament play. Marisol sensed that compliments made him uncomfortable, but that he, like she, had learned it was best to accept them graciously and move on.

"It's too noisy to talk here. Want to go outside?" he asked her, cupping his hand over her ear. He pointed to the courtyard to make sure she understood over the din.

Just then a handsome young man who had greeted them at the door reintroduced himself.

"Hi, I'm Jack. Would you like to dance?" he called out to Marisol, circling his index finger to get his question across.

Marisol looked at Adam, who nodded. She could feel his eyes on her as Jack led her toward the dance floor.

When they reached the floor, the DJ, who'd been playing Madonna, switched to Eric Clapton's "Layla," and Marisol began to dance slowly, with restrained, minimal movement in her slim hips and shoulders. When the raucous introduction modulated into the melodic anthem, she shifted gears, dramatically. In a blink, all eyes were on her. Jack did his best to match her movements, but no one was watching him. Marisol, who on stage was the epitome of control, had become woman incarnate.

When the song ended, Jack invited her to the bar, but she politely declined and returned to Adam.

"I've never seen anything like that," Adam said. "Guys will be lining up to dance with you."

"Let's get out of here," she said.

Marisol slid her arm through his and they strolled across the empty campus.

"At the basketball game, I got to see you in high gear. I wanted to show you mine. Now you've seen me choreographed and unchoreographed."

"I don't know which I like better."

"You don't have to choose," she said. He freed his arm and put it around her. Just then, the sound of a pealing bell reached them through the clear winter's night. Then another, and another. Bells were joining the chorus from all over town. They stopped and faced each other. Adam counted the chimes, and at the twelfth one, said, "Shall we celebrate the New Year in the customary fashion?"

"I'd like that." Closing her eyes, she tilted her head back and offered him her lips. He kissed her softly, just once.

"What a lovely custom."

Adam put his arm around her again and she adjusted her stride to match his.

When they got back to his rooms, Marisol disappeared into the bathroom with her dance bag and Adam did his best to straighten up his bed and then make up a place for himself to sleep on the sofa in the sitting room.

She emerged in her pajamas to find the lights out.

As she climbed into bed she called out, "Aren't you going to say good-night?"

He got up from the sofa and went to her. The soft light filtering through the window was just bright enough to illuminate her hair spread out on his pillow. Slipping his hands beneath her head he leaned down while gently lifting her upward till their lips met.

She wrapped her arms around him and pulled him toward her. He let himself be drawn down, but when they'd kissed, he pulled himself up to a sitting position and lowered her head to the pillow.

"I have a proposal," he said.

"What is it?"

"You're free New Year's week and I'm leaving for Paris tomorrow. How about going with me, as my guest?"

"You're crazy!"

"Yeah, I am."

"I've never done anything like that before." Her mind was racing. She'd always been a good girl. This felt like breaking the mold.

"I can't just disappear, can I? Plus, I don't have that kind of money."

"Don't worry. My dad's always urging me to see the world. He complains when I don't use the credit card he gave me."

"Carte Blanche?"

"Exactly, except it's American Express. So you'll go?"

"Can we get a ticket this late? And I'll need to pick up my passport." As the implications sunk in, Marisol was babbling, but she knew she'd passed the point of no return.

"I'll call the airline first thing in the morning. We'll stop by your place on the way to JFK."

"I'll leave my dad a note. He wouldn't try to stop me, but somehow I don't feel like talking it over with him."

They were too excited to sleep, and talked for an hour before Adam dragged himself off to the sofa.

§§§

From Charles de Gaulle Airport they took the train into Paris, the Metro to the Bastille, and walked the final few blocks to François Merle's town house at Place des Vosges. The usual gaggle of tourists stood gawking at the picturesque seventeenth-century structures bordering the grassy square.

Nearly four centuries old, the historic site had been the first residential square in the city. It comprised thirty-six matching buildings with red brick facades, white cornerstones, and steep, blue-slate roofs. A series of vaulted arcades formed the ground floor. Cardinal Richelieu and Victor Hugo had lived and worked there. Adam pointed out the fountain he'd cooled off in on hot days when he was a boy.

"Come on, I'll show you where you're staying," he said. "You've got a room with a view." He glanced at her to see if she'd caught the allusion to Forster, but couldn't tell. Taking her suitcase, he led the way up the steps to the front door.

On a table in the entryway there was a note from François. "We've got the place to ourselves for a week," he announced.

"Great! Let me unpack and change into my workout clothes." When they'd passed through New York, Marisol had phoned the ballet mistress there for help in finding a daily barre in Paris.

"You dance every day?" he asked.

"You practice every day, don't you?"

"Almost."

"There's a saying: 'Miss a class and you know it; miss two, and the teacher knows it; miss three, and the audience knows it.' I've missed two already."

"But everything's closed New Year's Day," he said.

"Oh, I can limber up here and take a real class tomorrow. And sometime this week I want to stop by and see the round studio at Palais Garnier. It's a mecca for dancers. Degas painted there."

After they toured the house, Adam carried Marisol's bag to the guestroom on the third floor that overlooked the square.

She said, "Actually, I could use a nap. All of a sudden I'm so sleepy, maybe I'll lie down for a bit and then stretch out."

"Okay, but if you're not down in two hours, I'm coming to get you. I want to show you Paris." He followed her footsteps up the stairs until he heard the door to her room close behind her.

§§§

"Beautiful table," Marisol said when she entered the room where Adam was reading. "A perfect circle. What's it made of?"

"Baobab wood, from our farm in Senegal. The Senegalese believe it brings good luck."

"And you have a round table made of it," Marisol mused, rapping lightly on it and, appearing satisfied, said her nap had put her in the mood for a walk.

"It's cold out there." He went to the coat closet and returned with a moss-green scarf. "I think this will look good on you," he said, putting the scarf over her head and giving the ends a playful tug.

They stopped at Mariage Frères for a pot of Russian Caravan tea, and as Adam added milk to his, he said, "Tea with milk reminds me of England. We lived there while my mom got her Ph.D."

"When did you come to the States?"

"I started high school in Cambridge while she was at Harvard, and finished at Jefferson when she took the job there."

"Will I meet your dad?"

"Yes, he's coming in from Africa on Saturday."

"Are you close?"

"Very. And you … to your dad?"

"Yes, close as father and daughter, plus, we're pals."

"Come on, you must see Notre Dame."

Walking through the streets at dusk, Marisol saw Paris as a well-lit stage on which she and Adam were anonymous extras in a show that would run long after they'd made their exits. To be beyond the reach of parents and friends, to be with a man she'd hardly known a week, was at once sobering and exhilarating.

§§§

The next morning, Marisol took an advanced ballet class at the Paris Centre Studio. It felt good to execute the familiar steps, to contract and lengthen her muscles, to reconnect with her body.

Adam was there to meet her when she left class.

"What would you like to do today?"

"If I don't go to the Rodin Museum while I'm in Paris, I'll never hear the end of it from my dad. He's a big fan."

§§§

"Well, this place is certainly not for prudes," said Adam as they passed a marble figurine configured to reveal every minute anatomical detail of the female body.

"Wow! Rodin doesn't leave much to the imagination, does he?" Marisol added.

"I wonder how he got his models to pose like that."

"Not hard to guess what happened next," she said with a giggle.

Before they left the museum, they sat on a bench in the lobby to rest their feet.

"I'll cook tonight. Would you like to try my specialty?" he asked her.

"Which is?"

"Pasta. My mother taught me how to make a good red sauce."

"Not only can he shoot a basket, he cooks, too! The crowd goes wild!" With that, Marisol gleefully threw her arms around his neck. Then she whispered in his ear, "I'm not going to be able to get this place out of my mind."

Adam kissed her. "Me either. Let's go home."

The week that followed was the happiest time Marisol had ever known. Her youth, like that of all dancers, had been highly disciplined. Now she was spontaneously giving her heart to a man she'd just met, yet felt she'd known all her life. In previous relationships with men, she'd been guarded; with Adam, she was fearless. It was the first time she'd felt the audacity she displayed on stage expressed in her life.

Their days quickly fell into a pattern: They got up late and hung out in the house till about noon. After a light lunch out, they explored Paris on foot. By late afternoon, they were back at the house at Place des Vosges making love.

One evening, they went to *Giselle,* and afterward spent hours discussing it. Adam wondered whether, when Giselle finds out that Prince Albrecht is betrothed, she dies of a weak heart or a broken heart. It's deliberately ambiguous, answered Marisol. In some versions she commits suicide. And, Adam continued, in the first act is Albrecht a cad, consciously leading a peasant girl on, or does he really love her? The role can be interpreted either way, Marisol replied, adding, "But in the second act Giselle's love is so strong and pure that it reaches beyond the grave. She shows him what love really is, and that knowledge changes him."

The next evening, he took her to the film *Casablanca*, another tale of impossible love. "'We'll always have Paris' isn't enough for me," was Marisol's reaction. "I'm glad you'll be heading back to the States soon too."

"I've got to go out to Jefferson to see my mom for a few days. She was away Christmas week," he said.

"Adam?"

He turned to look at her.

"Adam, I should tell you something. You'd find out anyway."

"What?"

"My dad and your mom are seeing each other. He told me just before he left to spend the week with her at his cabin in the Berkshires."

"No! You told me they knew each other but I had no idea they were … "

" … dating." Marisol finished his sentence.

"Wow! This is going to take some getting used to."

Marisol could see he was uncomfortable with the idea. "I think they're perfect for each other," she offered, but when Adam didn't respond she wished she'd kept her mouth shut.

"I'm sorry, maybe I shouldn't have spilled the beans."

"No, I'm glad you told me. We shouldn't have secrets between us. I think I'm still in denial about my parents' separation."

They were startled when the phone on the bed table rang. It was François calling from Senegal to confirm his arrival.

After Adam hung up, he said, "My dad's on the board of Doctors Without Borders. There's an emergency meeting on Somalia tomorrow and he asked me to stand in for him. It won't take us long."

§§§

Before the meeting started, Adam made a point of conveying his father's regrets to the executive director. Then he led Marisol to a seat at the back of the auditorium so they could duck out if it ran on.

The executive director set the stage for the event by explaining how chronic drought in the Sahel, coupled with fighting among Somali chieftains, was driving hungry refugees into the cities. He then introduced a young Indochinese woman who had just returned from Mogadishu. After completing her studies at L'Écoles des Médecins, Dr. Élodie Pham Fleury had signed up for a year of fieldwork in lieu of the typical hospital internship. Dressed in a lavender *ao dai*—the traditional Vietnamese silk tunic—over black pantaloons, she was the epitome of cosmopolitan elegance.

"I'll translate when she's done," Adam whispered. Although Marisol couldn't follow the substance of Dr. Fleury's presentation, she was impressed by her dynamism and passion. She tried to imagine herself in a world in which no one cared about *tendus* and *arabesques*. The satisfaction she presumed would come from saving people from starvation made her question her single-minded dedication to dance.

Dr. Fleury, who illustrated her talk with slides of emaciated children, argued that famine had become unavoidable and called upon the French press to get the story out. Then, speaking English with a light French accent, and with even greater urgency, she repeated her appeal to the world media.

Adam and Marisol were discussing the talk when Dr. Fleury joined them. She began in French but, after Adam introduced Marisol, switched to English.

"I'm told that you're the son of François Merle. He's one of our staunchest supporters."

"He's in Senegal and asked me to come in his place. This is my friend, Marisol, a ballet dancer in New York."

"I think your work is wonderful," Marisol interjected.

"Have you been following events in Somalia?"

"This is the first I've heard about the famine," Marisol admitted.

"No one's heard of it; that's the problem. We're looking for recruits. We've got nothing against dancers." She flashed Marisol a smile.

"When are you going back?" Adam asked the doctor.

"Next week. I go from Paris to Nairobi, then on to Mogadishu. Why do you ask?"

"Sounds like an adventure. I've lived in West Africa, but I've never seen the East. Who took the photographs?"

"I did, but they don't capture the extent of the tragedy. We're desperate for volunteers. Are you interested?"

Marisol's face froze and her heart pounded. Surely Adam wouldn't go off to Africa with this woman.

"Sorry, but I return to school in the States next week."

Marisol took a breath and smiled politely.

"Well, if you change your mind, you know where to sign up."

CHAPTER 21

François was due in from Dakar late that afternoon, and Marisol skipped class so they could spend their last day alone at home. After a quick trip to the market for supplies, they cleaned house and sat down to take stock.

"The talk on Somalia ... I can't get it out of my head," Adam began. "I want to do something like that."

"What are your friends planning to do after graduation?"

"Make as much money as possible."

"No one goes into dance for the money," Marisol said. "We're barely paid enough to live in the City."

"But you've got purpose ... passion. When did you know that you wanted to be a dancer?"

"I can't remember not thinking that ballet would be my life. I mean, I know it's not going to save the world but it does give people pleasure. There's a tradition in ballet that takes hold of you and makes you feel part of something larger."

"You're lucky. I wish I had a calling like that."

"Isn't basketball like that?"

"No, not for me. Putting a ball through a hoop is a distraction. I want to do something that matters. I won't find that on a basketball court."

"Are you thinking of quitting the team?"

"No, but it just doesn't seem important anymore." Adam stopped, then, with a grin, added, "Maybe I'll become a dancer."

He reached for her and gently pulled her down on top of him. With their heads together, her toes reached just below his knees. Placing his hands on her hips, he lifted her above him. She had the abdominal strength to hold herself like a barbell.

"You're about half what I bench press," he said. After he raised and lowered her a few times, he brought her down very slowly to the point where her lips were just inches above his. With her hair hanging around him in a rosy canopy, he lowered her until there was no space between them.

The sound of a key in the front door made them snap to attention. By the time François came into the room, they were seated at opposite ends of the couch. He was in his late fifties and of medium height and sturdy build. His dark, keen eyes accentuated a relaxed, intelligent face. Adam and Marisol went to meet him as he set down his bags and took off his overcoat. He shook hands with Adam, patting him on the back, and gave Marisol a welcoming smile. "Please introduce me to your lovely friend, Adam."

"This is Marisol Ellway. She's a dancer in the New York City Ballet. You won't believe this, Dad, but her father once held the same job that Mom has now."

Quite abruptly, François excused himself and withdrew to his study.

"He must be tired," Adam said. "He's usually very sociable. You'll see."

Minutes later, François called out, "Adam, would you please come in here for a moment?"

Marisol waited in the living room. She could make out the sounds of French coming from the study, and though she couldn't understand a word, she could tell that the conversation was intense. After ten minutes, her agitation was turning to fear mixed with anger. She was putting on her coat to go out when François came back to the living room and asked her to join them in the study. Adam was standing off to one side of the room looking out the window. He turned to face her but stayed where he was. François asked her to sit on the couch.

Adam looked ashen. With a feeling of dread mitigated only by mounting curiosity, Marisol asked, "What's the matter?"

"First, let me apologize for keeping you waiting. As you can see, something has come up. But to answer your question, nothing is the matter, with you, I mean," François said. "And nothing is the matter with Adam either. Something is the matter with me. Let me tell you what I've said to Adam."

"Please," Marisol said. She held out her hand to Adam to invite him to come sit beside her, but he didn't budge.

"Twenty years ago when I met Adam's mother in Dakar, she was carrying a child. I am not Adam's natural father. He was conceived in a relationship with your father while Adam's mother was a student at Jefferson."

Silence fell on the room. Marisol looked at François, then at Adam. "Adam, did you know this?"

"Of course not! Are you kidding? For God's sake!"

"But it can't be true! If it were, how come my father doesn't know? He'd have told me. I'm sure he doesn't know."

"That's right, he doesn't know," François said. "Until now, no one has known, apart from Easter and myself."

"Oh, my God," Marisol said, her voice falling.

"Adam tells me that you've known each other since Christmas. I'm very sorry for putting you through this. We never imagined that you'd meet."

"My dad is seeing his mom, what did you expect?"

"I didn't know." If François was upset by Marisol's revelation, he didn't let on.

An urge to scream battled Marisol's need to weep. She looked to Adam for help, but his face had become a mask.

"I don't expect you to forgive me," François said to Adam. "We can talk more about this later, but right now I should tell Easter what's happened." François got up to go. When he reached the door he turned and faced the couple.

"There's one more thing. I told Adam this and I want you to know too. From the very beginning, I've known the truth about Adam's paternity. I chose to accept him as my son and I will continue to do so as long as I live. He will inherit the family property. I realize this revelation is going to affect you both, but it does not affect my relationship with Adam. I have loved him as my son from the start and nothing will ever change that."

Without waiting for a response, he left the library, closing the door behind him. They heard his feet on the stairs as he headed for his bedroom to call Easter.

§§§

Adam busied himself with dinner while Marisol set the table. They weren't ready to talk, and both were thankful for the mindless routine. Within a half-hour, François returned to the kitchen where the cassoulet Adam had made that morning was warming in the oven.

"It's ready," Adam said glumly.

"Let's sit down then," François said. He pulled out Marisol's chair and seated her, gestured for Adam to sit opposite, and took his usual place at the head of the table. Adam set the dish he'd prepared on a ceramic trivet and took his seat.

"Easter and I have spoken," François said. "She's informing Rowan now. Before you were born, Adam, Easter and I agreed that this would be our secret, and ours alone, and that to keep it she would have to break off contact with Rowan."

"But she's been seeing him for over a year," Marisol insisted.

François, who was about to serve the cassoulet, set the ladle on the table. A pensive look came over his face, but after a moment, he said, "Since we've separated, that is perhaps understandable. Nonetheless, she has kept her promise regarding Adam."

"I'm not hungry," Adam said. He pushed back his chair and left the room. They heard the front door slam.

"I think he needs to be alone," Marisol said apologetically.

"I quite understand," François said. "This gives us a chance to talk."

"First, explain one thing: Why did Easter agree to all this in the first place? It's not like my dad to shirk responsibility. I think he's always loved her."

"You'll want to ask her about this, but as I understand it, when she realized she was pregnant, she tried to reach Rowan from Dakar but could not. She was about your age at the time and dreaded single-motherhood. I'd met her on a prior trip to Dakar, and when she returned that summer and found herself in trouble and alone, she turned to me in distress. Within a few weeks, I proposed."

"But why did you keep it all a secret?" Marisol pressed.

"To insure Adam's patrimony. If my parents had realized that he was not of their blood, they'd have left their property to me on the condition that it revert to the African branch of the family when I died. Easter and I felt that it was wrong to put Adam in the position of keeping the truth from his grandparents, and I always planned to tell him when his grandmother passed away. I just haven't … didn't yet …"

Marisol's mind had begun to wander. "I wonder how my father will react," she murmured.

"When Adam returns to the States I'm going to accompany him and introduce him to Rowan, assuming your father will receive me."

"He'll handle it," Marisol said distractedly. "But do you realize what a position this puts me in?"

"Yes, I think I do, and I'm very sorry. As I said, you and Adam are blameless. Your relationship is innocent, and surely everyone will understand that." He then got up. The cassoulet remained untouched. "Twenty years ago, when Easter and I chose this course, we thought we were doing the right thing. Tonight, it all looks different. I hope that someday you'll be able to forgive me. I'm going upstairs now. We all need time to let this sink in."

§§§

Marisol was in bed when she heard Adam's knock on her door. She called out to him, and when he opened it, sat up. Adam took a seat on the bed.

"Sorry to take off like that, but I had to be alone."

"I don't want to be alone," Marisol said. She had been crying.

Adam began, "I'm so mad at my mom and dad. Not only have they deceived me my whole life, I'm beginning to wonder if my mom ever really loved my dad, or if she deceived him too."

"Why do you think that?"

"The first chance she gets she goes back to Rowan. Plus, she's been keeping my dad in the dark about it."

"Well, they're divorced, aren't they? She shouldn't have to keep her ex up to date on her personal life."

"What does she see in your dad, anyway?"

"You'll have to ask her, but this I know—Easter is the love of his life. When you get to know Rowan as I do, I think you'll understand your mother better too."

"What about *your* mother? Did Rowan love her too? At the same time?"

"Not while I was in the picture. We never lived as a family."

"Well, I really don't want to meet him, not now anyway."

"When you're ready, you'll see that he's all right. I doubt he'll lose his cool, even over this. Guess I'll find out tomorrow when I get home. François told me that he's going to come over and introduce you."

"I don't want another father."

"My dad's not going to force himself on you."

"You mean *our* dad," Adam said, "which brings us to the big question: How are we going to handle *us?*"

"I wish we'd left yesterday. We should have kept our relationship to ourselves."

"I'd have told my mom about you, so it just would have come out then."

"I know, but I think we're meant for each other."

"I thought so too. I still think so, but maybe in a different way."

"So what should we do?"

"From the moment we met you seemed like my best friend. We have to keep that."

They were still for a while.

"Adam, there's something I've been wondering, ever since Princeton."

"What?"

"Why didn't you make love to me in your room on New Year's Eve?"

"You really want to know?"

"I do."

"There'd been other girls in that bed. My first year on the basketball team ... well, you know."

"You don't have to explain. It's the same in the dance world. But answer my question."

"With you it was different."

"What about this house? You must have brought tons of girls here."

"No, you're the only one."

Through tears, Marisol looked up at Adam and said, "You never told me what you called the third photo at the fountain."

"It was presumptuous."

"Tell me."

"I called it 'My Other Half.'"

CHAPTER 22

From JFK, Marisol took a cab straight to the Upper West Side apartment she shared with her father. She found Rowan in his running clothes, flushed from jogging in Central Park.

Her distress over the revelations of the past twenty-four hours had intensified as she'd flown across the Atlantic. A part of her wanted to blame her father, but he hadn't known either, and he had every right to be as upset as she was.

"Welcome home," he said as he opened the door. Rowan was always gladdened by his daughter's presence, never more than this time, and his greeting was effusive.

"Hi, Dad," she said, letting go of her suitcase and falling into his arms.

"So, our family is not just the two of us anymore," Rowan said. "Come sit. I've made us coffee."

After she explained why she'd made the impromptu trip to Paris, she asked him how he'd gotten the news about Adam.

"François called Easter's secretary, who reached us at the cabin. It must have been three in the morning. Then Easter called François in Paris."

"What did he say?"

"I couldn't hear his side of the conversation, but I could tell that Easter was upset. Finally, she told François he'd done the right thing and hung up. For a while, she just sat there by the phone. I was afraid her son had been hurt—or worse."

Rowan got two mugs from the cupboard and put them on the table. "Then she mumbled something about being sorry and broke down. She kept asking me to forgive her, but I didn't know for what. When she calmed down, she said there was something she'd wanted to tell me for a long time, but hadn't been free to do so. Then she told me."

"What did she say?"

"Her exact words? 'You have a son, Rowan. Adam is our son'."

"Holy crap. How did you feel? What did you think?"

"I couldn't take it in. I didn't understand what it could possibly mean. It seemed impossible that I could have lived my life without knowing something that important." Rowan poured the coffee and sat down across from her.

"We had a wonderful time in Paris, Dad. The best time of my life."

Rowan slowly shook his head. She couldn't tell if he was upset with her or sympathetic.

"I'm so sorry, Marisol. We'll all have to find a way to come to terms with this. When does Adam get back?"

"Next week. François is coming too. He wants to introduce you to Adam."

"I suppose that's the honorable thing to do."

"He wants me to be there. But not Easter. I won't go if she's there. I'm sorry, Dad, but it looks like she dumped you for a guy with more money. You should hate her."

"No, Marisol, that's not how it was. I didn't want to tell you, but it seems that your mother had a hand in this."

"What do you mean?"

"After I left Jefferson I holed up at the cabin. Easter couldn't reach me."

"Why didn't she call you?"

"It had no phone in those days. She repeatedly called the apartment in New York, but I'd left."

"So why didn't she leave a message?"

"Marisol, it was 1971; there were no answering machines. But one time, Sara answered, and told her to get out of our life."

"She could have written."

"I think Sara intercepted her letters."

"Oh God, I don't want to hear that either. It's so ... wait, why didn't *you* call Easter?"

"I did, and when I finally reached someone at François's place in Dakar I was told they'd gone to Paris together. That's when I realized I had to let go."

"So, you went back to Mom?"

"Not right away, but later that summer I came to New York for a job interview and she offered to let me stay in our old apartment. That's when you were conceived."

"Don't tell me more."

"Okay, but I want you to understand one thing. Easter believed that she had just two choices: Come home, abandon her fellowship, and be a single mother, or marry François. She went with the choice that offered security and avoided shame."

"Why didn't she just get an abortion?"

"For her, that wasn't an option."

"François told us that he made her break up with you. Something about his parents not finding out that Adam wasn't really their grandson. I got the feeling that jealousy was part of it too."

"Well, I never heard a word from her until after they'd separated, not until she invited me to Jefferson for the honorary degree."

"You didn't suspect?"

"It never crossed my mind. The pill, you know. In those days we thought it was foolproof."

Marisol, uneasy, was suddenly overcome by fatigue. It was midnight Paris time, and the next day she'd begin rehearsals for the new season. She excused herself to go to bed, but stopped to lean against the kitchen doorway.

"Dad, I've been thinking about getting a place of my own."

"I suppose that makes sense. Nearby, I hope."

"Just around the corner would be perfect." Rowan got up and kissed her on the forehead.

"I'm so tired I feel dizzy," she said, turning down the hall.

§§§

Within a week, François had made good on his promise to accompany Adam to the States and present him to Rowan. From the be-

211

ginning of this new phase in their relationship, François's advice to Adam was that two fathers could be better than one if they're both good men. And, knowing Easter as he did, he imagined that Rowan would prove to be a good man.

François had suggested that Rowan bring Marisol along, and the four of them met for dinner at a midtown restaurant. Marisol had given a lot of thought to her outfit and decided on a short, black, fashionable dress, with her hair pinned up for a more mature look.

When Rowan met Adam, he had the feeling that, apart from the mocha shade of his skin, in him, he was meeting a taller, younger version of himself. The conversation roamed from sports and math at Princeton to dance in New York. For Rowan's benefit, François repeated that Adam was his sole heir. He also made it clear that he was encouraging Adam to seek Rowan out for academic advice. The dinner was going smoothly, and Rowan attributed this to the fact that François was a loving father who made Adam's interests his own.

When, after the main course, Marisol and Adam excused themselves "for a walk," Rowan took the opportunity to ask François if he thought their romance had cooled, or simply gone underground. Easter had encouraged him to push François on this point, so when he demurred, Rowan said, "I hope you have more influence with Adam than I do with Marisol."

"After your daughter left Paris I shared something with Adam that might help him sort this out."

"That's good, because I'm at a loss."

"My father's sister had a daughter about my age, my cousin Viviane. As children, we saw a lot of each other at family gatherings. In adolescence, what began as child's play turned into flirtation. One summer, when my parents were in Senegal and I had the house to myself, flirtation blossomed into first love."

"Cousins are legal," Rowan noted.

"Genetically, half-siblings are no closer than first cousins. Couples of either type share two grandparents," François replied. "But for us, marriage was never in the cards. When my parents returned we tried sneaking around for a while, but soon realized that we were more important to each other as friends than as lovers. We've been soul mates ever since."

"I hope Adam and Marisol find their way to something like that," Rowan said.

"Viviane and I feel that our bond is closer because we were once lovers. I told Adam that a former lover always holds a special place in a man's heart."

"How did he respond to your story?"

"He hasn't yet, but I hope it's sinking in."

§§§

A week later, after a luncheon speech to Boston alumni, Easter drove to the Berkshires to spend the weekend with Rowan. They'd had several long phone conversations since Rowan had met Adam, but this was their first face-to-face meeting since this new phase of their lives had begun. He heard the car pull up and went out to greet her.

Ordinarily, he'd have stuck to their tried and true formula— "sex first, talk later"— but given all they'd been through, he sensed that an intermediate step was called for.

Easter hardly had time to sit down before he bundled her into a parka and ski boots and fastened on her skis. Two hours of cross-country skiing proved to be just the ticket. By nightfall she'd left her regrets and worries in the Berkshire hills.

After many hours of phone time devoted to children and their own lost years, Rowan was determined to make this weekend a new start. Relaxing before the fireplace with after-dinner coffee, he pulled out a small gray velvet box tied with a silk ribbon and set it on the table.

"I've been waiting for the right occasion," he said. "This is for the gift of Adam. Under the circumstances, I trust you'll overlook the fact that it's nineteen years late."

"That's the least I can do," Easter said with a rueful smile as she tugged at the ribbon. Inside the box she found a delicate brooch studded with rubies, pearls, and lapis lazuli—red, white, and blue.

"It's exquisite, Rowan!" Easter held it to her breast. "Where did you find it?"

"In Novosibirsk. The artist lives on the shores of Lake Baikal. I thought of you the moment I saw it and snapped it up in the hope that a day might come when I could give it to you. Some summer, I'd like to show you Baikal. We could rent a cabin and live like the natives—on mushrooms, berries, fish, and black bread. Wood fires at night, no electricity, no phones. I know just enough Russian to get by."

As he painted this rustic picture, Easter got up, walked around behind him, and, taking his face in her hands, tipped his head back and kissed him on the lips.

"Once upon a time, I was the president's lover," she said. "Now, you are."

"Just a permutation," he said, pulling her onto his lap. Easter had regained her footing and come back to Earth—to him.

The conversation went where it had so often gone: to college politics. A coalition of students and faculty women had drawn up legislation banning all sexual contact between students and faculty or staff. They had come to Easter early in the process, asking her to endorse their goals but, to their dismay, she'd refused to join their crusade.

"I told them I'll be presiding over the debate and must be seen as impartial," she explained. "They didn't buy it. They don't know where I stand, and for that matter, neither do I."

"Surely the faculty can tell the difference between consensual sex and harassment."

"You'd be surprised, Rowan. The idea of an outright ban on sex between people of different rank is gaining ground. One extreme group maintains that, so long as society is patriarchal, sexual intercourse is tantamount to rape. They're like fundamentalists. Rowan, I can't reason with them. I haven't seen such venom since the sixties."

"Haven't quite a few professors married students?"

"Yes, and many more are like me—they've done things the new code would prohibit, and they're against it. On the other side, there are women backing the new code who were taken advantage of by professors."

"Philpot," Rowan said glumly.

"He's Exhibit A. A few years after you left, one of his students charged him with offering to get her into Yale in exchange for sex. The president forced him to resign."

"I should have done that," Rowan said.

"Last fall, a football player wrote an anonymous letter to *The Jeffersonian,* charging an assistant coach with offering him playing time for sex. But he wouldn't identify himself or the coach, so my hands were tied."

"That's extortion, pure and simple. How do the French handle this? They've got a lot of common sense when it comes to sex."

"They're laissez-faire. But they draw the line at pressure of any kind, as should we."

"It seems impossible now … that we did what we did. Was it a dream?" Rowan ventured.

"I'd have left you alone if you hadn't been so young," Easter said with a smile.

"Yes, it was all your fault, you hussy. Anyway, whatever they do, it's going to look silly in a few years."

"But I've got to get through this semester."

"The job doesn't sound like much fun."

"Worse than that," Easter said, "it doesn't even feel important—like what we fought for. For the first time, I've begun to think about life after Jefferson."

"There is one, you know."

"You managed it pretty well. What could I do?"

"You won't even have to look. Opportunities will find you."

"Not if our story gets out. By the way, Marisol still understands the importance of keeping this in the family, doesn't she?"

"She moved into a place of her own last week. I'll remind her this weekend."

CHAPTER 23

A few weeks later, as Rowan was preparing for bed, his phone rang. It was Easter, in whose voice he heard a mixture of alarm and resignation. She told him that Marisol's full name had appeared in *The Princetonian,* and she'd been identified as Adam's sister. The news had already made its way to Jefferson and was spreading through the faculty like a firestorm. Rowan tried to calm her and promised to get to the bottom of it in the morning.

Before sunrise, he called Marisol and demanded an explanation. She had indeed been in Princeton for a game, and afterward a student reporter had asked her if she were Adam's girlfriend. Not content with her simple "no," he'd asked around, and Ellie had confirmed that they were half-brother and sister.

Easter's assistant traced the rumor's arrival on the Jefferson campus to Connie Wellstone, a Princeton professor who'd graduated from Jefferson during Rowan's tenure as president. From the article in *The Princetonian,* Connie had picked up on the implications in the half-siblings' surnames and phoned one of her old Jefferson professors who, in turn, had gleefully regaled the faculty with the news of an affair between a former and a current president.

Rowan's initial irritation with Marisol contrasted sharply with Easter's focus on damage control. She told Rowan that she'd immediately alerted the chairman of the board to a potential scandal.

"The timing couldn't be worse," she said in a call to Rowan. "I'm scheduled to chair an open forum on the sex code tomorrow evening. Do you think I should offer the board my resignation?"

"Hell, no. I think you can win this. Stand firm, and your critics will back down."

§§§

By noon the next day, Rowan was on a plane that would get him to Jefferson in time for the forum.

He left his rental car in the lot behind the administration building and, wearing sunglasses and a baseball cap, melted into the crowd pouring into Seeger Chapel. If he kept his head down and stayed way in the back, no one would recognize him, or so he hoped.

It was here, twenty years earlier, that he had given his inaugural address. A quick glance around the chapel assured him that for every minority student who had heard him then, there were ten who would hear Easter tonight.

On stage, the deans, President Blue, and the committee members who had drawn up the sex code were waiting to begin. As the chapel bell tolled eight, Easter rose and walked to the podium. The crowd was buzzing, but it lacked the earnestness and solemnity of assemblies held during the Vietnam era. Even when Easter called for order, bawdy laughter and nervous titters could be heard throughout the chamber. Finally, she brought the assembly to attention and introduced the committee chair, a youthful-looking female professor of gender studies, who spelled out three alternatives.

The first was the current hands-off policy labeled "laissez-faire"; the second, "limited ban," ruled out sex between faculty and students enrolled in their current classes. The third, "complete ban," prohibited all sexual relations between students and faculty or staff, a position supported by the majority of the committee members.

After committee representatives took turns defending each of the three positions, they fielded questions from students lined up behind microphones in the aisles.

As the first hour drew to a close, Rowan began to think Easter would get through the evening unscathed. Then, a well-dressed young woman took the mike and, in a soft but clear voice, respectfully announced that she had a question for the president.

Easter rose and walked to the podium.

"President Blue, there's a rumor going around that could have an impact on the subject of this forum. I think you should know that advocates of the complete ban on fraternization between students and faculty are using your personal story to support their proposal. I'm sure the community would like to hear your views on the matter."

Easter stood silently for what felt to Rowan like several minutes, looking out over the audience. An impatient buzz began to spread through the chapel. Then Easter spoke.

"Twenty years ago, in this chapel, I listened as a young president urged the faculty to do what was long overdue: to seek out and welcome people of color to Jefferson. I was one of his student supporters. We worked together in what was nothing less than a struggle for the soul of the college and, as is obvious from the diversity in this hall, the changes we fought for prevailed. In the process, what started as a friendship gradually turned into something more. By the time I graduated, the boundaries between us had dissolved."

A few hoots rose from the crowd.

"There is more to this story, but the rest of it is our business and ours alone. I do, however, have something to say to those who would use my story as an argument against any and all relationships between students and faculty or staff.

"I entered into the relationship I have described with my eyes open. I was an adult, I chose it, and I have never regretted that choice.

"In defending love I am not giving my blessing to promiscuity, let alone to sex between students and faculty or staff. We all know that many of the romantic relationships we imagine are unwise, and that we'd be better off not consummating them. But that does not mean that the faculty of Jefferson College should attempt to legislate matters of the heart between consenting adults."

This last remark was met with hisses sprinkled with a few bravos. Easter pressed on as if she'd heard nothing.

"In my view, legislating love is like regulating speech. Along with the founding fathers, I believe that the costs to liberty outweigh the benefits to society."

She paused to let them absorb the parallel.

"Legislation has a sorry record when it comes to love. Consider how often laws have been passed with pious certainty by one generation only to become an embarrassment to the next. We find ourselves today in the middle of just such a change of attitude toward homosexuality."

Scattered applause, a little stronger, but intense in several sections of the audience. Easter looked out across the chapel, made eye contact with two or three individuals, and resumed.

"The code recommended by the committee would disallow the defining event of my life and virtually criminalize a choice I made with all my heart, a choice I stand by today. If you want to do that, that's your prerogative. But for me to support it would not only be hypocritical, it would be to disavow the love of my life.

"John Keats spoke for me when he said, 'I am certain of nothing but the holiness of the heart's affections.' If the faculty adopts the 'complete ban,' I want you all to know that you have a president who transgressed it and who believes that you should have the right to follow your hearts as she followed hers."

Rowan listened in awe. When Easter finished, a stillness came over the crowd. It was broken by a few students carrying a placard reading NO FRATERNIZATION who got to their feet and booed.

But a wave of applause, rolling from the rear to the front of the chapel, soon drowned out the protestors. Rowan saw groups of students rising to their feet in a standing ovation. As he slipped out into the night, it was clear that the majority of students didn't want the College involved in their love lives.

He quickly crossed the short distance to the Archives, climbed the stairs to the guest suite, and found it unlocked. Twenty minutes later he saw Easter's car pull out of the lot behind the administration building. After giving her the five minutes he knew it would take her to get home, he dialed her number.

"I'm here, in the Archives."

"Oh, my God, you were there?"

"In the back. No one saw me. You won the day."

"Nothing's settled until the faculty votes, but I am sure of one thing—we're done hiding. I'll be right over."

He lay down on the bed in the darkness, trying to get used to the idea that their secret was out. The sound of a door snapping shut told him Easter was in the building. He listened to her steps on the stairs with growing anticipation.

She let herself into the apartment and walked toward him in the dimly lit room. As she settled down on the bed beside him, she put one finger over his lips to remind him of their rule.

§§§

"I don't like what's going on here," Easter said to Rowan in one of their daily calls between Jefferson and New York. "The lawyers on the board are arguing that colleges bear legal liability for sexual harassment charges brought by students. They're lobbying the faculty to ban fraternization of any sort."

"What about the consensus on campus? After your speech, they were with you."

"The students, yes, but as you know, they have little say."

"Did *The Jeffersonian* take a position?"

"They came out in favor of the limited ban, but Rowan, none of that matters. When it comes to questions of liability, the faculty's going to defer to the board. In any case, the board looks set to impose an outright ban. They see it as a matter of fiduciary responsibility."

"The whole thing has been blown out of proportion."

"I can't just carry on as if nothing has happened."

"Actually, that would be the best strategy. Stay aloof and in no time people will be talking about something else."

As if she had decided to take his advice, Easter changed the subject. "Marisol sent me an apology for blabbing to Ellie. I presume you suggested it."

"No, she's contrite. She's moved out now, and I'm feeling out of touch … with both kids, actually. Let's ask them for dinner next time you're here."

§§§

The following evening, Rowan responded to a knock on his door and found Easter standing in his hallway. Before she even said hello, she announced glumly, "The faculty caved." Disgusted with academic spinelessness, she'd driven straight to the airport and caught the first flight to New York.

Over a hastily opened bottle of wine she told Rowan that the Jefferson faculty, by a sixty-forty majority, had approved the "complete ban" that prohibited all fraternization, and then gone on to make violation of the ban cause for immediate termination.

Although several trustees had assured her privately that the board valued her services and wished her to continue, she took the faculty's action as a slap in the face. For the first time, she was seriously thinking of leaving.

Rowan poured her a glass of wine while she filled him in. "It's not that I feel they're wrong and I'm right, but they treated me as if my views counted for nothing, as if I didn't exist. Well, perhaps I don't."

As he listened, Rowan realized that one side of him relished the prospect of her moving on. If she left, Jefferson would be behind both of them.

"Getting out was the best thing that ever happened to me," he said.

"You could afford to lose your status. My dad would never have put it this way in public, but in private he'd say, 'Without a title, you're just another nigger.'"

"In his day, yes, but not today. You are in fact eminently employable."

"He believed that rank trumps race, that status could protect us from bigotry. If he were alive he'd tell me to hang onto my current title until I got a better one."

"He was right," Rowan admitted. "It's always been tough out there for nobodies. But come on, you won't be one for more than five minutes. Just offer your services to the Clinton campaign. They'll grab you and give you a top-level job when he wins."

§§§

Rowan invited Adam and Marisol for dinner the following evening. Over dessert, Marisol said to Easter, "Adam told me about your speech. I trust the heart's affections, too."

"Oh, that's from Keats," Easter said. "But it doesn't mean that anything goes."

"I don't think love can mislead us," Marisol said. "If it's holy, how can it?"

"When it's selfish. But so long as we put our beloved first, love is holy. I think that's what Keats meant. In any case, it's what *I* meant."

Before Marisol could reply, Rowan jumped in.

"Easter and I realize that we've put you in a pickle."

"We can take care of this," Adam said. "We don't want any advice."

"Please let me finish," Rowan said. "We know that our choices have caused you pain, and we're sorry."

"Well, you shouldn't be," Adam said. "If anything had been the least bit different, neither of us would exist."

Adam's remark put an end to the apologies. To move on, he passed the bowl of mashed potatoes to Marisol, saying, "I think you're losing weight."

"Dancing six hours a day is the ultimate diet plan," she said. "I agree with Adam. Please don't worry about us. We can handle this."

"No parent wants to see her child suffer," Easter said.

"No parent wants to see *two* of his children suffer," Rowan added. "But I'll say no more. We love you no matter what."

"We'll be fine," said Adam. "What we do want *you* to know is that in each other we've both found a best friend."

"You used to complain about being an only child," Easter said to Adam.

"Well, now I have a baby sister."

Rowan felt Easter nudge his leg under the table. He could see from her face that she was satisfied

.

CHAPTER 24

Marisol's apartment was six blocks from Rowan's. It had an airy living room and a tiny bedroom. She had painted the living room creamy apricot and trimmed it in a pale lavender. She furnished it with a navy-blue loveseat, a second-hand armchair, and a small, antique coffee table. The only window faced south, over the roofs of the buildings opposite, toward the skyscrapers in lower Manhattan. At night, the silhouettes of the World Trade Center's twin towers twinkled against a darkening sky.

Adam had come up from Princeton at her invitation to celebrate the end of his exams and the start of summer break. While she put the finishing touches on dinner, he curled up on the loveseat and dozed off to the sound of kitchen noises and soft music.

Before waking him, she changed into a filmy lilac skirt with matching tank leotard. When dinner was ready, she sat down on the edge of the loveseat and rubbed his chest.

"What are you wearing?" Adam said drowsily, gazing up at her.

"Oh, it's inspired by the Lilac Fairy in *Sleeping Beauty*," she said, rising and making a curtsey.

She spread a tablecloth on the floor of the living room and motioned for Adam to sit. She handed him a bottle of Chianti to open while she went to the kitchen to get the ratatouille from the oven.

"I've missed you," she called out. "I'm so glad you're here." Before she joined him on the floor she changed the music.

"Layla," she said. "Remember?" They listened as they ate.

When the song was over, she said, "Don't you wish that no one had ever told us?"

"Ignorance *was* bliss, but we can't forget what we know."

"But ... "

"But what?"

"No one would have to know."

"You mean sneak around? We'd never be able to keep it from our friends."

Marisol moved behind him. "Adam …" she murmured, and began rubbing his shoulders. When he relaxed, she nuzzled his neck.

"I thought we weren't going to do this anymore."

"Just pretend I'm the Lilac Fairy." When he didn't move, she whispered, "You don't want to?"

"It can't be right."

"So long as it's between us, right and wrong are our business."

"Rowan would hate me. The better I know him, the more that matters."

"It's not fair that the first time I fall in love, it's ruled off-limits."

"I love you too, Marisol, but that doesn't change the fact that we're brother and sister."

"Half … " Marisol insisted.

"I see you as family. I can't get past that."

"Why not?"

Adam spun around and grabbed his sister's wrists. "It's incest, Marisol! *That's* how everyone would see it."

Stung by his outburst, she shrank back.

There hadn't been a day since François had revealed his paternity that Adam hadn't struggled with the implications. He put his arm around her and gave her shoulder a squeeze. "I want my life to count for something," he said firmly.

"Well then stand up for *us*," she shot back. "I intend to!"

"I'm sorry, Marisol, but this is a fight we can't win." He stood up, picked up his jacket, and started toward the door.

"No, Adam, no," Marisol pleaded, tears flowing. She went to him and put her arms around his neck. "Please, come and sit down. I'm sorry."

"Marisol, you've got to help me with this." He opened the door and walked toward the elevator.

Marisol stood in her doorway, sobbing, until the elevator door closed. Then she went to the window and watched him walk away. He didn't look back.

The next day, without telling anyone, Adam left for Paris.

BOOK II

A PAIR OF US

I'm nobody! Who are you?
Are you nobody, too?
Then there's a pair of us—don't tell!
They'd banish us, you know.

How dreary to be somebody!
How public, like a frog
To tell your name the livelong day
To an admiring bog!
  – Emily Dickinson

PART 1

ADAM

The imagination roams widely over
the world until it finds a predicament
that reflects its own secret agonies.
  – Marcel Theroux, author, *Far North*

Every man has a Don Quixote in him.
  – George Balanchine

CHAPTER 25

Adam squeezed his six-and-a-half-foot frame into an economy seat for the transatlantic flight to Paris. The cramped space befitted his life at the moment—pressured by Marisol, and trapped by the expectations everyone—his parents, professors, and coaches—had of him.

When the plane was airborne he pulled a datebook from his breast pocket and flipped to June: "Princeton—BB camp" was scrawled diagonally across the month. Princeton's basketball program for kids with "hoop dreams" had been fun the previous summer, but he wouldn't have signed up again if his coach hadn't insisted.

Turning the page, he saw for July: "Berkeley—MSRI." Among mathematicians, the Mathematical Sciences Research Institute was affectionately known by its telling acronym, Misery. Indeed, most of the math that was done there was over his head, but he recalled being excited when the math department chairman had first broached the idea of a summer internship there. He briefly pondered the change in his outlook, then continued turning the datebook pages. Nothing he saw coming up thrilled him.

Come September, the dual grind of coursework and varsity basketball would again consume his every moment, especially basketball. The coach's dream was that the following year Adam, and Princeton's All-American forward, Ben Steinsaltz, would take them to the NCAA finals. He couldn't stand thinking about it anymore, and closed his eyes.

When he woke up, the datebook was on the cabin floor and the plane was over France. François would be picking him up at De Gaulle, and he tried to imagine how his dad envisioned his son's future. For as long as Adam could remember he'd known that the family's Paris home and the farm outside Dakar would someday be his. Still, when he tried to picture himself on the farm, he couldn't. It wasn't only because he couldn't imagine François gone, it was also that he just wasn't interested in agriculture *or* business.

A few hours later, Adam and François were sipping café au lait from the same out-sized porcelain cups that had held his cocoa when he was a child.

"It's good to be home, Dad."

"I'm so glad you've come."

"Mom sends her regards."

"How is she?"

"Fine. She's working for the Clinton campaign."

"She's always been ambitious—in a good way." Adam could tell his father still cared for Easter, which somehow in his mind made their separation easier to bear. "Have you seen Rowan?"

"A couple of times. He's not pushing things."

"He seems like a sympathetic fellow. And Marisol?"

"We've cooled it. She wants it to be what it was … before we found out. I can't go back."

Adam was truthful and direct. François was not a judgmental man, and by age fifteen Adam had learned that keeping his father in the know usually served him better than keeping secrets from him.

François had an off-handed way of offering useful advice.

"It must have been disconcerting—suddenly acquiring a grown sister."

"Especially when she's your girlfriend!" Adam blurted out. He was still angry, and François didn't miss his implied recrimination.

"For that I'm very sorry, son. At the time I married your mother, it seemed best to assume the role of father—in *every* respect. As I was an only child, it was extremely important to my parents that I produce an heir. Not that I hadn't tried before to give them what they wanted."

"What do you mean?"

"You know that I'd been married before, to a Senegalese woman."

"Yeah."

"It was long before I met your mother. We tried to have children but couldn't. It was my own medical issue. Our disap-

234

pointment, made worse by pressure from both sets of parents, was a factor in our parting. My parents were overjoyed when I remarried and Easter quickly provided them with a grandson and heir. It never crossed their minds that you weren't of their blood."

François looked at him over his coffee cup, trying to gauge his reaction. All Adam could come up with was "You never told me all that."

"Your anger is entirely justified. I wish I'd come to the States after my mother died and told you everything. Someday, I hope you'll forgive me."

If François had ever apologized to him before, it had been for missing a birthday party or a school play—the kind of things that occur in all parent-child relationships—not for a moral lapse of such consequence. His vulnerability made Adam want to comfort him. Barely able to get the words out, he said, "I forgive you, Dad."

"Thank you, Adam." Not one for effusive shows of affection, François reached across the table and placed a strong, loving hand on his forearm. Up until this point they'd been speaking English; now François turned to his native French. Adam knew it meant that the conversation was about to take an even more personal turn.

"And you—how are you doing?"

"It's been hard. I've never felt closer to anyone than Marisol. I don't think I'll ever find another woman like her."

"One thought, if I may?" Adam nodded. "Growing up with Rowan, Marisol lived a life that might have been yours. I'm not saying it would have been better than the one you had, but naturally it holds some fascination for you. I'm not disposed to the occult, but I've sometimes wondered if we don't sense the absence of someone who is missing from our lives—like amputees feel a pain in a missing limb. Is it possible that in getting to know Marisol you're accessing someone you missed without knowing it?"

Adam nodded again. It occurred to him that when someone tells you something you already know but haven't admitted to yourself, an echo of that knowledge can come from a deeper recess in your mind. He'd often had that feeling around his dad. He sat without speaking, letting the idea sink in.

François broke the silence, bringing up a current concern. "There's a meeting of Doctors Without Borders tonight on the famine in Somalia. As we feared, it's turning into another Ethiopia."

"I know. I've been following the story since January."

"Of course. You filled in for me at that meeting. If you come along tonight, you'll see some of the same people. Dr. Fleury is just in from Mogadishu and will have the latest news."

Adam remembered the young Indochinese doctor very well. Her passion. Her commitment. She had invited him to go to Somalia and see for himself, but he'd turned her down.

"Okay, Dad. I'll go with you."

§§§

The first speaker reported that the rains had not come to the Sahel that spring, and making matters worse, Somali chieftains were ruthlessly exploiting the famine as a weapon in their clan warfare. It was now certain that without massive international help, hundreds of thousands of Somali refugees would be dead by fall.

After the break, the chairman introduced the guest of honor, Dr. Élodie Pham Fleury. Large piercing eyes added drama to her delicate features. Straight black hair fell to her shoulders. Her animated face made her look twenty, but her MD degree told Adam that she had to be at least five years older. With soft-spoken intensity, she told simple stories of individual suffering and fortitude.

When Dr. Fleury concluded, Adam went up to her and reintroduced himself.

"I heard you in January. Looks like you were right."

"It's even worse than we predicted, and the world still doesn't know."

"Is that why you're here? To alert the press?"

"Not really. My main concern is medical supplies, but we all do a little bit of everything." She paused momentarily, then continued. "When we met at the beginning of the year you were with a young woman, a dancer. You were heading back to school in the States."

"I've just finished my second year. I'm home to see my dad."

"Are you staying for the summer?"

"I go back at the end of the month. Is the work dangerous? In Somalia, I mean?"

"We're under the protection of armed guards."

"How long will you be there?"

"As long as I'm needed."

Adam found himself envying her dedication. "Sounds like important work."

"Why don't you come see for yourself?" She took a card from her purse and handed it to him. We need volunteers more than ever. You'll have to pay your own way, but I can guarantee it'll be an eye-opener."

"I'm only home for a few weeks, but I'll talk to my dad about it."

The chairman called the meeting to order, and as Dr. Fleury returned to her seat, she called over her shoulder, "Let me know by tomorrow."

§§§

On their way home Adam mentioned Élodie's invitation, and François immediately urged him to accept it. He said they'd have time enough to see each other when Adam returned to Paris.

"I'd give a lot to know if it's as bad as they're saying," François said. "This soon after Ethiopia, we can't afford to be seen 'crying wolf.' The public has compassion fatigue, and the media are skeptical."

François never missed a chance to involve his son in African affairs. With Adam attending Princeton, and having an American mother, he believed the American part of his son's identity would take care of itself. And their home in Paris guaranteed that Europe would have as much allure as America. It was Adam's African heritage that most needed to be enriched. During Adam's youth, François had made sure they visited Senegal at least once a year, but his son's Wolof—the closest thing in Senegal to a national tongue—was childlike, and his feel for the land tenuous. If he lacked those ties, François feared that their property in Senegal would inevitably pass out of the family.

Adam needed no further encouragement. He'd been attracted by more than Élodie's beauty and energy. Her single-minded resolve intrigued him. He called Médecins Sans Frontières and when Élodie came on the line, asked her if she'd meet him for coffee. Before she answered, she wanted to know if he was seriously considering the trip. Only when he said yes did she agree to meet him.

From the moment they sat down, Élodie acted as if he were already committed, and began briefing him on the job at hand. Their mission was to make sure that a shipment of medical supplies reached the MSF office in Somalia. This meant escorting the precious cargo through customs in Nairobi and onto the small plane that would take them to Mogadishu. Once they were in Somalia, his job was to document anything that might help them persuade Western donor nations of the seriousness of the situation.

"I know how to use a camera," Adam volunteered, hoping to sound useful.

"MSF is always looking for compelling images. So are the media."

"Is getting supplies through customs a problem?"

"Having a man along can only help. Act like you're in charge and the officials in Nairobi will wave us through. If I were alone, they'd probably harass me and demand a bribe."

"Ah, I see," Adam said, though he had no experience in dealing with corrupt officials.

"Your being the son of François Merle should help. You should ask him for a letter of commendation, just in case. His name is known to the higher-ups there, as a businessman and as a board member of MSF. Wear a suit and tie, and get some shades. You want to look intimidating."

"Okay."

"Your height's a plus," Élodie added. He thought he saw a fleeting smile cross her professional face.

When she began to detail the conditions in Somalia, he grabbed a napkin and started a list of provisions he'd need: mosquito netting, sleeping bag, flashlight, extra batteries, protein bars, warm and cool clothing. Busying himself with mundane details like these was just what he needed. For the first time ever, he was signing up for 'the road not taken,' a sobering and exhilarating step for someone who had always taken well-traveled paths.

After she'd taken care of business, Élodie relaxed, and said, "This calls for a toast" as she waved to the waiter. While she ordered a carafe of Beaujolais, Adam looked around. The café she'd brought them to had a smoky, brightly-lit central room with a long bar, but they were alone in an adjoining alcove. She poured them each a glass and, after they toasted the success of their venture, asked Adam about himself.

Describing his soft life at Princeton made him uneasy, so he tried to get by with a few platitudes and generalities. She picked up on his apprehension and put him at ease with, "You don't have to apologize. Until I went to Africa, my life was just like yours."

"Tell me how you got into this," he said.

She pushed her hair behind her ears, narrowed her eyes, and looked at him as if to gauge his interest. She took another sip of wine, then began recounting her family history.

Her French father was a doctor who'd met and married her Vietnamese mother in colonial Indochina. When the Vietnamese rebelled against French rule, in the fifties, he'd brought his wife back to France where Élodie and her sisters were born. She'd been raised and schooled in Paris before enrolling in medical school at twenty.

"How did you get involved with Somalia?"

"Just before I graduated from med school, one of our professors said doctors were needed there. As soon as I got to Mogadishu, I realized I'd found my vocation. The work is exhausting, but it's never dull. I love that MSF takes healthcare to those who need it most, without regard for national borders. This sometimes means working in a war zone, but the danger is offset by the gratitude of the patients and their families, and it's a lot better way to see the world than as a tourist."

"I wish I could find something I'd be that passionate about."

"Aren't you—about your studies? You haven't said much about them."

"I sometimes wonder if I should even be in school now."

"What are you studying?"

"Math, basketball."

"Basketball?"

"Yeah, I'm on the team. It takes a lot of time."

"I should have guessed," Élodie said, looking him up and down. "You don't like it?"

"I'm looking for something more meaningful."

"Any ideas?"

"Not a clue."

"What you're about to see changed me. Maybe it will you."

"How? How did it change you?" Adam searched her face.

"I could try to explain, but it's better that you see for yourself. I don't want to risk scaring you off."

CHAPTER 26

On the evening of their departure, François drove Adam and Élodie to Orly Airport where, after they checked on the medical shipment, they boarded Air France's overnight flight to Nairobi.

Deplaning the next morning, Adam was pleasantly surprised by the cool summer weather. Although Nairobi is practically on the equator, at seven thousand feet it's spared the oppressive heat and humidity of equatorial Africa. But on this trip he wouldn't really get to see Nairobi, let alone Kenya.

From the commercial jet they were taken in transit to a remote part of the airport. Adam, dressed in a suit and tie, and striding across the oily tarmac as imposingly as he could, accompanied Élodie into the hangar where the life-saving cargo of antibiotics, rehydration kits, and protein biscuits awaited the scrutiny of customs officials.

An imperious little man blared, "Who is responsible for this shipment?"

"I am," Adam announced in a distinctly louder, deeper voice.

The man took a short step back and asked for their papers. Élodie had rehearsed Adam on the plane, so he handed over the documents, then made a show of examining the dollies holding their supplies.

"I trust it's all here," Adam barked. "I have a letter for Mr. Ojimbawi and I insist on presenting it to him in person. These supplies require *priority* handling, do you understand?" With that Adam presented the little man with a letter that François had prepared on MSF stationery.

It worked. "Yes, sir, of course," he said in a more obliging tone. "We need not bother Mr. Ojimbawi with this. It's my honor to serve you. Where is this shipment bound?"

"Mogadishu on the twelve-seater departing at eleven this morning."

The man shouted orders in Swahili to a crew of four wiry men clad in torn, oil-stained shorts.

"We're coming with you," Adam declared. He and Élodie followed the men as they pushed the dollies across the tarmac, and stood sentinel as the cartons were loaded into the bay of the chartered plane. When it was done, Adam handed the foreman a ten-dollar bill.

The two-hour flight to Mogadishu took them over the reddish sands of the Eastern Sahel known as the Ogaden Desert. From the air, Adam could make out patches of thorn scrub on the dunes below, but he couldn't imagine anything edible growing down there. Abruptly, the desert gave way to the sea, and the plane began a steep descent. A glimpse of waves breaking on the beach, and they were on the ground, taxiing along the runway.

The 12-seater pulled up alongside a C-130 cargo plane bearing the United Nations insignia and the inscription World Food Program. As Adam and Élodie climbed down the steps to the tarmac, a jeep mounted with an anti-aircraft machine gun drove up, and two European-looking men stepped out.

"Élodie!" one of them called. "Welcome to Mogadishu. Have you got the supplies?" There it was again, he noted—the same business-first approach he'd seen in Élodie.

"We saw them safely onto this plane," was her reply, and even before she shook hands with the welcoming party, she made for the cargo bay that lay open before the prying eyes of a group of Somalis.

Men from the jeep, armed with AK-47s, gathered around the cargo, and an official from MSF thanked Élodie for "a job well done."

"From this point on, we're under their protection," she whispered to Adam.

"Looks like a private army," he said. Surrounded by men carrying assault rifles, he felt like a bit player in an action movie.

"That's exactly what it is," the MSF official interjected. "They're called 'technicals.' Without these guards the supplies would be commandeered by a local gang before they left the airport."

Adam wondered if his dad would have encouraged him to go if he'd known things were this dicey.

They left the airport in a convoy, with the technical in command—who kept his finger on the trigger of his weapon—atop the lead vehicle. It was followed by an open truck carrying the shipment, then a van, and covering their rear, four heavily-armed technicals riding shotgun in a jeep.

The convoy moved so swiftly that Adam only caught glimpses of Mogadishu, scarlet splotches of bougainvillea clinging to pockmarked buildings; people scurrying everywhere, the women with baskets, the men carrying guns; children begging at intersections. The grim anarchy reminded him of Mad Max.

The four vehicles careened into a gated compound and screeched to a stop. The men in the trailing vehicle quickly closed the gates with a clang and locked them behind the last vehicle in the convoy. Adam and Élodie suddenly found themselves in a serene inner sanctum overhung with shade trees and bedecked with fuchsia spilling out of huge clay pots. A large stucco house with a verandah lay to the rear of the courtyard where the caravan had parked. Off to one side was a low whitewashed building that Élodie identified for Adam as the hospital.

Once they'd been shown their rooms, she gave him a tour of the hospital. Confronted with lifeless stares from emaciated children, he could only try to act normal. She whispered that these were the lucky ones. The real horror would be revealed the next day in a refugee camp 150 kilometers northwest of Mogadishu, in Baidoa, a country town that was the final destination of their precious cargo.

When Adam met the doctors at dinner, he was surprised that none of them looked the part. Their dress was informal—blue jeans or khakis; their topics of conversation, grisly—amputations, infections, dehydration, and starvation. But the staff's matter-of-fact attitude toward injury, illness, and death helped ease his squeamishness.

It was only when the talk turned to politics that the conversation became heated. They were furious at the United Nations officials in Nairobi for their callous indifference to the tragedy.

"They sit around in linen suits while thousands starve," one young Kenyan doctor said. He had just returned from the UN mission in Nairobi and reported that the top official had again postponed a long-scheduled visit to Somalia. "Until the media puts enough starving babies on TV they'll just go on lounging in their villas sipping gin and tonics. They learned nothing from Ethiopia."

Adam hung on every word, but said nothing. When the group broke up—some to make medical rounds, some to sleep—he said good-night to Élodie and went to his room where, to his relief, he found a real bed. A washbasin stood nearby, and after he'd sponged the dust off his face and limbs, he lay across the bed diagonally. A buzzing mosquito reminded him that Élodie's said he must sleep under his net, so he stood on the bed, suspended it from a hook in the ceiling, draped it around the bed, and crawled under its protective canopy. It kept the mosquitoes at bay, but gunfire repeatedly interrupted his sleep.

Breakfast consisted of cold fish, papayas, mangos, and bread. As they ate, the convoy for Baidoa was forming in the courtyard. Every vehicle had either the MSF logo stenciled on it or displayed a flag signaling its humanitarian mission. By nine, they were hurtling out of town in a SUV on dirt roads that ran like capillaries into the open desert.

Every twenty kilometers they had to stop at roadblocks to show their papers and fork over bribes. But what actually ensured their passage was the display of the technicals' firepower. Between roadblocks, they moved at high speed, passing slower vehicles at full throttle, and bullying oncoming pedestrians and vehicles into the roadside ditches. Once, Adam turned to see a man with a camel shaking a stick at the convoy as it sped away. Remembering a car he'd seen in Michigan after it had collided with a deer, he wondered if their driver had any idea what would happen to their vehicle and its occupants if it struck a camel at a hundred kilometers per hour.

Only after they reached the outskirts of Baidoa did Élodie explain that their private army was high on "qat," an addictive shrub cultivated for its stimulative effects. Adam had seen the Somalis stuffing leaves in their mouths and chewing them continuously; their gums and teeth were stained blood red from the juice. He'd assumed it was some kind of chewing tobacco, but Élodie told him it provided a mild amphetamine high, like speed, and was among the few stimulants sanctioned by Islam. Although driving under its influence surely increased the risk of an accident, the larger risk, she explained, was for your technicals to be suffering from withdrawal. Before they left Mogadishu, the convoy had picked up a supply of qat to keep the gunmen happy.

§§§

"This is why we're here," Élodie said, as their vehicle pulled to a stop. She gestured toward a vast field where thousands were camped, some in shelters made of sticks and cloth, many in the open air. They got out of the SUV and followed a dirt path. He could see families huddled together, sitting and lying on the ground. Élodie explained that the mummy-like objects lying everywhere were corpses, shrouded in white cotton cloth for proper Muslim burial. Adam knew he was there to take photographs, but he couldn't bring himself to look through the viewfinder and snap a shot; as it was, just being a well-dressed, well-fed object of envy among people in such distress embarrassed him, and he wished he could just make himself invisible. A couple of times, confronted by scenes of filth and degradation, he viscerally recoiled.

Whatever their condition, the Somalis sat immobile, staring at the visitors. To spare himself some of the anguish he felt, Adam quickly learned to look past people who tried to catch his eye. Élodie must have sensed his discomfort when she took him by the hand and led him toward a narrow, two-story, mud-speckled building that doubled as a hostel and a field hospital.

Inside, they were offered tea and biscuits by the administrator in charge, a middle-aged Englishwoman whose good humor was in sharp contrast to the grimness outside. For the first time in his life,

Adam declined refreshments. He feared he wouldn't be able to keep them down.

"The medicines you've brought will be gone in a few days," the administrator said flatly. Tell headquarters that we can use everything they can get us. We're receiving a thousand new refugees daily."

"How many are you losing now?" Élodie asked.

"Five hundred a day, and that's doubling monthly."

"How can we help? My colleague Adam has a camera."

"Triage. If they're going to die, send them over there." From a window she pointed to a ravine about a hundred meters off. "That's 'the valley of death.' By the time they reach us, most of the adults are beyond help. If a child has a chance, we put them in the hospital for hydration and protein biscuits. Above all, we don't give the antibiotics to anyone who's likely to die anyway."

Then, turning to Adam, she said, "There's nothing more important than letting the world know what's happening here. A picture really can be worth a thousand words. If you can, take some good ones, and get them published. In the long run, that will save more lives than the supplies you've brought today. Don't get me wrong. We're grateful for every little bit, but at this point only massive outside help can prevent a catastrophe."

"I'll do my best," Adam said, wondering how he could stick his camera in the face of such misery. Later that afternoon, when he did force himself to venture out among the refugees, he lasted barely ten minutes. The smell was almost unbearable. Reeling, he returned to the hut and found some of the MSF staff preparing dinner. He marveled at how the doctors and nurses handled the squalor, misery, and death surrounding them, and were generally cheerful, and had good appetites. As one of them told him, "If we don't take care of ourselves properly we won't last a week."

That night they dined by candlelight, and the conversation was disconcertingly upbeat. There was wine to go with hearty servings of rice and vegetables and a huge fish that had made the trip from Mogadishu on the floor of the SUV. It was all Adam could do to eat a little rice, but he did think to stuff his pockets with hunks of bread. It was awful to contemplate, but a crust of bread might give him a way to ask someone who was starving if he could take their picture.

The staff chatted over coffee, and by nine o'clock they had scattered. Élodie showed him to the storeroom where there were cots for guests. They'd accommodate her petite body comfortably, but Adam, clearly too tall for a cot, presented a challenge. She took a half dozen blankets from the shelves, folded them double, and stacked them on the floor to create an extra-long mattress for him. When they were almost asleep, she reached down and squeezed his hand.

"I had a hard time my first few days. It gets easier. I hope you're not sorry you've come."

"No, I'm not sorry, but it's an eye-opener all right. I can't say I'll be sorry to leave."

"Have you got what we came for?"

"What?"

"Photos!" Élodie said emphatically. "Images of famine."

"A few, maybe."

"Look, Adam, you heard the Englishwoman. Publicizing what's happening here is more important than the supplies. You've got to put yourself out there. This work is not sport. It's foul and disgusting, but we cannot fail these people. There'll be more time tomorrow morning. Please try again before we leave."

Adam was silent. What he'd seen that day reminded him of photographs he'd seen of prisoners in concentration camps. The ravenous famine outside felt like a plague stalking the world. He lay awake as Élodie's breathing grew less audible, masked by the wails and moans of people who lay starving meters away in the barren field that surrounded the makeshift hospital.

Early the next morning, with an hour to go before they were scheduled to leave, Adam set out again for the valley of death. He couldn't face Élodie empty-handed, or his dad. He used the bread to get closer to people than before, and improvised simple hand gestures to get permission to take their photographs. Astonishingly, no one rushed him for the bread, or offered resistance. Either they were too weak to respond or they sensed that images of their suffering were all they had left to give.

Adam had never been so close to human beings who were no longer living but not yet dead. A young girl covered by a rag sat vigil over her dead father; unmoving eyes peered up at him from a skeletal figure curled up in a wheelbarrow; an emaciated boy on stick-thin legs stared vacantly into space. Everywhere he saw children with the distended bellies that are emblematic of famine. Saddest of all were the eyes of parents helplessly watching the life drain out of their children.

As he worked his way deeper into the ravine he saw an emaciated teenage girl seated erect next to the dead body of a child, perhaps a younger sister. The way she held herself reminded him of something that he couldn't place; then it struck him. The line of her body was reminiscent of the way Marisol held herself. This girl had the poise and erect posture of a ballet dancer. Her noble carriage, in the midst of horror, was her attempt to uphold her family's dignity. When he indicated that he wanted to photograph her, the girl nodded unsmilingly, then elevated her chin ever so slightly. In that instant he pressed the shutter—and knew that *this* was why he was here. He vowed to get that image home, and make sure that as many people as possible would see it. To leave her with something, he draped his windbreaker around her shoulders before hurrying off. In a last look back, he saw that she had placed it over her sister's naked body.

§§§

The return to Mogadishu was even wilder than the outbound journey. Their bodyguards had exhausted their cache of qat and were desperate to reach their suppliers before withdrawal set in. Where the driver had slowed for bumps and potholes on the way out, he now drove as if he were trying to fly over them. The effect on his passengers' heads and kidneys was punishing.

They reached the outskirts of Mogadishu shaken and dirty, but intact. When the van stopped a few blocks from MSF headquarters to refuel before entering the compound, one of the doctors got out to buy cigarettes. Adam tagged along to get a look at the town from ground level, and two of their guards followed at a discreet distance.

Before he knew it, Adam and the doctor were surrounded by a gang of teenage hooligans, wildly yelling and gesturing. Adam turned around, frantically looking for a way to escape, but the doctor grabbed his arm to stop him. The mob's ringleader stepped forward and demanded the doctor's sunglasses and Adam's camera. A boy discharged a half-dozen rounds from his AK-47 into the ground, inches from their feet. Through the cloud of dust the shots made, Adam saw the glint of a knife cutting through the leather strap of his camera. Seconds later, the mob was gone. Adam was shaking uncontrollably.

When he looked at their bodyguards, they shrugged as if to say, "What could we do? If we'd opened fire, we'd have hit you."

The doctor and Adam ran the few hundred meters to the compound, and while they were telling the staff what had happened, the phone rang. It was an offer to return the camera and glasses for three hundred dollars. When a Somali gentleman on the staff said that yielding to the demands of the extortionists would only encourage such rackets, Adam listened quietly; then he asked where the goods could be ransomed. The camera was at a bike shop, he learned, near the corner where they'd been robbed. Leaving them arguing over the wisdom of yielding to extortion, he transferred exactly three hundred dollars from the money pouch around his neck to his breast pocket, then walked as fast as he could, past the scene of the crime, to the bike shop.

Inside, he slapped the wad of cash down on the counter and demanded the camera and glasses. An old man took the money and disappeared into the back, leaving Adam to wonder if he'd handed over the money for nothing. But within a minute, he returned with the goods. Ransoming stolen property was a business here, and future profits depended on customer satisfaction.

Adam opened the case and found the camera untouched. With a wordless glance at the old man, he turned and strode out, walking as tall and fast as he could. As soon as he dared, he broke into a run, determined to stop for no one. When he was safely inside the compound he immediately removed the exposed roll of film from the camera and secured it in his backpack.

Adam spent the remaining days accompanying Élodie on her rounds, photographing the doctors and their patients at the hospital. The physician-in-chief made him promise to show the photos to the MSF public relations people in Paris.

On the eve of his departure, word circulated that one of the relief agencies in town was throwing a party. The buzz built throughout the day, and Élodie seemed to lighten up. Moments before they left, she emerged wearing what looked like the same lavender silk ao dai he'd admired in Paris, and he hurried upstairs to change into his last clean shirt.

The host had gone to a lot of trouble to obliterate any trace of the party-goers' day jobs. A room that usually served as a dispensary had been transformed into a makeshift ballroom, strewn with flowers and decorated with paper lanterns. An artist had created two images, one on either side of the entrance, presumably to set the tone for the evening. With a start, Adam recognized them as an erect penis and engorged labia. When he and Élodie arrived, couples were already dancing to the Stones' *Let's Spend the Night Together*. With the exception of the explicit images, it could have been a post-game party at Princeton.

Usually it took three or four beers for Adam to overcome his inhibitions. Dozens of green Heineken bottles floated in huge galvanized tubs of melting ice. Élodie brought him his first one, and before it was half gone she dragged him onto the dance floor. When the music stopped, they finished their beers and went for seconds. Until the party, all of Élodie's considerable energy had been focused on the job. Now she was directing that same energy toward Adam. Something about the horror and danger of this place had him dancing with more abandon than ever before.

Around midnight the partygoers began drifting away in pairs. While Élodie chatted with a Japanese woman, an Englishman sidled up to Adam and whispered, "They say war's a great knicker-dropper. I've never been to war, but evidently humanitarian disasters have much the same effect."

When Élodie rejoined him, Adam said, "Everyone seems to be leaving."

"Actually, they're crashing upstairs," she explained. "This place used to be a hotel. How old are you?"

"Twenty," Adam said. His actual nineteen sounded so much younger, and he was, he reasoned, at least in his twentieth year. "And you?"

"Old enough to know better but young enough not to care. Come on." She took his arm and led him up the stairs. Moments later she paused at an open door to look at the large bed inside.

"Do you think that will hold you?" she asked.

"Definitely."

"With room for me?" she asked, standing on her toes and reaching up to take his face in her hands. She didn't need to stretch, because Adam had bent down to meet her halfway.

When they woke the next morning she said, "I have a boyfriend in Paris."

"No expectations," he replied.

"He doesn't ask questions. There's a freedom out here that doesn't exist at home. It's one of the fringe benefits of this kind of work. You work hard, you party hard."

"I understand," he said. "Paris is reality. I'm not so sure I want to go back."

"Don't you have a girlfriend in the States?"

"I did."

"What does that mean?"

"We're close, but it's no longer romantic."

"What happened?"

"It's complicated. I'll explain some other time. You know, I've felt more real out here than I ever do at home. What you're doing really matters, and I want to be part of it. Not just take classes, play sports, and party."

"Is that all college is?"

"Well, no, some of my friends really care about things that matter. But most of them just want to get rich."

As they got dressed, Adam pointed out that she hadn't told him her age.

"Twenty-four last month," she said. "An old lady to you."

"Hardly," he said, checking her out. "How did you get your MD so young?"

"I was the baby in the family and the only one to follow my dad into medicine. He pushed me along." She smiled and changed the subject. "Come on, you've got a plane to catch."

They joined a sleepy-looking group in the foyer, and Élodie's demeanor gave no indication of how they'd spent the night. But she did accompany Adam to the airport, and when she saw him off, she kissed her fingertips and reached them up to touch his lips.

"Once this crisis is over, I could be sent anywhere," she said. "You can always find me through MSF."

"I'll remember that." Adam put his arms around her waist and lifted her off the ground until her face was opposite his. She offered no resistance and seemed to float upward. For a long moment, she dangled there. He kissed her and then loosened his grip so she slid slowly down against his body until her toes reached the tarmac. The copilot was hollering at Adam to board, so with a quick good-bye he mounted the stairs and entered the cabin.

Winging high above the arid land, he thought about the horror below. Then his mind settled on Élodie—so earnest, so lovely, so gone.

CHAPTER 27

Princeton's summer basketball camp for high school players was no place to find the solitude that Somalia had left Adam craving, but he quickly realized that it was the next best thing—mindless. From breakfast till dinner the focus was basketball. He couldn't imagine a better way to distract himself from the wretchedness he'd witnessed. By day's end, the repetitive athletic drills, capped by a scrimmage with the younger, hungrier players never failed to produce the pleasant exhaustion that meant a sound sleep.

Like many Princeton undergraduates, he'd been admitted because he had something the University wanted. As point guard he'd led his high school basketball team to the state championship. Princeton's long-time coach, who'd seen the potential of pairing him with the team's top scorer, Ben Steinsaltz, had recruited him, and from day one Adam's job was to orchestrate an offense that capitalized on Ben's ability to put the ball through the hoop.

With the approach of Adam's third, and Ben's final year of varsity ball, both had bought the coach's argument that competing against the cream of American high school players during the summer was excellent preparation for their regular season.

As the weeks of camp passed, and the reality of his trip to Somalia slowly receded, it was hard for Adam to believe that the horrors he'd witnessed could be occurring on the same planet Princeton was on. More than once he tried to describe what he'd seen to his teammates; they'd listen politely for a few minutes, then cut him short and suggest they go out for pizza. Adam couldn't blame them; he'd been no different before he'd found himself walking in the valley of death.

During camp, Ben and Adam occupied the same adjacent rooms they did during the school year, and often spent evenings together. Ben, perhaps because of his own travels in the Middle East, was the only one who showed any interest in Adam's African trip.

253

The previous summer he and his parents had gone on a religious pilgrimage and retraced the steps of Moses from Egypt to Israel. Since then, he and Ben had spent hours discussing Middle Eastern politics. The day after Adam got back to Princeton, and he and Ben had time to talk, he brought out the photos he'd taken in Somalia.

"Who's the girl?" Ben asked.

"Dr. Élodie Fleury, one of the Doctors Without Borders. She's half French, half Vietnamese."

"She's damned beautiful is what she is, Ad."

"I know." His voice must have tipped Ben off because his next question was, "Did you sleep with her?" As friends, they'd always been able to read each other when it came to women. Ben had been the first of Adam's friends to see that he'd fallen for Marisol. There was no point in lying now.

"Yeah. On the last night."

"You lucky bastard."

Adam changed the subject, asking Ben if summer camp had affected his plans to play professional basketball.

"Your photos put pro sports in perspective. They're just part of the entertainment industry. I don't want to devote my life to that, do you?"

Ben acted as if Adam, too, were an NBA prospect. "I don't think I want to play pro ball badly enough," Adam said.

"You know what I think, Ad? I think we both have better things to do."

"Like what?"

"You're a born leader, Ad."

"I don't know about that. I haven't been able to get anyone besides you interested in Somalia."

"You've been talking to the wrong crowd."

"Listen to this," Adam said, pulling a book from his backpack. "It's a quote from George Bernard Shaw."

> The true joy of life is being used for a purpose
> recognized by yourself as a mighty one ...
> being thoroughly worn out before you are

thrown to the scrap heap … being a force of nature instead of a feverish, selfish clod of ailments and grievances.

"If I do go pro, it'll be for the money," Ben said, "so I can make a difference later. Promise me that you'll make me quit basketball before I turn into a 'selfish clod'."

"On the court, you are a force of nature," Adam said. As he spoke, he felt himself turning a corner that he'd been peering around since Somalia. With new clarity, he told Ben, "I don't know what I'm cut out for, but I intend to find out."

§§§

Marisol came off the Dinky at midday for that afternoon's end-of-camp trophy game between Princeton's varsity team and the high school all-stars. This was the first time they'd seen each other since Adam suddenly departed for Europe. When he'd called, hoping to smooth things over by inviting her to the game, they'd tacitly agreed to treat that evening at her apartment as if it had never happened.

She had a seat immediately behind the Princeton bench. In regular season games it was policy to ignore guests until the game was over, but for this exhibition game, Adam made an exception. In the minutes between the warm-up drills and the tip-off, while coaches were conferring with officials, and players milled around, Adam walked behind the players' bench to greet his sister. When the whistle blew and he left her to take his position in the backcourt, she wished him luck, and blew him a kiss.

The high school squad, led by a six-foot-eight shooting guard who moved like a young Magic Johnson, took an early lead but never opened up a gap of more than two baskets. Ben was outscoring all the high school players, in part because Adam was covering "Magic" so closely that by the fourth quarter he was saddled with foul trouble. The coach took him out to save him for the final minutes, but his substitute couldn't contain Magic so, despite the risk of his fouling out, Adam was sent back into the game.

That's when the trash-talking started. The other high school guard set a pick for Magic and, gripping Adam's arm, said in his ear, "Black pussy not good enough for you, nigga?" Adam pretended not to hear him, but on the next play the opposing player upped the ante. "After we whup you tonight, we're gonna pull a train on your skinny white bitch."

"Fuck you," Adam replied.

On Princeton's next possession, Adam positioned himself in the backcourt at a point where the trash-talking guard was directly between him and the basket, and called for the ball. Then he drove directly through the high school player, knocking him to the floor with such force that the crowd gasped. The trash-talker lay on his back looking stunned as Adam slammed the ball down through the net.

The whistle blew, the basket nullified, and Adam was charged with his fifth foul, a disqualification, and sent off to the locker room. To make matters worse, the referee judged the foul flagrant, and the high school team was awarded an extra free throw.

For a few mindless seconds, *Adam* had become a force of nature—a righteous, vengeful force. The target of his wrath had hobbled off the court supported by the attending physician. Ben tried to rally the team, but they couldn't contain the younger players. Princeton's coach was furious when his team lost by eight points.

§§§

"Sorry about the game, Adam." Marisol said. "What happened out there anyway?"

"Forget it. Let's get out of here."

They skipped the post-game party and immediately left for New York. Adam would spend the night with his mother and Rowan before he left for California and MSRI the next day.

On the train, going through New Jersey, Adam was still frustrated enough about the game to tell Marisol what was really on his mind.

"You know, if I'm honest with myself, nothing I'm doing in college is taking me where I want to go."

"You mean basketball?"

"I mean everything."

"Your mom would kill you if you dropped out."

"I know. Plus, I feel obliged to play with Ben until he graduates."

"What *is* important to you?"

"Not much, except I can't get Somalia out of my mind. Wait, I'll show you." After Ben's question about Élodie, Adam had taken out the photos of her, and it was this edited stack that he handed to Marisol.

She sorted through them in silence, then handed them back, her face a mirror image of what she'd seen. He'd already noticed that she was looking drawn and thin, and now, the stricken look on her face reminded him, for just an instant, of the Somali girl he'd given his jacket to.

"How's your dancing going?"

"What? Dance? It's fine; it's hard. But Jesus, Adam. These photos…"

"Powerful, huh?"

"Are you glad you went?"

"In the sense that not knowing about things like this is even worse than knowing."

"You should show them to everyone. When I feel something I want everyone to feel it too."

"It's easier to get an audience for dance than for … "

"…death?" Marisol finished his thought, putting it more starkly than he would have. "Come to think of it, many ballets end in death," she said. "*Romeo and Juliet, Swan Lake, Giselle.* Death and show business go hand in hand. Maybe your photos belong in a show."

"That's something I could get passionate about."

"You looked plenty passionate out there tonight."

"That wasn't passion, I was just pissed."

§§§

"Come in," Rowan said, grasping Adam's hand firmly. "Easter should be here in a couple of hours. I'll shut down my laptop."

"Marisol told me you're working on a history of nuclear arms treaties," Adam said to break the ice. It was the first time he'd visited Rowan's apartment without Easter being there, and for a moment, he felt awkward being alone with his "new" father.

"I finished that; it's being vetted by the State Department. How was basketball camp?"

"Less fun this year." Adam knew that it was not Rowan's style to spend much time on small talk, but he wasn't sure which of two competing desires was stronger—to hear Rowan's views, or avoid having yet another well-meaning advice-giver in his life.

"Letting go of one thing makes room for another," Rowan said. Adam could feel a lesson coming; stuck, he settled back in the sofa and tried to look interested.

"What's important to me has changed over the years," Rowan began. "Sometimes I hardly recognize the former me."

"How have you changed?" Adam asked to be polite.

"You really want to know?"

"Sure."

"I started out in math, like you, then switched to physics. It was the fifties, and physics was glamorous because of the bomb. But in the sixties my attention shifted to social issues. That's what brought your mother and me together. After I left Jefferson I went through a period of not knowing what to do. I read, I traveled, and gradually a new interest grew inside me that eventually displaced the others."

"What?"

"It's a bit embarrassing."

"Embarrassing?" Adam's ears perked up.

"In the sense that it can sound naïve."

"What was it?" Adam asked, no longer feigning interest.

"On a trip to the Soviet Union I'd been struck by how different the Russians seemed when we talked politics—but how similar they seemed when we talked about anything else. A question took shape, something like, 'Are the Russians Martians, or are they just like us?' It sounds dumb now, but at the height of the cold war that question consumed me. To my surprise, it took over my life, and for several years, gave it direction."

"How'd you respond to it?"

"I booked passage on the Trans-Siberian Railway, immersed myself in things Russian, and trained myself in strategic arms control. Within a few years, I was offered a job in Moscow with the State Department. That's when Marisol studied at the Moscow Ballet Academy and I reconnected with your mother."

"That part I know. So the Russians, they're not Martians?"

"Once they were free to speak their minds it became obvious that they were just like us. In a police state, people get bent out of shape. If you judge them by their external behavior, from what they say, they seem like Martians—even to each other."

"I wish I had a passion like yours." Adam was beginning to sound like a broken record to himself.

"How about some supper? A man never feels at a loss for purpose while he's eating."

Rowan pulled some leftover macaroni and cheese from the fridge and put it in the microwave. Getting out two bowls, he said, "As for finding a question of your own, one day you'll notice that something is turning over in your mind. At first you may try to ignore it, but it'll keep coming up. When you stop pushing it away, when you turn to embrace it, well, that's your question. If you're not too proud—because it may sound naïve, like mine did—it will generate a quest. I resisted my question for years. Once I took it to heart and began looking for an answer, it filled my life."

CHAPTER 28

Berkeley's Mathematical Sciences Research Institute provided residencies for about a hundred of the world's leading mathematicians. In addition, it offered a small number of internships for promising students.

Adam flew in to San Francisco and made his way across the San Francisco Bay to the Berkeley home of Professor Samuel Krimley. He had been Rowan's classmate in graduate school and, at Rowan's request, had agreed to put him up.

"So you've come to play with the big boys," were Krimley's opening words. Adam couldn't stifle a chuckle. Playing with the "big boys" was exactly what he'd been doing at basketball camp the month before. Krimley must have caught the look on his face because he added, "These are the smartest guys on the planet. What makes you think you're in their league?"

"Oh, for a moment there, I thought you meant basketball."

"A silly game for overgrown youngsters," Krimley declared. His open contempt for athletes drew Adam's attention to his wheezing as he lowered his overweight body into a leather chair. The entire house reeked of the stale, sweet aroma of pipe smoke.

"I'm here to learn." Adam knew it was a lame response, but he could think of nothing else to say to the pompous professor.

"My son, you're going to find out that math is a very rough game. In the academic world, the winners get tenure, perhaps even a chair at one of the top universities. The losers are never heard from again."

"I'm not at that stage. Mathematically, I'm just a kid shooting hoops in the backyard."

"Pursuing your metaphor, MSRI is the NBA. I'll take you up there tomorrow and show you around." He noticed that Krimley made a point of pronouncing the acronym "misery," and as he did, a sadistic grin crept across his face.

Adam had brought along Krimley's textbook on number theory, and on his way out to dinner he stopped by the living room, where he found the professor reading the newspaper.

"I was wondering if you'd sign my copy of your book," he asked deferentially. "Reading it is one of the reasons I went into math."

"With pleasure," Krimley said, beaming. "Not a bad job if I do say so myself. It still brings in enough money to pay for my tobacco."

He took the book, placed it in his lap, and with a felt pen wrote on the title page: "Prove Goldbach's conjecture and live forever." His signature was a hieroglyphic squiggle that covered the bottom third of the page and bore no resemblance to his name.

Every math major knows Goldbach's conjecture, the deceptively simple, but still unproven, statement that every even number after 2 is the sum of two primes. For example: $4 = 2 + 2$; $6 = 3 + 3$; $8 = 3 + 5$; $10 = 3 + 7$; $12 = 5 + 7$, and so on. Proposed two-and-a-half centuries ago by the Prussian mathematician Christian Goldbach, its meaning is clear to grade school pupils, but even today, no one knows if it's true or false.

"It's a ticket to a lifetime appointment at Princeton's Institute for Advanced Studies," Krimley said, peering up at Adam over his glasses.

When he didn't respond, Krimley continued, "Computer calculations have verified it for many large numbers, but a general proof still eludes us. I've spent a good bit of time on it myself."

"I think I'll start with something easier," Adam said.

"That may not be your best strategy," Krimley countered. "Let me tell you a little story." He reached for his pipe and spent a good minute packing and lighting it before he spoke again.

"When your father and I were graduate students at Princeton, there was an undergraduate who sat in on some of the advanced courses. He often came to class late and generally kept to himself. One day the professor wrote seven unsolved problems in number theory on the blackboard. When this chap arrived, he duly copied them down, and then we didn't see him for two weeks. When he finally came back, he looked terrible.

"After class, he went up to the professor and informed him that he was dropping the course because it was over his head. 'What makes you think so?' the professor asked. 'I could only do three of the homework problems,' he replied."

"You mean he thought the list of unsolved problems was an assignment?" Adam asked incredulously.

"They checked his proofs and made him a professor that same day," Krimley said, beaming with satisfaction that Adam had been impressed by his story. Taking a few quick puffs on his pipe, he leaned back in his chair and drove home his point: "Don't waste your time on trivial problems."

On his way to dinner, Adam began to suspect that Krimley had embellished the story. On Telegraph Avenue, he bought a slice of pizza at Blondie's and consumed it as he threaded his way along the sidewalk to Cody's, a cavernous bookstore known for catering to academic tastes. Evidence of Berkeley's glory days was everywhere— aging hippies selling jewelry on the sidewalks, stores devoted to pot paraphernalia, a building-sized "summer of love" mural near People's Park. Since Somalia, Adam had carried his camera in his backpack, and he took it out to shoot the mural. Lining up the shot, he felt like an archeologist photographing a cave painting.

Krimley's demeanor reminded him of the macho posturing of some of his fellow math majors—not so very different, really, from the bravado of some basketball players. Trash-talk and one-upmanship, whether from athletes or mathematicians, was inescapable.

But basketball and mathematics shared one trait that he valued highly. In both areas, the measure of success was unambiguous. Either the ball went through the hoop or it didn't; either a proof was valid or it wasn't. There was no wiggle-room when it came to a basket or to logic. Success was objective, measurable, irrefutable.

At Princeton, he had marveled at the ease with which some of his classmates handled mathematical abstractions. Although he'd done well at math in high school and entered college with almost a year's worth of advanced placement credit, his exposure to other math majors made him doubt he would be likely to end up among the elite. One thing he hoped to find out at MSRI was whether he was good enough at math to avoid suffering the fate of second-string athletes, who look on from the sidelines and play only in the final minutes of lost causes.

In the bookstore, he found his way to the math section and selected two texts to buy, one on probability theory, the other on elliptic functions. There were seminars under way in both areas at MSRI that he'd promised himself he'd attend, even if he couldn't follow every argument.

With Krimley's spare key, he let himself into the house and tiptoed to his room. He propped himself against a pillow, stretched his legs out on the bed, and examined the table of contents of the probability text. Then jet lag overtook him.

He woke a few hours later with his hand between pages two and three, and a stiff neck. Should he resume reading, or just go back to sleep?

Mathematicians divide themselves into two classes: "larks," who do their best work in the morning, and "owls," who work at night. He had long recognized himself as a lark, so rather than fight his nature, he crawled between the sheets. Before he drifted off he thought of Élodie, picturing her not in Somalia, but in a Parisian café. There, sitting beside her, an older man came into focus. He was smoking a cigarette. He mentally erased the café scene and replaced it with an image of Élodie in her lavender ao dai under a bougainvillea in Mogadishu.

The next morning, before his host was up, Adam plunged into the probability text. An hour later, Krimley padded into the kitchen in his bathrobe and slippers. Looking over Adam's shoulder, he snorted, "Kid stuff. They're way past that where you're going."

Adam wondered how anyone was supposed to get to the advanced stuff without first learning the "kid stuff." Krimley made himself some coffee, and as he left the room said, "I'll drive you up to MSRI at ten."

Housed in a modest three-story building, the Mathematical Sciences Research Institute sat atop the Berkeley hills, and had a panoramic view of the San Francisco Bay and its bridges. Though most of the space was devoted to offices for visiting mathematicians, it was also home to a lecture hall, several smaller seminar rooms, a lounge, and a library that stocked an assortment of mathematical books and journals.

The tables in the lounge were strewn with math paraphernalia—chess sets, puzzles, games of Go. On a low table ringed with child-sized chairs sat plastic models of tetrahedrons, cubes, octagons, dodecahedrons, and icosahedrons, in various sizes and colors. Adam had noted that many of his fellow math majors had a parent or two in the sciences. As in ballet, the most talented students had usually started very young and enjoyed a lot of parental support. Although he had Rowan's genes, he hadn't had the benefit of daily contact with him and other scientists.

On the wall outside the director's office there was a display of snapshots of the mathematicians in residence. They could have been of delegates to the United Nations—they came from every corner of the earth and, as with the UN, almost all of them were men.

As he walked down the corridor, in addition to English, he heard what he identified as French, Chinese, Japanese, Hindi, Arabic, and Russian issuing from offices. The impression he got was of something like the Tower of Babel tucked inside a cathedral.

After a brief tour, Krimley left Adam with the assistant director, who showed him to the office he was to share with three other students. One of them was a Russian from Moscow University, one a Japanese from Tokyo University, and the last a Texan from the University in Austin.

§§§

Adam spent mornings and most afternoons at his desk. Never once did the Russian appear; rumor had it that he spent all his time in the topless bars in San Francisco, scribbling in a notebook. The Texan was an owl who only twice arrived before Adam left for the day. Hiroshi Shinohara, the Japanese student, kept regular hours, and Adam liked him from the start.

Hiroshi was two years older and at least that far ahead of him mathematically. He was short and thin, a polite, unassuming fellow with wire-rimmed glasses. Adam soon discovered that Hiroshi was one of those rare mathematicians who took delight in sharing his mathematical insights, in contrast to the many who held onto them as if they were state secrets. When the two were together in public, the huge disparity in their stature prompted comments that Adam found tiresome but Hiroshi shrugged off with a smile.

Within a week, they were collaborating on a problem proposed in a lecture by a professor from the University of Rome. The Italian mathematician had suggested a line of attack on the problem based on techniques that were covered in the book Adam was reading.

After he made a little progress on a few special cases, he'd realized that a general solution was beyond his reach, so he'd shown the problem to Hiroshi.

Promoting international collaboration was one of the goals of MSRI, and soon Adam was experiencing it first hand. The next three weeks were the happiest and most productive in Adam's brief mathematical career. Hiroshi and he became inseparable. They worked together in the office they shared, and often took their mathematical conversation with them to lunch and dinner on Telegraph Avenue. After lunch, Adam liked to work out in the gym, and Hiroshi usually tagged along.

On one occasion, Adam was drawn into a game of pick-up basketball with some of the university's varsity players, and soon found himself in his usual role of playmaker. Later, Hiroshi, who was a keen observer of the game, asked him if he saw himself as a supporting player or a leader?

"In basketball, I'm more a playmaker than a high scorer."

"And in math?"

"I see myself as a collaborator, a partner. And you?"

"Same. Where are you a leader?"

"I don't know yet. I don't feel I have to be a leader, but I don't expect to be a follower forever."

"Does money motivate you?"

Adam didn't want to get into his family's business. Choosing his words carefully, he said, "I think you and I are alike in that making money is not what drives us."

"That's right," Hiroshi agreed. "I just want enough money to do what we're doing. Math is my reason for living. Collaborator, partner, or leader is not important to me." He paused and then asked, "Is math more important to you than basketball?"

"Definitely. I love doing math, especially working like this. Maybe it could be my life."

By the end of August the two young men had found a general solution to the problem posed by the Italian professor, and Adam suggested they show it to Krimley. They found him at home reading the paper, sucking on a briar pipe. The expression on his face reminded Adam of a baby with a pacifier. After introducing Hiroshi, he asked Krimley if he'd be willing to look at the fruits of their collaboration.

"Why sure. Show me what you've got."

Adam handed him three sheets of paper.

"Professor Veneti had posed the problem in a seminar," Adam explained. "We've been working on it together for several weeks."

"And you think you've got it? Have a seat," he said, gesturing toward the sofa.

Krimley studied the paper for a good five minutes without saying a word. Several times, Hiroshi and Adam exchanged nervous glances. Finally, Krimley put the pages down on the side table and picked up his pipe, which had gone out. Adam knew the suspense would last until Krimley had lit it again. Finally, Krimley leaned back in his chair.

"I see nothing wrong with your reasoning or your computations. Of course, they'd have to be checked, but at this level one assumes that such mundane details will stand up to scrutiny."

Adam began to relax. Hiroshi sat at full attention.

"Having said that, I feel I must advise you that problems of this kind are of little interest to real mathematicians. To my mind, what you've done is more properly seen as a homework assignment. Devoting a month to something this trivial is, quite frankly, a waste of your time and reviewing it is a waste of mine. I'm afraid Professor Veneti, whoever he is, has done you a disservice."

"But ... " Adam stammered. Krimley cut him off.

"Wait, I'm not finished. You may recall, Adam, that in our first conversation I advised you to tackle *significant* mathematical problems. This kind of schoolbook exercise is unworthy of a research mathematician. I was solving problems like this in high school. No, boys, I'm sorry. I have no interest in this kind of thing and it won't impress the king-makers either."

Adam glanced at Hiroshi, who sat immobile, his face an unreadable mask.

"Well, we had fun doing it," Adam said defensively, rising to go. "Thanks for your time."

"Perhaps you'll heed my advice in the future," Krimley called after them as they left the room.

Adam led the way out and he and Hiroshi set off together down the hill toward the campus.

"What a snob! I've never enjoyed math more than I have these last three weeks," Adam said.

"Me too," Hiroshi agreed glumly.

"He can go to hell. I'm sorry I subjected you to that. We should have just sent our results to Professor Veneti."

"Yes, but we'd better not show our paper to anyone else at MSRI. What if others think like Krimley? It could hurt our reputations."

"I don't care. If math is actually what Krimley makes it out to be, it's not for me." Adam paused. He realized with a jolt that it wasn't just Krimley. It wasn't even just math. At that moment, the entire academic world seemed like a cruel fraud.

Hiroshi was silent. "There were a few profs at Princeton like Krimley," Adam continued. "You know, the kind that make their lectures hard to follow so you'll feel stupid and they'll feel superior."

"Many professors in Japan are like Krimley," Hiroshi said. "They have absolute power, they're gods."

"It's sick."

"Do you think he'll tell the director? The director reports to my professor in Tokyo about my stay here."

"Don't worry. I'll tell Krimley that I asked you for input and you came to my rescue, that for you the work was a sideline to your main research."

"Would you?" Hiroshi said with a sigh of relief. "One negative letter could hurt me in Japan."

Adam went back to Krimley's place early that evening, packed his things, and left a note on the kitchen table offering a brief explanation of Hiroshi's contribution and ending with a curt, "Thanks for the room." Adam knew his hasty departure might be seen as ingratitude and could embarrass Rowan, but he didn't care. He set off down the hill and checked into a motel for his last few days at MSRI.

On the eve of his departure, he and Hiroshi put their results into an e-mail to Professor Veneti. Though they both understood that theirs was a modest contribution, it was the first original piece of research either of them had completed. Despite Krimley's dismissive appraisal, they were still hopeful that Veneti might find it interesting, and sure enough, he replied the next day offering to recommend it for publication in a small Italian journal of mathematics.

The night before Adam's flight to New York, Hiroshi took him to the best Japanese restaurant in San Francisco.

"Perhaps someday, we meet again, do more math," Hiroshi said over their sushi.

"For sure," Adam replied. "I'll be in touch." Adam treasured his first mathematical collaboration and held Hiroshi in his heart as a brother.

CHAPTER 29

Adam knew he was the product of a relationship that had cost his three parents dearly, and he attributed his untroubled childhood to François. He couldn't imagine ever being as close to Rowan as he was to his dad, but his initial resistance to having a second father had diminished. He welcomed Rowan's invitation to come tell him about his math internship.

En route to Rowan's apartment he stopped at a gourmet deli to pick up something, a token of his growing acceptance. After considering all sorts of imported sweets he settled on a jar of Italian apricot compote. It looked good to him, and he figured that if genes counted for anything, Rowan would like it too.

Adam was glad when Rowan opened the compote and set it down between them—along with some shortbread cookies. When he sat down, he said, "I had a call from Sam Krimley the other day."

Adam had scooped some compote onto a biscuit and, to keep it from dripping on the table, popped the whole thing in his mouth. When he could speak, he said, "I liked the Institute fine, but Krimley … sorry, Rowan, he's a pompous ass."

"I was afraid of that. He got tenure early and hasn't done anything since."

"Well, he sure laid a trip on me. I ended up moving out."

"He didn't mention that, but he thought you could have chosen a better collaborator."

"What a jerk! I learned a lot working with Hiroshi. Krimley thought I should have tackled Goldbach's conjecture."

"Sam always had a streak of grandiosity. Sounds like his fears have taken over in his old age."

"Fears of what?"

"Of being ignored."

That hadn't occurred to Adam. If it were true, it shed light on Krimley's attitude, and by extension, on the posturing of so many academics like him.

"I'm curious about why *you* left math and physics," Adam said.

"I used to do research, write papers, give seminars, the usual. I really tried to conform to the image I had of myself as a scientist. That's what everyone expected of me, and it paid the bills. But my attention had a will of its own. It's like love. Your heart can take you where you never intended to go."

"Sounds risky," Adam said, thinking of Marisol.

"Yeah, but at least you're alive. Denying that their interests have changed is why so many academics lose their spark. You have to choose between being a real nobody or a fake somebody. The heart chooses the real over the counterfeit every time. Krimley ignored the call of his heart and ended up a fake somebody."

"And you? Now?"

Rowan laughed. "Actually, I'm a nobody, and I like it that way, so long as I'm still trying to work things out. But in disarmament circles, I suppose people still see me as a somebody. Can you pass me the apricots again? They're good."

There was something else on Adam's mind, something he'd been wanting to ask Rowan about for a long time. This seemed like the moment.

"May I ask a personal question?"

"Sure."

"I've been wondering what brought you and my mom together in the first place."

"Ah. Twenty years ago, I'd have given one answer. Today, I'd give another. Which do you want?"

"The original one."

"Pretty simple, really. Of course, your mother was beautiful then too, but to me it was an unfamiliar beauty. When I was your age, most whites didn't see beauty in African Americans, and many black people went to a lot of trouble to make themselves look more like whites. But once you've recognized beauty as such, there's nothing so captivating as beauty you've overlooked.

"I'd seen your mother around campus; we often found ourselves working for the same things. I didn't expect to fall in love with her. I only realized I had when, one afternoon, she caught me staring at her, and called it to my attention. We resisted at first, tried pretending it wasn't happening, but in the end, well, you know the rest."

"Did the racial difference add to the attraction?"

"We were crossing a divide that had separated previous generations. There was extra excitement in that, yes. I've felt it a few times in my life."

"When else?"

"In Russia, during the Cold War. It's like tasting forbidden fruit. It wouldn't be much of an exaggeration to say that the cold war was settled amicably in hundreds of bedrooms in Moscow and Washington years before the diplomats realized it was over."

Adam reached into his backpack and took out his camera. "Do you mind if I take a few photos?" When Rowan agreed, he stood and circled him, snapping a half-dozen head shots from various angles.

Daily runs had kept Rowan fit into his fifties. His brown hair was graying at the temples, but Adam was glad that, despite the thirteen years between him and Easter, Rowan didn't look too old for his mother.

"What do you see?" Rowan asked.

"A rock star," Adam said with a smile.

"Just the right answer!" Rowan said, laughing and extending his hand. As Adam took it he realized that this was their first spontaneous display of affection.

"Mom's pressuring me to apply for graduate school this fall," he said, wondering if Rowan and Easter were in agreement on this. Instead of giving his own views, Rowan asked what François thought.

"He's not rushing me, but I know he's hoping I'll take over the family business."

"How do you feel about that?"

"I hate to disappoint him, but the fact is, I'm not interested in doing that. I don't think I ever will be." Adam had barely admitted this to himself, let alone to anyone else, but it felt good to say it out loud.

"What do *you* think I should do?" Adam ventured.

"You want my opinion?"

"Everyone else seems to have one."

"Well, if you don't have money, it's all you think about. But if you do have it—and for better or worse, that is your situation, Adam—you get to face the real issue."

"The real issue?"

"What to do when you own your own time. Gradually, as affluence spreads in the next few centuries, that's going to become a more common predicament. Now, only the rich have to deal with it. It's a much more complex problem than most people imagine because our schooling prepares us to follow instructions, work by the clock, and obey orders. Very few people even know how to identify their own true interests, or have the discipline to pursue them effectively.

"But," Rowan continued, "if somehow you're exempted from the money chase, I've always thought it best to do the thing that won't get done unless you do it yourself. For example, if you don't play basketball, no problem; others will swarm in to take your place. You'll hardly be missed. But if you don't do the thing that only you can do, that thing will remain undone."

"If only I knew what that was," Adam said, "I'd do it in a heartbeat."

"To find it you have to begin observing yourself even as you continue searching."

"I can't stand doing nothing."

"Observing is not doing nothing," Rowan said. "Seeing yourself search as you're doing so is harder than it sounds. Once I've found what I've been looking for I usually realize that I've actually been involved in it for some time, but in a small way, on the side, so I missed its significance. Spotting what you're in search of is like detecting a whisper amid a din. It's very easy to put off taking that whisper seriously, much less hear it. And even after it becomes audible, and you realize that it's what you really want to do, it can be risky and even embarrassing to pursue it. You have to overcome your own doubts, plus those of your friends and family."

"Reminds me of Don Quixote," Adam said. "Everyone made fun of him."

"Everyone except Sancho Panza. Once in a while, an ally appears who offers your dream some crucial bit of support."

"Like Hiroshi."

"I thought you were going to say Marisol."

"Yes, Marisol, too," Adam agreed, and as he did so he began to see her in a new way.

"Every time your interests change," Rowan continued, "you'll run into resistance. Others want you to stay the same, and each time your focus shifts you have to claw your way past their skepticism as well as overcome your own doubts."

Glancing at the clock, he said, "You're having dinner with Marisol, right? You better get moving or you'll be late."

"Would you like to join us?"

"Easter and I saw her last night. She's just back from tour and has some news. But I'll let her tell you herself."

§§§

Summer had not loosened its clammy grip on New York. By the time Adam reached their rendezvous on Broadway at 72nd Street, he felt his shirt sticking to his back.

Even from a distance, he could detect a new confidence in his sister. En route to the restaurant they'd agreed on for dinner, her assertive stride confirmed his first impression. But before he could ask her about herself, she asked him a question.

"Did you stop by Dad's place?"

"Yes. He's full of advice."

"Was it helpful?" she asked, as they were seated.

"Some of it was. Sometimes you don't see what's right in front of you."

"That's what he said?"

"Yeah. I kind of discount my own questions. I mean, I always assume that if I'm interested in something it can't be all that important."

"You mean because it's *just* you."

"Yeah, it's just me, and who am I?"

"You're as important as anyone else. We both are. That's one thing I've learned this summer."

"It's not that I think that others are more important than me. It's just that I don't think I'm anything special. There are better athletes than me, better mathematicians. It doesn't make sense to take myself *that* seriously."

"If you don't, no one else will. I used to dance around the living room to the music on TV. My mom asked me if I wanted to take lessons and I said yes without even thinking."

"Were you good from the start?"

"Not as good as the kids who'd been dancing for a while. But I was too young to care one way or the other. And the teacher had a rule—comparisons are odious, she would say whenever one girl put another one down. That gave all of us room to make mistakes and get better."

"In sports and math, put-downs are the name of the game."

"So, do something else. You seem pretty excited about photography. Maybe you take photos to see what's staring you in the face."

It was another of those moments in which Adam heard someone say aloud something he already knew but hadn't admitted to himself. At such times, he needed to let the insight marinate, not pursue it directly. He changed the subject.

"Rowan says you have some news."

"Yes! When I got back from tour yesterday, I had a letter from the director of the American Ballet Theatre. The company is offering me a position as soloist."

"Oh Marisol, that's wonderful." Adam noticed that Marisol had not reported her promotion in the giddy, school-girlish way she might have just months before. Rather, she conveyed the message in a matter-of-fact voice: "This is just a step on the way up." Her carriage and demeanor were that of a self-possessed artist. Even her face seemed subtly different. The starry-eyed girl had transformed into a mature woman.

"Did you know this was coming?" Adam asked.

"I knew that Sasha had recommended me to the director. You remember lecherous old Sasha, don't you? Even though I never gave him what he wanted, he still put in a good word for me, bless him."

"He's smart enough to realize that he's only as good as his partner."

"Could be. I do think I'm ready for this. I've felt a change coming over my dancing lately. My partners have noticed it too. ABT suits me now, so I'm going to accept."

"You'll be a principal in no time."

"They didn't promise," Marisol said with a fey smile. "But I think that if all goes well …"

"Congratulations!"

"ABT performs more full-length dramatic works like *Don Quixote* and *Giselle*—the classics. I'm ready for that now."

"So, when do I get to see your Giselle?"

"It's all up to the artistic director. Remember, I'm just a soloist."

When her chance came, Adam knew she'd seize it and never look back. Just as she was sailing into port, he was heading out to sea.

CHAPTER 30

While at MSRI, Adam hadn't once read a newspaper or watched the news on TV. As students returned to Princeton with stories of summer adventures, he realized he'd temporarily lost track of what was going on in the world.

When he *did* remember Somalia, what came to mind was not Baidoa, but Élodie. She had sent him a note asking if he'd placed any photos in American newspapers, along with a copy of MSF's latest appeal for funds, which featured two of them. Easter had some high-level media contacts through her work with the Clinton campaign, and gave him some leads. He reached out to three of them but none returned his calls.

He didn't fare any better with Rowan's contacts at the State Department. As the weeks passed and his studies and basketball claimed more and more of his attention, his memories of Somalia were fading like the autumn light. Occasionally, when he looked at the snapshot of Élodie in the corner of his mirror, he'd feel vaguely guilty about having lost his sense of urgency, but the feeling would pass.

Toward the end of September, Élodie called. She was speaking by satellite phone from the roof of the MSF building in Mogadishu. In a matter-of-fact voice she informed him that the death rate in Baidoa had reached several thousand a day, and would surely double again within weeks. Somalia was now the full-blown human catastrophe foreseen months earlier by workers on the ground. They spoke for less than two minutes; the urgency in her voice precluded further conversation, but just before the line went dead he heard her say, "Wish you were here."

Élodie had called in the afternoon Somali-time, but it was past midnight in Princeton and she had roused Adam from a deep sleep. He spent the next several hours wondering how to respond.

By morning he had inklings of a strategy. Before his first class he stopped by the offices of the *Princetonian,* and he was thrilled when they agreed to publish several of his photos in the campus paper. While he'd focused on reaching the national press he'd completely overlooked the daily college paper. In the days that followed, he used the *Princetonian's* story as an ice-breaker to solicit ideas on how to get the word out.

A few students and professors offered to send money, and he gave them MSF's New York and Paris addresses. But it was merging two ideas that led to a plan of action—one from Ben Steinsaltz and the other from Andy, a friend of Adam's at the Woodrow Wilson School of Public and International Affairs.

Ben suggested using a scanner and computer software to blow up the Somalia photos so they could be posted around campus. Captions with calls to action would be added along with MSF's address. For his part, Andy had maintained that the situation was beyond the reach of private relief organizations. He, like the MSF doctors Adam had met in Mogadishu, disparaged the United Nations' relief effort and insisted that only massive intervention from the Western democracies could end the famine. That, he was sure, wouldn't happen unless the US media were persuaded to run with the story.

That evening, Adam stopped by Ben's room and asked him just how large he could make the photos.

"What do you have in mind?"

"Big. Really big—car-sized."

"By when?"

"Yesterday."

Ben looked at his watch and whistled. "Technically tricky, but doable. What's the plan?" He listened carefully to Adam before he responded: "We're going to need help. I'll round up the geek squad."

§§§

As the sun rose over Princeton Friday morning, the University chapter of Women of Color was calling TV stations throughout the greater New York area to suggest they send camera crews to campus.

Historic Nassau Hall was draped, front and back, with enormous photographs of Somali famine victims. There were individual photos that covered the entire facade of the building, a panoramic shot showing row after row of skeletal human beings in rags stoically awaiting death by starvation. Captions like THIS IS HAPPENING RIGHT NOW, and WHAT CAN WE DO ABOUT THIS? were superimposed on the images in bold letters. From the steeple of the University chapel hung a gigantic image of the solitary girl in the valley of death, her head held high, sitting vigil over her sister's tiny body.

Crowds of students, faculty, and townsfolk had gathered at both sites, and the continuous buzz drew students from nearby dormitories and classrooms. Soon the two groups merged into a single body that stretched from Nassau Hall to the chapel. As people approached the scene they chattered nervously, but the moment they saw the photos they fell silent, transfixed by the images.

TV camera crews filmed the spectacle while print reporters, circulating through the crowd, questioned anyone who would talk to them: Who had done this? What did they want? How had they made such large images? How had they gotten them up on Nassau Hall?

It hadn't been so hard, really. After they'd scanned the photos into Ben's computer, he and his techie friends had created hundreds of files, each of which could be printed on a single sheet of photo paper. When they were mounted on billboard-sized canvas, according to a master paint-by-numbers design, they formed a huge enlargement of the original image of the girl. "It's like hundreds of spectators in a stadium holding cards over their heads," one of the conspirators explained. "No single card makes any sense, but from a distance it reads 'Go Tigers'."

Adam had a history class late that morning and the professor devoted it to a discussion of the famine and "the action taken by a group of students to bring it to our attention." Among the students in the class was the infamous Alexander Bludman, known on campus as a Renaissance man for his mastery of Greek and Latin as well as several modern languages, plus his broad knowledge in the humanities. Bludman, whose father had served as US ambassador to Belgium, had grown up on several continents. He was steeped in European culture, and it showed in the ease with which he navigated the curriculum at Princeton. No one doubted that he was destined for class valedictorian and a brilliant academic career.

On this occasion, he used his formidable critical faculties to cast doubt on the motives of those who had put on the demonstration.

"While the ends may have been well-intentioned, if a little naïve, the means are contemptible," Bludman declared to the class. "Frankly, I resent any group presuming to speak for me. I am not saying that our politics do diverge, simply that they could. Universities like Princeton must never be perceived as taking a partisan stand no matter how noble the cause."

"What's partisan about being against famine?" a young woman asked.

"Guerilla art, like that on display this morning, can arouse a nation to action, and any action taken by the United States will be seen as self-serving by the international community. Having lived abroad much of my life, I know whereof I speak. Europeans are suspicious of any American intervention, even if it's dressed up in humanitarian garb. Moreover, we cannot simply ignore the argument that bailing out one famine-stricken country after another undermines the incentive for Africans to get their act together."

Adam was trying to formulate a response when another student asked, "Are you saying we harm them by helping?"

"Exactly," Bludman said.

It was at this point that the professor blew Adam's cover. "Adam Blue, I noticed that some of the images draped on the library were blow-ups of your photos in The Princetonian. Would you care to explain what you hoped to accomplish with this demonstration?"

"Well, uh," Adam stammered. Caught off-guard, he hadn't prepared a fully thought-out rationale for the project and sought refuge in a defense he'd heard artists use: "I'd rather let the images speak for themselves." It sounded lame even to him, particularly after Bludman's smooth talk.

"That images of starving children stir up guilt in the West is well known," Bludman resumed. "Again, I'm troubled when others presume to speak for me. Your demonstration is presumptuous and I, for one, resent it."

Several students seated near Bludman were nodding their heads in agreement. Adam knew he couldn't win this argument, and he didn't feel the need to. He and his co-conspirators had made their point. The purpose was obvious: to move people to do whatever they could to end the famine in Somalia.

After class, Bludman sauntered over to Adam and said, "As you learn more about international politics you'll understand that sentimental gestures generally do more harm than good. I advise you to study the history of other societies before trying to change them. Athletic talent may bring recognition in college, but it won't take you far in the real world."

"My advice to you is to stop giving me advice," Adam said, glaring at him.

As it happened, people with more authority than Bludman shared his views. When Adam stopped by his room after lunch, he found a note summoning him to the dean's office.

§§§

Late that afternoon, Adam heard Ben's familiar knock on his door.

"We're going out to celebrate," Ben said. "Come on."

"I've been suspended," Adam reported.

"What?"

"You heard me. The dean told me to go home for the rest of the semester."

"What?" Ben repeated in disbelief.

"I can't go to classes or take exams, but they'll let me play in the holiday tournaments and come back next semester."

"What reason did he give?"

"Defacing University property."

"But we offered to clean up."

"They won't let us. The University would be liable for any injuries."

283

"Do they realize it made national TV?"

"That's what upset them most. He said they'd had lots of calls from alumni demanding to know why the University was taking a political position. The students in my history class this morning—Alex Bludman and his ilk—would agree."

"Bludman was born with a sneer on his face. This was humanitarian, not political."

"I tried that on the dean."

"Why did he finger you?" Ben asked, clearly puzzled.

"They were my photos."

"But the suspension is not about the photos, it's about displaying them on *University* buildings. I'm as involved as you are."

"You're indispensable here. I'm not. The dean said that, had it been up to him, I'd have gotten a full year's suspension. Higher-ups overruled him to preserve Princeton's chances in the tournament."

"How was it left?"

"I told him I'd clear out by tonight."

"What about next semester?"

"I'm not coming back, Ben."

"You're dropping out?"

"Yep."

Ben was silent. He paced around the room, then stared out the window at the quad below.

"We'll see about this," he said through his teeth, and without another word, he left. From his window, Adam saw him march off toward the administration building.

A half-hour later, Adam's phone rang. It was the vice president for student affairs calling to rescind the suspension. Adam told him that his room would be empty within the hour. The vice president urged him not to make a hasty decision, and Adam said that *they* were the ones who'd made a hasty decision, and he accepted it. As soon as he put down the phone, Ben knocked.

"What did you do?" Adam asked him. "The VP just offered to reinstate me."

"I told the president that we were in this together, that if you don't play, I don't play. You're our leader, Ad."

"Thanks for sticking up for me, Ben. That was … wow … valiant. I feel terrible about leaving you and the other guys, but my heart's just not in it. I'm out."

"I understand, and my commitment stands—if you don't play, I don't either."

"But you'll finish your senior year, right?" Everyone except Ben himself was sure he'd win one of the Rhodes scholarships to be announced in November. He'd need to graduate to claim it.

"Yes, I'll finish up. I need that degree."

"What about the NBA?"

"I don't need Princeton to go pro."

"Without you, there'll be no championship."

"Who cares? No Ad, no Ben, no trophy."

CHAPTER 31

Adam dreaded telling his mother what had happened. He called her Washington number, got no answer, then tried her at Rowan's.

"She's on the campaign trail with Clinton till tomorrow," Rowan said. "What's up?"

The urge to tell someone had grown so insistent that Adam decided to confide in Rowan.

"Could I stay over with you tonight?"

"Of course. Are you okay?"

"I'm done at Princeton."

"What happened?" Rowan asked evenly, which Adam appreciated.

"I'll tell you the full story when I get there."

"Does this have to do with the Somalia demonstration? I recognized your photos in the TV coverage."

"It has everything to do with the demonstration. I should be there by eight."

As he hauled two suitcases and a trunk onto the Dinky, Charlie took the smaller suitcase from him and carried it to the top of the steps. When Adam retrieved it, Charlie said, "Leaving's what you make of it." Before Adam could respond, Charlie was back on the platform ushering others aboard.

What would he make of his leaving? Adam wondered. He could blame the University. He could blame its officials. He could blame students like Bludman. He could blame himself. Or, he could interpret his unexpected departure as an opportunity to do exactly what he wanted.

§§§

Had Easter read the sports pages en route to New York that Saturday morning, she'd have learned that sportswriters were shocked that Princeton's lock on the Ivy League championship had been thrown into doubt by the sudden loss of star forward Ben Steinsaltz, and point guard Adam Blue—and not through injury, but a disciplinary issue.

Rowan met her at the door and, before she'd even taken off her coat, filled her in on the news. Adam, hearing their voices, joined them in the living room.

"Why didn't you tell me?" Easter bore down on him. "I know Princeton's president. I could have given him a call. A college degree is indispensable in this brutal world."

"But, Mom, I don't want your help on this. It's my problem."

"I'm proud of what you did," Rowan weighed in, "but your mother is right about the degree."

"Thanks," Adam said, his confidence building; with each passing minute his departure was feeling more like an escape than a suspension. But from Easter's expression, he knew she wasn't finished arguing her point.

"I'm sure they'd take you at Columbia or New York University," she continued, unfazed. She wasn't going down without a fight.

"Look, Mom, I'm okay with this," Adam said firmly. "After the election, I'm going to go to Paris to see Dad."

"I know he'll feel as I do about your finishing college. Promise me you'll get that degree."

"I'm making no promises to anyone until I've had time to think things over," Adam said, his voice rising. Then, the words spilled out before he had consciously formed the thought: "What makes you and Dad think you can tell me how to live? For most of my life, you fed me a lie."

Easter was speechless; Rowan came to her rescue.

"Adam, that's not fair. Your mother has always put your interests first. If I can live with that, so can you."

Adam wished he could take back his words, but he was in no mood to apologize. He got up as if to leave.

Again, Rowan interceded. "It's understandable that you're upset, Adam. When you've had some time, I'm sure you'll see that we're on your side."

Easter turned to her son. "Please stay, Adam."

Rowan looked at the two of them, then exhaled. "All right, good. I'll put some supper on the table."

After the meal, Easter tapped her glass with a knife and looked at Adam.

"Given everything that's happened," she said, "I'm afraid this isn't the best time for more news, but we think you should be the first to know our plans: Rowan has asked me to marry him, and I've accepted."

"Better late than never," Rowan said with a smile, reaching for Easter's hand.

"When?" Adam asked. Suddenly he felt that the family he'd been part of since birth was disintegrating, but the one he'd been part of even longer was taking its place.

"Sometime before the inauguration."

"So, you think Clinton's going to win?"

Easter nodded.

As Adam stood up to go to his room, he said, "I'm happy for you, Mom. And you too, Rowan."

CHAPTER 32

The day after Adam cast his first vote for president of the United States, he flew to Paris. He was relieved when François treated his visit as a pleasant surprise and didn't ask any questions.

When he did tell his dad about what happened at Princeton, François said that, in his opinion, university learning was vastly overrated. As if to prove his point, he told Adam that contributions to MSF had doubled during the week following the Princeton demonstration. Adam was elated. He knew now that his images could have consequences in the real world. He was ready, even eager, to embrace his newfound freedom.

A few days later, he accompanied François to an MSF meeting that François had said Élodie would be attending, and he was delighted when he felt a familiar hand on his shoulder.

She flashed her beautiful smile and presented both cheeks to be kissed.

"I'd like you to meet Gérard," she said, indicating the man at her side. Adam figured Gérard was the older boyfriend she'd mentioned in Somalia.

"Gérard, this is Adam Merle-Blue. He took the Baidoa photos."

"Very moving shots. I hear they brought in a lot of money."

"Thank you," Adam said, shyly adding, "I'm glad."

"You'll have to tell me the full story," Élodie said, but just then an older woman pulled her away to introduce her to a board member. Two hours later, on her way out with Gérard, Élodie slipped him a note. It read:

Tomorrow at 4:00 Café Vavin

§§§

The minute he got home, Adam phoned Ben Steinsaltz at Princeton.

"You sound like you're next door," Ben said.

"Did you get the Rhodes?"

"Yup, heard a few days ago."

Adam congratulated him on the scholarship and then shared the news about the impact of their demonstration.

"I'm not surprised, Ad. Those were moving photos."

"I'm going to start looking for more images that move people."

"Where?" asked Ben.

"One place I want to go is Israel, particularly the West Bank. I was wondering if we could meet up in Jerusalem."

"I'd love to be there without my parents. I know my way around the club scene. The girls are very friendly there."

"How do you think I'd fit in?" Adam knew Ben would take his meaning. Recently, a flare-up between Jews and blacks in Brooklyn had made headlines, prompting many conversations they'd had about race and religion.

"Israelis come in all shades. They're closer to being colorblind than most people. Look, without basketball I'll have time on my hands over Christmas break."

"You'll come then?"

They quickly hatched a plan. Adam would go on ahead, visit the usual tourist sites, and take some photos. Ben would join him for the last two weeks of December. They'd develop a specific plan once they knew more about the local situation.

§§§

Élodie was waiting for him at an outside table. It was a bright Paris day and she wore a short-sleeved apricot blouse over a cream-colored skirt. Her long, straight, black hair hung below the rim of a white cloche hat. When Adam's shadow fell on her she looked up through her sunglasses and spoke his name in a way that made him want to pull her to her feet and wrap her in his arms. Instead, he sat down opposite her.

"I've ordered a treat," she said just as the waiter arrived with two slices of Tarte Tatin, a deep-dish apple pie topped with crème fraîche. The sight of it made him recall her ravenous appetite.

"You're a gazelle who eats like a horse," he teased.

"I burn a lot of nervous energy," she said, drumming her slim fingers on the table and tapping her feet on the ground, as if to show where the calories went.

"Where's your next posting?"

"They're sending me to Peshawar early next year. It's home to several million Afghans, refugees from the war with the Soviet Union."

"Peshawar?"

"It's in Pakistan, just east of the Khyber Pass near the border with Afghanistan. They call it the Northwest Territories. Picture your Wild West with land mines."

"What will you do there?"

"Everything—surgery, obstetrics, pediatrics, wounds. Plus, we fit prostheses and teach amputees to use them."

"Is Gérard going with you?"

"He won't leave his private practice here. He's been trying to persuade me to join him."

"And?"

"I want to see the world before I settle down."

"Does Gérard know anything about us?"

"Of course not. So tell me, what are you doing now?"

"I got kicked out of college."

To his surprise, her response was that, given the jump in MSF's revenue, any sacrifice on his part had been worth it. Then she abruptly turned to the future. "We're looking for a volunteer in Peshawar—to drive the ambulance. The fundamentalists in charge of the camp won't let women drive."

"How enlightened of them!" Adam said sarcastically, leaving her suggestion unanswered. As they got up to go, Élodie suggested a walk in the Luxembourg Gardens.

On the sidewalk their exotic looks turned heads; Parisians took Adam for a North African and Élodie for Indochinese. Inside the park they sat down near the octagonal pond and watched the children sailing their model boats. Every so often the wind sent a fine spray from the fountain across their faces.

Élodie spoke first. "You didn't answer my question."

"What question?"

"Would you consider working with me? In Peshawar, starting in February?"

"Hmm, maybe. I do want to take photos that show what's going on in the world."

"Your Baidoa photos were so effective. You may have thought I was doing more good than you, but the truth is that your photos can support five like me in the field."

"Actually, the credit should be reserved for the people who let us use their images."

"That's true, but someone has to take the shots. You were that person in Baidoa. You could be that person in Peshawar."

"You *know* I'm interested."

"Let me know when you're sure. I want to have something to look forward to."

"Okay, go ahead and look forward. I'll find a way."

§§§

That evening, as Adam often did, he was dining with François at their home on the Place des Vosges. Just as he was about to tell his dad about his plans for Israel, and possibly Pakistan, François spoke. He told him he'd had a call from Nabil Diop, the caretaker and cook on their farm outside Dakar.

"I think of Nabil whenever I eat a crêpe," Adam said.

"He asked after you. But the reason for his call was his son. Ousmane is in trouble."

Adam remembered Ousmane as a childhood playmate. He had never been as tall as Adam, but he was lean, angular, and quick, and could out-climb and outrun his bigger friend. "What's he doing now?" Adam asked.

"He went to South Africa to work, and ended up in prison."

"For what?" Adam felt his back and neck muscles contract, as for a tip-off in a basketball game.

"Protesting conditions in the mines. Even with Mandela's release, unrest is growing. Nabil has asked for our help but I can't seem to make any progress from this distance. I was wondering if you'd be willing to go to South Africa and get the facts. Stop off in Dakar to see Nabil and his wife en route. Our firm has an attorney on retainer in Johannesburg who could intervene once we know the charges."

"Sure, Dad, I'll go. I'll do my best."

They spent a long, leisurely evening around the table, ending the meal with espresso and fresh fruit. As they rose, Adam rested a hand on his father's shoulder, and in return got an affectionate pat on the back. Theirs was not a physically demonstrative relationship, but Adam's heart was full. His dad had eased his mind and given him a mission that fit into a larger plan he was bringing into focus.

He would begin in Africa, connect with Ben in the Middle East, and then make his way to Peshawar where he'd work with Élodie. He would take pictures everywhere. He'd miss Easter and Rowan's wedding—and Christmas at home, but they'd understand. As he drifted off to sleep, it occurred to him that the trip he would begin the next day would be his *Ad*-venture. He smiled and felt at peace for the first time since the demonstration at Princeton.

CHAPTER 33

A Jeep was waiting at the Dakar International Airport to take Adam to the farm south of the city. The hot, sticky climate of equatorial Africa and the brightly-colored dresses of Senegal's women awakened fond memories of his childhood visits.

Nabil's wife met him at the front door of the main house and led him to the room he'd stayed in as a child. This same room had once been his father's, and he wondered if a child of his would ever sleep in it. François always spoke of the farm as if it were an ancestral trust and he were its steward, responsible for the land and also for the livelihoods of the people who worked it. His relationship with them had a curiously medieval flavor, as if they were all members of his extended family.

The farmhouse stood on a hundred hectares of fertile rolling land devoted primarily to what the locals called groundnuts, but which Adam knew as peanuts. They also grew millet and sorghum, and recently, François had taken steps to further diversify the crops, adding sugar and ornamental flowers for export.

After he washed up, he paused to peer out the window at the old baobab tree behind the house. If the farm had a hub, the baobab was it. He recalled hiding from Ousmane in a hollow in the tree's huge trunk, then climbing up into its branches behind his friend.

As he entered the kitchen, the caretaker, Nabil Diop, rose from a prayer rug spread on the floor. Though François's parents had been Catholic, most of the people on the farm were Muslims.

Nabil smiled and spread his arms in welcome. Adam embraced him, and they exchanged greetings in Nabil's native Wolof. Then, taking mercy on Adam, Nabil switched to French.

"Thank you for coming, Adam. It's been too long."

"The farm looks like it's flourishing," Adam replied.

"Yes, it's better than ever, but I'm afraid I'm a little the worse for wear." He did look thinner than Adam remembered, his worry lines more pronounced.

Mrs. Diop called them to the kitchen table for tea and biscuits, and Nabil immediately turned to the business at hand.

"Ousmane is in Johannesburg. Sadly, he didn't see himself spending his life on the farm and left us last year to make his way in the world. Two months ago his letters stopped. Last week we received a note from him from prison. It seems he was arrested for participating in a demonstration over conditions in the coalmines."

"We're glad you let us know. My dad wants to help."

"Ousmane needs an attorney. We were wondering if …"

"No problem. Our attorney in Johannesburg is at your disposal."

"Would you explain things to him?" Nabil's eyes welled with tears. "As I told your father, I've never traveled and my wife is afraid for me to go."

"I'll leave for Johannesburg tomorrow. Did Ousmane say exactly where he's being held? And what the charges are?"

Nabil handed his son's letter to Adam. It was in French, not Wolof, suggesting Ousmane had anticipated that someone other than his parents might have occasion to read it.

"It's not really clear from this, but I'll be in touch as soon as I know what's going on."

The next morning, as Adam was about to leave for the airport, Nabil handed him a little box. "This is for Ousmane."

"I'll see that he gets it."

"Please give my respects to your father, and our thanks. We'll be waiting for word. Farewell, my son, and Godspeed."

§§§

Adam went straight from the Johannesburg airport to the office of François's attorney, Mr. Vishveshwara, a lawyer of Indian descent. A man in his fifties, he insisted on being called "Vishu," and considered himself to be of the distinguished lineage of Indian lawyers in South Africa that included Mohandas Gandhi. Vishu had been born in South Africa and held South African citizenship. Under the apartheid system he was classified as "coloured," a status higher than that of the black majority, but below the ruling white minority. François had chosen Vishu to represent him in South Africa because his intermediate social status gave him access to both white and black communities.

After hearing Adam out, Vishu began placing calls. Adam sat in a cramped reception area and waited. Three tense hours later, the intrepid Vishu had determined where Ousmane was imprisoned and learned that his release could be secured by posting as bail bond the equivalent of five hundred dollars. Such a figure put freedom completely out of reach for most prisoners, so it was tantamount to indefinite detention. By paying it, Ousmane would be free until his court date. Political conditions in South Africa were changing rapidly, and Vishu thought that by the time the matter came to trial the case would either be dismissed or the defendants would be let off with sentences of time served.

Adam instructed Vishu to post bail in the courthouse, then he paid the bail as well as the attorney's fees.

The next morning, Adam was waiting in a taxi at the prison gate when Ousmane was released. He was shocked at his old friend's appearance. Slumped and walking with a limp, he seemed to be dragging himself toward the taxi. His once bright eyes were sunken, his face pallid and drawn. There appeared to be bruises on his neck, and his handshake was limp. Dazed by his sudden freedom, all he wanted was to put some distance between himself and the prison.

They returned to Adam's small hotel so Ousmane could bathe and rest. Later that evening, they settled in a café on the other side of town. Adam explained how his freedom had been secured and gave Ousmane his father's present.

Ousmane unwrapped the package and found a bracelet and necklace made from the bark and seeds of the baobab tree. "The very tree we used to climb in. We believe that no harm can come to the wearer. If I'd had them during the demonstration I might have avoided jail. How can I ever thank you for getting me out?"

"We're even. You got me out of the baobab tree," Adam said, laughing at the memory.

They stayed awake late into the night, catching up. Ousmane recounted what had happened since he'd arrived in South Africa, and reported on the nation's evolving politics. To Adam's question about prison life, he said, "They treated us like dogs. You cannot imagine …" He trailed off, then abruptly turned the conversation to Adam and his family. Adam found it embarrassing to speak of life at Princeton in the wake of Ousmane's experience in the shantytowns, pits, and prisons of South Africa. Instead he told Ousmane about the famine in Baidoa and the Princeton demonstration—but stopped short of mentioning his suspension and departure.

Ousmane was quiet for a while, then said, "I wish you could show your countrymen what it's like in the mines here. On our TV, we see how you live, but you have no idea about conditions here."

"I think I do," Adam said. "I …"

"No, you can't know," Ousmane interrupted. "No one who hasn't worked here has any idea of the degradation. I didn't know what slavery was until I worked in the pits. Forgive me, Adam, but you've never been hungry, not for a single night. You've never been so tired you couldn't stand. Try spending even an hour two miles underground. Miners are old before they're forty and dead by fifty. But to quit means you lose the roof over your head, and your family starves. We are slaves, without chains, but slaves nonetheless. Don't misunderstand, I'm very grateful to you and your family for getting me out, but so long as we depend on whites and foreigners for our livelihood, there will be a cost—to our pride."

Adam said nothing. After a silence, Ousmane asked him if he'd brought his camera.

"I never go anywhere without it."

"Then there's something I'd like to show you. We'll need a car and a guide."

§§§

The next day they took the train to Soweto, where Ousmane introduced Adam to two men who, for ten dollars each, would not only take Adam into their world, but could also protect him from its dangers. The bargain reminded Adam of the technicals in Mogadishu. Over the next few days, he realized that the "protection" they provided consisted mainly in knowing what situations to avoid.

Ousmane provided a running commentary on everything they saw. The driver and the guide spoke to each other in Xhosa, a language Adam recognized from the staccato clicking sounds that punctuated it. The guide spoke Afrikaans to obtain permission for Adam to take photographs, and blunt English to tell him when to put the camera away if he sensed trouble.

By day's end, Adam had shot five rolls of film in and around Soweto. He left them at a photo shop near the hotel, but when he saw the prints the next morning, he was disappointed. The images were not nearly as moving or powerful as the ones of the Somalis. The photos of starving children went straight to the heart, whereas his shots of poverty and injustice aroused only feelings of helplessness. This would take more thought, he realized, but far from discouraging him it bolstered his determination.

The next morning he stopped by Vishu's office to tell him that Ousmane had decided to return to Senegal and forfeit bail.

"Are you going with him?" Vishu asked.

"No. I'm heading for the subcontinent via the Middle East."

"May I make a suggestion?"

"Sure."

"My ancestors came to South Africa from Banaras, India's holy city. Banaras is to Hinduism and Buddhism what Jerusalem is to Judaism and Christianity. But there the similarity ends. Whereas Jerusalem is a city of conflict, Banaras is a city of peace. If you go there, look up my guru. His name is Lahiri. By day, Professor Lahiri teaches geology at Banaras Hindu University, but in truth he's a sage. His students see him as a holy scientist because in his teachings he sticks to the evidence and debunks the charlatans. Lahiri taught me to see the sacred in the mundane."

"If I get to Banaras I'll look him up."

Ousmane and Adam shared a cab to the airport. When it came time to part, Ousmane slid the baobab bracelet that Nabil had made for him onto Adam's wrist.

"The griots say the baobab's powers are useless to Muslims and whites. Since you're neither, you should be covered."

Though Adam doubted the power of amulets, he liked the idea of wearing this one. "I'll wear it till I'm home," he promised Ousmane.

CHAPTER 34

Running along the east coast of Africa, the Great Rift Valley is a gash in the earth's surface created millions of years ago by tectonic movements of the earth's crust. Prominent enough to be visible from the moon, it was clearly visible to Adam from thirty-five thousand feet.

In recent decades, archeologists had discovered the fossilized bones of early human, and much older hominid ancestors there. Squinting through the window, he tried to imagine his own ancestors, fifty millennia earlier, making their way northward through the valley to North Africa, the Middle East, and beyond. From this initial exodus, splinter groups of *homo sapiens* fanned out and populated the earth.

On a world map in the seat pocket, Adam traced the routes of his own parents' ancestors. Rowan's earliest human forebears, after leaving Africa for the Middle East, had taken a northwesterly route to Europe, settling in Italy and Scotland before they'd sailed to North America in the seventeenth century.

Easter's ancestral route was longer and more complex. It included European genes with a travel history like Rowan's, African genes (from slaves imported to America from West Africa in colonial times), and Native American genes carried to the New World via Siberia and Alaska by Asian descendants of those who'd once walked through the Rift Valley below. It struck Adam as absurd that racial differences, the source of so much misery and grief, were nothing more than consequences of the geographical barriers and climate variations that these forerunners had encountered as they spread around the world.

Tracing the path his earliest ancestors had followed he felt as if he were closing a great circle. He saw his life as a single tick of the cosmic clock, and himself as the descendant of humankind's first refugees.

Before he boarded he'd phoned François to let him know the happy outcome of their rescue mission, and tell him he was now on his way to Israel. François suggested a hotel near the Old City in Jerusalem and offered to book him a room. When Adam expressed misgivings about putting the cost on his dad's credit card, François said that he'd always expected to pay Adam's college expenses, and felt deprived of the opportunity when Princeton had awarded him an athletic scholarship. More important, he felt that travel would teach his son more than any college, and he was glad to provide "tuition." All Adam could do was promise to be frugal.

§§§

The Boeing 747 set down at Ben Gurion airport, about fifteen miles inland from Tel Aviv, and less than an hour by car to Jerusalem. He shared a taxi with an Israeli couple who provided a running commentary on their young nation's history. They pointed out the rusty tanks abandoned on the side of the road, grim monuments to the battles that broke out at the moment of Israel's birth, pitting Israeli forces against a coalition of Arab nations determined to prevent the creation of a sovereign Jewish state.

It took him a few days to realize that a campaign for his allegiance had begun within minutes of his arrival. When the taxi pulled up to his hotel, his fellow passengers made him promise to visit *Yad Vashem*, the museum devoted to the Holocaust. Only there, they asserted, could an outsider gain an understanding of the depth of Israeli determination to create a secure homeland and defend it to the death. It was not the last time Adam would hear the phrase "Never again" uttered through clenched teeth.

François had booked a room for him at the Jerusalem Garden, a small, inexpensive pension that catered to young travelers, and was just minutes from the Damascus Gate in the Old City. After he'd checked in, he stopped there to compose a photo before he passed through the arched gateway. It struck him that for millions of people—Christians, Jews, and Muslims—Jerusalem, this little piece of ground, was the center of the world, or as the city's natives call it, "the navel." He navigated the narrow streets of the Old City to the Church of the Holy Sepulchre, and inside, he saw a sign pointing to the Chapel of Adam. He figured he'd begin there. The text on the sign read that the chapel was built against the Rock of Golgotha, reputed to cover the burial place of Adam's skull. Though Adam regarded the biblical account of creation as myth, he took quiet pride in bearing the name of the first man.

He'd been exposed to religious rituals all his life, but the extent of his participation had been limited to the few occasions on which he'd lit a candle in a cathedral. At home, the amber glow of candlelight helped him dispel angst; he lit candles at meals or while reading, so why not light one where others did—in a church. He put a few coins in a slot and picked out a small white candle. Igniting it from the dying flame of another, he stuck it on a metal stand below the altar, then sat down on a stone bench to watch his candle burn. In the darkened chapel, the flame was a polestar shining down through the centuries.

On the way back to his hotel he stopped at a café, wrote postcards to Easter and Élodie, and debated sending one to Marisol. He'd often asked himself if he'd left the United States primarily to get away from his sister. Now that his mind had begun to clear he thought that it may have been a factor at first, but it wasn't driving him any longer. With her appointment at ABT she also seemed to have turned a corner. Her commitment to her vocation strengthened his resolve to settle on one of his own. He ended up sending her the only dance-related postcard he could find—Whirling Dervishes.

Next, he phoned the town house in Paris to let his dad know he'd arrived at the hotel. François insisted that he take down the name and number of Le Monde's Jerusalem correspondent, and consider calling him. "Paul Maffre is one of our best journalists. I've known him for years and I still read everything he writes. I'm sure he'll be glad to show you a few things." François then said, in a pointed way that Adam recognized, "Tell me, Ad, how are you doing?"

"Feeling a little lost, but I'm okay."

"Seek and ye shall find," François quipped. "And enjoy the seeking, because once you find what you're looking for, it may take over your life."

"Okay, Dad."

"Let me know when you move on. I don't want to be a nuisance but I'd like to know where you are. One more thing, Adam. Your mother called the other day and she's quite concerned about your future. Be sure to keep her in the loop too, okay?"

"I just sent her a postcard."

"You owe her an occasional call. If you let her in on your doings, I think you'll find that she wants to be part of the process more than she wants to control the outcome."

"Don't worry. I know things were tense before I left, but all that's behind me now. I'll stay in touch with you both."

Although Adam felt utterly alone, he also felt absolutely free. In this novel state it was as if he were seeing everything, including himself, for the first time.

§§§

The next morning, he put in a call to Paul Maffre. Hoping to predispose Maffre in his favor, he spoke French.

"This is Adam Merle-Blue. My father thought you might give me some pointers."

"Pointers for what?" came Maffre's gruff reply.

"I take photos."

"So?"

"I'm hoping to document the conflict here. I want to …"

"Listen," Maffre interrupted him. "To get even the faintest idea of what's going on here, you've got to get out of Jerusalem. Go to the Palestinian refugee camps. I'm taking a film crew out to one this morning. We could probably squeeze you in."

"That would be great. Thanks! I'm at the Jerusalem Garden."

"Be outside in a half-hour."

An SUV pulled up and, before it had come to a full stop the rear door swung open. From the backseat Maffre yelled impatiently at him to jump in. A cameraman in the front passenger seat nodded his greetings as the driver merged with onrushing traffic, and they were off.

"I met your father here in the late sixties, just after the Six-Day War," Maffre said. "He was traveling and I was a rookie reporter. What brings *you* here?"

"Same as my dad, I guess—exploring—but with a camera."

"Most people come here for either religion or politics."

"For me, it's not religion, and I'm baffled by the politics."

"Don't be fooled by the religious labels. The conflict is primarily political, not religious. Both sides claim the same real estate."

The car reached the outskirts of Jerusalem and stopped at a roadblock. After Israeli soldiers inspected Maffre's press credentials, they waved them through.

"I'm doing a story on the camps," Maffre continued. "Most visitors to Israel just visit the religious sites and Yad Vashem. The Kalandia Refugee Camp will give you a peek behind the headlines."

Not since Somalia had Adam been so agitated. Late that afternoon, back at his hotel, he wrote to Élodie.

> Dear Élodie,
>
> I've just been to a Palestinian refugee camp outside Jerusalem. One thing I've realized on this trip is that outsiders have no idea what's going on here.
>
> The main thing I saw in the camp was kids. Kids everywhere, from toddlers to teenagers. They've spent their whole lives in camps—hot, dusty, crowded places, with nowhere to play.
>
> My presence drew a crowd. The older boys wanted to talk sports. When I said that I played basketball, they asked if I knew Michael Jordan. They insisted on showing me a hoop they'd nailed to a telephone pole, no backboard. We played a few games, and although it

was the most pathetic basketball court I've ever seen, it was very satisfying.

The miracle of the Jews surviving Nazi death
camps to become citizens in a sovereign Israel
is matched only by the irony of them now being accused of genocide by the Palestinians. So
long as the Palestinians have nothing to call
their own, it's hard to imagine an end to the
uprisings.

Is there no way out of the cycle of indignity,
indignation, and revenge?

I'm planning to arrive in Peshawar on
Groundhog Day. That's a pagan version of
Easter observed on the second of February.

See you then,
Adam

§§§

In the days that followed, Adam explored Jerusalem on foot, twice
getting terribly lost in the backstreets of the Old City. He visited
sites sacred to Jews, Christians, and Muslims, and kept his promise
to visit *Yad Vashem*. When it came to indignity writ large, nothing
compared to the Holocaust.

At first, he seized every opportunity to discuss the political
situation. But whether he talked with Jews or Arabs, Europeans or
Americans, they were all brimming with passionate conviction, and
he soon grew weary of partisan polemics.

In early December, he received a note from Ben confirming
his arrival on the fifteenth. Ben's parents, who were prominent
supporters of Israel and spent at least one month a year there, were
treating their son to a stay at the posh King David Hotel.

He had time before Ben arrived, and he took a bus trip around the
country. Its proximity to Africa suggested that the first humans to leave
that continent had settled in this area before they'd dispersed and popu-

lated the rest of the earth. If there were a crossroads of the world, this land had a strong claim to the designation.

§§§

A garden terrace at the King David Hotel looked out over modern Jerusalem toward the Old City. Guests lay sprawled on lawn chairs taking in the sun and sipping drinks delivered by waiters in formal attire. Nowhere else in Israel had Adam seen sumptuousness, and it made him vaguely uncomfortable.

He spotted Ben at a table typing on his laptop, and after they got caught up, Ben regaled his friend with stories of his amorous adventures the last time he'd stayed at the hotel.

"I hooked up with an Aussie, a Brazilian, and an Indonesian," he said.

"How did you keep them apart?"

"Hell, serial monogamy. They were tourists looking for a good time. We're likely to meet some like them tonight."

In years past Adam would have welcomed a chance to go clubbing, but now his response was a noncommittal shrug.

"What's wrong, Ad? Is it Marisol?"

"No, we've resolved it."

"Élodie?"

"Not her either. I'll be joining her in Pakistan in February, but she has a guy in Paris." Eager to forestall further questioning about his love life, or lack thereof, Adam said, "This place is way more complicated than I thought."

"I suppose, but a few things are perfectly clear."

Leery of another harangue, Adam was silent.

"Israel can never expect peace so long as it has settlers on Palestinian land. You've been to the West Bank, haven't you?"

Adam nodded. In the last few weeks he'd learned enough to recognize Ben's position as one that was common among liberal intellectuals in Europe and America. In this view, the Israelis were occupying land that they would relinquish to the Palestinians in a trade for peace, a peace deal patterned on the Camp David Accords with Egypt.

"Yes, I visited a refugee camp. It was pretty awful."

"As a Jew, I'm embarrassed by Israelis who argue for a 'Greater Israel.' The Palestinians have lived here for centuries and have a strong competing claim to parts of this land."

Adam had heard this and counter-arguments many times, and changed the subject.

"I've got lots of photos. From all over Israel and the West Bank."

"Your last ones sure had an impact."

"I don't think a show of images would work here."

"I don't see why not, but let's leave that for tomorrow; today, let's party."

§§§

"Did you get laid?" Ben was yelling into the phone. His call had awakened Adam from a troubled sleep. He sat up in bed and propped himself against the headboard, trying to relieve a punishing hangover by closing his eyes.

"I have an awful headache. Why are you calling so early?"

"It's noon. What did you do after I left with Ruth?"

"I had a few more beers, and came home," Adam said, omitting to mention that he'd had several more at his hotel. He opened his eyes and counted six empty green Heineken bottles around the room, then remembered what he'd been trying to forget. After just one day, he had doubts about the value of meeting up with Ben in Israel, and they'd multiplied to the point where he was questioning the rationale for his entire journey.

"Alone?" Ben asked, incredulous. "Ruth's friend seemed ready and willing."

"I'm not in the market."

"What's come over you, Ad?"

"Do you want to see my photos?" Adam said, closing the subject.

"Come on over."

§§§

310

Grabbing a table in the hotel café, Ben ordered a full breakfast while Adam settled for a café au lait.

"I never had sex with an Israeli soldier before," Ben said. "You sleep with Ruth, you sleep with her rifle."

"Did it give you performance anxiety?" Adam joked.

"It *was* kind of exciting," Ben admitted.

The waiter arrived with the order and, after a few mouthfuls of his omelet, Ben started looking through Adam's photos.

There were several hundred, sorted by subject: panoramic views of the old city, ancient sites, sacred places, and people. There were photos of the Mediterranean and Red Seas and desert landscapes taken in the Negev and Sinai. Ben zeroed in on images of teenage faces from the Kalandia Refugee Camp.

"These show the squalor of the camps," he said. "Maybe they could get people thinking."

"You know Israelis better than I do, but I don't think making them feel guilty will improve things."

"Why not? Making Americans feel guilty about the famine in Somalia sure loosened the purse strings."

"That wasn't guilt; it was empathy. The Somalia photos didn't reproach anyone, they simply aroused compassion."

Ben nodded and turned back to his omelet.

"I learned something when I was ejected for charging the high school player at basketball camp, remember?" Adam asked.

"How could I forget? I've never seen you so pissed."

"I let his trash-talk get to me. It felt good to flatten him, but it hurt our team and helped theirs. Answering one indignity with another won't help in this situation either. Somalia was beginner's luck."

"What do you wanna do, then, Ad?"

"How about if we put on a basketball clinic at a refugee camp? Teach the kids the basics, and perhaps organize a tournament including both Israeli and Palestinian teams."

"Now you're talking! I like it. But we'd have to put on two tournaments—one for boys and one for girls."

"That's okay. Now, who do we know here who can help us? I did meet this journalist…"

"And through my dad's connections I'll bet I can get to Israelis who can cut the red tape."

Their partnership rekindled and their energy redirected, the two old friends spent the rest of the morning making plans, and the rest of December bringing joy to a few hundred teenage boys and girls.

§§§

At year's end, Ben left to resume his Rhodes at Oxford, and Adam's thoughts turned to the East. Since he'd left South Africa, every time he'd opened his notebook his eye had fallen on the name Lahiri—Vishu's guru at Banaras Hindu University. Vishu had characterized Indian philosophy as nonpartisan, nonjudgmental, and nonviolent. That seemed the perfect antidote to the bitter quarrels of the Middle East. Why not spend some time in India, he thought, before he joined Élodie in Pakistan?

CHAPTER 35

Adam's flight from Israel to India flew over the route of the original human migration from the near Middle East to the Fertile Crescent, across Persia, and to the Indus River Valley.

A taxi driver deposited him at a small hotel in New Delhi, and for a few days, he wandered around in a daze, glad for the temperate winter weather. He made himself take in some of the principal tourist sites, but felt disconnected and isolated. Getting his pocket picked at the Red Fort didn't help. He only lost about twenty dollars worth of rupees, but it made him feel like a naïve tourist.

Remembering his promise to François, Adam wrote his mother to let her and Rowan know where he was, and to give his letter a little heft, he included his out-of-Africa ruminations.

As he wrote Easter's address on the envelope, the baobab bracelet on his wrist caught his eye. It was ragged and dirty, but so far, so good.

On his way to the train station for the day-long trip down the Ganges to Banaras—where he hoped to find Vishu's guru—he stopped one last time at American Express to check for mail. There was a letter from Marisol, and in an envelope postmarked Moscow were separate letters from his mother and Rowan. He immediately opened and read these two.

> December 31, 1992
>
> Dear Adam,
>
> On the spur of the moment, we decided to fly to Moscow for our wedding.
>
> Moscow is where we first realized we might be able to give our story a different ending. We returned to a park on the Moscow River outside the city where we'd picnicked during the summer of 1990. Back then, we sat on the ri-

verbank amid the flowers, drinking champagne and watching the boats drift by. This afternoon we huddled in a shelter, drinking vodka and watching boys play ice hockey. Rowan, who still has friends at the Embassy, had the chef make us a lovely little wedding cake.

In marrying Rowan, I feel I've closed an open wound and come back to myself. But I want you to know that I have no regrets about my life with François. I don't need to tell you that he is a fine man, but perhaps I do need to let you know that he will always have a place in my heart.

Your loving mother

Adam folded his mother's letter and put it back in the envelope. Then he opened Rowan's.

Dear Adam,

I knew the dollar was strong in Russia, but I didn't realize it was *this* strong! On short notice, I managed to rent an entire church—complete with a Russian Orthodox priest—for just two hundred dollars cash. The ceremony was conducted in old Russian, an archaic language that's no longer understood by anyone, including a former Russian colleague who stood in for you as best man.

After consenting to the vows—we had no idea what we were agreeing to, by the way—the priest sang a soulful dirge, presented us with icons of Russian saints, and topped it off with shots of hundred-proof plum brandy. Then, waving a pot of incense, he led us around the beautiful old church and out onto Sparrow Hill, from which Moscow could be seen under a blanket of snow. It was a glorious day.

As you know, your mother's and my relationship has not been an ordinary one (if such exist). So we wanted to do something extraordinary to mark this milestone. We also wanted an unassailable excuse for not inviting any of our friends to the wedding. A Moscow marriage filled the bill. Your mother tells me that she mentioned our return to Fili Park in her letter to you. Yes, that's where we first realized that our love had persisted through the years of separation. The result is that you and I both get to know each other as adults. I'd never have planned it this way, but I couldn't be happier about how things have turned out.

I love you, Adam.

Rowan

He stuffed Marisol's unopened letter in his pocket and raced off to the train station.

Boarding the train at the last minute, he discovered that every seat was taken and he'd have to stand in the aisle for hours. But hearing from his parents, who'd obviously forgiven him for what he'd said in anger before he left, had the happy effect of rendering him oblivious to physical discomfort. People were huddled in the spaces between cars, teenage boys swarmed over the roof with the agility of spiders, and bicycles were strapped to the train's sides. At every stop, wiry men sold thimble-sized earthen cups of milky tea that were passed up through the windows, consumed in one sip, then dashed on the ground below.

§§§

In Banaras Adam found a pension that for a pittance provided room and board by the week. From that base, he set off every morning to explore the city on the west bank of the Ganges River, sometimes heading north toward the confluence of the Varana River, and sometimes toward the Asi River that marks the city's southern boundary. These tributaries gave the city its modern name—Varanasi.

The city itself was a web of narrow lanes teeming with vehicles, pedestrians, animals, and rickshaws. He wanted to capture its soul on film, and shot several rolls of film every day. He vowed he'd never ride in a rickshaw, that ancient mode of transportation in which one human being, in harness like a draft animal, tows another through the streets.

A few days later, several miles from his pension, he had a severe intestinal attack and had to rescind his vow. He gave the fellow who hauled him home in a rickshaw a big tip to assuage his guilt. Later that afternoon, he stumbled ashen-faced into a local pharmacy and, before he could speak, the man at the counter seemed to know he was looking for anti-diarrheal medicine.

He spent the next day in his room. His weakened condition opened him to the sounds of the ancient city: birds chirping, cows mooing, humans talking and singing, cars honking, scooters revving, awnings flapping, and his landlady sweeping the courtyard. Banaras was slowing him down, making him listen and inviting him to widen his gaze. In contrast to Jerusalem, which had jangled his nerves, this ancient city cooed a lullaby. The illness humbled him and left him content to do nothing, expect nothing, and want nothing more than an end to his nausea.

While temperatures regularly reach 120 degrees Fahrenheit during the summer, the balmy January weather helped him recover. On the third day, after a light breakfast of bread and tea, he sidestepped his way through the churning streets to the dusty calm of a neighborhood bookstore.

Though the window display featured travel books, novels, and comics, inside he found a vast collection in philosophy and religion. One wall was devoted to Hinduism, another to Buddhism. At least half the books were in English, India's second language. No distinction was made between new and secondhand books. A back room was full of comics of epic Hindu myths.

He soon tired of standing and, in addition to a map of the city, he chose a fat book entitled *Philosophies of India* and a thin one called *The Great Equation*, which the elderly gentleman at the counter assured him would explain the fat one. When Adam asked him if that meant he could dispense with the fat one, he recommended that he take it too, as it would answer any questions left unanswered by the thin one.

Adam realized that he'd been drawn to *The Great Equation* because its title evoked the elegance and certainty of mathematics. If Indian philosophy could be expressed as an equation, he might be able to understand it. He hurried back to his room to read it.

The equation of the title was "Atman = Brahman." As best he could make out, this meant that the Soul is not different from absolute, divine, cosmic reality. The equation was simpler-looking than those he'd studied in higher math, but like many of those, its meaning was not immediately apparent.

CHAPTER 36

The next morning Adam set out on foot along the Ganges for Bana-ras Hindu University to find Vishu's teacher and guru, Dr. Lahiri. As he walked south along the riverbank his eye was drawn to two old men seated side-by-side in an ancient wooden rowboat, and he took out his camera to capture the image. Draped in wrap-around cottons that hooded their heads, and pulling in unison on thick rough-hewn bamboo oars, they were making steady progress against the current. At this point in its long journey to the sea, the Ganges was very wide, and moved with the solemnity of an elephant.

When he reached the confluence with the Asi River, he turned away from the Ganges to follow a sign for the university. A map posted near the campus entrance guided him to the geology build-ing, where a cheerful secretary directed him to Lahiri's office. "His door is always open," she said. "Just poke your head in."

As he approached the office, he overheard voices speaking in Hindi, and even before he peeked in he heard a voice he took to be Lahiri's call out in English, "Come in." Either the old man had the hearing of a fox or he could see around corners.

Lahiri was busy pouring tea from an earthen pot into clay cups, and did not immediately look up. When he did, it was to ask if Adam would take tea, and to introduce the woman he'd been speaking with.

"This is Malika Kapoor. You'll have to introduce yourself, young man."

"I am Adam Merle-Blue. I met a student of yours in Johan-nesburg and he suggested I look you up."

"That must be Vishu!" Lahiri exclaimed. "You are most wel-come, Mr. Blue."

"Nice to meet you, Adam," said Malika, offering her hand. "Where are you coming from?" Malika was tall and athletic-looking. Dressed in a violet sari, she looked so much like a Hindu goddess that Adam imagined her with four arms.

"America, France, Africa, and the Middle East."

"Where are you going?" Malika continued.

"Continuing around the world and then back to New York where I began." Adam hoped his itinerary would make him seem more adventurer than tourist.

"Malika is one of my students, in geology and other subjects," Lahiri interjected. "Tell Adam what we're discussing," Lahiri prompted. "It's a common concern."

"All right," Malika said. "In geology we study the formation of the earth. In astrophysics I'm reading about the origin of the universe, the formation of stars and planets. It's all very mechanistic."

"That's the goal of science," Lahiri interjected. "To explain how things work."

"Yes, but …"

"But what?"

"But an asteroid could destroy us at any time—like what happened to the dinosaurs." Malika paused. "The universe seems to have no regard for us, for life. It's heartless, indifferent."

"Pitiless," Adam put in to signal his agreement.

"Nonsense!" Lahiri exclaimed. "You exclude love, and then you complain that the world lacks it. Taste the tea. Look at each other. The tea is delicious. You are both warm, sentient, lovable creatures. And you do not stand apart from the cosmos. On the contrary, you are *part* of it."

Lahiri looked at his guests in quick succession.

"Do you have feelings?" he asked. "Do you have heart?"

Adam and Malika nodded affirmatively.

"Then how can the universe lack them? Its heart beats in your breast. Let me put it this way: The universe has evolved for more than thirteen billion years, the earth more than four billion, and life somewhat less. Our species has been around for several hundred thousand years. We feel. We think. We love. Therefore, the universe is hardly devoid of these things. On the contrary, they are close at hand. So close that we overlook them. Quite simply, *we* are the mind and the heart of the universe."

If someone had said that to Adam in New York, he'd have dismissed it as verbal gymnastics. However, in this simple office, on the far side of the world, coming from this humble man, it moved him.

"But what if Malika is right?" Adam persisted. "What if a comet slams into the earth and destroys everything?"

"If you don't want that to happen," Lahiri said with a grin, "you must either deflect the comet or get out of its way. We're far from helpless, you know. We understand gravity and we can predict the movements of planets and comets. We know enough to avert such a catastrophe. You have the expression, 'God helps those who help themselves.'"

"God?" Adam said, surprised at the religious turn in the conversation.

"Oh, I don't mean some omniscient, omnipotent being in heaven who responds to our personal prayers. That god was a human invention—a father figure to comfort ourselves. That god won't save us from a comet."

"God?" Adam repeated.

"I'm agnostic," Lahiri replied. "Agnostic with an asterisk."

"An asterisk?"

"If there were a God, he'd want us to act as if there weren't." Lahiri smiled, then elaborated. "I use the term "god" as shorthand for the whole inner thrust of things, for the mystery and the intelligibility of nature. Nature includes human heartfulness and mindfulness. Leave those out and you're omitting the most interesting phenomenon in our corner of the cosmos. Now, with the advent of science, for the first time in our species' history, we're assuming the role of our planet's steward. A hippie in California put it nicely: 'We are as gods and might as well get good at it.'"

Lahiri rose and went to the window, inviting Adam and Malika to join him. Standing between them, he pointed at a banyan tree in the courtyard below.

"See that old tree? Doesn't it have a kind of dignity? But if a comet strikes Banaras, it won't be able to get out of the way. Neither will I. We're counting on you to save us. Now run along and get busy."

Malika led the way out. Adam felt like he sometimes did after seeing a movie: reluctant to break the spell by talking.

He followed Malika to a bicycle stand. "It was nice to meet you," she said as she climbed on her bike.

"Do you see Lahiri regularly?"

"Every Wednesday at four."

"Would it be okay if I went along with you sometime?"

"Sure," Malika replied, offering him a warm smile. "Meet me next Wednesday at three o'clock, at the café opposite the university entrance, and we'll go together."

§§§

A week later, Adam was waiting in the café as Malika rode up, dismounted, and chained her bicycle to a post. She was wearing a luminous pale blue sari. Her long black hair hung in a braid to her waist.

"Hello," he said, rising to greet her. When the waiter came, they ordered coffees. After some small talk, Adam pressed her on Lahiri's attitude toward religion.

"He has studied Vedanta, Buddhism, Islam and the religions of the West, and focuses on what they have in common. He sees their differences as ritualistic and theological, and no more or less significant than other cultural differences."

"If rituals and dogma are secondary, what's primary?"

"On the basics of man's place in the universe, ethics, selfhood, and death, the religions are far more alike than is generally recognized. They diverge on customs, style, and theology, but Lahiri would say that none of these are subject to either verification or disproof, and therefore they should not be disputed."

"A lot of wars have been fought over such distinctions."

"Lahiri maintains that doctrinal distinctions serve primarily to bolster the solidarity of the groups that adhere to them, and provide rationales for preying on others. He maintains that our age-old strategy of picking on the weak can take us no further. That globalization heralds either the end of human predation or the end of our species. You should ask him about his political views. Nothing is off-limits."

CHAPTER 37

On days that Adam didn't visit Lahiri, he scoured Banaras for images that, in one way or another, reminded him of the old man's teachings. He took photos of an old couple seated under a bougainvillea, a young couple leaning against a sprawling fig tree, shopkeepers, street sweepers, and rickshaw drivers.

At one meeting with Lahiri, Adam and Malika found him poring over a map spread on his desk. "Can you show me Mount Everest?" Adam asked. Lahiri put his finger on it.

"Here's the second tallest mountain," Lahiri said, pointing to K2 on the map. It lies a thousand miles northwest of Everest, and is visible from the Karakoram Highway connecting Pakistan and China. Shortly after the road was constructed, I traveled on it to a conference in Urumqi, China. Getting there was better than being there. That's true in life as well. See if it's not, Adam, as your journey unfolds."

"Could I take that road?" Adam asked.

"During the summer months, yes. But from November to April, it's impassable. If you want to see mountains in the winter, Darjeeling is the place. It's home to Mount Kanchenjunga, the world's third tallest peak. At twenty-eight thousand feet, it's only one thousand shorter than Everest but much more impressive because it rises four miles above one's vantage point."

Lahiri's tone had softened until it sounded almost reverential.

"You speak of the mountain as if it were alive," Malika said.

"I do love Kanchenjunga," Lahiri said. "To me, the mountain has a holy dignity."

The three of them went silent. Finally, Malika spoke. "Dr. Lahiri, I have a philosophical question, but one that's personal at the same time."

"The best kind," Lahiri said expectantly.

"I'd like to know your views on arranged marriages." Malika blushed, then quickly recovered and continued, "Many of my friends are rejecting their parents' choices and marrying for love. What do you think?"

"Before I respond, let me say that my views are nothing more than one old man's opinion. People's circumstances, once you're aware of the details, are rarely comparable, so it's important not to impose your beliefs on others."

"Okay," Malika and Adam said in unison.

"For me, marriage is about more than procreation. It is also about the growth and creativity of the partners. I was married to my beloved, Viveka, for fifty years. Our love has survived her death. She is always within me. When I speak of her it is as if she is again *beside* me. I valued our relationship for the companionship and for its subtler effects on the nature of my connection to the world."

"Was it love at first sight?" Malika asked. Adam was surprised by the question—and even more by Lahiri's response.

"No, it was *infatuation* at first sight," Lahiri said. "Love grew as we built a sanctuary in which we felt safe. The golden rule of relationships is "Cause no indignity." A loving relationship is one in which both partners take care to protect each other's dignity. A wounded soul heals more slowly than a wounded body, so it is as important to avoid indignity as it is to avoid outright harm."

CHAPTER 38

On what was going to be Adam's last Sunday in Banaras, he heard a knock on his door and rose to answer it. The receptionist told him a young woman wished to see him. Adam knew only one woman in Banaras and so was not surprised to find Malika waiting for him in the lobby.

"What's the matter?" Adam asked.

Malika led him to a divan out of earshot of the reception area before speaking.

"Professor Lahiri died last night."

Adam reached for Malika's hand and took it between his palms. Words were superfluous. Time stopped. They were together with Lahiri.

Finally, Adam said, "What kind of service will be held?"

"Cremation along the Ganges. It's being planned for tomorrow night. His students are coming from all over the country."

"The Ganges? What about his ashes? Where will they …"

"He has no relatives, so the funeral is being organized by his students. They all know that he worked to clean up the Ganges. He asked several of us to make sure that his ashes do not add to the contamination." Adam guessed what she had in mind.

"Kanchenjunga," he said. "If it's not inappropriate, I would like for us to go together."

"That should be fine, if my mother goes along."

"How do we take possession of the ashes?"

"I'll put it to the student who's in charge of funeral arrangements. His name is Narinder. All Lahiri's students know what Kanchenjunga meant to him. I won't be surprised if Narinder wants to come with us. What you can do is get an urn and a carrying case for the trip."

§§§

327

The cremation was held the next evening at Manikarnika Ghat near the place on the Ganges where Hindus believe that Vishnu sat for fifty thousand years creating the world. Lahiri's corpse was wrapped in a white shroud, with logs of aromatic sandalwood stacked around his reclining form. Because Lahiri had no sons, the pyre was lit by Narinder. It burned fiercely, casting its light on a throng of hundreds. When the fire began to subside, Narinder punctured the skull with a stick, and a rushing sound sent a gasp through the crowd. According to traditional Hindu beliefs, this was the moment when Lahiri's enlightened soul was liberated from the cycle of rebirth, and took up eternal residence in nirvana.

§§§

Darjeeling lies about four hundred miles northeast of Banaras, and a mile and a half higher in elevation. The trip up the southern foothills of the Himalayan Range from the Ganges River Valley to Darjeeling is one of the world's most awe-inspiring train journeys.

The final leg of the trip on the Himalayan Railway is via a nineteenth-century, narrow-gauge track that snakes upward through the foothills into the clouds to reveal a panoramic view of the surrounding snow-capped peaks.

All around Darjeeling lay the plantations whose tea made the mountain town known to the world. The air is a smoky blend of burning dung, yak butter, and fermenting tea leaves.

Across a steep valley nestled in the mountain kingdom of Sikkim, Mount Kanchenjunga towers over Darjeeling, a glittering white peak of perpetual snow that pierces the sky. Its vastness provides a lesson in humility. It was obvious why Lahiri regarded Kanchenjunga as a special mountain. As the sun set, Adam thought he heard the mountain whispering to him in a language he did not know. In the moonlight, Kanchenjunga seemed to stand sentinel over all that stood in its shadows.

Narinder had indeed decided to come, as had Malika's mother. Adam had called ahead to book two rooms, one for the ladies and one for the men. Each room was equipped with a little coal-burning stove. After supper in the inn, they asked the hotel manager for advice on the best way to accomplish their mission. He offered to rent them a car and hire a driver who would take them into the nearby kingdom of Sikkim and part way up the mountain on special day-passes.

Early the next morning, with the urn on the backseat between Malika and her mother, the foursome set out. They had told the driver what they were looking for and he took them to the outskirts of a sunny mountain village at about twelve thousand feet with a view of the summit.

As they stood wondering what to do with the ashes, the wind rippled Malika's sari and lofted the ends of her scarf toward the snowy peak. She took it as a sign and, with a scoop, released a portion of Lahiri's ashes to the wind. By turns, they each scooped ashes into the updraft and watched as they were carried aloft toward the icy summit.

With Lahiri's ashes falling like snowflakes on the upper slopes of Mount Kanchenjunga, Adam felt at peace. The railway that took them to the passenger trains bound for Banaras reminded him of the Dinky, which had so often carried him from idyllic Princeton into the real world. He smiled inwardly at the thought of Charlie, and wondered what Princeton's "Siddartha" would make of his Himalayan adventure.

On the journey back, he wrote a newsy letter to his mother and Rowan. He knew Easter would be skeptical, but he told her he'd met a man in India from whom he'd learned more in a month than he had in the two years he'd spent in college.

When the train reached Banaras, Adam's time with Malika would end. The following morning he was to leave for Pakistan. He had shared the most precious learning of his life with this young woman, and as their taxi drew up to her residence, his heart was full. They got out and faced each other to say good-bye. He took her hand in his.

"I don't know if we'll meet again," Adam said, 'but I do know I will never forget you."

"I think it is our destiny to meet again," she said. "You have my address. Please let me know where your quest takes you and what you learn from it. I wish you the very best, Adam."

CHAPTER 39

Groundhog Day, 1993

From the day he arrived in Peshawar, Adam made himself useful in MSF's operation. He was strong and fit enough to carry the sick and injured Afghan refugees to the van from dawn to dusk and deliver them to Élodie and her colleague, Dr. Donald Lighthill, at the hospital in the MSF compound.

Lighthill, a Canadian in his mid-forties, was on his fifth tour of duty with MSF. He was an expert in the use of prosthetics, and the millions of live landmines left behind from Afghanistan's war with the Soviet Union ensured he always had too many patients. He did much of his work in the refugee camps where, as a male, he was accepted by the Muslim religious leaders (mullahs) who controlled them.

The compound, which was situated near a refugee camp, was within a walled enclosure. At its heart stood a decaying two-story colonial building dating from the British Raj. Stairs led up to a broad verandah decked out with hanging plants that, Adam noted, were in dire need of water. Just a few miles to the east of the refugee camp lay the narrow Khyber Pass that threaded its way into Afghanistan.

Adam was not only a one-man ambulance crew. Once a week he used the van to make the hundred-mile trip to Pakistan's capital twin cities, Rawalpindi and Islamabad, to replenish the infirmary's medical supplies. His route was a section of the legendary Silk Road traveled by Marco Polo in the late thirteenth century. It passed through the lawless Northwest Frontier, legendary for gun-running and drug-smuggling. Consequently, his trips were punctuated with impromptu inspections at checkpoints manned by uniformed Pakistani police and Afghan "watchers," but once the gatekeepers were satisfied that he worked for MSF, they waved him through.

On one of his trips, when he was giving an Afghan couple a lift into town he got a lesson in local etiquette. When the husband caught a checkpoint guard peering into his wife's eyes through the slots in her burka, he berated him, shrilly and at length. To Adam's surprise, it was the man with the gun who backed down.

On the day he'd arrived at the compound, Élodie had made it clear that Adam was welcome in her bed, and as soon as the dishes were done, that was where they went. By ten they were asleep, her alarm clock set for six, his internal alarm for five-thirty, so he could write in his journal while the house was still quiet.

Donald and Élodie worked from seven to seven, six days a week. Donald took Saturdays off, Élodie, Sundays. Though most of Adam's time was taken up with shuttling patients to and from the clinic, he got good at snatching idle moments to take photos of the camp and the people who lived there.

The staff regularly gathered for dinner, and two Afghans prepared the main course, typically kabab with rice and lentils, or the delicious Afghan lamb stew known as korma. Warm, freshly-baked bread accompanied every meal, sometimes in the form of a hot sandwich of spinach, onions, and spices.

As talented as the Afghans were in the kitchen, they knew nothing about the desserts Westerners enjoyed at the end of the meal. Adam offered to fill the gap. With help from a tattered cookbook left by a previous resident, he experimented with baking at elevations well above sea level, and within weeks he was turning out cakes, pies, crêpes, and puddings. After his day job as transporter of the sick and dying, his night job as dessert chef was a pleasure, and he quickly came to appreciate the comforting role that food, and especially treats, played in the lives of relief workers.

One evening, the staff was lingering at the table, chatting, when Donald told a tale that made Adam question the mission itself. "Last month, Élodie and I were vaccinating teenage boys at a religious school in an Afghan refugee camp. The students are in training to become mullahs, and are called Talibs while they're being groomed to exercise secular and ecclesiastical power. While we were giving vaccinations a boy ran into the room and said someone in the camp had been knifed. I left immediately to deal with it. When I returned an hour later, Élodie was gone. We knew the Talibs are strict fundamentalists who object to being ministered to by a woman, so I was afraid that she might be in danger. I spent hours looking for her; finally, I found her at a detention center, but it was morning before they released her into my custody."

"My god, Élodie. I can't … how did they treat you?" Adam asked.

"They were very angry, and for the most part I couldn't even understand what they were saying. They treated me like a criminal."

"She had a bruise on her head," Donald said.

"One of them hit me with a cane," Élodie added in a matter-of-fact tone. "Then they took me to the mullah in charge. In French he told me that I had insulted Islam, and severe punishment was called for under their religious laws. I was to be held in solitary confinement until I could be tried in an Islamic court."

"In order to get her out," Donald continued, "I had to threaten to go to the Ministry of Police in Islamabad. The Afghans have no legal jurisdiction in the camp because it's on Pakistan's side of the border, but the Pakistanis have given them de facto authority. We see the brutal effects of their brand of justice every day."

"Women suffering from beatings, lashings, and burns," Élodie explained. "Half of them are severely depressed. Suicide is common. The mullahs' authority is growing. Their ultimate goal is to depose the rulers in Kabul and bring the entire frontier and ultimately the country under 'Sharia' law. They call their organization the Taliban."

"Élodie was lucky," Donald said. "As a condition of her release, I had to promise that she wouldn't leave the compound. We can't risk offending them again. I've worked all over the world and I've never seen such fanaticism."

"I tried reasoning with them," Élodie added, "but the men simply wouldn't allow their religious beliefs to be questioned. The women see things very differently, but can't speak up in public."

"What do they say privately?" Adam asked.

"That when their men fight they have no choice but to support them."

"And the men have been fighting forever," Donald interjected, "fighting either the British or the Russians or each other. The struggle for control of Afghanistan—'The Great Game' as it's still known—is centuries old; it's a way of life."

"The violence has metastasized," Élodie said. "The longer it continues, the weaker the position of women becomes. In less militant times, I think women would be able to temper the religious fanaticism."

"And you're committed to stay here through March?" Adam asked.

"Yes."

"I'll stay as long as you do."

Later that night, in the bed Adam and Élodie shared, he confronted her: "Why didn't you tell me about this? You said you couldn't get back to the compound that night because there was a skirmish on the route."

"I knew how you'd react, and I didn't want to turn you against some of the mullahs we have to work with."

§§§

Every Saturday evening Donald took the van to visit a friend who worked at the American Embassy in Islamabad. He left a phone number "for emergencies only" and unfailingly returned by noon on Sunday. From his vague language and avoidance of gender-specific pronouns, Élodie told Adam she thought Donald could be gay. Among the Taliban, homosexuality carried a death sentence, so if that was the case, Élodie admired him all the more for accepting an assignment from MSF that put him in mortal danger. A dedicated, versatile physician, he also took the time to mentor Élodie in frontier medicine.

"I can't imagine having had a better internship," she told Adam. "I've learned more in the last six months than I did in medical school."

"Too bad you can't follow Don into the field," Adam said.

"My quarantine to the compound puts an extra burden on him. I'm sure my replacement will be a male."

"When we do leave, we could take the Karakoram Highway to China," Adam proposed. He hadn't forgotten how Lahiri's face had lit up when he described his own journey through the snowcapped Karakorams over the Khunjerab Pass into Western China.

"Aren't the mountains snowed in?"

"The pass opens in the spring."

"So if we get to China, then what?"

"The Trans-Sib from Beijing to Russia."

"I'm game!" Élodie said. One of the things Adam loved most about her was her appetite for adventure.

On the last day of February the Paris office sent word that Élodie's replacement would arrive in three weeks. Adam had obtained visas, and learned that Pakistani truckers began traversing the Khunjerab Pass in early April, and for a price, would take passengers. He figured they could get from Pakistan to Beijing in less than a week, and Élodie could be in Paris a week after that.

§§§

Due to the malnutrition and unhygienic conditions in the camp, in pregnant women complications were frequent; they often died in childbirth, and infant mortality was high. Donald provided most of the prenatal care in the women's homes but encouraged his patients to come to the clinic at the first signs of labor, so they could give birth there. Élodie had assisted Donald in several difficult deliveries and a few lifesaving Caesarians.

On a Saturday night, sometime after midnight, Adam was awakened by a voice calling out in Dari, the Afghan-Persian dialect spoken by many of the refugees. Since Donald was in Islamabad for the night, he went to the door. An unkempt man, gesturing frantically, kept repeating the Dari words for "doctor" and "baby," and tugging at his arm as if to drag him outside.

This was not their first late-night emergency. The previous week, at two in the morning, Adam had driven Donald deep into the camp to tend to a sick young boy, and Donald had performed an emergency appendectomy on the spot.

The commotion brought Élodie to Adam's side, and she told him to bring the van around to the front while she spoke to the man. When Adam pulled up, she pushed the Afghan in beside him and jumped in.

"You shouldn't leave the compound," Adam said. "Let me go and bring the patient to you."

"There's no time," Élodie said. "Drive." She spoke with such authority that he simply followed her orders. Ten minutes later the husband told them to stop. They got out in front of an earthen hut with a plastic tarpaulin that served as a roof. Inside, the only heat came from a kerosene lamp that lit the one-room shelter. A hugely pregnant woman lay gasping for breath on a floor mat soaked with blood. A tiny foot could be seen protruding from the birth canal. Several Afghan women stood around helplessly. Two small children cowered in the corner.

Élodie gave the woman an injection, and a few minutes later, cut into her abdomen with a scalpel and lifted a blue-toned baby boy out of her womb. She handed the child to Adam, told him to cut off the placenta, clamp the umbilical cord, and massage the baby until it began breathing. He did as instructed, and almost immediately the infant's hue changed from lifeless purple to rosy beige. The little body reminded him of those light bulbs controlled by a rheostat that go from dim to bright with the turn of a rotary switch.

Élodie hooked up an intravenous transfusion and spent twenty minutes sewing up the woman's belly. The husband, who until now had stood against the wall, approached Adam offering a worn but clean blanket. Adam laid the tiny baby boy in the blanket and placed him in his father's arms.

As the transfusion took effect, the new mother's color improved and her breathing steadied. After Élodie checked her vital signs, she approached the father, still holding his new child, trimmed the umbilical cord and tied it off.

In halting Dari, she said "beautiful boy" to the father. "Wife sleep now. Tomorrow, Dr. Lighthill come."

The mention of Donald's name was a grim reminder to Adam of the risk Élodie was taking in violating Taliban orders, and he urged her to finish up so they could return to the safety of the MSF compound. Élodie told him to take their things to the van while she checked the mother's vital signs. As he stepped out into the chill night air he was startled to see a bearded man peering into the hut through a window. His first thought was "peeping Tom," but then he realized he was dealing with something far more dangerous—one of the spies who worked for the Taliban and kept watch over the camp. Suddenly, the interloper broke into a run. A dormant athletic reflex kicked in and Adam chased him down and seized him by the arm. The man struggled to break free, but Adam spun him round and marched him back to the hut and into the dimly-lit room.

"Woman doctor," the man spat out, shaking a fist before going limp in Adam's grip.

"What are we going to do?" Élodie said. "He'll report me."

"Would you be safe in the compound? We could take him back with us and release him once we were inside."

"We couldn't keep them from coming in after me," Élodie said. She began to tremble. The new father glowered at the spy.

"We'd better get out of Peshawar," Adam said. "If we get a head start, we can get you to safety in Islamabad. I'll tie this guy up."

"But then they'll find him here and blame the family," Élodie said. "I have a better idea." She went to the black bag that Adam had dropped to run after the spy, and took out a hypodermic needle. She drew a dose of anesthetic into it. "Get him on the ground and hold him still," she said to Adam.

He used his weight to immobilize the man while Élodie jabbed the needle through his pants into his thigh. Within moments he looked like a sleeping seal.

"Let's drop him somewhere. He'll come to in a few hours and be able to walk back under his own steam," Élodie said. "He'll either report me or hold his tongue in shame, but regardless, we'll be long gone."

"Leave him in the van?" Adam asked.

"No, Donald can't function without it." Turning to the new father, she said, "Car. At compound. Twenty minutes." She demonstrated her instructions with hand gestures. Adam grasped her plan.

The new father nodded, handed his newborn to one of the women in attendance, and ran out.

"We have to trust him," Élodie said.

"You just saved the lives of his wife and son. If that doesn't earn you a few points, I don't know what would."

Adam drove to the compound, stopping halfway to drop off Sleeping Beauty, as they'd taken to calling the Taliban informant. When they arrived there, Adam threw their things into backpacks while Élodie wrote Donald a note. They were waiting anxiously on the front steps for a car when it pulled up.

"I take you to Islamabad," the driver said in English. "I am Ahmed Farani, baby's uncle."

"Thank you," Adam said, opening the rear door for Élodie. He tossed their backpacks in beside her and climbed in.

"We very happy … you good doctors," Ahmed said, looking over his shoulder at them. Adam was amused to be thought of as a doctor but felt no need to correct his assumption.

Minutes later, Ahmed barked, "Roadblock. Put on burka." From the seat beside him he took a traditional, all-concealing garment and handed it to Élodie. He took off his hat, which marked him as one of the Afghan warriors known as "mujahedeen," and told Adam to put it on. Élodie put the burka over her head and, with some difficulty, managed to pull it down to her feet. In the dark, Adam could only make out the glint of her eyes behind the veil that obscured them.

At the checkpoint, the driver slowed to a stop and exchanged words with the guards. One of them poked his head in the car and peered at Adam and Élodie. Adam immediately put his hand up to the intruder's face to signal that he objected to another man eyeing his woman. To his relief, the guard backed off and waved them through. From under the burka came a muffled "It's claustrophobic in here."

"I rather like my hat," Adam said.

"Souvenir for you," the driver said to Adam over his shoulder. "Cold in mountains. Now we go to nice hotel."

CHAPTER 40

On Sunday morning Élodie phoned Donald at the compound from the Marriott in Islamabad. She told him the whole story, and he agreed to look in on her patient and make discreet inquiries about the anesthetized Talib. He regretted that the crisis was a result of his absence, and assured her that she'd done the right thing. She asked him to notify the home office of her early departure from Peshawar and let them know that she'd report to headquarters in Paris by the end of April.

Before Ahmed dropped them off at the hotel, he gave Adam contact information for his cousin, Mohammed Farani, in Gilgit. He managed an apricot farm in the Gilgit hills, and Ahmed assured them that hospitality would be extended to them both, and that Mohammed, though a devout Muslim, was no fundamentalist. "Taliban bad for Islam" was Ahmed's considered opinion.

They spent a few days holed up in the hotel and then made their way by taxi to the airport. They'd decided it would be best to get themselves to Gilgit, then find transport across the Karakorams into China. If anyone was looking for them at the airport it would be in the international concourse, not the domestic terminal they'd depart from. As an extra precaution Élodie donned a burka for the ride to the airport and didn't take it off until she'd boarded the plane. In the cab, Adam adjusted the baobab bracelet on his wrist, glad that Ousmane's lucky charm had survived his ordeals in Peshawar.

Landing in Gilgit they felt safe for the first time since they'd left Peshawar, but not quite safe enough to ditch the burka. When they left the airport, Adam stuffed it in his backpack.

"One more detail," he said, pausing in front of the terminal. "I think we'd better pose as a couple."

"As in 'married'?"

"We don't want to shock these folks, and if we're not husband and wife, they'll give us separate rooms."

"I do," Élodie said, ceremoniously holding out her ring finger. Taking his cue, Adam removed a ring from her right hand and slipped it on her left ring finger, and they kissed.

They found a driver to take them to the address Ahmed had given them, and Adam presented Ahmed's note to his cousin, Mohammed. As its message sank in, Mohammed's eyes lifted to meet Élodie's, and his swarthy face broke into a warm smile. Then he reached for Adam's hands and took them in his own.

"Ahmed writes that our family is in debt to you both. It is an honor to receive you." With that he ushered them into the house.

After introducing them to his wife and children, Mohammed showed them to a guest house that clung to the face of a cliff overlooking an orchard of leafless apricot trees. He said he'd have a basket of bread and fruit sent over for breakfast, and invited his guests to take their other meals in the main house with his family.

In the days that followed, Adam realized that, as foreman for an absentee owner, Mohammed held a position of considerable authority. Conditions for apricot farming were perfect in Gilgit, Mohammed told the couple, and his orchards produced a surplus that went to China over the Karakoram Highway. He encouraged his guests to relax and enjoy Gilgit until the road opened to traffic in mid-April. He also promised to find them a reliable driver.

Mornings in Gilgit were crisp and cold. After breakfast, they went hiking in the hills surrounding the farm. During their wanderings they often came upon people whose blue eyes marked them as descendants of the Macedonian soldiers who'd marched through these parts some two thousand years earlier with Alexander the Great.

Over the years, guests had left a small library of books at Mohammed's house, and they spent their afternoons reading. Adam, anticipating his upcoming journey through Russia, tackled *War and Peace* in an English translation. Élodie read *Les Misérables* in French.

Despite occasional squabbles, they got along well. Whereas Élodie liked things organized, Adam made the case for leeway, and sometimes thought of her as a control freak.

Usually, after dinner they spent evenings in their cottage talking by candlelight; the daily grind in Peshawar had left no time for deep conversation. In the aftermath of Lahiri's discourses Adam had been content simply to let them sink in while he drove the van. Now, having come to a stop in Gilgit, he was glad for the chance to reflect on everything that had transpired since he'd left Paris.

A topic they returned to again and again was the notion of "making a difference." The cliché held questions for them both. Was it vanity to insist on making a difference? What proof could there possibly be that the difference that was made was beneficial in the long run?

"But your medical work, that's clearly positive," Adam insisted.

"It does relieve immediate suffering," Élodie acknowledged.

"And it sets a standard," Adam added. "The people you treat begin to expect quality care."

"But when they don't get it, they're all the more unhappy. So long as the Talibs are in charge, there won't be any real improvement. They want to keep people ignorant and weak so they're easier to control."

"So, what can outsiders do? How can one make a positive difference?"

"There are a million other ways to do good, and they're right under our noses. Most people who say they want to make a difference actually want to be heroes. I don't trust do-gooders who don't acknowledge what's in it for them."

"Go on," Adam said.

"People are drawn to social issues that reflect their personal problems. But often they present themselves as altruistic. There's nothing wrong with working on a societal problem that mirrors a personal issue. It's often better than discussing it with a shrink. But is it too much to ask that do-gooders acknowledge what they themselves get out of their work?"

"What do you get out of MSF?"

"As half-Vietnamese, I've never felt accepted in France. I want a world in which ethnicity and nationality don't matter—a *world* without borders. By working for Doctors Without Borders I'm helping create the world I want for myself."

"I'm not sure of my motives," Adam said, "but I do feel driven."

"Clarity comes from bringing into focus what's already in plain sight," Élodie said.

"Like what?"

"No one can help you there, Adam. I think you've got to discover that for yourself."

§§§

Spring was beginning to show its face in Gilgit. Wild flowers, buds on the apricot trees, and swelling mountain streams all signaled that the snow was melting and the Khunjerab pass would soon open to through traffic. They were pleased when Mohammed announced that in two days a convoy of trucks was going to attempt the year's first crossing.

"I found your driver," he said. "Mustafa lives in town with his family and makes many trips to Kashgar. After the harvest, he will carry our apricots."

"Sounds perfect," Adam said.

"You'll need to pay him something."

"Gladly. What would be appropriate?"

"Perhaps a hundred dollars."

"That's a bargain." Adam said. He took two hundred dollars from the pouch that hung from his neck and gave it to Mohammed. "This should cover us both."

Adam had been trying to figure out how to reimburse Mohammed for his out-of-pocket costs of putting them up, but was reluctant to offer him money for fear of offending him. This way, their host could work this out for himself and pay the driver accordingly.

On the day of their departure, Mohammed drove his guests to the edge of town where a convoy of garishly decorated trucks was assembling. He introduced the couple to Mustafa. He spoke no English, so Élodie's rudimentary Dari, plus the usual pantomime, would have to bridge the gap.

The first day's destination was the mountain town of Hunza. The second day they'd tackle the Khunjerab Pass. Once over the Karakoram Range and in China, it was a straight shot to Kashgar, one of the most fabled way stations on the Silk Road.

The trucks in the caravan clung together like a train of circus elephants. The highway followed a river that carried the snowmelt all the way to Banaras and beyond. The roar of the torrential stream reverberating off snowcapped peaks reminded Adam of the crashing cymbals in Beethoven's "Ode to Joy."

As they approached the inn where they'd spend the first night, Élodie remarked that it looked like it hadn't been remodeled since it had hosted Alexander's troops. They were served a rich stew of potatoes, onions, carrots, and lamb that made up for the hardscrabble accommodations. Spent from the extreme altitude and the sustained exhilaration of the drive, they were asleep within minutes.

Six hours later, a clanging bell summoned drivers and passengers to a breakfast of dried apricots, bread slathered with yak butter, and milky tea. The truckers did not talk during meals, but Adam sensed a subtle shift in their mood from the suppressed gaiety he'd observed on their departure.

They hadn't gone ten miles when the convoy came to a stop. Using hand gestures, Mustafa indicated that his passengers should stay in the truck while he went ahead on foot.

With the engine off, the temperature in the truck rapidly dropped, and after thirty minutes with no sight of Mustafa, they got out to look around.

"Out of the fridge, into the freezer," Adam said as they passed between the line of trucks and the sheer cliff from which the road had been carved. Their truck was somewhere near the middle of the convoy, and before they reached the lead vehicle they saw what was holding things up. A gigantic boulder had fallen onto the road, blocking traffic.

Some of the men were clustered around it while others watched from a distance. From his vantage point near the front of the convoy, Adam could see that sticks of dynamite were being placed in and around the boulder.

About an hour later, Mustafa led them back to the truck. When they were inside, Mustafa peered intently into his rearview mirror, then slowly began to back up, with the truck behind him doing likewise. Slowly the entire convoy backed down the mountain, putting some two hundred meters between it and the boulder.

Silence. Walking around outside had kept Adam and Élodie warmer than they'd been sitting in the truck; now, the suspense made them oblivious to the frigid temperature.

Suddenly a blast echoed through the canyon. Up ahead they could see debris flying across a darkened sky. Then they heard the rumbling of rocks falling, and finally, eerie stillness again.

They all climbed out. By the time they had made their way back to the spot where their truck had stood before the blast, men were at work shoving rocky debris into the ravine. Rocks a meter in diameter caromed down the mountain, decapitating trees as they gathered speed.

Adam ran to the truck for his camera. Hundreds of laborers had lost their lives constructing the Karakoram Highway, and he could see why. After he'd attempted to shoot the boulders in free fall, he focused on the faces of the men who, with crowbars, were inching them across the road to the edge of the abyss, and over. If ever he'd seen pride and awe on the human face, it was at the precise moment when gravity caught hold of one of the boulders. As one the size of a cow tipped over the edge and plummeted into the ravine, he saw on Élodie's face the unguarded wonder of a nine-year-old child.

Opening the road took the better part of the morning, but from then on it was clear sailing to the international border at the Khunjerab Pass. The guidebook Adam had picked up at the Marriott explained that "Khunjerab" means "River of Blood" in the local Tajik language. No one knew if the reference was to the rusty color of the mountain streams or the predations of the bandits who had once terrorized the area.

At its summit, the pass gentled out into an empty windswept space of frozen streams and glistening glaciers. The Pakistani-Chinese border crossed the highest paved highway in the world. That Marco Polo made it over these mountains seven centuries earlier would not have been credible, except for the fact that tens of thousands of years before that, aboriginal humans had somehow managed to do so too.

It was a tradition among the truck drivers to stop at the summit for a smoke. Élodie had been looking for a place to dispose of the burka, and when Mustafa pulled to a halt near a stone monument marking the three-mile-high Pakistan-China border, she and Adam climbed out to give it a ritual burial. What they hadn't anticipated was that the ground at that altitude would be tundra-solid.

"We'll have to cover it with stones," Adam said.

They walked a distance from the truckers and Adam did his best to scrape out a shallow depression where Élodie laid the folded burka.

"Thanks for saving my life," Élodie said to the burka as she placed the first stone over it.

As the stones grew into a cairn, a plump ginger-colored marmot circled them warily and then, sitting up on its haunches, stared at them from ten yards off.

"I think that fellow is making plans," Adam said. "By tonight his family will have a new mattress."

"Lining a rat's nest is the perfect use of a burka," said Élodie.

"Not a rat, a marmot, a Himalayan marmot," Adam said. He'd seen pictures of them in a guidebook. "Don't you think he's cute?"

"In Vietnam, we'd put him in a stew." She was not one to get misty-eyed over furry animals. He wondered if she was sentimental about anything, but her toughness was one of the things he loved about her.

He took a photo of her standing beside the entombed burka. A breeze rippled through her long black hair and her breath showed white in the cold thin air. A last look around, and they hurried back to their truck to cross into China.

As the convoy descended, it picked up speed. The only sign of life was a herd of two-humped, shaggy-haired camels grazing in the desert. Seven hours of driving across a vast brown plain brought them to Tashkurgan.

They took a room in the truckers' hotel and, after a supper of lamb and noodles, Élodie went back to the room to lie down. Not ready to call it a day, Adam headed out into town for a walkabout. Night had fallen, and the heavens looked more like a chandelier hanging from a lofty ceiling than stars that were light-years away.

After the exhilaration of traversing the pass, Adam felt uncommonly happy. When he asked himself why, he remembered how Lahiri had described his own road trip to China. Yes, getting somewhere was often more interesting than being there.

Alone in this silent vastness beneath the brilliant low-hanging stars, his mind roamed the centuries. He propped himself against a boulder and imagined that Marco Polo had once leaned against it, gazed at the same sky. He wondered if his celebrated forerunner had savored the journey itself, or simply yearned to get where he was going.

Don Quixote was another man with a mission, but hadn't he, at the end of all his chivalrous adventures, returned home disillusioned? Quixote came to see his romantic ideals as sadly misplaced, his heroic striving as desperately misguided. The message in that, Adam was coming to believe, was that striving to "make a difference" or "do good" was like trying to fall in love; you just have to recognize it when it happens.

If Marisol had not been an impossible love, they'd have dated while she danced and he completed his studies at Princeton. Then, they'd have married and raised a family. Instead, fate had blown him off that path and onto the Silk Road. *Where would it take him next?* he wondered.

He walked back to the inn and slipped into bed beside Élodie.

"Are you all right?" she whispered.

"Better than ever."

§§§

Late the next afternoon, Mustafa deposited his passengers at the one hotel in Kashgar he judged suitable for Westerners. A sign described it as "Hotel with Civilization."

"I hope 'civilization' means a hot bath," Élodie said.

"I'll be satisfied if 'civilization' means hot water," Adam countered. They hadn't seen plumbing since they'd left Gilgit, and their last encounter with hot running water had been at the Marriott in Islamabad.

Kashgar's Sunday bazaar is a centuries-old institution. Spread out over an esplanade of twenty acres, there is nothing a traveler can't buy, including household wares, bejeweled daggers, horses, motor scooters, and camels. The sheer variety of goods reminded Adam of a billboard for an enormous American hardware store he'd once seen on a country highway. It advertised: IF WE DON'T HAVE IT, YOU DON'T NEED IT.

As they entered the bazaar, a student rode up on a bicycle, dismounted, and, walking beside them, explained that he was working toward a graduate degree in chemical physics, and wanted to practice his English. In response to Adam's questions about his mathematical training, he pulled several textbooks from the basket on his bike. In one of those cosmic coincidences that seem to violate one's sense of causality, one of his textbooks was the book Rowan had written decades earlier when he was teaching math at Columbia.

In another part of the bazaar they watched a vendor turn a large ball of pasta dough into long strands of spaghetti without benefit of any culinary appliance. The graduate student, who'd appointed himself their guide, explained that pasta was of Uighur origin, and Italians owed their national dish to Marco Polo's expedition.

At a stall that displayed fur hats and coats, Adam was shocked to see several snow-leopard skins. A vanishing species of singular mystique, snow leopards had eluded countless wildlife photographers and spiritual seekers, yet apparently not a local pelt-hunter.

§§§

It was soon apparent that if Élodie were to reach MSF's Paris headquarters by month's end, they'd have to fly to Beijing. The one travel agent in Kashgar assured them that they would not regret skipping the long bus trip across the Taklimakan desert to Urumqi, and when they realized how much train travel lay beyond Beijing, they decided to fly to the Chinese capital.

Once again, Adam pressed the American Express card into service, silently thanking the gods of finance for the gift of plastic, and François for providing a two-by-three-inch piece of it to cover his "tuition."

CHAPTER 41

In Beijing, rather than use public transportation, Adam and Élodie rented bicycles and joined the flow. The image of Beijing that Adam carried with him was the bird's-eye view from high above Tiananmen Square. From their hotel window, the ponderous buses moving among swarms of bikers looked like whales passing through schools of minnows.

The smog was so bad that they ceased to regret having only forty-eight hours there before boarding the train for Russia. For a small extra charge Adam had booked them a private compartment. Not far out of Beijing they passed the Great Wall of China on the route north that led through Mongolia to the Russian border. Before the train could cross into Russia, however, it had to undergo a "wheel transplant." Always fearful of invasion, the Russians had designed railway tracks to be wider than those of neighboring countries, so when they crossed the border, a new undercarriage had to be substituted to accommodate "Russian gauge" tracks.

Not far into Russia, the line from Beijing joined the Trans-Siberian Railway, which stretched almost six thousand miles from Moscow to Vladivostok on the Sea of Japan.

Adam had decided to accompany Élodie westward as far as Irkutsk. After seeing her off to Moscow he would retrace this segment of the trip and continue eastward to the Pacific. He told her that he wanted to go along on this leg so as not to miss the Lake Baikal shoreline, but actually he had another reason: The day of their arrival in Irkutsk would be Élodie's twenty-fifth birthday, and he had a surprise for her.

Ordinarily, there's little to do aboard a train besides gaze out the window, read, and eat. But with a room of their own, and their separation looming, they put their private compartment to good use.

Somewhere in Mongolia, rolling through the Gobi Desert, lying together and making love, Élodie asked, "How long have we known each other?"

"Almost a year."

"You've changed. A lot."

"For better or worse?"

"When we first met I was aware of our age difference. It vanished in Peshawar, perhaps when you caught that Taliban spy."

"Every man wants to rescue a damsel in distress," Adam teased.

"My knight in shining armor."

"Merely a lady's seneschal. It was your show."

"What's next for us, Ad?" As he'd seen her do on numerous occasions, Élodie abruptly changed the direction and mood of the conversation.

"You tell me."

"I don't believe in 'all you need is love'; just being good together—and we are—isn't enough. The timing also has to be right … for both of us, like the last few months. Neither of us knows what lies ahead."

"Will you stay with MSF? Go wherever they send you?"

"I want to spend a few weeks at home before I recommit to the organization. But I think you and I may have found our pattern. We meet when we can, and we're good together. We separate when we must, and we're good on our own."

"Don't be surprised if I come looking for you."

"I hope you will, and when you show up it'll be as if you've just come home from a day's work. But when we're apart we'll make no claims on each other. My relationship with Gérard has not run its course."

Adam felt a surge of jealousy, but sadness quickly replaced it.

Élodie paused in reflection. When she continued, it was not Gérard she spoke of.

"I know that Marisol occupies a place in your heart."

"No, not really …"

"You needn't deny it with me. I saw you together in Paris. It's hard to miss it when you see two young people in love. You've never told me why you broke up with her, and I'm not asking you to, but it's possible that that story isn't finished either. At this point, our life situations are carrying us apart. Let's accept that and use the distance to see what's next. Is that okay with you?"

"I guess that makes sense," Adam said, promising himself that, someday, he would explain to her why he had broken off with Marisol. What had he done, he wondered, to deserve a friend, and yes, a teacher, so true as Élodie?

To seal their new understanding, Adam opened a bottle of vodka he'd picked up at a kiosk at the station in Ulan-Ude. It was Ryabinovka, steeped in rowanberries, a Siberian specialty. Its name reminded him of his father.

After pouring them each a shot, he said, "First, a toast to us: Together or apart, we're good."

"Either way, we're part of each other," Élodie said, downing her vodka.

"Will you join me in a toast to my two fathers? They've both had a hand in this trip."

"Gladly. I know François, and someday I hope to meet Rowan."

"To François Merle, whose support made this journey possible, and to Rowan Ellway whose questing spirit … " Adam faltered. He couldn't finish his thought. Élodie did it for him.

"… lives in you," she said.

On their last day together, less than an hour out of Irkutsk, he pulled a little package out of his backpack and presented it to her.

"Happy Birthday."

"How did you ever remember? Where did you get this?"

"A few thousand miles back. Before you open it, I want you to close your eyes."

Élodie did as he asked.

"Open." Her eyes widened in disbelief. On the little table between them there was a small round cake with a single blue candle in the center. Adam lit it.

"A cake … in the middle of nowhere! With chocolate frosting, no less."

"Now open your present."

Élodie removed the wrapping paper without tearing it, and from the small box she took out a pair of sapphire earrings.

"They're beautiful!" she said, putting them on. "Two drops of pure blue sky."

"I found them in Gilgit; the candle is from Kashgar."

She was not one to display her feelings, but her eyes glistened. He'd never seen her so moved, and the thought that she might cry unsettled him. She composed herself and asked, "How did you come by a cake in Siberia?"

"A small bribe to the dining-car chef."

"Very sweet."

"The frosting is a melted Cadbury bar."

"I didn't mean the frosting."

As the train approached the outskirts of Irkutsk, Adam stuffed his belongings in his backpack. At the station, they got off and huddled together on the platform as new riders climbed aboard for the westward journey. At the last moment, they embraced, and Élodie returned to the compartment that had, for three precious days, been theirs alone. She pressed one hand against the window and Adam reached up and placed his opposite. With a lurch, the train separated their palms. Adam barely had time to wave, and she was gone.

§§§

By mid-afternoon, Adam had boarded the eastbound Trans-Siberian. For the next few hours he sat in a trance, gazing out the window at the spring flowers along the shore of Lake Baikal as he retraced the route he'd travelled that morning with Élodie. Baikal's surface is smaller than Lake Superior's, but because of the lake's great depth—more than a mile in some places—it's the world's largest body of fresh water. From the train, one could easily mistake it for a sea.

For two days, the train made its way through the dense Siberian forests of larch and birch and, at every stop, night or day, Adam got off to stretch his legs. He shared the compartment with three Russians, but the language barrier precluded all but the most elementary communication. Stripped of meaning, the pure sounds of their chatter served as a background murmur that kept him from feeling alone. Between Irkutsk and Vladivostok, he made time to chronicle his adventures in Peshawar, the respite in Gilgit, and the drive over the mountain pass to Kashgar.

For the first time since he'd left Paris he felt that he'd taken in all he could. Once he reached the end of the rail line, all that lay between him and home was the two-day cruise to Tokyo, where he hoped to find Hiroshi, and the long flight to New York. Curled up in his bunk, lulled by the train's rhythmic sounds, he felt unaccountably open to whatever might happen.

He awoke in the middle of the night with an image in his mind of a bent-over old woman he'd seen selling roast potatoes in the Siberian town of Petrovsky Zavod. Clad in a ragged greatcoat, she was pushing a dilapidated baby carriage full of her offerings alongside the train. In response to Adam's gestures, she'd rolled a newspaper into a cone and filled it with golden brown potatoes flecked with garlic, chives, and salt. As she worked, he'd snapped a few photos, and finished by catching her lined face looking straight into the camera as she passed up his portion. At that moment, peering through the viewfinder, a sense of déja vu had come over him and a chill ran up his back. Now, still under the spell of the lucid dream that had awakened him, he saw her anew.

What he'd seen in the weathered face of the babushka was what he'd seen in the starving Somali girl watching over her dead sister—dignity under duress. It's easy to keep one's dignity in the absence of hardship. What's rare are individuals who manifest dignity when they're under pressure and struggling.

The faces of the people he'd photographed—miners in South Africa, Palestinian children, rickshaw men in Banaras, Afghan refugees in Peshawar, Talibs—passed before his mind's eye. Faces in which dignity was uncertain vastly outnumbered those in which it was secure.

In that moment, Adam knew what he'd been looking for—not just on this trip, but all his life. There had been many clues, from childhood on. He wondered why it had taken him so long to see where the signposts on his journey were leading him. His holy grail was dignity.

After breakfast he took out his notebook and tried to describe his epiphany to Élodie. The train was moving, but he was at rest. Somewhere in the Siberian wilderness the words came to him:

> I've been preoccupied with dignity long before
> I had a name for it. Why? Probably because
> I'm not sure of my own, especially now that
> I'm an unemployed, college drop out. But out
> here no one cares about my status or my
> résumé. I feel unseen, but not unworthy.
> There's a place for me and I'm in it. That's the
> crux of dignity.

I know that when I get home my worth will be questioned, my dignity, like everyone else's, will come under attack. Why do we accept this state of affairs? What would it take to secure dignity for all? To make everyone's dignity inviolable, as sacrosanct as life itself?

I intend to find out.

§§§

In Vladivostok Adam boarded the ocean-going vessel, *Baikal*, that would carry him across the Sea of Japan to Tokyo's port city of Yokohama.

As the ship plowed through choppy, frigid waters, he began to think about Marisol. He was ashamed for not having written her, and hoped it wasn't too late. He pulled out paper and pen and, for the second time that day, described his discovery—but then took it one step further:

> George Bernard Shaw challenges us to serve a
> mighty purpose, but says nothing about how

to find one. Rowan says that purpose emerges little by little, from things that catch our eye and lift our spirit. On this trip, I've come to prefer our father's practicality to Shaw's grandiosity.

I don't think I would have found my purpose if we hadn't been forced off the path we were on. But, while away, I've learned that that doesn't mean we must go our own ways. Please forgive my absence and my silence.

Your loving brother,
Adam

CHAPTER 42

Adam reached Hiroshi at the phone number he'd kept in his address book since their days in Berkeley, and they met a few hours later in Hiroshi's office at Tokyo University. On the door was a polished brass plate inscribed "Dr. Hiroshi Shinohara." From a crystal vase on his desk a tall slender lily reached for the last rays of morning sun that streamed through a window.

"You got your Ph.D. I see," Adam nodded toward the brass plate with a wide smile. "Congratulations."

"The work we did in Berkeley was part of it. I have a copy of my dissertation for you."

Hiroshi showed him to the room he'd reserved for him in lodgings the University maintained for visiting scholars. "I hope you can stay long enough to renew our collaboration," Hiroshi said.

"My math has gotten a little rusty, but sure!"

"Tomorrow. Today, I'll show you the city. You've come a few weeks late for the cherry blossoms; still, there are other flowers, less celebrated but no less enchanting."

The first thing Adam did was take his film to a photo shop. Later, in a restaurant over a flask of hot sake, he told Hiroshi about his quest, using the prints to illustrate what he'd encountered.

His travelogue was interrupted by the arrival of a steamed fish and a second flask of sake. Hiroshi ceremoniously extracted the fish's upward-facing eyeball and presented it to Adam on the tips of his chopsticks. Screwing up his courage, Adam swallowed it with the eerie expectation that he would now come under surveillance from within.

When the table had been cleared, Adam, without speaking a word, laid out two rows of photos, ten to a row. One row consisted of faces manifesting dignity; the other of faces that seemed to lack it. He set them before Hiroshi without comment.

Hiroshi's face mirrored what he was seeing; once or twice he seemed to flinch.

"I see," he said at last.

"What do you see?"

"I see man as he can be and man as he is—included and excluded. You must show your photographs to others."

That night in bed, Adam found himself thinking about the moniliths on Easter Island. The effect of dozens of faces, side-by-side, was to multiply their mysterious power many times over. Similar to the effect of the Somali photos at Princeton, but with the added impact of repetition, as in the silk screens of Andy Warhol, and aurally, in the musical compositions of Philip Glass.

He imagined an exhibit juxtaposing faces of dignity with faces of indignity. Knowing he wouldn't be able to sleep, he turned on the light to write in his journal. An hour later, his exhilaration had subsided, and he turned off the light. Alone in the dark, questions crept in. Nighttime was a time of doubt for him, but he knew from experience that dawn often renewed his faith.

He woke the next morning with a fresh idea: Just let people react. Don't try to persuade them. Proselytizing doesn't work. It was enough to show people the images—as he had done with Hiroshi—stand back, and let them react as they would. Emerson was right: The proper goal was provocation, not instruction. People could like or dislike the photos; they could like or dislike him. Either way, they would be face to face with dignity, and the anguish of its absence.

§§§

After a week with Hiroshi, Adam took a nonstop flight to New York. On the plane, shuffling through all his photographs, he realized that Hiroshi had seen something in them that he himself had missed. Hiroshi had detected subtle signs of indomitability in the faces of indignity, and hints of vulnerability in the faces of dignity. This complicated the picture, but by allowing for change, it provided hope that dignity might eventually take root even where it was now lacking.

Somewhere on the great circle route high over the Bering Sea, the plane crossed the International Date Line, and Wednesday became Tuesday.

§§§

His mother and Rowan were in the apartment to welcome him home. Adam sat with them for as long as he could keep his eyes open; then, with the promise of a full report the next day, he headed for the guest room. Before he got into bed, he snipped off the baobab bracelet Ousmane had given him. The talisman had seen him through his quest.

The next day, Adam showed his parents his photos. Rowan asked him if he'd thought of writing about his journey, but before he could answer, Easter raised the question of finishing college.

Adam had seen it coming, and asked her for time to think about it. Rowan, ever the peacemaker, suggested that for certain colleges that required a senior thesis, Adam could probably submit an illustrated account of his around-the-world trip for credit toward a degree.

Adam thought about the five notebooks that lay at the bottom of his backpack, and thanked Rowan for his suggestion. His mother offered to come up with a list of colleges that gave credit for experiential learning, and he saw a way to make her happy without submitting to the lockstep of graduation requirements.

With confrontation avoided, the conversation moved on to Marisol. Rowan and Easter had gone to the ballet whenever she danced a new role, they told Adam, and evidently she was on her way to the stardom that Sasha had foreseen.

"Does she know I'm back?"

"I called her after you'd gone to bed," Rowan said. "She's dying to see you."

§§§

The next day, Adam was up before sunrise, his body clock in some foreign time zone. He let himself out and took a long walk in Riverside Park. He chanced upon a feral cat, looking cold, damp, and hungry, but it wouldn't let him get near it. He settled for taking a photo from twenty feet off, wondering if someday, dignity might be extended to animals.

Back at the apartment, but too restless to read or write, in midafternoon he joined Rowan for a few laps around the reservoir in Central Park. He was so out of shape from months of traveling he had to struggle to keep up with his father.

When they got back, dripping sweat, there was a message from Marisol on the answering machine. In a voice higher and more excited than either of them had ever heard it, she said,

"Dad, Adam, I'm on tonight. *Giselle*. The lead sprained her knee. I've been rehearsing all day. There'll be four comps at Will Call. Mom's on her way down from Boston. See you all after the show. Welcome back, Ad!"

"Injuries are a dancer's worst enemy but an understudy's best friend," Rowan noted as he, Easter, and Adam left for the show. Shortly after they took their seats on the left orchestra, Rowan spotted Sara on the other side. He went over to greet her, and then returned to his seat between Easter and Adam.

The conductor struck up the overture, and the curtain rose above a village on the Rhine. Adam immediately recognized Prince Albrecht as the same Sasha from Leningrad who, in real life, had often come on to his sister.

In the ballet, the peasant girl Giselle dies, but, in the name of love, she comes back as a ghost to save the two-timing prince from an evil queen. As Marisol danced, Adam imagined that she was forgiving him for not standing up for their love when it had collided with a taboo. She'd been ready to fight for what they had, but he'd been unwilling to go against convention. By the time the curtain fell, he understood what Lahiri had meant when he'd said his love for his wife "reached beyond the grave."

Audiences adore an understudy who exceeds expectations. Not only does it make up for the disappointment of having a known performer replaced by a novice, but there's also the excitement of being present at the birth of a star. The audience, on their feet, summoned Marisol for one curtain call after another. It was a coronation.

After she changed, Marisol, pale and exhausted, clung to Adam. Rowan, Easter, and Sara were waiting at the stage door, and greeted her with hugs and flowers. Rowan had thought they might walk to the Russian Tea Room, but when he saw Marisol, he hailed a taxi.

"Actually, Dad, I'm not feeling up to supper tonight," Marisol said. "I think I'd better go home and lie down."

"Okay, Marisol," Rowan said. "We're all so proud of you. We'll celebrate Sunday. See your sister safely home, Adam."

"Sorry to be a party-pooper. Thank you for the lilies, Easter. Mom, thanks for taking me to all those ballet classes way back when."

"You did the work," Sara said, giving her daughter a hug and patting her on the back. "Tonight, you gave me something I thought I'd lost forever."

"Dad, if you hadn't taken me to Moscow this couldn't have happened. And Ad, thank you for coming home just in time."

As their taxi left Lincoln Center, brother and sister caught a glimpse of the fountain on the plaza where they'd innocently fallen in love eighteen months before.

"Let's meet there tomorrow noon," Adam said. "I'll take you to lunch after company class."

"That's where my life changed. I'm sorry I've had such a hard time letting go."

"I envy your bravery. You're true to yourself. And you were true to me."

Adam walked her to her door, and kissed her on both cheeks.

"Till tomorrow," Marisol said.

"I'll be waiting."

§§§

By eleven-thirty Adam was at Lincoln Center keeping an eye out for Marisol. A few intrepid pigeons had inched toward his feet, and after studying them for a while he took out his camera to get some close-ups.

Sirens were blaring, but they were so common in New York that he didn't look up until he saw an ambulance stop in front of the plaza. Moments later, paramedics were wheeling a gurney past the fountain.

Something made him stand up, and he found himself following the medics. A guard stopped him at the door to the building where company class was held, and he had to stand on his toes to see inside. The paramedics were strapping a dancer to the gurney. Sunlight dancing off her hair told him it was Marisol.

As they lifted the gurney into the ambulance, he demanded to know where they were taking his sister. One of the medics yelled out "Cornell Med Center," and the ambulance sped away, siren blaring. Adam ran to a phone booth and called Rowan. While he yelled into the receiver, he used his free hand to flag a cab. Forty-five minutes later, he was waiting in Cornell's emergency room when Rowan ran up.

Eventually, a doctor emerged and called out Adam's name. Drawing the two men aside he told them that steps were being taken to stabilize Ms. Ellway's condition, and that evidently she was suffering from severe dehydration and fatigue, probably exacerbated by flu.

Adam guessed that Marisol had gone straight to bed without eating, and then skipped breakfast to make company class. She'd been caught with dangerously low blood sugar, and collapsed.

§§§

Adam declined Rowan's invitation to join him for lunch; he wanted to be alone, and after a change of clothes, left for Central Park.

After he'd circled the reservoir twice he stopped, sat down, and took off his shoes and socks. An angry blister had formed on one heel; he felt he deserved the pain. Marisol had borne the brunt of their separation, alone, while he had traveled the globe. What if she had died? The idea of it made him vow to do whatever it took to help her back to health. Let her be okay, he bargained with fate, and he'd see to it that she got on her feet, and onto the world stage.

In the last year, he'd learned something about love, from his mother and both his fathers. He'd learned from Élodie, from Ben and Hiroshi, and from Ousmane, Lahiri, and Malika. Most of all, he'd learned about love from Marisol herself.

He couldn't follow his heart, but it showed him where he must go. In the nameless faces he'd captured on film, he'd found something he wanted to show the world.

Barefoot and sore, he limped back to Rowan's apartment. Looking south, he could see the silhouette of the World Trade Center. He imagined gigantic images hanging on the sides of the twin towers: faces of dignity on one tower, faces of indignity on the other. Show people the difference, he thought, and let them choose.

PART 2

MARISOL

O body swayed to music, O brightening glance,
How can we know the dancer from the dance?
  – William Butler Yeats, *Among School Children*

Love's mysteries in souls do grow,
But yet the body is his book.
  – *John Donne, The Ecstasy*

Le coeur a ses raisons que la raison ne connait point.
  – Blaise Pascal, *Pensées 277*

CHAPTER 43

Marisol opened her eyes. A nurse was taking her vital signs. Through a tangle of tubes she saw Rowan looking down at her. She tried to raise her head, but couldn't.

"What happened?" she asked in a whisper.

"You fainted in company class. They say you'll be fine."

"In due time," the nurse interjected. "You were unconscious when they brought you in."

"How long have I been here?"

"Since noon," Rowan said. "It's Thursday evening."

"I'm dancing Saturday."

"No chance," the nurse said. To Marisol's attempt to protest she added, "None whatsoever, young lady. You won't be dancing for a while."

"Why not?"

"Because your body shut down and needs time to recover."

Marisol lay there taking in this news; looking up at Rowan's face, she saw anxiety and tender concern.

"Adam was here this morning," he said.

"He saw me like this?"

"No, they wouldn't let us in. He followed the ambulance that brought you here."

"What did he say about Giselle?"

"We all loved it, Marisol. Adam was proud of you."

"We were supposed to have lunch."

§§§

She drifted in and out as the nurse took her blood pressure and removed the intravenous drip. Then the poking and shuffling had stopped and she went back to sleep.

Someone had taken her hand. She opened her eyes and saw Adam's face where Rowan's had been, but the sun was streaming through the window. She made an effort to smile, to push her hair back.

"Hello, Marisol," he said softly.

"How long have you been there?"

"A little while."

"I must look awful."

"You look beautiful to me."

"I'm sorry I missed you at the fountain."

"I saw the paramedics wheel you out."

"Oh, God."

"I was pretty worried." The nurse came in and told him his time was up.

"Come back tomorrow, okay? Make them let me out of here."

"One step at a time," the nurse interjected. "Before then, you have to walk, and before that you'll have to stand."

Adam went to the door. "I'll see you tomorrow. Love you."

§§§

Marisol's parents came bearing gifts. Rowan brought a potted hydrangea, spilling over with strawberry-blonde blossoms. Just like her dad to try to match her hair color, she thought. How sentimental. Sara brought a tidy box of artisanal chocolates, and the Gumby doll that Marisol had played with as a child. Gumby elicited a big smile from Rowan and, for a moment, Marisol felt as if she were seeing her parents when they were young and in love. She persuaded the nurse to let them stay beyond the fifteen-minutes allowed by the doctor, but when they did leave after a half-hour, she immediately fell asleep. She woke Saturday morning ready to go home—until she ventured into the hall. Yes, it would take a while to get her dancing legs under her.

A nutritionist, after a probing interview, gave Marisol a stern lecture: Inadequate glycogen reserves had likely been the cause of her collapse. Six small nutritious meals a day and eight hours sleep a night was the prescription. Plus, whatever she could do to reduce the stress in her personal and professional life.

"Follow the nutritionist's rules and you won't be back," the doctor affirmed. "You're a healthy young woman, so eat better, sleep more, and worry less. That should do it."

At noon, two dancers stopped by. One was her childhood friend Ellie Liang Stewart, now in the corps at the New York City Ballet. The other was Sasha. Though he still hit on her every chance he got, Marisol didn't hold it against him. He generously shared his knowledge with his partners, and never let his amorous intentions affect his professionalism on stage.

Knowing that Sasha would carry word of her condition back to the company, Marisol took pains to assure him that there was nothing wrong with her.

Nearing the end of a long and illustrious career, Sasha had seen everything. He'd known ballerinas who had never recovered from a setback like the one Marisol had suffered, and others who'd learned from the wake-up call and gone on to realize their full potential.

To Marisol's protestations that it was just a fainting spell due to dehydration, he responded bluntly.

"Shut up, girl, and listen to me. You get just this one chance. Either you take care of yourself from now on or you're finished. You know I think you're good. But you waste yourself if you don't listen to your body. Your body is your instrument and you must treat it like a Stradivarius."

"I thought I was doing that."

"You weren't. If you were taking proper care of yourself you would not have fallen down."

"Okay," Marisol said meekly.

"The difference between good dancers and great dancers is that great ones have a life, and they see dance as an expression of life."

"Don't you think I have a life?"

"Not yet. To be your best, you must build a life apart from dance. Only those who do can make it to the top. That's what you want, am I right?" Marisol met Sasha's gaze, and felt he was peering into her soul.

"You're right."

"Then remember: Dance is what we do, not who we are."

§§§

"Sasha was here this morning," Marisol reported to Adam as he took a seat beside her. "He and Ellie came together, but Sasha did all the talking."

"What did he want?" He had not forgotten Sasha, nor his reputation.

"He gave me a piece of his mind."

"What?"

"He told me to get a life."

Adam didn't respond.

"I tried to make dance my life when … " Marisol began.

She turned her face away and tried not to cry. She felt small and stupid lying in that bed. But it was true. Her life was off-balance. She had let her career consume her. Ballet was like a drug she had used to numb and distract herself.

"When what?"

"When we found out. When you left."

"Oh."

"Nothing has changed for me. I'd give up dance in a heartbeat to be with you."

"You don't mean that, Marisol. That'd be a waste of your talent."

She locked eyes with him. "It's how it is."

"Well, I won't let you. I can't let you. I can't let myself."

"Why not? Love can't be wrong, can it?"

"I can't devote my life to fighting taboos. The interracial taboo may be dying but the incest taboo is as strong as ever. We have better things to do than devote ourselves to a hopeless cause."

"Why can't you just love me? No one needs to know. We could go away, live abroad."

"No, Marisol."

"Don't you feel anything? Didn't you think about us at all on your damn trip? You didn't even answer my letters!"

"I'm sorry, Marisol, I had to try to put it behind me, but ..."

"But what?"

"Then this happened."

"What do you mean?"

"I almost lost you. And I don't think I could go on without ..." Looking at the floor, he continued, "without you ... without my other half."

Marisol reached for his hand and held it tight.

"I can't not love you," Adam said. "I don't know what that means, but I promised myself I'd do whatever it takes to get you dancing again. When are they letting you out?"

"Tomorrow."

"Okay, I'll pick you up and take you to Rowan's. You've got to make some changes. I'm staying there too, and I can help you make them."

Getting up to leave, Adam said, "Call me when you're ready and I'll be here in a flash."

"Adam, can you do me a favor? Can you find out who's dancing Giselle tonight? I was supposed to."

"Whoever she is, she'll be just a placeholder. You own the role now."

"You don't know nothin'. Until I dance again, I'm a nobody."

"Well, then be a nobody. One thing I learned on my trip was that only nobodies can change."

CHAPTER 44

With her doctors' approval, Marisol had resumed taking the barre a week after leaving the hospital, and a week after that she was back on her regular schedule. "No big deal" was the message she wanted to communicate, especially to the artistic director and ballet masters who cast ballets.

But there were differences between her old and new life that Marisol kept to herself. She was living with her family now, and Adam was doing the shopping and cooking, and handling other mundane matters to help her recover, and to support her professional life.

He'd learned that toward the end of a full-length ballet a lead dancer is like a marathoner nearing the end of a twenty-six-mile course—running on empty—yet she's expected to leap and pirouette *and* make it all look effortless. He did some research and fueled her with the combination of carbs, protein, fat, vitamins, and minerals she needed if she was to reclaim her stature in the company.

Once she got used to Adam's support, Marisol wondered how she'd ever managed without it. She came to understand that taking responsibility for her well-being was his way of expressing his love. Knowing that was as important to her as the meals he prepared to restore her body.

Even more importantly, shortly after she'd moved in with Rowan and Adam, Adam's commitment to her recovery had mysteriously enabled her to accept the impossibility of their living as a couple. She was surprised to find herself becoming accustomed to the idea of Adam as her brother, and in accepting the fraternal tie, they both regained the easy familiarity they'd enjoyed before they'd learned they were siblings.

In July, the company was on break for two weeks, and she and Adam used the time to read and hang out. On a walk, they stopped by her unused apartment near Lincoln Center and bumped into

Ricardo, the friendly superintendent of her building, who was giving a fresh coat of paint to an apartment that had recently been vacated. After they left, Adam said it was probably time to give Rowan back his privacy. They both embraced the idea of becoming neighbors, and Adam soon settled in there.

§§§

They were having lunch in Adam's kitchen when he told Marisol that he'd met with the dean of Columbia College, then asked Columbia to accept him as a transfer student with three years credit, so he could graduate in the spring.

"I thought you only finished two years at Princeton."

"That's true, but the math research I did with Hiroshi Shinohara goes a long way toward meeting the requirements for a math major. We've already published a paper, and we have another in the works. And during my trip, I gathered materials I can use for a senior thesis in photojournalism. That'll give me some more units toward the undergraduate degree.

"When I showed the dean my portfolio he offered to talk to the journalism school about my taking some graduate courses. I begin in September and graduate next May."

"Then what?"

"Photojournalism is a ticket to the world. I've had a first look, and I want to go back. I think people need to see what's out there."

"That's great, Adam! You're so lucky, studying just what you want."

"There was one condition. Just before he signed off on the deal he asked if I'd play basketball for Columbia. I could tell that if I said yes he'd agree to everything. Anyway, basketball will keep me in shape this winter."

"Wouldn't it be sweet to beat Princeton?" Marisol said. She knew he was still mad about his abrupt departure.

"Sweet is the right word," Adam said, savoring the prospect. "I don't expect you to come to my games, but you might want to be there when Princeton comes to town."

Until she was cast in a principal role again, Marisol continued to be afraid that her fainting spell would be held against her. The director had kept her waiting for months, and when he finally let her dance the lead in a contemporary pas de deux, it was only for a matinee.

Whether it was a reward for her debut success or to bolster her confidence, the director had cast her opposite Sasha again. He was every ballerina's choice as the most dependable danseur in the company. Dancing opposite him made better dancers of whomever he shared the stage with—men and women alike. He rarely made a mistake himself, and his ability to improvise enabled him to cover the inevitable mistakes of others. One more thing; Sasha's name in the program guaranteed a full house, despite the afternoon curtain.

She phoned Adam with the news, and was disappointed when he said he'd be in Los Angeles that weekend to deliver a paper with Hiroshi at the annual meeting of the American Mathematical Society.

Thinking it over later, however, she saw an up side to his absence. When he was in the audience she'd sometimes found herself dancing for him. She recalled her first *Giselle*, and admitted to herself that having him there had contributed to her stress. What she needed now was a routine performance. She'd tell Adam all about it when he got back from the West Coast.

§§§

Marisol saw Adam from her window and was waiting for him when he stepped off the elevator. They were hugging again now. The awkward time when he had kept her at arm's length was over. She jumped into his arms and he momentarily lifted her off her feet.

"It must have gone well," he said. "You're buoyant."

"I'm still floating. How was your trip?"

"Routine."

"Ha! That's what I was trying for. I made a point of taking company class today to prove to everyone that I'm 100 percent again."

"Did the audience like you?"

"I think so. I missed a few steps, though no one noticed except Sasha. Dad was there with Easter *and* my mom. This time they all sat together."

"What was Sasha's verdict?"

"He wants to work with me on my jumps on Monday. Unless they're perfectly timed, they can put a strain on a partner."

"Did he say anything positive?"

"That he offered to work with me is the real message. I couldn't be happier."

"I hope that's all he wants."

"If I see him outside the studio it will only be to practice my Russian. I thought you wanted me to have a normal social life."

"Not with that guy. I know he's a great dancer but I don't think he'd make a good boyfriend."

"Would anyone?"

"There aren't many men worthy of you," Adam said.

CHAPTER 45

Easter had worked for the Department of Education in Washington since she'd left the Jefferson presidency. She spent weekdays in Washington, and alternate weekends at Rowan's in New York. Every other weekend, he traveled to Washington on Friday afternoons and returned on Monday mornings to New York, where he'd reclaim the solitude he needed to write. Mindful that their own relationship had developed during Rowan's commuting marriage with Sara, they never skipped their weekend rendezvouses. They described their arrangement as "living apart together," and as far as Adam and Marisol could tell, it suited them perfectly.

On the evening of the day Adam received his Bachelor of Arts degree from Columbia University, Easter and Rowan invited him and Marisol for dinner at Rowan's.

Easter was relieved that Adam had finished his degree on schedule, and Rowan thought the degree he'd assembled suited him better than a traditional BA.

"No doubt about it," Adam said. "I think everyone's education should include at least a year of travel."

"Well, take this along on your next trip," Rowan said, handing him a gift-wrapped box.

Adam weighed it in his hands.

From the look and feel of the package, he'd guessed its contents: a telephoto lens. Easter said, "Now you can take photos from a safe distance."

"You're right, with this I can be a hundred feet away and get a close-up."

"He's been talking about Rwanda," Marisol said, then looked at Adam. "Wouldn't that be awfully risky?"

Ignoring her question, Adam asked his mother if she thought President Clinton knew what was going on there.

"I'm sure State is briefing him. Somalia has made him hyper-cautious."

"Black Hawk down?" Adam said.

"Seventeen Americans died," Easter reminded him.

"But intervening saved a half-million Somalis. President Bush deserves credit for that."

"We should have left when the famine eased," Rowan said.

"My friend at Doctors Without Borders—remember I went to Mogadishu with her a few years ago?—she's in Rwanda now and says the world has no idea what's going on. She wants me to come and help get the word out ... like Baidoa."

"Those photos got you kicked out of Princeton," Easter said.

"There's no one to kick me out this time."

"I'm proud of what you did at Princeton, Adam, but genocide by famine is one thing, genocide by machete is another. Marisol is right: Rwanda is much more dangerous now than Somalia was then."

When they had finished dinner, Easter brought in a sweet-potato pie; she smiled fondly at Rowan when she gave him a slice.

When everyone had been served, Marisol said, "I have a bit of news too."

They all looked at her.

"It's good news, not bad. I've been promoted to principal, and ..."

"And what?" Adam drew her out.

"And they've asked me to learn the Odette/Odile part in *Swan Lake*."

"Bravo! Does your mother know?" asked Rowan.

"I phoned her just before coming over. It'll be in the *Times* tomorrow."

Adam and Marisol slapped a high five and whooped.

"It's due to him, you know," she said. "Adam put a proper foundation under me."

"I just pick up a few more groceries and double the recipe. No big deal."

"Just everything," said Marisol, her eyes welling with tears. "Without you, it couldn't have happened."

Presently, they moved to the living room where Rowan turned on CNN. Horrendous images of bloated bodies in Lake Victoria changed the course of the conversation. The correspondent was saying that the dead were Tutsis massacred by Hutus. Their bodies had floated down the Kagera River separating Rwanda and Tanzania.

Adam was transfixed. Marisol turned away. Easter insisted that Rowan turn it off.

"It's tribal," Rowan explained. "Hutu militias versus the Tutsis and moderate Hutus. Hundreds of thousands have been slaughtered already."

"Why?" Marisol asked.

Rowan took the floor. "There's always an incident that sets things off. In this case, it was the assassination of the Hutu president. The Hutus claim that the Tutsis were planning to seize power and enslave them, so they launched a preemptive genocide.

"Humiliation, remembered and imagined, fuels most conflict," Rowan continued. "It goes on until someone breaks the cycle. That's what's so extraordinary about Desmond Tutu and Nelson Mandela. Instead of seeking vengeance for the indignities of apartheid, they're proposing to break that cycle even though they could choose to get even."

"I take it there's no Mandela in Rwanda," Adam said.

"Too late for that, nor is there any world leader willing to intervene."

"Clinton's keeping quiet," Easter put in.

"He's learned the wrong lesson from Somalia," Rowan said.

"Guys, I really want to go," Adam said. "I have to see it for myself. Dr. Fleury thinks photos will help, and I know people in the journalism school who'll get them published."

"Oh, Adam, it's too dangerous," said his mother.

"This lens will keep me out of harm's way. Thanks, Mom. And thanks, Rowan. Do you mind if I turn up the sound?"

"I can't stand to watch," Easter said. "Come on, Marisol, help me load the dishwasher."

Adam and Rowan remained in the living room, mesmerized by the horror.

§§§

They were silent while they waited for the elevator. After they'd ridden down to the lobby and were on the sidewalk, Adam asked "What's wrong?"

"You're not really planning to go to Rwanda, are you?"

"Actually, I am."

"Why?"

"Same reason I went to Somalia."

"To see Melody?"

"To get images that open people's minds. You're not jealous of *Élodie* are you?"

"Élodie, Melody. Every time you go abroad, you hook up with her."

"Look, Marisol, this is silly ... for several reasons. First, you and I are not a couple."

"But I have feelings."

"So do I," Adam said. "I found a safe place for them and I want to keep them there—locked away."

"So you're content with feeding me."

"My supporting you while you deal with being a ... you know, a star, is working for us."

"But I hate seeing you with another woman."

"Élodie is in Africa."

"You know what I mean. What is she to you, anyway?"

"She's older. She doesn't attach herself to me, or to anyone. She's a free spirit. When we're together, we're together, and when we're apart, we're apart."

"Out of sight, out of mind?"

"Not exactly, but when we're apart, I don't miss her. I'm sure it's the same with her. We're fond friends but we make no claims on each other. We have no plans. We'll never live together."

"I don't understand how a woman can be satisfied with that."

"I am."

"What if she asked you to stay with her?"

"She wouldn't ask that of me. I wouldn't ask it of her. If either of us did, it would be the end of the relationship. We work together professionally, then we go our separate ways."

"Sounds like a business arrangement."

"Work comes first, that's true. I wouldn't go somewhere *just* to be with Élodie."

"Couldn't she take the photos?"

"She's a doctor, not a photographer."

"Isn't there enough TV coverage?"

"TV doesn't capture images that can work in newspapers. Plus, Doctors Without Borders needs photos to raise money."

"Well, then just don't stay with her, that's all."

"You don't expect me to be celibate for the rest of my life, do you?"

"Not for the rest of your life. Just for now."

"You're the one in my heart, Marisol. Not Élodie, not anyone else."

"Hurry back," she said, taking Adam's hand. "I still need you."

§§§

"Adam!" Marisol cried, recognizing his voice over the transatlantic line. She hadn't heard from him in three weeks. "Where are you?"

"London." He had waited till Marisol's usual wake-up time, an hour before company class, to call. "Did you make yourself some oatmeal?"

"Who cares about oatmeal? You just got out of a war zone! Are you okay?"

"Yes, I'm fine. Rwanda's a hell-hole but I got what I came for. I've just sent François my best shots. He knows people at *Le*

Monde, Deutsche Zeitungen, and *Liberazione.* I've got an appointment with an editor at *The Independent* in a half-hour."

"That's good, but when are you coming home?"

"I get in tomorrow night. Tonight I'm going up to Oxford to have dinner with Ben."

"Say hi for me." She debated whether to ask about Élodie and decided against it. She had no room to be Marisol, let alone Adam's jealous non-girlfriend. She couldn't risk losing her focus on what she had to do that day, and every day for the next two weeks. She had to transform herself into Odette and Odile.

Reading her mind, Adam asked, "How are rehearsals going?"

"It's the part of a lifetime. Good swan, bad swan. Good girl, bad girl. I'm both, and I'm learning to project them on stage. In addition to the usual ballet police, I've got a drama coach."

"I feel guilty for not being there. Please pick up an egg bagel on your way to class."

"I promise."

"Do you have time to do one thing before you go out?"

"What?"

"Call my mom and ask her if she got through to the White House. I called her from Rwanda. Some of the experts think that a simple show of force by the UN peacekeepers could stop the genocide. In any case, it's irresponsible of us to stand by and do nothing. Easter promised to try to reach someone near the president. Would you follow up with her before you go out?"

"Sure. It's the least I can do. Ballet seems frivolous by comparison."

"No way. I'll need *Swan Lake* to recover from Rwanda. Now promise me that you'll get enough sleep and eat right."

"I promise," Marisol said, and this time she meant it. That Adam cared made her care. No one else did, except maybe Sasha, and he was not her Prince Siegfried. She thought of Michael, the new danseur she'd been paired with, a real "prima don"—vain, selfish, narcissistic, one of those people who don't converse; they just wait for their chance to talk. That's how it was dancing with

Michael. The moment he ceased to be the center of attention, he lost interest.

None of the girls were truly rooting for her either; that she got the role meant they did *not*. Within a half-dozen years, most of the corps, men and women alike, would be sucked dry and unceremoniously discarded. Only a few would make it to soloist, even fewer to principal. And while the stars got the spotlight, dozens of others served in anonymity in the corps. Marisol had been one of them until Sasha had intervened with the all-powerful director. But not to complain—in this chancy business, you had to take what came your way and not look back.

§§§

Ben met Adam's train from London and they walked to his rooms at Christ Church College. Ben had let his curly black hair grow longer, and, as always, he was in superb shape. The two tall Americans drew looks as they made their way across town.

"*Brideshead Revisited*?" Adam asked as they entered the college courtyard.

"You may call me Lord Sebastian."

"I don't see the teddy bear."

"Lost it. No plover eggs or scouts either, but the place still reeks of tradition."

"Is it worth two years of your life?"

"I'll let you know in a decade. Sometimes I feel like this is a detour, but there's enough basketball here to keep me in shape. Plus, living outside the United States is an eye-opener. You know that."

"My guess is that in ten years you'll look back on this as the best time of your life. What are you going to do after?"

"Play for the 76ers."

"You're going pro?"

"For the money. Bill Bradley's the model. The money and name recognition are a ticket to politics. That's why I signed with Philadelphia."

"Senator Steinsaltz of the great state of Pennsylvania?"

"That's the plan."

"Well, then, you'd better either score a lot of points or make a lot of money."

"I plan to do both, but it won't be like Princeton because I won't have you. You got us to play *together*, Ad. You led by example. In the NBA there are a lot of glory hogs."

"I'm done with basketball, Ben, but hey, I haven't told you—did you hear about Columbia versus Princeton?"

"What happened?"

"Probably my best game ever: 42 points, 12 assists, 15 rebounds. We beat 'em 92 to 88. The Lions hadn't beaten the Tigers for decades."

"A triple double. Sweet revenge."

"Well, it's over now, basketball and college. I finished up at Columbia."

"What next?"

"I'm going to look for images that will move people, like the ones we put up at Princeton."

"You called that beginner's luck, Ad, but it won't surprise me if your Rwanda photos are just as influential."

"It's *The Killing Fields* all over again. *The Independent* plans to publish a few photos tomorrow, and I'm going to try the American papers when I get back. I'm hoping they'll get President Clinton off his ass."

"I doubt the British will get involved," Ben said.

"Some Rwandans are saying that a force of just 500 troops would put the brakes on the slaughter—just by showing up! Like the bully who backs down when his bluff is called."

"Sounds worth a try. If the victims were white, we'd have intervened already."

"I'm glad you said that, not me. Rwanda is not going to be something Clinton's proud of."

"If you really want to change things, you can't avoid politics. Images show people the problem, but what's needed is action. Somalia and Rwanda can't wait for public support. Where have all the leaders gone?"

"I'll leave that to you, Ben. I see my role as alerting people to the problems. Leaders can't get much ahead of public opinion and survive the next election."

The two old friends talked into the evening, then went out to a pub where the talk turned to women.

"Marisol says 'Hi'," Adam said.

"Are you over her?"

"She's my sister."

"Same question." Ben knew him too well. He added, "She's probably the most beautiful girl in the world."

"It was more than her beauty. Maybe someday science will explain it. My theory is that the fact that she and I share half our genes intensified the connection."

"So, have you gotten over it? I'm still waiting for your answer."

"I've made my peace with it … by taking care of her after her collapse."

"Are either of you dating?"

"I've just been with Élodie in Kigali."

"Élodie doesn't count."

Adam changed the subject. "Marisol tells me that Ellie Liang is waiting for you."

"I told her not to."

"So she's not your girlfriend anymore?"

"Well, she is, kind of. I am looking forward to seeing her, but I can't live like a monk. I'm a sucker for these English beauties, and Oxford's crawling with them. I know those girls at the corner table. Want to meet them?"

"Nope. I've got an early flight tomorrow."

CHAPTER 46

Toward the end of 1995, with his two-year stint as a Rhodes Scholar at Oxford behind him, Ben returned to America. Ellie Liang picked him up at JFK, and they took up as if he had never been gone. Whenever the schedules of the New York City Ballet and the Philadelphia 76ers permitted, they were together.

Ellie and Ben are lucky to see each other twice a month, Marisol thought, as she compared her own life to her friend's. She saw Adam every day, but that was when he wasn't off in some exotic place on a shoot.

The coming Sunday evening would be an occasion. The 76ers were playing the Knicks at Madison Square Garden, and Ellie had comps for herself, Marisol, and Adam, who'd be back from London by then.

When the three of them took their seats behind the Philadelphia bench, Ben spotted them from the floor and trotted over. Ellie pulled the green elastic band from her ponytail and gave it to Ben, who slipped it on his left wrist. The first time he'd worn it in a game, his triple double had led Philly to victory, so wearing her colors when she was at a game had become a ritual.

"Ben's superstitious," Adam said to Marisol. "In college, he played the same song on his Walkman before every game."

"In college, he had you feeding him the ball," Marisol said. "It was your passing, not his music, that made him a star."

"A part of me wishes I was still out there. It's a lot more fun to play than to watch."

"You've got better things to do," Marisol whispered.

"I hope so, but, I couldn't play at this level even if I tried."

"One athlete per family is enough," she said, poking him playfully. "And you're it."

§§§

They were all outside the dressing room when Ben emerged, bearing the sheepish grin of defeat, and returned Ellie's green token with an apologetic bow.

"Worked like a charm. We only lost by nine; it could have been twice that."

"That looked like punishment," Adam said. "I can't believe you're still standing."

"The game is getting more physical every year." Once up at street level, they strolled to a restaurant where Ellie had made reservations. As they sat down, Ben continued, "I'm going to quit before I'm a cripple. A walker or a cane wouldn't look good in politics."

"When do you see yourself running for office?" Adam asked.

"Oh, that's a ways off; early in the next century, if there's an opening. But I'm not going to play till then. Three or four years max, then I'll buy into a computer start-up. That's where fortunes are made these days. You should go in with me, Adam."

"I'm not a money guy. François wants to groom me to take over his business, but I love what I'm doing."

The waiter interrupted to take their orders. When he left, Marisol said, "Tell them about our idea, Ad."

"You've probably heard that the siege of Sarajevo has finally been relieved."

"Yes, I know."

"During the siege, Susan Sontag staged *Waiting for Godot* there. So now, Marisol and I want to celebrate the city's survival by taking some dancers there to perform."

"I'd like to form a small troupe, half from New York City Ballet and half from ABT, and go for about a week," Marisol said. "We could perform by night and hold classes for kids during the day. What do you think, Ellie?"

"Is it really safe?"

"A ceasefire has been in effect since October," Adam replied. "Peace accords are being signed next week in Paris. I have contacts in Sarajevo at Doctors Without Borders who can advise us on safety and logistics."

"You'll need funding," Ben said.

"Will you help us? Aren't there a few Croatians in the NBA? They sided with the Bosnians, and might want to celebrate the end of the siege."

"Possibly, but don't forget Jews like me who have no stomach for genocide, period. I'll see what I can do."

"I've already talked to my friends at ABT," Marisol said and, turning to Ellie, asked, "Can you think of anyone at City Ballet who'd be game?"

"Count me in. I'll ask around tomorrow."

When the waiter brought their entrées, Adam ordered a bottle of champagne and requested four glasses.

"This is not an occasion for jubilation," he said as he poured the champagne, "just a sober toast to the power of art to open eyes and heal wounds."

§§§

Élodie met the troupe at the Sarajevo airport. Marisol had recruited one man and one woman from ABT, and Ellie had brought two men from New York City Ballet; that made three couples. There were no distinctions of status within the troupe, nor any reference in promotional materials to the rank they held in their home companies. For publicity purposes, the dancers were all described as "Stars of American Ballet."

After much discussion, the dancers decided to perform several classical and contemporary pas de deux. The Sarajevans, in addition to taking free daily ballet classes taught by the Americans, would also perform in the gala, dancing an ensemble piece choreographed by the troupe.

Élodie got the visitors settled in their quarters and pointed out a few nearby restaurants. After that, she had absented herself for several days. The dancers were lodged in the town house of a businessman who had entrusted its use to the Arts Council, and Adam stayed there too. Élodie and the other MSF staff occupied rooms in an annex to the hospital where they worked.

On the afternoon of their first performance, as Marisol left the theater where the dancers had been rehearsing, Élodie intercepted her at the stage door.

"I'd like to take you for a cup of tea," Élodie said. "Do you have time, or would another day be better?"

"We're as ready for tonight as we're ever going to be," replied Marisol, making a conscious effort to hide her ambivalence. "Sure, let's go," she said.

Élodie led the way to an outdoor café. After they were seated she said, "I thought we might talk, the two women in Adam's life."

"I hadn't thought of it like that," Marisol said. She was nervous. Though Élodie was only four years her elder, Marisol found her maturity oddly intimidating.

"I was there at the beginning," Élodie began, "in Paris, four years ago, when you were innocent lovers. Adam has since told me the whole story."

"Then you know I'm his younger sister."

"Yes, I know. But what you may not realize is that I'm his older sister."

"No way."

"Not literally, not genetically, but in a sense that's possibly the equal of your relationship with him, my relationship to your brother is that of a sister, an older sister."

"I thought you were lovers."

"We have been, from time to time."

"Adam and I were too, but now he rules it out."

"I didn't know, but this I do know. You and Adam were meant to be. I knew it the minute I saw you together. That you have the same father is a technicality. That Adam and I do not share a parent is an accident—we're so alike. The deeper truth is that you're his mate, Marisol, and I'm his sister."

Marisol was stunned, aghast. This imperturbable stranger, this feared competitor for her brother's affections, had put her own heart's reasons into words.

"Does this mean you've given up Adam as a lover?" Marisol asked.

"I reject convention. It's a lot of rubbish and I refuse to be bound by it. You shouldn't be either."

"I don't feel so bound by it, but Adam does."

"A love like yours is too rare to ignore."

"Tell me about your relationship with Adam," Marisol said, "that is, if you don't mind my asking."

"As the women in his life, we should not have secrets, don't you agree?" Without waiting for Marisol's reply, Élodie continued. "Adam is not an ordinary man. He is driven, driven by forces that are larger than he is and of which he is unconscious. I see him as carried along on the current of history on a mission that no one can yet make out. From the start, I've sensed that our role is to help him grasp that destiny."

"Well, at the moment, it's the reverse; Adam is my support system."

"That's part of his preparation for what's to come. With Adam, everything is preparation. I'm preparation. There are a few things I can teach him, but he is a man with many teachers."

"He has always been like that. He learns from everybody. No one asks questions like Adam."

"Here's how it is with Adam and me," Élodie continued. "When we're together, we live as a couple, and when we're apart we pursue our lives independently."

"Adam told me that."

"There are other men in my life."

"What about this week? What about Adam now?"

"He told me that he's with you this week. I take no offense. This city is wounded and we're both here to do what we can to heal it. I wouldn't do anything to jeopardize that."

Marisol reached across the table and covered Élodie's hand with her own.

"I like having an older sister," she said. And then, to her own surprise, she added, "Even if now and then she fucks my brother."

CHAPTER 47

On the morning of September 11, 2001, Adam and Marisol were in New York City. So was Rowan.

Rowan was at the kitchen table drinking coffee and reading the *New York Times* that had arrived, as it always did, while he was still asleep. Shortly before 9 AM, NPR was interrupted for breaking news. A massive explosion had blown out the upper floors of the World Trade Center's north tower. There were reports that a plane had crashed into it. Emergency personnel from all over the city were rushing to the scene.

Rowan turned on the TV and saw live video of the tower engulfed in flames and smoke. He knew Marisol would be preparing to leave for company class; he quickly got her on the phone and told her to turn on her TV.

They were watching the mayhem, transfixed, listening to reporters speculate on how this could have happened, when they saw a second plane fly into the south tower and explode in a fireball. In an instant, it was clear that this was no accident; it was a terrorist attack.

Marisol ran to Adam's apartment. By the time she got there he was in the hallway, camera in hand, heading for the Trade Center site. Marisol tried to talk him out of it, but he wouldn't listen.

§§§

"Where's Easter?" Marisol asked Rowan when he opened the door.

"Washington. She promised to hunker down till this is over."

"What do you think, Dad?"

"Feels like Pearl Harbor. I was just five when that happened and all I remember is my parents' emotions—grim determination on my dad's part, lust for revenge on my mother's. I expect that's what we'll see this time."

"War?"

"Not armies and navies in battle, but military action of some sort. The problem will be identifying the planners."

"Even if we do, won't there be more where they came from?"

"It's worse than that. The real problem is not finding the terrorists, it's winning over the much wider group that wants them to win."

"What do you mean?"

"Terrorism is a tactic used by the weak to protest chronic indignity."

"We can't just let them go free."

"No, we can't. And we won't. We'll hunt them down and bring them to justice, one way or another. But until we break the cycle of indignities that fuels terror, the threat will remain."

The phone rang. It was Adam. Marisol picked up the extension.

"Adam, where are you?"

"As close as they'll let me get. My cell wouldn't work. I'm at a pay phone. Have you heard from my mom?"

"I got through to her in DC," Rowan said. "She's okay."

"It reminds me of Somalia and Rwanda. Smoke, debris raining down. Panic in the streets, everyone running away from the disaster."

"That's what you should be doing," Marisol said.

"The only way I could get this close was to duck into shops and catch my breath."

"Well. you've never been one to go with the flow," Rowan said.

"I picked up some face masks at a medical supply store. Don't worry about me."

"I'll worry till I see you," Marisol said. "Come home now."

"Not till I …"

The phone went dead, cutting him off in mid-sentence. Marisol panicked, and Rowan reminded her that phone service had been spotty all day.

After they'd watched video of both towers collapse for the twentieth time, Marisol left Rowan's and went back to Adam's apartment so she'd be there when he got home.

He came in late that afternoon covered in grainy soot. "Get those clothes off," she told him. "They look contagious. I'll make supper while you shower."

Adam emerged in fresh clothes and sat down at the kitchen table. Marisol turned off the TV and put a plate of instant macaroni and cheese in front of him. "Comfort food," she said.

"After this, let's go donate blood," Adam suggested. "The Red Cross is looking for donors."

"I'd like to do *something*. I've felt useless all day. Did you get some photos?"

"Hundreds. But they don't capture the horror. How'd Dad react?"

"Philosophically. I didn't realize he remembered Pearl Harbor."

"What did he say?"

Marisol did her best to convey Rowan's ideas, but when Adam asked her what their father would do if he were president, she had no answer.

"You should ask him," she said, and went to look out the window for the hundredth time on that most traumatic day in the city's history.

"Oh, I almost forgot. Ben called. He's here on business. I told him you were out taking photos."

§§§

Ben was the person Adam most wanted to talk to about the attacks. After three seasons, he'd retired from the NBA, and for the last few years had been devoting his prodigious energy to an Internet start-up. It was obvious to Adam that Ben took more satisfaction in being a geek than in being a pro athlete.

During his last year as a 76er, while his teammates were carousing after games, Ben had been in his hotel room working on his laptop. His transition from sports to business was seamless. As soon as he'd saved enough money from basketball to turn entrepreneur, he announced his retirement and never looked back.

Adam emailed Ben suggesting dinner with him and Marisol the coming weekend. Over dessert, Adam asked Ben if 9/11 would accelerate his switch to politics. "Not till I'm financially independent. A politician who can't say no to corporate money is a lapdog. Our company leads the field in digital imaging—the kind of thing we did in Princeton. Within a few years everyone's going to be sending photos over the Internet. That's when my investment will bring top dollar. When I run for office, it won't be to read from some lobbyist's script."

"Democrat or Republican?" Marisol asked.

"Doesn't matter to me. Truth is, I'm neither and I'm both. But I'll probably have to choose before I run. Once I'm in office, I'm going to establish myself as an Independent."

"You're talking about Pennsylvania, right?" Marisol asked him. "Where most of your fans are."

"Pennsylvania is my best shot. I want to do there what Bill Bradley did in New Jersey."

"Philly's a short hop by train," Adam said. "Just let us know how we can help."

"Seriously, Ad, you should take a look at politics too. You've got what it takes to be effective—presence, experience, and money. Plus, you're a visionary."

"No one's interested in the future, Ben. Politics is still about "the economy, stupid." Plus, there are tons of qualified leaders, but not many worker bees willing to go to Mogadishu, Peshawar, Kigali, Sarajevo, or Kosovo. The public has to know what's going on. Images change the world as much as political speeches."

"More, if you ask me," said Marisol.

"Images sow seeds," Ben said, "but it takes decades for them to bear fruit. What's needed now is politicians who can explain things to the public. The wrong policy in Washington can do more harm than all those conflicts put together. You're a born teacher, Ad."

"For now, I want to show, not teach. To show people the effects of dignity affirmed and dignity denied. Then stand back and let them choose for themselves."

Marisol listened as the two old friends argued over the best way to change the world. Their friendly jousting ended in a mock fight over the check. Outside the restaurant, they looked south to where the silhouettes of the Trade Center had been and noted their horrible absence.

Marisol invited Ben and Adam back to her apartment for a nightcap. "How's Ellie?" she asked, putting on her coat.

"Lots to tell there, lots."

When they were settled in the living room, Marisol said, "Okay, Ben, out with it."

"Ellie and I have been together—except for England—for ten years." This was as close as Ben had ever come to the subject of his love life in Marisol's presence. She and Adam both knew that his NBA road trips had given Ben many opportunities for meeting women, but they didn't want to know about it, and had never asked.

"She's wanted to be married for most of the time I've known her, but it made no sense when I was abroad or on the road."

"You always came back to her," Marisol noted.

"Yes, I did. It was great to have a home base, and during my playing days, Ellie was 'home'."

"Is she still 'home'?" Marisol pressed.

"Thing is, I'm hardly ever home. I'm spending more time on the West Coast than here."

"Sounds like you're ambivalent," Adam ventured.

"I guess so."

"About marriage or about Ellie?" Marisol asked him.

"Both, to tell the truth. I can't decide if I'm not right for marriage or Ellie's not right for me."

"Best make up your mind before you go into politics," Adam said.

"I know. This is the one area of my life that's out of control."

§§§

After she'd spent almost a decade at New York City Ballet, Ellie's contract was not renewed. Over the years, she'd seen Marisol rise to the heights of the dance world. The two had been able to remain close only because Ellie was devoid of resentment or jealousy.

Marisol was debating as to whether she should let Ellie in on what Ben had said, or wait for her to open up. When Ellie called, proposing lunch the following day, Marisol decided to let her take the lead, and support her regardless.

Ellie went right to the point. "I'm pregnant, Marisol. Ben and I are having a baby."

This was the last thing Marisol expected to hear. All she could think of to say was, "When?" hastily adding, "Oh, that's wonderful." Years of regarding pregnancy as a career-killer had conditioned her, like most dancers, to treat it like a disease.

"Nine months post 9/11," Ellie said. "Terrorism has a silver lining."

"How does Ben feel about it?"

"He doesn't know. I wanted to tell you first."

"Really?"

"I'm not sure how he'll react."

When Marisol didn't respond, Ellie went on. "You can never let on, but I took things into my own hands. Ben always had a reason to wait. You know, the Rhodes, the NBA, and now his start-up. I decided to help him make up his mind."

"What are you saying?"

"I went off the pill."

"Without telling him?"

"I couldn't stand it any longer, so I put it in God's hands. If I have to, I'll raise the baby on my own."

"But Ben is the father."

"I had to do this … for me. I'm getting older. After ten years, I couldn't come away with nothing."

§§§

After first swearing Adam to secrecy, Marisol told him about her conversation with Ellie. A few days later, Ben called to say he and Ellie were getting married. Adam hated play-acting with him, but managed to sound pleasantly surprised at the news.

The wedding would take place that weekend, at the Office of the Justice of the Peace in Philadelphia. After Adam agreed to be best man, Ben told him that Ellie was expecting in June.

CHAPTER 48

July 4, 2004

"Who's the Nordic princess?" Adam asked Ellie, indicating the striking woman who was steering Ben from one prospective supporter to the next. Ellie shifted their two-year-old daughter, Galia, from one hip to the other and shaded her eyes to get a look.

That morning Marisol and Adam had taken the train to Philadelphia to attend a fundraiser for Ben's senatorial campaign. Held in the spacious garden of a mansion owned by a former teammate of Ben's who was still playing for the 76ers, the gathering was unusual in that there were as many blacks present as whites.

Players from the New Jersey Nets, the Washington Wizards, and the New York Knicks, many of whom appreciated Ben's efforts to ease racial tensions, had also been invited. It was not hard to pick out the ballplayers, who towered over the rest of the crowd. A live band played so loud that meaningful conversation was all but impossible.

"That's Gwyneth," Ellie said. "Gwyneth Lionel. She's got family money—from a toy fortune—and good connections."

"Model trains, I'd guess," Adam said. "Will you introduce me?"

Ellie took Adam's arm and walked him toward Ben and Gwyneth.

"This is our next senator, Ben Steinsaltz," Gwyneth was saying to a small group of supporters. "I trust we can count on your help."

Ben was so good at this, Adam thought. He knew who should introduce him, and just how long to spend with each person before moving on: long enough to make people feel they mattered; not long enough to discuss policy.

Ben would take his interlocutor's hand and leave him or her with the impression that, but for the call of other obligations, he would have liked nothing better than to spend the rest of the afternoon discussing the matter at hand.

"Adam, I'd like you to meet Gwyneth Lionel," Ellie said. "She's been such a help to us, right Ben?"

"Best in the business," Ben said, smiling at Gwyneth. "Thanks to her, I may not need to pour my dot.com earnings into the campaign."

"Hello, Gwyneth," Adam said. Her skin was so fair she seemed to emit a rose-colored light, and although she looked about 28, she had naturally white hair. She immediately brought to mind his favorite animal—the polar bear. Big grayish-blue eyes looked up at him. The hand she proffered, palm down, asked to be kissed.

"Adam and I and go way back—to college basketball at Princeton," Ben explained. "Without him, no one would have heard of me."

"You were unstoppable, then and now," Adam said.

Gwyneth looked up admiringly at Ben, who at six-foot-seven stood an inch taller than Adam.

"Back to work everyone," Ellie said. "We can talk when this is over." She drew Ben after her, leaving Adam and Gwyneth on their own.

"What do you do?" Gwyneth asked.

"I'll finish law school at NYU this year. I'm specializing in healthcare legislation, and Ben wants me to join his staff to work on it. I gather you're already with the campaign."

"As a volunteer. I'm from New York, actually, but the country needs senators like Ben, regardless of party."

"How did you get involved?"

"It's the man, not the politics. I heard Ben speak in New York and knew I had to help him."

"His heart's in the right place."

"Above politics," Gwyneth continued. "He'll do what's right for America, and others will follow his lead."

"Actually, his aim is even higher," Adam said. "Ben will do what's right for the world. We must stay in touch."

They were exchanging cards when Marisol joined them. She was wearing a chic straw sunhat with a wide brim. He introduced the two women to each other and asked if he could get them a drink.

"Pinot Grigio," Gwyneth said.

"Make it two," said Marisol.

"I'll be right back."

"I'm Adam's half-sister," Marisol said to Gwyneth. She'd learned from experience that it was better to lead with the full facts of their relationship than subsequently disabuse people of the idea that they were a couple. Or, what was equally annoying, to backtrack from "sister" to "half-sister" to account for their racial difference.

"Yes, there is something alike about you," Gwyneth observed. "I hope you don't mind my saying so."

Marisol smiled politely.

"Adam tells me you're a dancer."

"I do other things too. Like this. Whatever Adam needs, I do."

"Sounds like you're close."

"Two halves of a whole," Marisol said, not unaware that in saying this she was warning Gwyneth that to deal with Adam was to deal with her.

Marisol could spot women who had power over men. Gwyneth was one of them; she herself was another, but there was a difference. Apart from Adam, Marisol wanted nothing from men save that they admire her as an artist. In contrast, Gwyneth used her feminine power to get powerful men, men like Adam and Ben, to do her bidding.

§§§

A few days after they returned to New York, Marisol had a rare day off and called Adam. After they caught up on mundane matters, she brought up what was on her mind.

"You certainly didn't wait long before calling Ms. Lionel."

"She's compiling a list of New Yorkers we can ask to support Ben's candidacy. She wants my input."

"But why dinner?"

When Adam didn't reply, she added, "I'm sorry. I know it's none of my business."

Adam had been pleased when Gwyneth immediately accepted his suggestion that they meet over dinner. He and Marisol had been over this ground before, and he should have seen her reaction coming. It didn't help that Gwyneth was beautiful—Marisol's equal in repose, though no one compared with his sister in motion.

Marisol was off limits, but the special place she held in his heart usually left him apathetic about other women. Perhaps Gwyneth's charms could break him out of his lassitude. He needed to find out.

Marisol had dated a few times—most recently an actor—but she'd been relieved when he was cast in a Hollywood movie and had to leave town. When Adam had encouraged her to try again, she said she was too busy.

"Adam," Marisol began, her tone softening, "Gwyneth is not like other women you've gone out with. Promise you'll take care."

"I'm not looking to get involved."

"Women like Gwyneth get what they want."

"How do you know?"

"Because I'm one of them. I get what I want. Except for you."

"You have me. In the only way that really matters. That's never going to change."

"She's … Oh, forget it. Never mind; have a nice time."

Of all the evenings to have off, Marisol thought. She'd rather have been cast as a spear carrier in *La Bayadère* than sit home while Adam was out with this woman.

She tried reading, but couldn't focus. She remembered Sasha's warning, "Dance is what we do, not who we are." Could she now say to him, to the world, "dance is what I do, not who I am?"

She pondered the question for a while and found her answer—yes. Tonight she wasn't dancing. She was home alone worrying about her brother, but she hadn't fallen apart. Adam had helped her find her balance, but she was no longer dependent on him. She would survive.

§§§

Election Day, November 2, 2004

After they voted in New York, Marisol and Adam went to Philadelphia to be with Ben and Ellie for the returns. Polls indicated that Ben held a small lead, and they were hoping to end the evening with a victory party. The campaign had rented the ballroom in the Crowne Plaza Hotel, and by eight o'clock it was filling up.

During the four months since they'd met, Gwyneth had worked full time for Ben's election. Her inheritance enabled her to do what she liked, and her passion was politics. Marisol saw her as a contemporary Madame de Staël, presiding over a salon. It was hardly surprising that she would attach herself to a charismatic candidate for high office.

Adam's first dinner with Gwyneth had been followed by walks in Central Park, movies, more dinners, and by summer's end they were a couple in every way, except that they were not living together. There was no urgency to do so with Gwyneth spending at least half her time in Philadelphia organizing the team to get out the vote. Polls indicated that, to win, Ben would need to take 90 percent of the minority vote. Thanks to the support he would get from professional athletes, that was not out of reach—if enough minority voters went to the polls.

Ben was no ordinary man, and he proved himself to be no ordinary candidate. His progressive views on social equality and justice made him an atypical Republican. In predominately Democratic districts he argued that, if elected, he would be a senator who was not beholden to the ideologues in either party.

For those who cared, Ben went into detail. A loyalty to Republican principles, yes, but that was just part of the story. As he'd become familiar with America's diversity and inequities, he'd also found something to like about the Democratic party. Still, he considered both parties too narrow. He saw himself as a political hybrid—fiscally conservative, socially liberal. He knew that if he won the election this would be awkward, and probably untenable, so he decided that, if he did win, he wouldn't wait long before he declared himself an Independent.

§§§

Adam and Marisol were sidestepping their way through the packed ballroom when Gwyneth announced her presence with a tap on Adam's shoulder. He pivoted and gave her a quick kiss.

"Hi Marisol," she said.

"We just got here, and I'm looking for Ellie."

"She and Ben are in a suite on the tenth floor. They're not coming down till it's decided. Exit polls look good. We're getting the votes where we had to."

"Let's go up," Marisol said to Adam, tugging on his sleeve.

"Mind if I come along?" Gwyneth asked.

In the elevator, Gwyneth asked Marisol if she had the night off.

"*Swan Lake* tomorrow. We get the night off before a full-length."

"Adam took me two weeks ago. He must have told you how much we loved it."

"He's in love with Odile," Marisol said, poking her brother in the ribs. "The bad girl."

"No, I'm not," Adam protested. "I prefer Odette."

"And you, Gwyneth?"

"Rothbart."

"The evil sorcerer? What's to like about him?" Adam asked.

"His hold over his women."

"But Rothbart loses in the end," Marisol said. "Odette's faithfulness wins out. Love breaks the evil spell."

At that moment the elevator doors parted, and Ben was standing there waiting to welcome them.

§§§

After Ben's victory speech, Marisol and Adam had dashed off to catch the last train to New York. "I don't trust her," Marisol said.

"Why not?" He knew who his sister was talking about.

"She doesn't listen."

"Sure she does."

"What turns her on is the scene, not individuals. She's not your soul mate, Ad."

"That role is already filled, Marisol; you know that. But I need someone like Gwyneth in my life. She helps me connect with people."

"She's always in motion. Even when she's standing still her eyes are darting around the room in search of her next target."

"That's an asset in politics. Without her, Ben probably would have lost, and I wouldn't be going to Washington to work with him."

Marisol was aware of his growing interest in health policy. Being a wonk suited his nature, and the goal of healthcare for all resonated with Ben's campaign watchword—Dignity for All.

"Have you noticed how she looks at him?" Marisol went on.

"Everyone admires Ben, you do yourself. Anyway, he's got Ellie, and now there's Galia."

Absent Galia, they agreed, Ben would probably not have gotten married. Women were drawn into his orbit and he'd always had his pick. Adam couldn't help but think that if Ben were free, he might have chosen Gwyneth. But he was not free; his role as a family man was now integral to his public image.

"For your sake, I hope I'm wrong about Gwyneth."

"Just drop it, Marisol, you're not being fair. What I love about Gwyn is that she's serious. She won't be stopped. With or without the trappings of office she's going to be a formidable political force. I need her, Marisol. Together, we can accomplish twice as much as either of us could alone."

§§§

Adam took Gwyneth to meet his mother and Rowan, and she took him upstate to meet her parents. That spring they went to Paris so she could meet François and see where Adam had grown up. She adored the town house on Place des Vosges.

On their final day in Paris François took Adam aside and asked him what his plans were. When he indicated that he had marriage in mind, François offered to buy the couple a house in Washington.

"I've been looking for a way to get some of your inheritance to you early, when you need it, instead of decades from now when I'm gone."

"We can manage, Dad."

"I know you can, but I don't want you to find yourself in the position of living off your wife's money. That could put an unnecessary burden on the relationship."

"I was concerned about that. No way I can support her lifestyle on a staff salary."

"Real estate looks like a very good investment now. I'll buy the house in both our names, but it'll be yours for all practical purposes. Let me know when you've found what you want."

On the homeward flight, Adam asked Gwyneth to marry him, and she consented. The nuptials were set for the day after Adam's graduation from law school. Immediately afterward, they would move to Washington where he anticipated joining Ben's staff.

Even before their wedding, Gwyneth had begun scouring the real estate ads for a town house in Georgetown. Marisol was right: She saw herself as a hostess on the Washington social scene, and her first order of business was to equip herself with a proper venue for her salon.

CHAPTER 49

As moving day approached, Adam was developing reservations about working for Ben. To avoid saying no to the offer he knew would be coming, he made an appointment with Ben and asked him for help finding a staff job with a member of the House.

"I belong in the House, Ben, not the Senate," he explained. "The people's house, not the *upper* chamber."

That wasn't Adam's real reason, and that Ben had so easily accepted his dubious explanation suggested that he was aware of it. Their relationship had always been that of peers, and both men sensed that it might be better to keep it that way. In addition— buried so deep in Adam's psyche that even he would have denied it—there was yet another reason. As a senator, Ben was a somebody; as a staffer, Adam would be a nobody. Only the powerful were welcome in Gwyneth's world. Why burden their marriage with the constant reminder that he was working for Ben?

Adam also asked Easter to check her connections for an opening, and it was she who came up with the lead that panned out. Dr. Valerie Gruber, a prominent member of the House Committee on Education, was the representative of a district in the Berkshire Mountains in western Massachusetts where Rowan's family had long owned property. Easter, using Rowan's tie to the district and her own familiarity with it, had befriended Congresswoman Gruber soon after going to work in the Clinton administration. Over the years they'd worked together on numerous education bills, and Easter was delighted to have an excuse to reconnect with her old colleague over lunch. If Congresswoman Gruber was not in the market for someone with Adam's skills herself, she would likely know who was.

Gruber's legislative interests had widened since the Clinton years, and she now also served on the health committee. The Democrats needed to have health legislation ready to go if they regained a congressional majority in 2006 and/or won the presidency in 2008. Gruber was looking for someone to represent her on the task force of congressional staffers that was drafting a comprehensive healthcare bill.

Easter didn't need to say much about Adam to get him an interview, and after Gruber and her chief of staff met him, they offered him the job on the spot. The old girl's network was becoming as fecund as the old boy's. Connections, connections, connections, Adam mused, wondering how people who lacked his extended family network ever found work.

§§§

On the day of Adam's wedding, Marisol was making a guest appearance with the Houston Ballet. Adam didn't press her to explain her absence, but he knew it was no accident.

Gwyneth spent their honeymoon in Washington looking at real estate. Adam soon tired of it, and pleading the pressure of his new job, left the choice to his wife.

François followed through on his offer to pay for the house. Without the constraint of price, Gwyneth had little trouble finding a property suitable for the entertaining she envisioned. It was a Georgetown colonial whose façade bore a remarkable resemblance to the Merle town house on Place des Vosges. The dining room opened through French doors onto a patio that ended in a spacious lawn surrounded by dozens of old rhododendrons.

Gwyneth's father, impressed by François's generosity and not wishing to look the miser, offered to furnish the couple's new home in the style of their choice. After consulting Adam, Gwyneth decided on English Country. Its pièce de résistance, which had influenced their choice of décor, was a large circular oak table that Adam had admired on his first visit to the Lionel family home. Shortly after they took possession of the house he had come home from work to find it dominating the dining room.

It was on this table that hors d'oeuvres would be laid out at their housewarming party. Gwyneth had drawn up a guest list that reached deep into Valerie Gruber's network, and then, to provide gravitas, she'd added Senator Ben Steinsaltz and his staff, and the media figures and pundits whom she'd gotten to know while working for Ben's election.

Gwyneth operated on a "two degrees of separation" rule. She felt at liberty to invite anyone known by someone she or Adam knew themselves. This formula, applied to their circle of friends and colleagues, had yielded a guest list of almost two hundred. The house and garden would look full but not crowded.

§§§

Back in New York, Marisol had acceded to Rex Urey's suggestion that they meet. A balletomane, Rex seldom missed a performance of Marisol's, always sitting unaccompanied in a choice orchestra seat. On a few occasions, he had waited for her with flowers outside the stage door after the performance.

She'd been polite to him, but done nothing to encourage him to think of himself as anything more than one of her fans. Unlike some admirers, Rex had never made a nuisance of himself.

Then, after having been vaguely aware of him for several years, she ran into him at an opening in an art gallery. They exchanged nods, and a few minutes later Rex approached her and thanked her for the joy her dancing brought to his life. Marisol was experienced at handling such compliments, and reflexively struck a pose of modest gratitude while maintaining an emotional distance. But even in this brief encounter, she noticed something in Rex's expression that moved her. He didn't want anything from her. He was merely offering his personal recognition.

To her surprise he didn't immediately attempt to build on her thank you, but simply accepted it and moved on. However, a half-hour later, on his way out, he approached her again.

"The relationship between the artist and the audience is inherently unsymmetrical. You do your job, which is to dance, and I do mine, which is to appreciate your artistry. We've fulfilled those roles and we can continue to do so without ever speaking. But if you would care to talk sometime, I would like that. You need not worry that I'll become a bother. It's simply that, over the years, I've admired your art, and I've come to think that it would be remiss of me not to propose one meeting. Here's my card, should you ever care to talk."

Rex met her eyes. Again, she felt strangely moved by his appearance and his appeal. She tucked his card into her purse and, without speaking, offered her hand and said good-bye.

A week later she sent him an e-mail suggesting that they meet at the Lincoln Center fountain on the following Sunday afternoon.

Their meeting at the fountain was followed by coffee in a nearby café, and within a week, they met for a light supper. Rex turned out to be the most sensitive observer of dance Marisol had ever known.

§§§

On their second meeting, Rex made a reference to the experience of "single, gay men" in New York in a way that identified himself as one of them. Unlike many of the gay men Marisol had known, there was nothing about Rex's dress or manner that announced his sexual orientation. In the company of a woman like Marisol no one would have taken him for anything but straight.

Rex's sexual orientation did not concern Marisol; she would not have cared if he were manifestly gay, but she took an impish delight in seeing people take them for a couple. That Rex passed for straight had the merit of shutting up those who nagged her about dating, and those who accused her of being too picky when it came to men.

What did matter to Marisol was that she found Rex intelligent, kind, and observant. What she was learning from him was exactly what a mature dancer needs to take her art to the next level. She soon discovered that the comments he made about dance were having a salutary effect on her performances.

Rex saw ballet not from backstage like her fellow dancers, but from a seat in the theater as a member of the audience. The two perspectives were not always the same. And, at this late stage in her career, the most important audience was the one Rex spoke for, not her colleagues, let alone the artistic director and his inner circle.

Marisol realized that dancing for those with the power to decide if you dance again is a trap that dancers must avoid if they are to imprint their own vision on ballet. Great dancers see themselves through both near-sighted and far-sighted lenses, and it was Rex who was helping her, at a stage in her career when most dancers have stopped improving, to see herself as she was seen from afar.

§§§

The guest list for the housewarming included all of Adam's and Gwyneth's family members. Rowan was spending the weekend in Washington and he and Easter would be there. Marisol had decided to take this opportunity to present Rex to her family, but stone-walled her sister-in-law's attempts to find out more about her mystery companion.

Marisol had toyed with the idea of keeping everyone in the dark about the nature of her relationship with Rex, but at the housewarming, the quizzical expression on Adam's face as he shook hands with Rex made her reconsider.

Steering Rex and Adam through the crowd to Ellie's side, she made the introductions and then, after chatting briefly, said "Ad, let's give my oldest and my newest ballet friends a chance to gossip while you show me the house."

Marisol and Adam watched as Ellie took Rex's arm and led him into the garden. Judging that they had at most fifteen minutes before their absence would become awkward, Adam said, "You can see the house anytime. Let's talk in my study."

Adam had hardly closed the door when Marisol said, "Rex is a good friend, but we're not lovers. He's gay."

"Oh," Adam said. "I'm …"

"glad?" Marisol finished his thought.

"Well, kind of."

"Chivalrous of you to be jealous of the sister you've jilted."

"I don't have a leg to stand on, I know, but I had to find out ..."

"... if you could live without me?"

"Stop finishing my sentences!"

"I'm moving on too. Rex helps."

"Doesn't that make you a 'beard'?"

"Oh, please, I couldn't care less what people think."

"No one would ever guess. You make a handsome couple."

"So, how are things with you?"

"I go along with all this," Adam said, fully extending his arms. "Gwyneth loves being a political hostess, and I love my new job. It's great to put my law degree to work on something that can really improve people's lives."

"I can't picture you partying like this very often."

"She's held several events already. They're more useful than I thought they'd be; this is where deals are made. There are several Washington hostesses who are as powerful as senators. Gwyneth is determined to be one of them."

"I can imagine that," Marisol said. "Come on, I haven't even said hello to her yet."

Adam led Marisol down the back stairs to the kitchen, and they found Gwyneth huddled in a corner with Ben amid a swarm of tray-wielding servers bustling in and out.

Ben grabbed Adam and they disappeared into the dining room. Marisol heard them talking politics as they receded. Gwyneth guided her to the veranda off the kitchen and pointed to a pretty TV anchor chatting up a senator.

Marisol complimented Gwyneth on the house and the party, and was looking for a way to make a graceful exit when Gwyneth turned to her and asked point blank, "I want to be the first to know. Is marriage in the works? Your beau is a lovely man."

Taken aback, Marisol almost spit out "none of your damn business." Instead, with exaggerated theatricality and a little curtsey, she replied, "Alas, I'm wedded to dance."

Not to be denied, Gwyneth followed up, "Come on, now. When the jumps aren't so high and the turns so quick, surely you must think of giving those knees a break."

"I never think about life after dance."

Ellie and Rex, who had come up and overheard Marisol's riposte, both had something to say.

"Nor should she," Rex added. "Marisol is at the top of her game and still improving."

"She has bionic knees," Ellie said. "They'll last till she's ninety-five."

"Thanks for the vote of confidence," Marisol said. "I don't know what I'd do if I couldn't dance."

"Well," said Gwyneth softening her tone, "we all have to leave the stage someday, don't you think? It's almost as certain as death and taxes."

§§§

Marisol sat in her darkened apartment. The bitch was right, she thought. I'm thirty-two. Most dancers are done by thirty-five. But how could anything replace dance? It made her feel alive, free. Nothing could compare with the magic of being onstage, where she could forget technique and just trust her body to take her into the zone where she became one with the music and her character. But it wasn't only performing. She had some of her most fulfilling moments in the studio, simply working on new choreography or rehearsing a role. No audience, no applause. Just dance.

What could she do? What other skills did she have? None. Zip. Nada. How depressing: to go from having roses thrown at your feet to working at the perfume counter at Macy's. That's what happened to Laura, one of the ABT dancers whom she used to admire. Dear god.

Marisol thought about Ellie, whose situation was different in that she had already had a post–dance career lined up when she'd retired—motherhood. But maybe she could help. I'll call her tomorrow, Marisol decided.

"Do you still get Dance Magazine?" Ellie asked Marisol. They'd already spent a half hour gossiping about the party when Marisol casually broached the subject of retirement.

"Yes, but I don't have time to read it. They just stack up."

"There's something in the latest issue about life after dance."

"Yeah?"

"There's a new degree program for people like us, professional dancers. You can earn a bachelor's degree while you're still performing. And they offer classes in New York."

"Really? Maybe I'll look into it," Marisol said. "I always wanted to go to college."

§§§

In the midterm election of 2006, both houses of Congress went to the Democrats. Electing Nancy Pelosi Speaker of the House was not only a historical first, it also put Congresswoman Gruber, a long-time Pelosi ally, close to the seat of power. The two women had dreamt for years of extending healthcare to all Americans, and with the new Democratic majority, Adam's work took on greater urgency. All it would take to realize long-held liberal dreams was winning the White House in 2008, and after six years of George W. Bush, it was beginning to look possible.

When Congresswoman Gruber's chief of staff left to take up a position at the John F. Kennedy School of Government at Harvard, Gruber offered the job to Adam. From this vantage point, he had an overview of the House, and gradually acquired an insider's knowledge of legislative strategy.

During the 2008 campaign, it had occurred to him that he might someday step out of a behind-the-scenes role and run for Congress himself. He increasingly found himself yearning to speak up rather than prepare position papers for his boss; to negotiate deals with other representatives, instead of with his counterparts on their staffs.

Gwyneth was always one to encourage Adam to think big. Since their marriage three years before, she'd acquired a stellar reputation as a political hostess. What set her salon apart was that by leveraging her connection to Ben Steinsaltz, who straddled both parties, she had managed to build a nonpartisan guest list of politicians, journalists, lobbyists, business leaders, and celebrities. The Lionel-Blue residence was one of the few places in Washington where Democrats and Republicans actually socialized with each other. Whereas Congresswoman Gruber was persona non grata in the offices of many Republicans, Adam, as Gwyneth's husband, had entrée. This did not easily translate into votes, but no one had a better record of negotiating legislative compromises than he did.

Despite his distaste for pressing the flesh, Adam appreciated his wife's labors. He and Gwyneth did not share many interests, so he was doubly grateful that they had found an area where their ambitions coincided.

§§§

The election of Barack Obama, and simultaneous retention of the Senate and the House, heralded a new day—in America and the world. Adam and Gwyneth spent election night at Ben and Ellie's. Ben, who had done so much to combat racism as an athlete, and who had endorsed Obama early and campaigned for him tirelessly, was elated. No one was surprised when he received a personal call from the president-elect late Tuesday night.

Adam had never seen Gwyneth look happier or more radiant. A Republican senator from the South came over to Adam and quipped, "There go your chances for the White House." Adam would normally have made light of such an obtuse remark—as if the emergence of the first president of color had filled a quota—but on this night, he spoke his mind. "On the contrary, the White House will be home to many minority candidates in the years to come."

As he was saying this, Ben's daughter jumped up on his lap. Adam loved little Galia. Half-Chinese and half-Jewish, she already possessed an exotic beauty that would deepen as she grew up.

He and Gwyneth had tried to have children but none had come. It often occurred to Adam that her prodigious hosting might be her way of compensating for the lack of a family. Galia, who regarded Gwyneth and Adam as her aunt and uncle, was the beneficiary.

"Will you knit me a new sweater, Aunt Gwyn?" Galia asked. "I'm too big for this one."

"Yes, it's too tight," Gwyneth agreed. "Would you like a winter hat too?"

"Oh, would you?"

"Do you have a favorite color?

"Red. Could you put a silver tassel on it?"

"I think so," Gwyneth said. "In time for the first snow."

CHAPTER 50

Now in her thirties, Marisol had been spared most of the injuries that commonly plague dancers. The key to her relative immunity from major injury was a fortuitous mix of flexibility and strength.

During the 2008 season, however, she twice had to take time off to rest a hamstring prone to crippling spasms. Recently, those spasms had moved up into her lower back. She was also battling chronic tendonitis in her right ankle.

Marisol's box office appeal—with her name on the program having long ago come to guarantee a full house at Lincoln Center—blinded management to the hazards of over-scheduling their star. Those responsible for the bottom line tend to downplay injuries until they see their meal tickets on crutches. At the other extreme, some of the younger dancers were salivating at the opportunities Marisol's retirement promised.

Who could Marisol confide in about the most difficult decision a dancer ever faces: when to bow out?

She had raised the subject of retirement with Rex a few times, but not without signaling that she expected him to talk her out of it. As the 2008 season drew to a close, she raised the issue again.

"I've been thinking about leaving the company," she said over supper after a performance of *Romeo and Juliet*. "I'm twice Juliet's age."

"You can't tell from the orchestra," Rex said.

"But, I *feel* too old. And if I feel too old now, I'll look too old in a year or two. I want to go out on top."

"Then make next year your last," he said. She was shocked by his bluntness. She had expected at least token resistance from him. But she knew he was simply putting the implacable truth into words. She hung her head to hide her tears.

"If you leave a year from now, you'll leave them begging you to stay—not just your average fan, but the connoisseurs as well.

You don't want critics praising your port de bras because your jumps aren't as high as they expect."

"Well, they aren't. I feel a caution coming over me lately, like I can't trust my body anymore."

"Spending more time at the physical therapist's than in the studio?"

"Hey, it's not that bad. Yet. It just feels a bit risky to be dancing parts like Juliet and Giselle."

"Not so fast with Giselle. That was your debut, and it should be your swansong."

"My swansong is Odette/Odile," Marisol joked, mainly to cloak the sadness that was welling inside her. It didn't work.

"It's a death, Rex," she whispered. "Death of an identity. Plus a loss of my community and my income." She let out an involuntary sob, but recovering quickly, added, "I hope you're paying for this dinner."

"You said that the college classes you were taking were helping, right?"

"Yes."

"So take more classes to fill the void while you look for your new self. You'll survive this, and come out on top. I know it."

Rex signaled for the waiter and ordered two flutes of champagne. When they came he proposed a toast that had nothing to do with Marisol's career.

"To us. To me for suggesting we meet, and you for taking the chance."

"Thank you, Rex, and thank you for not telling me that every ending marks a new beginning. The end of a dance career is an unmitigated disaster. Nothing will ever be as glorious, not even a Ph.D. I know that."

"I'll be at your side for as long as you like."

"Even when the house lights go out?"

"More than ever."

§§§

A few days after the swearing in of Barack Obama as the forty-fourth president, Adam received a call from Valerie Gruber's husband. His wife had been experiencing abdominal discomfort since Christmas, and at the inaugural lunch the pain had become serious enough to require a trip to the emergency room. Instead of spending the evening at one of the many balls, Valerie had spent it in the hospital. Within days she had been diagnosed with ovarian cancer.

"Valerie hasn't been right for some time," her husband concluded.

"I'm so sorry to hear this," Adam said.

"She wants to see you, Adam. I'm bringing her home today. Could you stop by around eight this evening?"

"Of course. Can I pick up anything for you?"

"Just bring yourself. *You* are what she needs, Adam. She'll explain when you get here."

Valerie's husband answered Adam's knock and led him upstairs where the congresswoman was sitting up in bed.

"They've given me a sedative and some pain-killers," she began, "but I can still think straight."

"That's always been your strong suit," Adam said. "Tell me what you need from us. We'll do whatever it takes to help you through this."

"For an indeterminate period I'm going to need a lot of help. The doctors are alarmingly vague about my prognosis."

Adam grasped her implication but decided not to touch it.

"Since we're at the start of a term, I want to hold on to my seat during treatment. I may miss a few votes, but with your help we can still serve the people of Massachusetts as well as if I were healthy."

"What are the doctors proposing?"

"Surgery with chemo both before and after. But cure or no cure, I'm planning on using the illness to make my exit."

"I wouldn't have thought it was time."

"Without this, I wouldn't have either. But in the last few days I've begun to think that twenty years is enough. We deserve to spend the rest of our days, however many, in the hills of western Massachusetts," she said, smiling at her husband.

She paused and took a deep breath. "What I'm thinking, Adam, is that we're both of us ready—me to step aside, you to fill my seat."

"There's the little matter of being elected."

"With my endorsement, and that of the governor, which I think I can deliver, the nomination is yours to lose."

"And the nomination is tantamount to election," her husband added. "The district has been in Democratic hands since Kennedy was president."

"But I don't live there."

"Neither do I, but like us, you have a residence in the district. I recall your telling me that your family has long had property there."

"That's true. Gwyneth and I are planning to ski on it next month."

"This time, we'll make something of your visit. If I'm up to it, we'll schedule a few joint appearances."

"You're really serious about this, aren't you?"

"Dead serious," Valerie quipped. "Adam, I've been in politics a long time. I know a leader when I see one. The best leaders are not ostentatious. Often, their followers don't even realize they're being led. You have that gift. I've seen you in action. What's more, you and Gwyneth make a great team."

"She's a force in her own right."

"And she'll be even more effective as your career unfolds."

Valerie was tiring, and her husband noticed. "She's a tough old bird," he said, "and we intend to beat this. But we're both thinking it's a good time to bow out. Your availability makes this all a little easier."

When he got home, Adam told Gwyneth the news. Within days, she began compiling guest lists for a series of salons designed to build support of her husband's candidacy for a seat in the U. S. House of Representatives.

§§§

In May, 2009, a gala evening of ballet marked the retirement of one of ABT's luminaries, Marisol Ellway. She danced three numbers chosen to showcase the highlights of her career. The program opened with the Rose Adagio from *Sleeping Beauty*. After a video presentation that included clips from *Swan Lake* and *Romeo and Juliet*, she danced in Twyla Tharp's ensemble piece set to Philip Glass's score, *In the Upper Room*. Following intermission, the evening concluded with a pas de deux from *Giselle*, the role that had made her a star. As she had done dozens of times on previous occasions, Marisol forgave Prince Albrecht for forsaking her, and saved him from death with the power of her undying love.

Rowan, Easter, and Sara had box seats. Adam had suggested to François that he and Marisol would both love him to be there, and he had come from Paris with his cousin, Viviane.

Ben had flown Adam and Gwyneth to New York in a private plane and booked them a suite at the Pierre Hotel. Sasha, who had left ABT a few years into Marisol's career, had come over from Copenhagen where he was spending a season as guest choreographer.

Rex was not in his usual aisle seat in mid-orchestra, but with Marisol's help, had a seat in the second row, adjacent to Adam, Gwyneth, Ellie, and Ben.

No one in the audience except Rex noticed that, as the curtain came down on Giselle, Adam was in tears. Marisol noticed too. From the stage, on one of her many curtain calls, she took two roses from a bouquet and tossed one to Rex and one to Adam. With a final bow in the spotlight, her dance career was over.

When the theater had emptied, champagne and finger food was served on stage for dancers, critics, friends, and patrons.

In social settings, Adam always took note of who was talking to whom, who looked comfortable, and who seemed left out. By midnight, family and friends had made their exits, but Marisol was still surrounded by well-wishers. Adam could see that the smile on her face was frozen, and when he saw Rex fetching her a bottle of water, he intercepted him.

"She's about had it, don't you think?"

"I can't free her up," Rex said. "Maybe if we work together."

"Okay, you grab her coat and I'll get her. We'll converge at the stage door in two minutes and just keep moving."

In the street, Marisol asked Adam to meet her at noon at the fountain the next day. As she and Rex left, she assured Adam that she wouldn't stand him up a second time.

§§§

She was at the fountain when he walked up. In blue jeans and blazer, he thought she looked more beautiful than she was the day they'd met eighteen years earlier.

"Are you glad it's over?" he asked.

"Relieved I didn't fall on my face. Devastated that it's over."

"I know. I won't whistle a happy tune."

"Where's Gwyneth?"

"She had to be in Washington this afternoon for one of her charities. She caught a ride with Ben on his plane. Ellie and I are staying on for a few days."

"I've got some food in the fridge. You see? I don't need you to feed me anymore. Come on, I'll make us lunch."

As he savored the lentil soup Marisol served him, she asked about his life in Washington.

"Valerie has finished her chemo. They won't know for months if she's clear of cancer, but regardless, she's stepping down. She says the cancer was a blessing in disguise."

"I don't get it."

"Cancer gave her the excuse she needed to leave Washington, to live a country life. She hasn't hidden the illness from her constituents. Gives her speeches bald."

"The lady has guts."

"She wants me to replace her."

"Run for office?"

"Exactly. I'd have to win the Democratic nomination, but after that I should be a shoo-in."

"I think you'll be great."

"Will you vote for me?"

"I don't live there."

"You'd only have to change your voter registration from New York City to our cabin in the district."

"I might be able to do more than just vote for you. As part of the bachelor's degree I've been working on, I choreographed a few short pieces to Yann Tiersen's music. He wrote the scores for *Amélie* and *Goodbye Lenin!* For my senior project I put together a little troupe of ballet dancers who performed the dances, kind of like in Sarajevo. I think they'd be willing to stage a benefit for your campaign."

"Perfect! Perhaps they could even join me on the campaign trail."

"It won't be an easy act to follow. You'll have to polish your stump speech."

"Does your offer mean you'll stay in New York?"

"I have friends here, Rex, most importantly. But once I have my BA and you've been elected I'll be footloose and fancy free."

"Any dreams?"

"Not in focus yet. How are things with Gwyneth?"

"Okay."

"Only okay?"

"Well, after four years, we're kind of on automatic."

"That sounds dull."

"When it comes to work, we have a wonderful partnership."

"She likes playing queen."

"Yeah, and while she holds court, I make friends, friends who'll help … when the time comes."

"Friends are nice, but what about love?"

"It'll always be there."

Marisol reached across the table and cupped his hand. "Giselle was for you."

"I know. Have you forgiven me?"

"I forgave us both a long time ago, but I still believe in the holiness of the heart's affections, don't you?"

"I think my mom was right about that, but if we hadn't changed direction, neither of our careers would have happened as they have. Love doesn't have to mean living together, or having babies."

"Heaven forbid!"

"We couldn't go the usual way, so we found another path."

"And now? Now that I'm a nobody again, starting over?"

"Our story begins anew."

BOOK III

DIGNITY

Dignity is not negotiable.
– Vartan Gregorian

PROLOGUE

April 28, 2029

Adam Blue put another log on the fire, then settled himself on the sofa facing the hearth. He took the manuscript on the end table and leaned against the sofa's high arm. Stretching his legs, his stockinged feet just touched the other arm. He began to read.

The writing was nothing like the presidential memoirs of his predecessors. It was more intimate and revealing, and he knew it. Across the top of the first page he had printed "As It Happened : 2009–2029," followed by a quote from a prose poem by Robert Browning. In a score of titled entries—narrated in the first-person and using dialogue he'd reconstructed from memory—he retraced his journey from his first run for Congress to his last day in the White House.

AS IT HAPPENED

2009–2029

Man is not Man as yet,
Nor shall I deem his object served, his end
Attained, his genuine strength put fairly forth,
While only here and there a star dispels
The darkness, here and there a towering mind
O'erlooks its prostrate fellows: when the host
Is out at once to the despair of night,
When all mankind alike is perfected,
Equal in full-blown powers - then, not till then,
I say, begins man's general infancy.
 – Robert Browning, *Paracelsus*

After my father resigned as president of Jefferson College, emotionally spent, he needed the solitude and healing powers of his cabin in the Berkshires. Rowan Ellway decamped there, alone, and in the years following his exit from academia, few sought him out. The place didn't even have phone service until the late 1980s.

When I left the White House in 2029, I did as my father had done a half-century before me. I repaired to the family cabin.

During my time in office I had used it as a getaway—a retreat from the official Camp David one. So, what had been a nineteenth-century cabin well into the late twentieth had to be equipped with twenty-first century technology and a secured perimeter. Somewhere, out of sight, the Secret Service still makes sure that no one sets foot on the property without permission. I wish it were otherwise, but I know it can't be, not so long as the world remains an angry, vengeful place.

My latest sojourns in the cabin have one thing in common with my father's, though, and it outweighs the inevitable consequences of my former presidency. He was leaving one life and looking to begin another, and so am I. During his solitary retreat, Rowan came to think of the place as Nobodyland, and in our family, the sobriquet has stuck.

Since I left office I've read several presidential memoirs that, for the most part, I found self-serving, score-settling chronicles written by men bent on burnishing their legacies. Sadly, there is little in them that can't be found in the public record.

When I realized that I had no interest in writing yet another version of the public story, I was drawn to the place where my public story and my private life intersected. This, then, is a personal journal. It's not a memoir, and not for publication. Until the lives that I and those closest to me led can be accepted for what they were—muddled quests for dignity by once and future nobodies—the details must remain unknown.

§§§

When a guy says he fell for the wrong girl, it's usually a story of unrequited love. Not so in my case. We met when we were nearing the end of our teens, and were instantly attracted to each other. For one glorious week together, alone in the Place des Vosges town house, we talked, laughed, and made love, passionately and often. The girl I fell in love with loved me back—and loved me unconditionally. The same can not be said of me. I did have a condition, one that couldn't be met: I needed Marisol, the love of my life, to not be my half-sister.

It was shortly after that unforgettable week that we found out we had the same father. It changed nothing for Marisol, but I couldn't get past it; our blood tie stopped me cold and, for almost a year, I couldn't even accept a fraternal hug from her. Marisol ached to share her life with me, and I needed to obliterate what I felt for her. My need to put as much space between us as possible was largely the impetus for the around-the-world quest I undertook when I turned twenty.

In Paris, I was fortunate to meet a mature woman who was not looking for commitment, and helped me come to terms with losing Marisol. Élodie—Dr. Élodie Pham Fleury in full—a physician, five years my senior, was working with Doctors Without Borders. I volunteered to photograph the victims of famine and war that she treated in the refugee camps that dotted the globe. When our paths crossed in faraway places, whether by accident or design, we did the work we were there to do, and together, we did what came naturally. She's spent her life with Doctors Without Borders, and I've visited her in a good many of the places she's been posted to over the last thirty years: Somalia, Pakistan, Sarajevo, Darfur, Haiti, Gaza, Dhaka, and, most recently, the Maldives.

After years of trying to bury my love for Marisol, and feeling guilty for the pain I was causing her by withholding it, I met and married Gwyneth. Beautiful, elegant, cosmopolitan, and brilliant, she's admired by everyone who knows her.

In her early twenties, Gwyneth had played a key role in the election of my closest friend, Ben Steinsaltz, to the U. S. Senate. Had she not been by my side, pushing me forward and connecting me with the right people, I would have ended my political career where I'd started it—as a back-bencher in the House of Representatives.

§§§

A Heartbeat Away

My road to the White House was an untraveled path. Every president before me was either elected to the office or ascended to it from the vice presidency.

Here's a little history. When, on the death of President Franklin D. Roosevelt in 1945, Vice President Truman became president, the vacancy that resulted moved a series of cabinet secretaries up in the line of succession, beginning with the secretary of state.

Then, in 1947, the Constitution was amended to insert two *elected* officials between the vice president and the cabinet secretaries—the Speaker of the House and the president pro tem of the Senate. From then on, the secretary of state and other cabinet members would ascend to the presidency only if these two elected legislators were rendered unable to serve.

With that modification, the Speaker of the House would become president only if the offices of the president and the vice president simultaneously became vacant. Until Thanksgiving Day, 2023, such a double vacancy had never occurred. Previous holders of the Speaker's office knew that they were second in the line of succession to president; a few had probably fantasized about landing in the top spot. I had not.

The 118th Congress, with a Democratic majority, had chosen me as Speaker of the House for my part in our party's victory in the midterm election of 2022. Thus, although I had no desire to be president, the Constitution put me just two steps away from it.

As is seared into the memories of all my contemporaries, Republican President Mike Mulroney was halfway through his second term when an aortic aneurysm took his life. Just the month before, his Vice President, Sally Myers, had perished in a helicopter crash, along with the premier of Russia, en route to the site of an earthquake in Almaty, Kazakhstan.

Before Mulroney and congressional leaders had been able to agree on whom to nominate to replace Vice President Myers, the president was also dead—and the Constitution catapulted me into the White House.

There are so many questions one could reasonably ask about my unexpected fate. Why wasn't the vacancy left by Myers's death filled more quickly? Answer: Because more was at stake than just finding someone to serve out the last two years of Myers's term. Unless Mulroney nominated a mere place-holder, his pick would immediately become the front-runner for the party's next presidential nomination. Republican contenders were jockeying for Mulroney's favor when his death dashed their hopes. That the failure of Congress to act expeditiously resulted in putting a Democrat in the White House could not have been more ironic.

With the tragic death of Sally Myers, Mulroney had seemed to lose interest in his job. I say "tragic" not only because the cruel and sudden death of a young leader on a humanitarian mission must, out of respect, be seen as such; everyone recognized Sally as an extraordinary leader. Her death devastated the members of both parties, and the American people. Conservatives loved her All-American brio, and liberals loved her manifest compassion. She would have been a shoo-in for her party's presidential nomination and—not in my judgment alone—would have won the presidency in 2024.

As Speaker, I had been looking forward to working with Sally on a broad range of reforms that were stalled by the inertia of the Mulroney administration after the Republicans lost control of Congress; it was the election that brought me the speakership.

Mulroney's attempt to pump new life into his agenda and win a second term as president had led him to replace Vice President Timothy Fisher in favor of Sally Myers on the Republican ticket for the 2020 election. I'd always liked Fisher and, while I understood why Mulroney made that choice, I was sorry to see him dumped. In fact, later, bringing him back into government was one of the first things I did when I became president.

With Sally as his number two, Mulroney had regained some of the enthusiasm he'd exhibited during his first term. Then, suddenly, she was gone. A bereaved nation mourned Sally's loss as if she'd already been the president that most people believed she would have become. At her funeral, Mulroney looked like a broken man.

From that day on, he spent much of his time at his home near Charlottesville, Virginia. It was there, playing with his grandchildren after Thanksgiving dinner, 2023, that he had collapsed and died.

Given the accidental nature of my ascension to the Oval Office, the real explanation of it lies in the story of how I became Speaker.

§§§

Becoming Speaker

Although I rose to the speakership at the relatively young age of forty-nine, Henry Clay, one of the most influential Speakers in our nation's history, was first elected Speaker when he was only thirty-five. More recently, Newt Gingrich was chosen Speaker at fifty-one, and it is his rise that mine most resembles.

Both of us were awarded the speakership in return for putting together a set of principles that brought our parties to power: Speaker Gingrich as architect of the Contract with America, me for crafting what I dubbed the Dignity Deal.

I got the idea for the Dignity Deal from the rhetorical and electoral success that both Roosevelt's New Deal and Truman's Fair Deal had had. After Democrats campaigned under that banner in 2022, they replicated the Republican feat of winning the midterm elections of 1994. My party rewarded me, as the Republicans had Gingrich, by electing me Speaker.

My political career got its start in 2005, when Easter put me in touch with Congresswoman Valerie Gruber, who represented the First Congressional District in Western Massachusetts. She hired me as her staffer on a congressional task force, and a few years later when her chief of staff resigned, she gave me his job.

Shortly after Barack Obama took office as the forty-fourth president, Congresswoman Gruber was diagnosed with ovarian cancer. Early in the second year of her two-year term, she announced that she wouldn't stand for reelection, and endorsed me as her replacement. Though my opponent attempted to undercut me by depicting me as a carpetbagger, I had the Ellway family's history in the district on my side. My great-grandfather, Rowan's grandfather Calvin Ellway, had settled there in the nineteenth century, and I had spent many vacations hiking and skiing in the Berkshires. My crevice-by-crevice knowledge of the backcountry had dissipated any skepticism that citizens of this rural district might have had toward a candidate of mixed race who'd lived most of his life in one metropolis or another.

That, Congresswoman Gruber's support, and my familiarity with the issues that were important to her constituents, which I'd acquired while serving on her staff, were enough to gain me the Democratic nomination for the special election that was held to fill her seat.

Looking back on my career in politics, I don't think I ever enjoyed campaigning as much as I did during that first run for office. With a vivid New England autumn as a glorious backdrop, the crowds were buzzing with energy. I loved the give and take with voters. Addressing a large group of them, responding to their concerns, and wading into the crowd to personally win them over, was more exciting than a basketball game decided by a last-second shot.

I had another incalculable advantage over my opponent: Marisol Ellway. After she'd retired from her position as a ballerina at American Ballet Theatre, she'd put together a small troupe of musicians and dancers that I enlisted to participate in my campaign. They performed in virtually every town and hamlet in western Massachusetts, and word of Marisol's multiethnic troupe—Dignity Rocks, she called it—spread among the young, drawing larger than usual crowds to my stump speeches. It not only endowed our campaign with vitality and momentum, it gave artistic expression to what was new and distinctive about our message—that the paramount purpose of politics should be to secure and defend equal dignity for all. The cumulative result was that voters were disposed to give me a chance.

The Dignity Rocks troupe would warm up the crowd, then I'd make the case that, along with liberty and equality, dignity was essential to individual wellbeing and the common good. In previous eras, Republicans had emphasized liberty over equality, and Democrats had done the reverse. I argued that voters did not have to choose between these traditional American values; if legislation was conceived and vetted for its impact on dignity, they could be reconciled.

Dignity for all meant dignity for everyone, I told the voters of western Massachusetts—young and old, black and white, immigrant and native-born, progressive and conservative, urban and rural, gay and straight, blue- and white-collar, people with and without disabilities, those of every ethnicity and religion, and, I'd say—pointing to folks in the audience—that includes you, and you, and you.

On foreign policy, I took the position that affirming other nations' dignity was in *our* national interest. While I was speaking, volunteers went through the audience handing out bumper stickers that read NOLO: NO ONE LEFT OUT, or HUMILIATION IS MORE DANGEROUS THAN PLUTONIUM. Then, after my stump speech, never longer than five minutes, I opened the floor to questions.

When the votes were counted, my opponent had lost by ten points overall and, more important to my future, we had the support of 70 percent of voters under thirty.

That first victory, in November 2010, halfway through President Obama's first term, came in the face of Democratic losses nationwide. That Americans had by then grown accustomed to biracial political leaders made my ethnicity a non-issue for the most part. With every election since Obama's, the issue of race has faded in importance until, this last time around, injecting race into electoral politics, no matter how subtly, would have hurt anyone who tried.

§§§

It took me several years to find my proper niche in the House. On the advice of several congressional mentors I specialized in legislation on science and technology, and globalization. I managed to get myself appointed to the Committee on Foreign Affairs, the Committee on Science and Technology, the House committee on Homeland Security, and the House Permanent Select Committee on Intelligence. My service on the Select Committee's subcommittee on Terrorism, HUMINT, Analysis and Counter Intelligence, gave me a rare appreciation of just what our intelligence agencies knew and did not know of others' intentions.

It was while I was seeking a fourth term that I realized that the idea of a Dignity Deal might have national appeal. Some of my colleagues in Congress thought so too, and with their support, I submitted my name for the position of chairman of the Democratic caucus. After I was reelected to my seat in 2016, my fellow democrats elected me to the House leadership.

At that time, no one symbolized America's will to power as unequivocally as the man in the White House, President Mike Mulroney. The contrast between dignitarian and traditional politics was especially clear in international affairs. The presidential campaign of 2020, in which Mulroney sought a second term, came down to a national referendum on his foreign policy.

Mulroney's commitment to a muscular approach had been made clear when he dumped Vice President Fisher in favor of Sally Myers. Though Fisher was held in high regard by foreign affairs professionals, he had long been depicted by conservatives as soft on terrorism, weak on national defense, and naïve about China's threat to American dominance in the Pacific.

Consequently, he had gradually been marginalized by the hawks in his party. Sally Myers contrasted with him less in substance than in style. She too shunned the version of American exceptionalism and bellicosity favored by the hawks, but she cut a figure that made voters proud, and to attack her was politically risky.

Mulroney's pollsters believed that Myers's presence on the ticket would cut into the Democrats' share of the women's vote, which they depended on, and her youth would compensate for the president's increasingly visible infirmities. The election proved them right. As Republican strategists anticipated, the public saw them as father and daughter figures, and took comfort in the idea that the "father," to whom they had grown accustomed, would groom the "daughter" to take the reins when he left office.

Republicans had carried the House in the elections of 2016, 2018, and 2020, but in November, 2022, that string of victories came to an end. As in the midterm election of 2006, they lost their majority to the Democrats. By that time I had become Democratic Party Whip, and I used my position to put the package of proposals known as the *Dignity Deal* at the heart of Democratic policy. That, in brief, is the story of my rise from comparative obscurity. For my perceived role in our party's victory, my fellow Democrats elected me Speaker at the opening of the 118th Congress, in January, 2023.

That the speakership put me second in line for the presidency wasn't in anyone's mind at the time. We were all under the spell of Myers's charisma and vitality when her unthinkable death made replacing her as vice president a matter of the greatest urgency. As Speaker, I met with President Mulroney and urged him to act quickly, promising him that whomever he nominated to replace Sally Myers would receive the most expeditious consideration.

Meanwhile, the cliché that a Democrat stood "a heartbeat away from the presidency" was on every conservative's lips.

To their dismay, it came true.

§§§

Twice-Taken Oath, Thanksgiving Day, November 23, 2023

I was scrambling to get my clothes on when Karen burst in, dragging a photographer behind her. She handed me a tie, waited while I put it on, and then slid a Bible under my left hand.

"Raise your right hand and repeat after me," she said. "I, Adam Blue, do solemnly swear … "

"I, Adam Blue, do solemnly swear," I began. Following her prompts, I continued, "that I will faithfully execute the office of president of the United States, and will to the best of my ability, preserve, protect and defend the Constitution of the United States."

Karen did not add "So help me God" to the oath, and neither did I. We both found it hard to believe in a God who would become involved in politics.

Karen Parker and I had begun working together in 2005, when I joined the staff of Representative Valerie Gruber. Five years later, when I assumed Valerie's seat in the House, Karen became my chief of staff, and she has continued in that role ever since—when I was Speaker, then president, and even now, in my retirement.

Karen and I have no secrets from each other. She has two rare and priceless virtues. First, she lives by Lao-Tsu's adage "Those who know do not tell and those who tell do not know." Second, she can be blunt and irreverent, and she always speaks her mind to me. Perhaps because she'd known me from the very start of my political career, even taught me the ropes when I joined Gruber's staff, she never showed a deferential attitude toward me. From her, I got the truth, and others got nothing.

Karen had a life partner in Washington—her college roommate, Letitia. As first-year students at Oberlin College, they were thrown together by chance, roomed together for four years, and have lived as a couple ever since. Theirs is a loving, loyal, and long-lasting relationship, and I'm a grateful beneficiary of its stability (and its childlessness).

During my years in politics, Karen and I often worked overtime. Eighty-hour weeks were common, hundred-hour weeks not unknown. She planned my domestic and foreign trips overseas, and it was on one of those—to the low-lying Maldives, then being evacuated in advance of the rising sea level—that she woke me, on Thanksgiving Day, 2023, to tell me that President Mulroney was dead. In that instant, I knew that my life was no longer my own.

Karen immediately began to organize our return to Washington, instructing her assistant, Theo, to arrange for a police escort to the military transport plane that had brought us from India to Malé, capital of the Maldives, the previous day.

I was there to draw attention to the impact of climate change on low-lying island nations, and, for me personally, it was a chance to see Élodie Fleury, now a vice president of Doctors Without Borders. Élodie was in the Maldives planning for the evacuation of its population, and had arranged a tour of the island for me, followed by a briefing from the country's chief environmental scientist, and dinner with the Maldivian president.

Within minutes after I took the oath, the Secret Service was hustling me toward a waiting van. Before I ducked inside I heard my name called, and turned to see an agent blocking Élodie's approach.

"Let her through," I said (my first presidential order).

Élodie came forward with a startled look on her usually imperturbable face.

"How'd you hear?" I asked her.

"I couldn't sleep and had the TV on. I rushed over."

"I'm glad you did. At least we had yesterday."

"If ever I can help …"

"I know how to find you. I don't know what lies ahead, but I'm sure you'll be part of it."

"Remember the Trans-Siberian and you can't go wrong."

I puzzled over her meaning for a moment, and then it hit me. Everything I'd done since our Siberian sojourn, thirty years earlier, had been seeded on that trip, and she was reminding me not to forget what I'd learned there.

Élodie reached up and cupped my shoulders with her palms. I bent down so she could whisper in my ear.

"You'll always have my love," she said.

"And you, mine," I replied. I was conscious that cameras were recording my every move, so I resisted the impulse to lift her off her feet in a bear hug. Then I got in the van and left her to her work, as I had so many times before. When I leave people I love, I feel like a robot lacking in volition.

As we pulled up to the military aircraft I overheard the Secret Service agents referring to it as Air Force One.

The plane's captain, waiting at the top of the stairs, saluted me as commander-in-chief. When I asked him if we could make it home in one hop, he said it was too risky. The great circle route to Washington was nine thousand miles—the outer limit of the aircraft's range—and we'd be approaching North America over open ocean with scant room for error. We'd have to stop to refuel.

"When will that put us in Washington?"

"Flying westward, we gain ten hours, so we should have you on American soil early tomorrow afternoon."

I nodded and asked him to send Karen to me as soon as she boarded.

§§§

Without knocking, Karen poked her head into the small office in the rear of the plane. "Mr. President ..." she began.

"'Adam' in private, please. I'll need you to keep me grounded."

"I've had plenty of practice doing that, but if I don't call you Mr. President in private, I might slip up in public. Don't worry, it won't interfere with my candor."

"Alas, probably not," I joked. "Please ask the switchboard to put me through to the secretaries of state and defense."

She turned to leave.

"One more thing. I'm appointing you White House chief of staff."

"You should think it over, Mr. President. My experience does not qualify me."

"Do you want to speak to Letitia first? It'll be more work than even you are used to."

"No need. I know what she'd say."

"And what is that?"

"That it's my duty and I'm lucky to be needed."

"Then please don't argue with me about this, Karen. Anything else, okay, but not this. It's official and takes effect immediately."

"Thank you, Mr. President. I will do my best to serve you and our country."

The secretary of state, who on several occasions during the Mulroney years had stone-walled the House Committee on Foreign Affairs, immediately began angling for face time. He even offered to meet my plane when it landed to refuel, and accompany me to Washington so he could brief me in person. I told him to remain at his post and asked him to call his counterparts in a score of countries and assure them that the transfer of power would be smooth.

The secretary of defense asked for an appointment as soon as possible to acquaint me with the nuclear codes.

I then made a series of personal calls, first to Marisol, whom I asked to meet the plane; then to François, who promised to come see me in the White House; and then to my mother who, until I forbade it, addressed me as Mr. President.

She passed the phone to Rowan, who tried to reassure me by saying that my life had prepared me for the role.

Then I asked the operator to find Gwyneth, and when she came on the line I asked her where she was.

"At Ellie's and Ben's. Thanksgiving dinner, remember?"

"Oh, yes."

"We're all reeling," Gwyneth said. "Ben wants to talk to you."

"Before you put him on, Gwyn, you'll be managing our move into the White House. Please give Mulroney's people a few days to adjust. I'm thinking we could simply stay put in Georgetown till the White House is ready."

"Don't worry about that. You've got enough on your plate. They tell me you're landing at Reagan National. I'll be there."

"Thanks, Gwyn. I know you'll be a great first lady."

"I think I'm ready. Here's Ben."

"Mr. President, how may I be of service?"

I decided to skip the 'Call me Adam' bit and get straight to the point.

"I believe it's urgent to fill the vice presidency, Ben. The majority leader will take my place as Speaker as soon as the House meets, but at this moment, the next in the line of succession is the president pro tem of the Senate."

"That's on everyone's mind here. The media have already begun fanning doubts about his capacity."

"Even though we should have a new Speaker within days, I want to fill the vice presidency immediately. Ben, I want to nominate you. As an Independent and a four-term senator you've got two essential qualifications—you're not seen as partisan and you have the experience to be president. Your appointment will reassure the nation. I'll consult with the Speaker and the leaders of the Senate before announcing this, but first, I need to know that you'll accept."

"I would be honored to serve with you, Mr. President."

"I expect this to go through without a hitch."

"I'll meet your plane tomorrow, and be with you as long as you need me. You're the right man for this job."

I made courtesy calls to the leaders of the United Kingdom, China, India, Russia, Japan, Germany, France, Brazil, and our neighbors, Canada and Mexico. And then, because I thought it would reassure the country, I put in a call to the chief justice and asked him to administer the oath of office on American soil for live TV.

§§§

How had it come to this? I gazed out the window at the brightening sky and reflected on my life and fate.

Was I prepared, as Rowan said? Of course not. There's no adequate preparation for the role of president. But I'd served six terms in the House, and been fortunate in my committee assignments. Equally important was what I'd absorbed from François growing up and from Rowan in our many conversations about politics. He'd shown me a new way to think about the wars, famines, and genocides I'd seen abroad, and the partisan political struggles I'd experienced at home.

A leader must stake out a position and hold the torch high in the hope that people are drawn to the light. Then, they either make your cause their own, or blame you for leading them astray.

I vowed then that in place of politics as usual, my presidency would espouse the politics of dignity. If everyone's right to dignity were recognized and secured, this would mark a turning point in human affairs. The idea made my heart soar.

But then my mind turned to the personal. How could I connect to "the people" when I hadn't been able to bond with my own wife? Although our professional partnership was solid, our personal relationship was fragile.

Marisol believed that Gwyneth valued me for the opportunities my political career gave her. I'd been in the House only two terms when she began urging me to run for the Senate. In contrast, Marisol argued that I could do more from a leadership position in the House than as a senator. Ironically, if I'd taken Gwyneth's advice then, she would not now be realizing her dream of becoming first lady.

From the start, Gwyneth had cultivated her own agenda, and when it coincided with mine, we made a formidable team. Marisol's agenda was simpler—it was to share my fate.

§§§

As Air Force One taxied toward the area cordoned off for its arrival at Reagan National Airport, I could see the raised dais set up in the open air. Row upon row of chairs—for Congress, President Mulroney's cabinet, military leaders, and the Supreme Court—had been placed in a circular pattern facing it.

Karen had arranged for Marisol to board Air Force One, and she led her to my quarters. As I rose to greet her she rushed into my arms. There was no need to hide our feelings from Karen. She understood everything and would never say anything. My life wouldn't have worked if these two women I was so close to hadn't also trusted each other.

Between Marisol and me, words were not needed. As we embraced, we both knew that our fate had been revealed. I would use the forum that had been given to me to suggest an alternative to the dead end toward which America and the world were hurtling; she would do what she had done in my campaigns—help me frame this life or death choice in a way that predisposed the public to risk the unfamiliar and move forward. Was the world ready to ground human relations and governance in dignity for all? Would the

American people go along? Or would the predatory cycle of indignity, resentment, and revenge continue?

Though making the case for dignity would fill most of my days in office, Marisol surprised me on that first day of our new life by saying, "Remember, this is a wake, not an inaugural. No grand ideas yet."

I immediately realized that the forward-looking speech I had in mind was inappropriate; inwardly, I cringed. "You're too lofty," Élodie used to tease me. "Come down to Earth." The American people were in shock and they needed reassurance. I'd have to shelve my hopes for the future until people had come to terms with the past.

§§§

"The Marine band will play 'Hail to the Chief' as you exit the plane," Karen said. "The chief justice is standing by to swear you in. Then you're on."

I had quickly revised my remarks to express the nation's grief, acknowledge that the White House had changed parties without the voters' say so, and reassure the American people that we would not take partisan advantage of the tragedy.

Karen handed me my overcoat. "We're ready, Mr. President. The first lady is waiting for you at the bottom of the steps."

Karen and Marisol followed close behind as I stepped through the exit onto the stairway and into a bright, cool Washington afternoon.

The familiar bars of "Hail to the Chief" boomed out across the airfield. At the bottom of the stairs I embraced Gwyneth, and then the leaders of the House and Senate welcomed me onto American soil. The congressional delegation led Gwyneth, Marisol, Karen, and me to seats on the elevated platform, and as soon as everyone was seated, the chief justice took the podium.

"All rise," he intoned. Gwyneth and I approached him together. He handed Gwyneth the Bible.

"Repeat after me, I, Adam Merle Blue, do solemnly swear ... "

As I was about to remove my hand from the Bible, the chief justice asked, "So help you God?"

"So help me God," I echoed. This was no time to make a point of my beliefs, or lack thereof.

§§§

Day One in the White House, November 27, 2023

I asked Mulroney's White House staff to stay on during the transition—with the exception of his chief of staff, whose job had gone to Karen. She would want to bring some of her people with her to the West Wing, and I encouraged her to do so, but not all at once. Out of respect for the deceased president, I asked that no one move into the White House before the memorial service that Sunday.

After the service, a motorcade drove Mulroney's coffin from Washington Cathedral to his country estate near Charlottesville. He was buried in a family plot not a hundred yards from where he had died, and just a few miles from Monticello, the home and burial place of our third president, Thomas Jefferson.

On Monday, November 27, 2023, Gwyneth, Karen, and I made a low-key visit to the White House. I had decided to devote the week to a series of meetings, and Karen had begun scheduling them over the weekend. In addition to Mulroney's cabinet, I planned to meet with congressional leaders of both parties; business, labor, and religious leaders; educators and directors of research laboratories; and of course the media.

Before any of them, however, at eight o'clock that first Monday morning I met with the director of National Intelligence and the director of the Central Intelligence Agency, William "Bill" Dickinson. Within minutes, the full weight of the presidency fell on me.

"Mr. President," the CIA director began, "As you know, the investigation into the cause of the helicopter crash that killed Vice President Myers and the Russian premier is ongoing."

I already knew this. President Mulroney and his press secretary had been taking refuge in boilerplate of that sort ever since the day of the crash. Although there was much speculation about terrorism, there had been no midair explosion, and the data provided by the black box was consistent with either sabotage or mechanical malfunction.

"The Kazaks and the Russians have given our experts full access to the crash site. Debris was scattered widely in a remote, mountainous area. We completed the painstaking task of reassembling the aircraft only last week. We now have unambiguous evidence of foul play."

I asked when the agency had reached this conclusion and if they had any idea who did it.

"We weren't certain it was sabotage until yesterday. We have no specific leads yet on who did it. Our best hope of identifying the perpetrators lies in intercepting their communications. Needless to say, the National Security Agency is listening."

When I asked if any group had claimed responsibility, he replied that while there were many claimants—evidently there always are—none were credible. He explained that the method of sabotage had made use of advanced technology that interfered with the helicopter's onboard computers. Russian and American experts thought this was the work of a sophisticated new network—with multiple nodes in the "Stans," which they'd recently become aware of.

"Which Stans?" I asked.

"We've picked up transmissions from a half-dozen of them, including Uzbekistan, Dagestan, Tajikistan, and Pakistan."

"Who else knows this was terrorism?"

"Only Defense Secretary Chilton and General Harris. Defense is drawing up some retaliatory options for your consideration."

"First, we need to know who did it," I cautioned.

"We'll find out, Mr. President," Mr. Dickinson said confidently.

At this point, I asked the two directors to work with my staff and the Russians on a joint statement that would inform the American people of this development.

When Bill Dickinson protested that his Russian counterpart did not want this made known, I told him that I wasn't going to dissemble with the public, and I would call the Russian president to explain why keeping the truth from our citizens was unwise: If the perpetrators were to claim responsibility, and do so convincingly, we would have to admit to incompetent intelligence-gathering to avoid being seen as liars—not a choice any leader wants to make.

As it happened, the Russian president put up no resistance, and our phone call laid the groundwork for what would in time prove to be a very fruitful relationship.

Next up was a meeting with Mulroney's holdover cabinet. Again, I asked them all to stay on the job, but as it turned out, one would be gone by the end of the day.

Truth be told, I was delighted when the secretary of state promptly gave me a reason to fire him. I'd had occasion to meet President Mulroney's appointee, Thaddeus Pritchett, when he testified before the House Foreign Affairs Committee on Capitol Hill. At that time, we got nothing but ambiguous diplomatic clichés out of him, and when we pressed for specifics, he patronized us.

His message to the legislative branch had been that international affairs called for expertise we lacked. He didn't say so in so many words, but his point of view had been as clear as if he'd said, "It's none of your damn business."

At the cabinet meeting, where protocol had him seated to my right, Pritchett registered his objection to my announced intention to meet in person with the leaders of Russia, China, and India in the coming weeks. He felt it necessary to advise me, in front of the cabinet, that preparing for talks with heads of state took months, if not years, and in any case, we should avoid giving the impression of being over-eager. Solicitude was beneath the dignity of a great power, he concluded.

I let his remarks pass, but an hour later I was shocked to see him giving a live interview on the White House lawn in which he repeated his views in a way that was clearly intended to limit my options.

With Pritchett's unctuous tones ringing in my ears, I asked Karen to get Timothy Fisher on the phone. Unlike many of my congressional colleagues, Fisher never impugned anyone's patriotism. I'd already decided to bring him back into government, but hadn't imagined that the chance would present itself so soon.

When Fisher came on the line I told him I wanted to make a change at State and asked if he could see himself working with a president not of his party. His response was immediate and direct. "I would be honored to serve you and the country, in whatever capacity you deem appropriate."

I told him I'd run the idea by the congressional leadership, and I expected to make a public announcement by noon.

I knew that the leaders of both houses of Congress believed that in dropping Fisher from the national ticket, Mulroney had treated him shabbily. But politics is politics, and Republicans and Democrats alike had understood the move as a poll-tested maneuver to retain the presidency in what looked likely to be a close election.

I now hoped that the Republican leadership would jump at the chance to make it up to Fisher and place one of their own at State. Most likely, my fellow Democrats would agree to this, not only because it was my first appointment, but because everyone understood that our party had gained the White House by succession. Moreover, most Democrats regarded Fisher as a pragmatist, and they appreciated the civility he had shown them when, as vice president, he had presided over the Senate. In short, Fisher, though a Republican, was a welcome change from Pritchett's partisanship and condescension.

My successor as Speaker of the House, Daniel Perkins, had been elected over the weekend, and after my opening remarks, he offered the support of Congress during the transition.

At that point, I surprised them by saying that something had come up much sooner than expected, and I invited their comments on my intention to replace Secretary of State Pritchett with Fisher.

Not a single voice was raised in objection, and the few who did speak up could barely conceal their delight at Pritchett's departure.

"Then I gather you anticipate no problem with confirmation," I said to the majority leader.

"Oh, there might be objections from a few quarters but, no, Mr. President, I don't see a problem." He paused, then broached what was on everyone's mind.

"The tragic events of this last month have reminded us all of the importance of filling the vacancy in the vice presidency expeditiously."

"Thank you for bringing that up," I said. "I have a nominee in mind and I would appreciate knowing if you think he'd be confirmed by both houses as required under the Twenty-fifth Amendment."

"You have our full attention, Mr. President," said the new Speaker.

"You may be a heartbeat away from the presidency," I said to the Speaker, "but since it's my heart we're talking about, you ought to know that my doc thinks it's got a lot more beats in it."

As I'd hoped, this broke the tension in the room.

"I don't think any of you will be surprised by the name I'm going to propose. To the office of vice president of the United States I intend to nominate the senior Senator from Pennsylvania, Benjamin Steinsaltz."

I waited for this to sink in. Everyone in the room was thinking about how it would affect his or her prospects for reelection.

"As some of you know, Ben and I go way back. There is no one better qualified to be president than he, and I include myself in that estimation. Absent the tragic events that bring us together today, none of us would have been surprised if Senator Steinsaltz had emerged as a candidate for president in the upcoming election."

"He may still intend to run," Senator Jones put in. "Couldn't his appointment to the vice presidency be seen by some as a move to keep him from becoming a presidential rival?"

"Not if he embraces the role," I said.

"Have you sounded him out?"

"I have," I said.

"And?"

"He has told me that, if the offer is made, he would be honored to serve."

"I think I can speak for my fellow Republicans," the senate majority leader began. "You'll have it. And, as we were saying, the sooner the vacancy is filled, the better." The majority leader then glanced at the Speaker of the House, and added, "Nothing personal, Dan."

"I believe we're all agreed on this," the Speaker replied. "The nation won't begin to heal until both a president and vice president are on the job. As for the nomination of Senator Steinsaltz, I think President Blue is right not to nominate a Democrat given the manner in which the party has come to the White House, but we can hardly expect him to choose a Republican either. As an independent, Senator Steinsaltz will be a noncontroversial placeholder until the voters weigh in next November."

I asked Karen if Ben had arrived, and when she told me he was waiting in the Roosevelt Room, I asked her to show him in.

We locked eyes for a moment, and I smiled. Ben's instant grasp of my intentions reminded me of our days on the basketball court. His uncanny ability to know what I'd do almost before I knew myself had made him a college star. We still played basketball occasionally, on a court remodeled in honor of President Obama after he left office. In excellent physical condition and taller than most younger players, Ben could still compete with them. Though I'd never been at Ben's level as an athlete, I'd stayed relatively fit by joining in a game whenever my duties in the House had permitted. When we played on the same side, we were invincible.

"I guess you've told them that you want me on your team," Ben said.

"And we agree with the president," the Senate majority leader volunteered, reaching out to shake Ben's hand. "We'll have to go through the motions, but none of us expects any trouble. Not at a time like this."

"Thanks for your confidence," Ben said. "I've known this fellow for thirty years," he continued, indicating me. "The nation couldn't be in better hands."

I detected a few obligatory sounds of approval in response to Ben's endorsement, but I had what I wanted: congressional backing for two of the most important appointments a president ever makes.

After lunch with Ben, and before I headed into my afternoon meetings, I asked Mulroney's press secretary to notify the networks that I would shortly make an announcement.

At two o'clock, with Ben at my side, I told the nation and the world that I had nominated Senator Ben Steinsaltz for vice president of the United States, and that former Vice President Timothy Fisher had agreed to serve as secretary of state.

When a journalist asked me if I thought the Senate would act swiftly to confirm these nominations, I referred him to the congressional leadership.

Within minutes, ex-Secretary Pritchett called to protest his dismissal. Karen told him I was unavailable.

Acting Secretary Tim Fisher was in his car en route to the State Department from his home in Virginia when Karen reached him and asked him to come directly to the White House for an emergency meeting of the National Security Council. I also asked Ben Steinsaltz to attend.

I wanted Ben and Tim to hear firsthand what the director of National Intelligence had told me that morning—that the helicopter crash in Almaty that killed our vice president was an act of terrorism—and also to hear what other members of the NSC had to say about it. In attendance were the Secretary of Defense, Hazel Chilton; and Chairman of the Joint Chiefs, General Tobias Harris, known to everyone as Toby.

I knew General Harris from his frequent appearances before congressional committees, but I did not call him Toby. General Harris had a reputation for toughness that had shielded President Mulroney from any charges of waffling or weakness. I'd seen Harris flash hot with anger in public, and thought it largely an act for the cameras, but when he did so at the first meeting of my National Security Council, I sensed trouble.

No sooner had the director of National Intelligence and the director of the CIA repeated their briefing than General Harris jumped in to present a few military options "for our consideration." All of them involved firing cruise missiles or drones at targets in the Stans.

I let others take the lead in the questioning, and almost immediately it became obvious to everyone that nothing was known of the perpetrators' identities or locations.

Nonetheless, General Harris thought it was imperative to show the terrorists that we meant business and do anything we could to discourage another attack.

When I asked him if he knew something more than what we'd just heard, he insisted that it wasn't necessary to know every last detail before we sent the terrorists a message they could not possibly misunderstand. Showing weakness in the face of the murder of our vice president would simply encourage them to plan bolder acts. "You could be next, Mr. President," he warned, as if this clinched his case.

I was not persuaded. Neither was Secretary of Defense Chilton, who I could see was put off by the chairman's grandstanding.

After a brief but heated discussion during which uncertainty was piled on uncertainty, I drew things to a close with the hope that better intelligence would soon enable us to craft a suitable response. Then I let the group know that, first thing tomorrow, I would inform the nation that our vice president had been killed in a terrorist attack, and that a worldwide manhunt was under way to bring the perpetrators to justice.

General Harris grumbled audibly, but Hazel took his arm and walked him out of the room in a move designed to keep him from buttonholing me.

Back in the Oval Office, I asked Karen to catch Fisher before he left—I needed to talk to him. Fisher explained that, as President Mulroney had become increasingly weary of his presidential duties, he had allowed Harris to assume a policy role that no general had played since General Douglas MacArthur.

"How does Hazel put up with his insubordination?" I asked.

"Duty. She sees her job as limiting the damage."

"We'll have to keep an eye on this," I said.

Before my first day in the White House was over, the TV pundits had turned from retrospectives on the Mulroney-Myers administration to examining the Steinsaltz and Fisher nominations. Secretary Fisher called a secure video meeting of the entire staff, some at far-flung outposts around the globe, and skillfully fielded their questions.

At day's end, I sat alone in the Oval Office at the desk that President Mulroney and many of our predecessors had used. The dead president's books and mementoes had been hastily packed, and a few cartons lined one wall.

I heard a knock, and before I could call out, the door swung open and Gwyneth came in with two flutes of champagne on a silver tray.

"Champagne, Mr. President," she announced with a big smile.

"You are the perfect image of a first lady," I said, moving to a sofa where we could sit together.

"How do you feel?" she asked.

"That this can't be happening to me ... to us."

"It is," Gwyn said, "it really is. I've already begun thinking about how to use the opportunity. Tell me about your first day."

§§§

State of the Union, February 14, 2024

The combined efforts of Russian and American intelligence agencies provided our first good lead to the terrorists who killed the American vice president and the Russian premier. The NSA captured signal intelligence that pointed to a minor player in the conspiracy, and the Russians were able to trace the source of the intercept to a transmission tower in Mazur-i-Sharif in northern Afghanistan, broadcasting in the local Uzbek language.

Next, Russian agents of Uzbek ethnicity were sent to Mazur-i-Sharif to infiltrate suspect groups. They found and befriended the minor player and through him learned the identity of a participating programmer in Dagestan. Dagestan proved to be the hub of a network that reached into the other Stans, and Russian intelligence methodically planted ethnically-compatible double agents in a half-dozen nodes of the terror network.

In the aftermath of the attack, Russian President Anatoly Kostikov and I began conferring on a regular basis. One early result was the creation of a joint Special Ops capability, codenamed AmerRuss. Sooner than anyone thought possible, AmerRuss would make its existence known to those who had assassinated Sally Myers and the premier.

But before we were ready to act, I was scheduled to deliver the annual State of the Union address. Amid a crescendo of calls for military action, I addressed a joint session of Congress, knowing that nothing I could possibly say would slake the nation's thirst for revenge.

Joint Chiefs Chairman Harris had continued to press his view that merely condemning the villainy and promising retaliation would embolden the terrorists, unless it was backed up with a missile strike on at least one of the targets we had identified. He brushed aside the argument, made by Bill Dickinson, that attacking even one target before we had the full network in our sights would drive the rest of the network further underground.

Secretary of State Fisher agreed with the CIA director, and argued strenuously—to General Harris's face—that military action was premature and would achieve the terrorists' goal of provoking the United States into an indiscriminate attack, causing collateral damage that would strengthen local support for the assassins.

As satisfying as it would have been for me to announce in the State of the Union speech that the terrorists had been brought to justice, we just weren't ready to act, and I dared not even hint that we were making good progress. To Congress and the American people I could only repeat my promise that when we had the perpetrators in our sights we would strike, and leave none who attacked our nation, or who might be planning to, in doubt about the long reach of American justice. I concluded with this:

"If Vice President Myers could speak to us tonight, I know she would counsel patience. Do it, but do it right, she would say.

"Until we are in a position to do it right, anything you hear about our plans will not be true, and anything true, you will not hear. I know you understand why it must be so."

My vows did little to cool the inflamed passions sweeping the country and, to my dismay, voices in the military, most notably that of its highest ranking officer, Chairman Harris, continued to stoke people's appetite for immediate action.

Within a week of my speech, in an address to the Veterans of Foreign Wars, General Harris described the reach of our military as sufficient to inflict lethal damage anywhere in the world, and went on to wonder aloud what was keeping us from doing so. "Above all," he intoned, "the most powerful nation on Earth must never look weak. Our enemies interpret inaction as an invitation to walk all over us."

What does Harris want? I wondered. Is he begging to be sacked?

The very next day, following a speech Harris gave to the cadets at West Point, he upped the ante. When a journalist asked him about the morale of the Armed Forces under the new president, Harris, knowing that he was being recorded, said, "There aren't many commanders in chief like Mike Mulroney. He was someone we looked up to."

The journalist followed up. "And now? President Blue?"

"Where's 'tough,' when we need it?" the General barked.

That evening, sound bites of Harris's remarks aired on every media outlet. I asked Defense Secretary Chilton to come to the White House, without aides. I had already decided to relieve General Harris of duty, but I wanted to give the secretary a chance to declare herself on the matter, as well as to sound her out on a replacement.

When Hazel was seated in the Oval Office she asked me if she could tell me something before we took up the matter at hand—which was obvious to her. She wanted me to know that she understood why President Mulroney had appointed her—just as he had named Sally Myers vice president—to increase his percentage of the women's vote.

"I knew I was window dressing when I took the job," Hazel went on, "but I took it in the belief that I owed it to my gender to demonstrate that a woman could serve as defense secretary."

"It was clear from the outset that President Mulroney and Chairman Harris had an understanding: Harris would provide key military advice; I was supposed to show the flag. I've been planning to submit my resignation in December."

"Are you still determined to leave?"

"There's something I'd like to do before I answer your question, Mr. President."

"What's that?"

"Fire General Harris."

We had a good laugh. I thought, Hazel Chilton is someone I could work with. She even brought some levity to the job. Whoever established the post of court jester had done governance a true service.

"I'd say go right ahead, Hazel, but I think that's my job. What do you say we do it together?"

"When?"

"I can't think of a better time than now, that is, if you'll promise not to quit after the deed is done."

"If you think I can still be of use, I would be honored to continue serving, Mr. President. Regardless of my job status, I do have something I'd like to discuss with you at the first opportunity. It concerns Operation AmerRuss. General Harris has done his best to keep me out of the loop on it, but I have my sources."

"We'll talk about AmerRuss tomorrow, but first I'd like to know who you recommend to replace Harris as Chairman."

Hazel didn't skip a beat: "Chief of Staff of the Army, General Magdelena Cole."

Two women in the two top spots, I thought. That'll make the hawks crazy—but if they tried to use it, they'd be shooting themselves in the foot. General Cole was no wimp.

"Thank you, Secretary Chilton. Now, let's meet the press."

§§§

General Harris did not take his dismissal lying down. Unlike General MacArthur, who gave a mournful old-soldiers-never-die-they-just-fade-away speech to Congress, then proceeded to do just that, General Harris held a news conference the next morning and announced his candidacy for president. He described me as the "illegitimate heir to the legacy of President Mulroney and Vice President Myers," and promised to restore the days when America "counted for something on the world stage."

In the days following Harris's firing, a few members of Congress floated the idea of impeaching me, but when it drew little support they let the matter drop.

For a day or two, I wondered if it might have been wiser to delay firing Harris until the primary season was too far advanced for him to compete for the nomination. But wasn't the choice between our two visions of America's future precisely the one I wanted to ask the country to make? General Harris had framed the debate. Time would tell whose case Americans found more convincing.

§§§

The House at Place des Vosges, March 5, 2024

What Hazel Chilton wanted me to know was that she had a personal connection to the Russian defense minister. She thought it might help us develop AmerRuss into a surgical foreign policy tool. Thirty years before, during the Yeltsin era, Hazel had spent a year in Russia as an exchange student. There she'd befriended Dimitri Ivanov, who now presided, as did she, over his nation's defenses. As students they had shared an interest in World War II history, and read and discussed Vitaly Grossman's classic account of the Battle of Stalingrad, *Life and Fate.* They also had visited the sites of the decisive battles in Stalingrad and Kursk together.

They'd stayed in touch over the years, and marveled at the uncanny parallels in their careers, and since they'd become defense ministers they'd exchanged visits to each other's countries.

General Harris, as the de facto head of President Mulroney's Defense Department, had marginalized Hazel, but her connection with Ivanov was alive and well. Because of their personal friend-ship, there was the potential for uncommonly effective military collaboration. I didn't probe the nature of their long-standing friendship, but whatever it was, Hazel was right in suggesting that we pursue this avenue.

Immediately after our talk I asked Hazel to go to Moscow to see if anything could be done to hasten the date when AmerRuss could take action. My State of the Union speech had given us some breathing room, but I knew that the pressure to retaliate would increase until, by summer, to resist it would be political suicide. All I had to do to ensure Harris's election in November was—nothing.

To keep Hazel's mission to Moscow out of the headlines, Ka-ren suggested that we fold it into the March G-20 Summit in Paris. It was decided that, in addition to Defense Secretary Chilton, the AmerRuss task force would consist of the director of the CIA, and the new Joint Chiefs Chairman, General Cole, whose confirmation had been surprisingly uneventful, even in the wake of Harris's noi-sy exit.

Earlier in Cole's career she had commanded Special Forces Operations, and in addition to her native Spanish, she spoke a half-dozen languages, including Urdu, Farsi, Turkish, and Arabic.

Filling out the AmerRuss team were two personal representa-tives of mine, Rowan and Marisol Ellway. Like Hazel, Rowan had friends in the Russian Defense and Intelligence agencies, dating from his days in Moscow as a SALT negotiator. Marisol had built on the Russian she'd acquired in Moscow in the early nineties to earn a Ph.D. in Russian Politics and Culture from Johns Hopkins University. Throughout my political career Marisol was my person-al advisor on all things Russian. By including Rowan and Marisol in the delegation I was signaling the Russians that they should not doubt the strength of my commitment.

§§§

Since that fateful day in January, 1992, after Marisol and I had spent a week at François's Place des Vosges town house, and he'd returned and informed us of our kinship, I'd visited him there on many occasions. But for most of the period after that, Marisol had refused to set foot in the place.

Then, in 2005, on a Paris tour of American Ballet Theatre, there had been a mix-up over hotel reservations. Marisol, after checking with François, had taken three of the dancers with her to stay at his house. A week of playing hostess there must have diminished any lingering trauma she'd experienced from her ill-starred sojourn with me there years before, because from then on (with François's blessing) the town house was her Paris home.

Gwyneth and I also had made it our home when my work in Congress took me to Paris. I'd have liked to stay there during the summit, but since I'd become president, the Secret Service controlled logistics. When they told me that if I slept there, the police would have to close off access to the Place des Vosges for days, I dropped the idea.

So, only Marisol stayed at Place des Vosges. Rowan and Easter preferred a small hotel in the Marais, and I was locked up in a presidential suite somewhere. Had it not been for a dinner party that Marisol organized for my fifty-first birthday, I probably wouldn't even have seen François and my old home on this trip.

In addition to my family members, Galia Steinsaltz, Ben's daughter, who'd flown to Paris with us on Air Force One, was expected to drop by the town house on her way to a private party at the Chinese Embassy.

Galia had picked up spoken Chinese from her mother, former New York City Ballet dancer Ellie Liang, and by the time she graduated from the University of California at Berkeley, she had spent a year in Beijing and was almost as comfortable there as in Washington, D.C. At Berkeley, Galia, who had her father's strength and her mother's agility, was a standout on the women's tennis team. On and off the court, she evinced a sense of high purpose. Most college-age men were too shy to approach her, but she had a steady stream of international suitors.

Galia had pursued a doctorate at Johns Hopkins while she was interning in her father's Senate office and, at Ben's suggestion, I'd brought her into the West Wing as a junior member of the National Security staff. She was a natural at politics, and there was already speculation that someday she'd follow in her father's footsteps.

If my generation had traveled the world, Galia's friends were at home in it. My friends had studied French, Spanish, or German, and tended to speak one of these "foreign" languages haltingly. Galia had friends who were fluent in Arabic, Chinese, Hindi, Bangla, Farsi, Malay, Tagalog, and Swahili.

By her early twenties, she'd met the cultural and political elite of the world. Her voracious curiosity had exposed her to rural poverty in China, Indonesia, and Brazil, and to the urban slums of Dhaka, Mumbai, and Karachi. On one occasion, when I'd heard her discussing politics with her friends, it crossed my mind that if human beings managed to create a just and equitable world, it would be the achievement of her generation, not mine. The most Ben and I could hope for would be to catch a glimpse of it from our rocking chairs.

§§§

At Place des Vosges, when I arrived everyone had gathered and, knowing that Galia had to leave before dinner, I engaged her first.

"How are your folks?" I asked.

"Mom's hosting an event at the Kennedy Center tonight; Dad's in New York."

"What for?" I asked, surprised that Ben wasn't in Washington. Our understanding was that when I was away, he would hold the fort in the capital.

"He didn't say, but he sounded tired. You should make him take a vacation."

We dined at the baobab table I had played under as a child, just six of us—François and his cousin, Viviane, Rowan and Easter, Marisol and me. As always, the Secret Service stood guard, but by this time I was used to its unobtrusive ubiquity.

Gwyneth was at the United Nations, chairing the first ever global conference of Dignity Now!, the women's organization she had founded soon after becoming first lady. If I won a full term she planned to establish chapters of Dignity Now! in every bastion of male supremacy the world over. I knew our marriage had suffered from my heavy schedule and frequent absences, but I took some comfort in the idea that Gwyn had an important project of her own.

Viviane had brought in a French chef who prepared a six-course dinner served with a different wine for each course. When it was time for dessert, Marisol presented me with a rectangular cake with fifty-one candles arranged in three rows of seventeen. She knew I was fond of prime numbers, and the configuration of the candles expressed my age in prime factors. The inherent (a more devout man would say God-given) structure of the whole numbers is about as close as I come to experiencing religious awe.

As I prepared to leave, Marisol pulled me aside and asked me if I knew why Ben was in New York. We'd both thought he'd be with Ellie at the Kennedy Center gala. I meant to ask Karen to find out, but the unceasing whirl of the presidency drew me into the vortex, and I didn't follow up.

§§§

AmerRuss, April 9, 2024

I returned to Washington immediately after the G-20 Summit, and several days later the *AmerRuss* task force arrived home from Moscow. Marisol came straight to the White House to brief me before my meeting with the whole group.

It had been a sentimental trip for her. The last time she'd been in Moscow with Rowan was the day of the Gorbachev coup, when they sped by taxi to the airport, sausages in hand. "Dad wanted to be here," Marisol said, "but I made him go home to rest."

"How did he hold up?"

"No one would believe he's eighty-seven, but Secretary Chilton went out of her way to make things easy for him. She insisted that he take her room on the plane."

"Gallant," I said, making a mental note to thank her with a bouquet.

"We dropped by the Embassy to see our old apartment, and I went by the Ballet Academy and found one of my old classmates. But the best thing was Dad running into his old Russian girlfriend, Katya."

"What?"

"Before he reconnected with your mom. She was his interpreter in the arms negotiations. I gave her a hard time then."

"Why?"

"I thought she was using Dad to get to America. Plus, she was too young for him."

"Maybe you were jealous."

"Probably. When I saw them light up, I realized they had really meant something to each other. Anyway, she married one of Yeltsin's staff and now manages the pool of interpreters that work in the Kremlin."

"Was it worth Dad's going?"

"Yes, very much so. He kept our eye on the ball by reminding everyone that the goal was not to kill terrorists, but to put terrorism out of business."

I wanted to understand everything about the terrorists—their identities, nationalities, motives, means, funding, and connections. Marisol reported that the Russians had indeed proceeded, step by step, to place undercover agents in cells in Uzbekistan, Dagestan, and Kazakhstan. The plan was to identify as many nodes of the network as possible, and then send in the Special Forces.

I asked her when the Russians thought we'd be ready to go, adding, "If we don't act by summer, the voters will turn me out and Harris will send in the bombers."

"Ask Hazel and Maggie," Marisol answered.

"*Hazel* and *Maggie*?" I exclaimed in comic disbelief.

"That's what we called them. The group bonded. Maybe it was because there were so many women. From the start, Dimitri

Ivanov and Secretary Chilton called each other Mitya and Hazel. Then Mitya asked Magdelena if he could call her Maggie, and she suggested that we all dispense with formalities. It was the most fun I've ever had in government."

"AmerRuss sounds like a movie."

"A thriller, with a love story at its heart."

"Now you've got my attention!"

"Hazel and Mitya behaved like former lovers. I think they may still be friends with benefits. They regaled us with stories of traveling around the Soviet Union when they were in their twenties. Russians know how to party. Hazel dropped fifteen years before our eyes. Mitya got me to demonstrate the Russian dance in *Nutcracker*, and everyone joined in. Picture Maggie doing the Trepak?"

"Time to revert to 'General Cole.' I hear them in the Oval Office."

Karen had seated the AmerRuss task force, and when Marisol and I entered through the side door they rose as one.

After Secretary Chilton gave a progress report, Bill Dickinson told us that his Russian counterpart had informed him that they had planted an agent in a cell in Peshawar. At the sound of "Peshawar," memories of Élodie's run-in with the Taliban and our escape over the Karakoram Highway flooded my mind.

As I quickly brought myself back to the present, General Cole was describing plans for putting commando teams in positions to execute a simultaneous takedown of a half-dozen terrorist cells spread across Central Asia.

After absorbing this, I asked the two obvious questions. Regarding possible collateral damage, the answer was "very little, if any." Maggie's plan was to rely entirely on elite professionals on the ground. No planes, no cruise missiles, no drones. "You don't want to know how the terrorists will die," she added, "but be assured, they will die, and very quickly. There will be no explosions larger than a percussion grenade."

"Once we hit one group, won't others be alerted?" I asked.

"Remember the scene in that old film *The Godfather*, when Michael Corleone's men take out five mafia bosses while his son is being baptized? It'll be like that. There will not be time for phone calls."

"How many targets have we got now?"

"Four and counting. Ideally, we'd like to wait till we've infiltrated the whole network."

"How many cells in the network?"

"Eight that we're sure of, so we've got our people in half of them. Of course, there's a point where the risk of being found out exceeds the value of identifying additional cells. We hope to pull the trigger within a month."

"Anything more you want me to do?"

"Defense Minister Ivanov asks that you stay in frequent contact with the Russian president."

"I fully intend to. I see AmerRuss as the beginning of a beautiful friendship. I'd like to build on this joint effort to reconstitute our World War II alliance. It's time for a reset. That war was about territory. This one is about justice and, once again, Russian participation is indispensable."

When they'd all left I wondered if I'd spoken too freely. If AmerRuss failed and the assassins of Sally Myers were not brought to justice, I'd be gone in six months.

Six weeks later, I addressed the nation from the Oval Office:

"As I speak, the president of Russia is addressing the citizens of his country. In the last few hours, in simultaneous attacks at nine locations throughout Central Asia, joint American and Russian forces have conducted precision raids on the terrorists who killed Vice President Sally Myers and the Russian premier.

"By sharing intelligence and collaborating on the application of lethal force, we have eliminated the threat posed by a terrorist network with cells from the Black Sea to the Indian Ocean.

"Vice President Myers would be glad to know that justice has been dealt to her murderers without the loss of innocent life. Russian and American troops accepted risk to themselves in order to protect the lives of those among whom the terrorists were hiding.

Our casualties were minimal, and the brave men and women who carried out these raids are now out of harm's way.

"For reasons of security, I will give no further details. But I will say this: America and Russia are prepared to act together against terrorism whenever the need arises. Anyone who is considering a career as a terrorist should know that he or she will face the combined resources of our two nations. What I am saying to would-be terrorists is: Your career will be brief, your death certain, and your legacy as shameful as that of the common enemy we destroyed in World War II.

"But if, instead of forming clandestine groups to plot against us, you choose to talk to us, to lay your claims before us, and to work with us toward a fair and just resolution of legitimate grievances, then we will welcome you as partners in building a world of dignity for all.

"I will have more to say about dignity and justice in the coming months. But tonight, the first lady and I, accompanied by the vice president and Mrs. Steinsaltz, will proceed from the White House to Arlington National Cemetery to lay a wreath at the grave of our beloved Vice President Sally Myers, in whose name justice has this day been done. May she rest in peace."

Had Operation AmerRuss failed, I would surely have been one of the briefest-serving presidents in American history. With its success, Ben and I had a chance to win election to a full term.

§§§

Four More Years

There had been many in the Democratic Party who believed that its candidates would fare better in local elections if the ticket were headed by someone other than me. Political cartoons often depicted me with my head in the clouds. But despite the misgivings of party stalwarts and progressive pundits, no one had stepped forward to challenge me for the nomination.

As expected, the Republican nomination had gone to the bellicose General Harris, and until the success of Operation Amer-

Russ, he had enjoyed a comfortable lead in the polls. But TV images of Ben and me and our wives, heads bowed, at the Arlington gravesite of Vice President Sally Myers, proved to be a turning point in the campaign of 2024.

Overnight, my image morphed from Wimp to Top Gun. Suddenly, Ben and I led the polling in several states that General Harris had thought were his, and without which he could not carry the electoral college.

To capitalize on our good fortune, Ben spent a lot of time in traditionally conservative strongholds. Appearing together, we appealed to Independents in states where voters had become disenchanted with social conservatism, and fearful that Harris's belligerent foreign policy could take us into another war.

Easter managed our appeal to the boomer generation. The majority of baby boomers, still nostalgic for the activism of the sixties, could be counted on to vote Democratic. Easter's job was to make sure that our political ads reminded them that their natural home was still with the party that had brought the country civil rights for minorities and equitable treatment of women.

At Karen's suggestion I hired Brad Alvarez, the whip-smart political operative who'd guided Senator Johnson to a win in Florida, to direct the campaign for our reelection. Marisol continued in her role as political advisor. For the duration of the campaign, Gwyneth focused Dignity Now! on issues affecting the lives of American women and girls. And me—the candidate—how did the campaign propose to use me? There was a tug of war within the staff as to whether to unleash me or muzzle me.

Having devoted my political career to persuading voters that our future lay in a less bellicose direction, I was determined not to trade too heavily on the Top Gun image. But Karen and Marisol warned me not to let "the pussycat out of the bag" before the election. I was reminded of Saint Augustine's prayer for "chastity, but not yet." Throughout the summer and fall of 2024, Brad kept up a chorus of "not yet."

"Let the public savor a macho moment," he counseled. "Many Americans, especially Harris's backers, still love their guns. With AmerRuss, you stole the general's thunder. Save talk of the future for the Inauguration."

As it happened, we did keep the foreign policy implications of our dignitarian agenda under wraps, but I gave voice to its domestic implications in my acceptance speech at the Democratic National Convention. It would have been hard not to because all my congressional campaigns had been based on translating the principle of Dignity for All into political policy.

The difference between those campaigns and this one, however, was that then I was a lawmaker. As president, I could not only influence legislation, but also advance dignitarian ideals from the bully pulpit.

Despite Karen's and Brad's advice, on a few occasions I did comment on the *global* implications of Dignity for All. Whereas General Harris dwelled on past acts of terrorism, and advocated preemptive attacks to prevent future ones, I argued that a vital part of a strong defense was to avoid giving offense in the first place.

My staff tensed up every time I touched on foreign affairs, but as it happened, the hints I dropped about the need for a new system of global governance received little attention. Pundits of the right were too busy stoking fears of the nuclear terrorism General Harris had alluded to in our presidential debates, while pundits of the left were still basking in the afterglow of AmerRuss.

§§§

Inauguration, January 20, 2025

It was from my mother, Easter Blue, that I got the question that gave direction to my life. At bedtime she'd often read aloud to me from *The Once and Future King*, T. H. White's retelling of the story of King Arthur and the Knights of the Round Table. In my teens, at a time when I was troubled over a girl, she reminded me of the tale of "Sir Gawain and Lady Ragnell," which turns on the answer to the question, "What do women want?"

As I grew up, Gawain's question morphed into a more general one: What do *people* want?

Like Arthur's knights, I combed the world for an answer. I found pieces of it in many places, and they all came together on a railway platform in Siberia. Ever since, I've been trying to show others the centrality of dignity in personal and political affairs.

Before I describe the fateful events of the term to which Ben and I had just been elected, I want to explain what I mean by dignity, and why I see it as an indispensable foundation for human relationships and governance.

At bottom, dignity means belonging, membership, a secure place in the "tribe." Quite simply, dignity means "in"; indignity "out."

Psychologically, dignity means inclusion and recognition. Socially, it means equal opportunity to contribute. Materially, dignity means having the essentials required to pursue happiness—health, education, income sufficient to live securely, and a voice in governance.

I planned to use the inaugural address to suggest that the only thing as important as how we treat the planet is how we treat each other.

Of the three men who contributed most to my philosophical outlook, one was absent and two remained. Gone to the icy slopes of Mt. Kanchenjunga was Professor Lahiri of Banaras. With me still was the man who had raised me, François Merle, the primary source of my philosophy of life; and my biological father, Rowan Ellway, who I thought of as my personal Jefferson.

Before I wrote my inaugural speech I asked Rowan for his thoughts on how best to use the opportunity. A few days later I received this memorandum:

> To: Adam Blue, President
> From: Rowan Ellway
> Date: November 9, 2024
>
> The last time I was in Jerusalem, I met the president of Al-Quds University, a Palestinian writer named Sari Nusseibeh. The Nusseibeh family traces its ancestry back to the time of Jesus. For two thousand years, the Nusseibehs

have been the custodians of the Church of the Holy Sepulchre, by tradition the place of Christ's Crucifixion and Resurrection. Sari and I got to talking about his family's place in Jerusalem's history, and he told me something his father had taught him.

The elder Nusseibeh maintained that virtually all family dynasties, including their own, can trace their privilege to an act of brigandage. Think about that. It is an admission, by an aristocratic family, that its social status originated in a theft, one it got away with.

I find this revelatory. We, who enjoy privileged lives, are the beneficiaries of crimes airbrushed from history. Our initial advantage, the head start upon which our subsequent gains depended, was the result of a crime sanitized by time. In this important sense, our elevated status is not of our own making. While hard work and luck are part of the story, so also are opportunistic predation and chicanery. It's a humbling recognition, and it has implications for political policy.

The impact of the senior Nusseibeh's insight is all the greater because it was not intended to instill guilt. Rather, it is a nonjudgmental acknowledgment that current inequalities rest on a foundation of past iniquities. The moral is: Do not decry the past. The implication is: Change the game going forward.

How must the new game differ from the old?

The answer is so simple it's usually overlooked. We blind ourselves to it because we don't want to admit that our relative success is mostly due to unfair advantages.

That's what it is going to take to make the "game of life" work for everyone—

unimpeachable fairness. Our challenge, from here on out, is to identify and root out every instance and every kind of unfairness, as if unfairness itself is our enemy. Because it is.

Unfairness is experienced as indignity and indignity breeds indignation. No wonder that angry protests ensue. They can be violent or non-violent. Either response is disruptive. Nonviolent protest is usually more effective in the long run than armed uprisings because it's more likely to permanently break the vicious cycle of reciprocating indignities.

If the dispossessed cannot live in dignity, they increasingly have it within their power to see that no one else does either. The price of social peace and economic prosperity is equal opportunity and equitable recognition for everyone in the global community. In short, an end to the indignities that are still the daily lot of many. The issue is whether we'll invite those who are currently taken for nobodies into the human family or force them to crash our gates.

People want dignity for themselves more than they want to humiliate their oppressors. In this proposition lies hope for humanity. If it's right, the poor will choose an escape from relative poverty over the fleeting satisfaction of bringing down the privileged.

Every act of indignity can be traced to a prior indignity, but it's rarely possible to identify the first link in the chain. So we have to start, not with the first indignity, but with the most recent one, and work backward until we've identified as many precursors as possible. Then, we survey the entire sequence, from initial acts of brigandage to indentured servitude to the form indignity takes today—subsistence labor maintained by chronic poverty—and acknowledge the lot, without blame or guilt.

With the history of indignity spread out before us, we're in a position to strike a grand bargain. In return for acknowledging past indignities and forswearing future ones, past indignities are forgiven. The slate is wiped clean, but *only insofar as future indignities are scrupulously disallowed and rigorously eliminated.* Instead of indulging in recrimination and revenge, we get on with the task of building a dignitarian world.

The guiding, inviolate principle is dignity for all. Since most manmade indignities stem from abuses of power—*rankism*—the operational recipe for building a dignitarian society is to disallow rankism (in much the same way that building a multicultural world required that we dismantle racist institutions and disallow racist practices).

To gain support for the grand bargain, we must not frame it as either a victory or a defeat for liberty or equality. To move beyond libertarian and egalitarian ideologies, we need a dignitarian synthesis that incorporates the partial truths the Right and Left have long championed.

Such comprehensive bargains are not unprecedented. Examples of previous realignments of power include Britain and India; France and Algeria; whites and blacks in the United States; and the USSR and the former Soviet Republics. The transition in South Africa from apartheid to democracy was exemplary.

I foresee a two-stage process. The first is to communicate the dignitarian idea in every language, culture, and society. Then, when a broad social consensus is in place, a worldwide institutional base will have to be built to secure dignity at all levels of human interaction.

Your life has equipped you for the first of these tasks. It's apt to fall to future generations to institutionalize the politics of dignity.

§§§

At the beginning of my first full term as president, just moments after I took the oath of office on January 20, 2025, I addressed the nation from the west portico of the Capitol. After outlining plans for a domestic Dignity Deal, I concluded with my reasons for believing that securing global peace and prosperity depended on replacing the UN Security Council with a new institution that I called the Dignity Council.

For our own security, we must secure human dignity, not just for Americans, not for any one group at the expense of another, but dignity for the entire human family. In this shrinking world, we're all members of one tribe—humankind.

If there *were* a more effective way to make Americans safe, I would be duty-bound to pursue it. But there is no way to make anyone, or any people, secure so long as anywhere on Earth there remain pockets of indignity.

Any such pocket is a time-bomb. By not defusing it, we accept the inevitability of retaliatory indignities.

The world we share has become so interconnected and interdependent that it won't work for anyone unless it works for everyone. There is no fortress strong enough to protect us from both weapons of mass destruction and techniques of massive disruption.

Building a *dignitarian* world requires a reset that will be the work of many generations, long beyond my time in office. I intend to make a start by proposing the creation of a Dignity Council.

The world has undergone an epochal change since the United Nations was designed at the time of World War II. Our institutions of governance have not kept pace with the new realities of development and globalization.

I will seek the support of other world leaders to update the composition and the structure of the UN's Security Council so it can serve a global community.

The design of the Dignity Council must itself emerge collaboratively. In the coming weeks I will begin the process by conferring with the leaders of the European Union, Russia, India, China, and others.

As we attempt to lay the foundation for a new global institution to safeguard dignity and justice, there is something of equal importance you can do.

Ask yourself, "Am I willing to accord dignity to others in return for dignity for myself, my family, and my countrymen?"

If your answer is Yes, then, wherever you are, start to look for ways to remove the indignities that diminish the lives of those around you, and begin building homes, schools, communities, and a world, of dignity for all.

§§§

The Dignity Deal and Dignity Council, 2025

Following the inauguration, we set to work. Ben's focus was domestic; mine was global. The vice president campaigned nationally to build public support for passage of the Dignity Deal. In a half-dozen venues where he thought my presence would be a plus, we appeared together.

Ben, from his position as president of the Senate, also lobbied his senatorial colleagues to make the Dignity Deal the law of the land. He made a strong case: Its passage would cap a century-long journey that included President Roosevelt's New Deal, Truman's Fair Deal, Johnson's Great Society, and Obamacare. Key provisions of the Dignity Deal were: equal access to higher education, strengthened agencies to safeguard against predatory financial practices and environmental depredation, a living wage, and campaign finance reform to curtail the influence of money in politics.

The Dignity Deal aimed to do for people who lacked the protection of rank what the New Deal did for labor and civil rights legislation did for minorities. If it were adopted, rankism wouldn't vanish, but it would be stripped of its legitimacy; and those who engaged in it would find themselves on the defensive.

While Ben built domestic and congressional support for the Dignity Deal, I traveled abroad to introduce our proposal to modernize the United Nations by transforming the structure and composition of the Security Council and, to signal these fundamental changes, renaming it the Dignity Council.

A key difference between the Security Council, which gave dominant roles to the victors of World War II, and the Dignity Council, was in their composition. The members of the Security Council were nations; the components of the Dignity Council would be supranational entities that qualified as credible guarantors of dignity. Their treatment of those within their boundaries, and their conduct internationally would determine whether they qualified.

§§§

Everywhere I went, I got an earful. Countries that had once been colonies of imperial powers seized the chance to vent their anger over past humiliations. The United States came in for criticism for its support of dictators who had served American interests, and for domestic subsidies that undercut free trade.

Where there was still bitterness over past humiliations, taking my cue from Rowan's memo, I suggested that mutual dignity might be found through a process like that of the Truth and Reconciliation Commission, or TRC, that had been used in South Africa to deal with the crimes and injustices of apartheid. For any people or nation that made a credible case that it had suffered an indignity, the Dignity Council would provide a safe forum for confronting the party it holds responsible. The "deal" would be that the victims of past abuses forswear revenge in return for the opportunity of a fair hearing, and a guarantee going forward of truly equal opportunity to compete for rewards and recognition.

TRCs would operate at all levels, from local to national to regional to continental to global. Under their aegis, the watchword Dignity for All would be made operational—among states, tribes, groups, sects, ethnicities, religions; between the rich and the poor; between those who take themselves for somebodies and those whom they have mistaken for nobodies, and seen fit to exploit.

One of the responsibilities of the Dignity Council would be to operate international TRCs and provide expertise to local ones. Since indignity is a consequence of rank abuse, TRC staff would function as ombudspersons charged with distinguishing legitimate uses of rank (e.g., holding office), from rankism (e.g., corruption), and upholding the former while delegitimizing the latter.

I believed that once the TRCs were in place, the dignitarian approach to conflict resolution would gain traction.

§§§

Back home, the response was lukewarm. It wasn't so much that people disagreed with this form of conflict resolution—there was none better. It was rather that Americans felt I should be focused on *their* problems. Much as I tried to show them that peace abroad would redound to our benefit, and as much as Ben showed up at the scene of every hurricane and flood, there still was mounting criticism of my foreign travels and international focus. They were only to increase—the travels and the criticism.

Before I continue, I must mention a tireless champion of dignity—my wife, First Lady Gwyneth Lionel. If my approach was top down, hers was bottom up.

Gwyneth was a master of grassroots organization. Within months of my assuming the presidency she gave form to her dream of making the right to dignity gender-neutral by founding Dignity Now!. She spent a lot of time away from the White House, traveling the globe, meeting with government officials, and holding conferences, with the goal of making women's and girls' claims to dignity as strong as those of men and boys.

Since the 1970s, Americans have recognized NOW as the acronym of the National Organization for Women which, from its founding in 1968, spearheaded equal rights for American women. For women and girls on every continent, Dignity Now! embodied the message that they had a right to fulfill their individual potential and enjoy coequal partnerships with men in the global economy.

By putting the female half of humankind in the spotlight, Gwyneth's organization introduced dignitarian values in homes, schools, workplaces, and religious and healthcare organizations. Some saw it as a Trojan Horse intended to undermine traditional gender roles. In public, Gwyneth always denied the accusation; in private, that's exactly how she described Dignity Now!.

Gwyneth's message of dignity for women and girls and Ben's message of dignity for all Americans complemented each other, and sometimes the two leaders appeared together on the same stage. Of those they made their case to, few were immune to their combined appeal.

§§§

Russia, April 2025

As crucial as it was to get the United States and European Union aboard, the participation of Russia, India, and China was indispensable to the viability of the Dignity Council. The residents of these five giants comprised two out of every three people on Earth. Here's the story of how, with the help of France, we secured Russia's participation.

France was no longer a world power, but its good offices were nonetheless critical to the Russian initiative. As a prominent businessman, François had access to the French president, Jean Massengale. As a senior officer of Doctors Without Border, so did Élodie. On my behalf, François and Élodie met with President Massengale to let him know that I would be asking him to accompany me to Moscow to make the case for the Dignity Council to the Russian president. Along with drawing on the historic ties between France and Russia, I believed that France, as the nation that had given the world "Liberté, Égalité, Fraternité," should have a say about the addition of "Dignité." In an auspicious coincidence, it was Massengale's turn as president of the European Union.

Meetings between heads of state are always carefully prepared through diplomatic channels. If I know people with on-the-ground experience that's relevant to the issue at hand, I try to deploy them as personal intermediaries, as François and Élodie were with the French president. For the Russian president, the choice was obvious. In the aftermath of their diplomatic roles in project AmerRuss, Rowan and Marisol would make the perfect advance party.

Rowan had spent the week prior to my visit in briefings, seeing old colleagues, and making new connections. Marisol, whose fame as a ballerina was further bolstered by her fluent Russian, had paid a visit to the Bolshoi before she accompanied Rowan to his meeting with President Kostikov. It never hurts to bring a beautiful and gracious woman to a meeting of male dignitaries. Her presence functions to remind them that they're human beings before they're VIPs. That this woman was my sister was icing on the cake.

President Massengale and I flew to Moscow on Air Force One and were shown into the Kremlin office of the Russian president together. Before taking up the business at hand, Anatoly Romanovich Kostikov turned to me and joked that Operation AmerRuss hadn't hurt either of us in our respective countries' polls.

After President Massengale and I outlined the case for the Dignity Council, President Kostikov jolted me with, "Is dignity your Holy Grail?"

His question was blunt enough to push me to a new level of candor. "God has long served Man as the dignifier of last resort. Victims of indignity look to Him to affirm their dignity when their fellow men deny it. So the answer to your question is *yes*—dignity is the Holy Grail of human relationships."

Then I asked Anatoly if he knew Tolstoy's story *Master and Man*, in which a coach driver and his employer are marooned in a snowstorm. As he nodded affirmatively, I saw him lower his eyes as if to control his feelings. "To many Russians, Tolstoy is a saint," he said.

"It was from him, and that story in particular, that I came to understand dignity as the social counterpart of love," I said. "I believe that if we can secure dignity for all, we will have put in place the prerequisite for peace on Earth. Indignities and injustices will surely still arise, but they will not persist, because they will be diagnosed and treated as curable maladies, not used as pretexts for hostility and war."

"I hope you're not deluding yourself," the Russian president countered.

"I know I sound like the man who claims the sun is coming out when it's been raining for months and dark clouds still fill the sky. To be sure, such optimism is usually misplaced. But not always. Once in a while the rains stop and the sun *does* come out. I'm saying that this is one of those times—but only if Russia participates; only if Russia and America act together. That's why I've come to you first."

"I see."

"If America, Russia, India, and China, along with the European Union, stand together for dignity, no domestic tyranny and no international aggression can stand against them."

"Why can't this be done through the UN Security Council?" Anatoly asked.

This was the jackpot question. Now, for the first time, I would be trying out my answer on someone with the power to bury the idea simply by refusing to consider it.

"The Security Council consists of nation states. Naturally, members put national interests over regional and global ones. I'm proposing that the Dignity Council consist of regional supranational entities."

"The model for this is the European Union," Jean added. "By virtue of its composition, it embodies a transnational perspective. If the nations of North America were to form a union, that would be another example of a supranational entity. Each entity would undoubtedly bear the stamp of its history. Some might have open borders, others not."

I jumped in. "In the case of Russia, your recent history suggests a possible answer. As a regional organization, the Confederation of Independent States would be a natural candidate for membership on the Dignity Council. Likewise, geography suggests a union of South American states for charter membership. To an initial handful of regional entities we could add others until the Dignity Council became the principal forum for global affairs."

"Of course, it would be … what do you say, "dead on arrival" without the Indian Subcontinent and China," Anatoly remarked.

"I think there's a good chance that the subcontinent will want to participate," I said. "And, if it did opt in, China might conclude that it's better to be in than out."

"But wouldn't China first have to make some changes to qualify for admission?" Anatoly asked. "As far as democracy goes, it's still where Russia was decades ago."

"True enough," I said, "but from what I can tell, the Chinese leadership is acutely aware of the need for political change. They just don't want to risk chaos. President Zheng and I have begun a correspondence and we've agreed to an exchange of summits."

I stopped myself, fearing that Anatoly Romanovich was finding my words naïve. He surprised me by moving beyond the issue of the Dignity Council's composition to its governance.

"The five victors in World War II have veto power in the Security Council. Would the Big Five in the Dignity Council have it too?"

"That's to be determined. I can imagine arguments for and against it, or something quite new such as requiring a two-thirds vote to adopt a resolution."

The Russian president persisted, "How many 'Guardians of Dignity' do you envisage?"

Guardians of Dignity. GODs. I thought of making a joke, but resisted the impulse.

"In addition to the charter members, I'd guess there will eventually be a half-dozen more, each of them multinational entities," I replied. "For example, the African Union, Oceania, the Association of Southeast Asian Nations, one or perhaps two entities in the Middle East."

"The Mideast is surely going to be a challenge," Anatoly remarked.

"Perhaps, but it's integral to the vision, and for reasons that go beyond preserving the peace in a volatile region. First, the Mideast is the crossroads of the world; the first stop, as it were, on the original migration out of Africa that eventually populated the world. And second, the Middle East is where, during the Arab Spring, Dignity found its feet and resumed its march around the globe. On the day the United Nations adopts the Dignity Council as an instrument of world governance, I hope we'll pause to remember the courageous men and women who stood up against despotism and corruption by occupying the public squares of Tunis, Cairo, Benghazi, Damascus, and elsewhere."

Anatoly appeared to be thinking this over. I knew he was already sizing up his domestic allies and opponents in the event that the idea garnered enough initial support to receive serious attention.

"Without Russia's strong support, the Dignity Council will be stillborn," I continued.

"I'm afraid that you overestimate Russia's influence. We're no longer a great power."

This was easy for me to counter, and I did so with absolute conviction. "Russia reaches almost halfway around the world. What's more, the influence of the Russian people far exceeds their numbers. In the long history of warfare, no people has ever evinced more will in repelling aggression than the Russians."

At this, the French president jumped in.

"Twice, no less. First you defeated Napoleon's army, and then, to make sure no one missed the point, you drove Hitler's troops back to Berlin. Heroics on such a scale leave an indelible mark on the collective memory. Our friend Adam is right, Anatoly Romanovich. Among nation states, there are four giants. France is not one of them, alas, but the CIS, of which Russia is the hub, deserves charter membership in the Dignity Council."

That was why I'd stopped in Paris—to have the Russian leader hear those words from the president of a nation that had once occupied Moscow.

Anatoly ordered tea and cakes. "I think I can take it from here," he said. "I'll begin by convening a meeting of the CIS in Moscow. This opportunity may put new life into that organization."

I wanted to get more of Anatoly's thoughts on China, but it became clear that we had covered enough material for this session when Anatoly abruptly turned to his vacation plans.

"I've long dreamed of spending some time in Malibu. In California, you know? So beautiful. Do you think it would be possible?"

"I've got a number of backers who live there. Movie stars and the like. I'll have my staff make some inquiries."

"Thank you. Have you been there?"

"Well, I've driven through. Seen the beaches. It is spectacular, and close to Los Angeles."

"Yes, Hollywood. And how about you, Adam? Is there anywhere you still want to go?"

There was, and my smile told him so. "Ever since riding the Trans-Siberian, I've dreamed of a cabin on the shores of Lake Baikal."

"Your presence would honor us, Mr. President." Anatoly replied. "Our Defense Minister, Dimitri Ivanov has a place there that he seldom uses. I will speak to him about it."

Was he serious? I flashed back to the train ride with Élodie. Maybe someday, I thought, but no time soon. "No Siberian tigers, please," I said. "Somewhere I'll feel safe combing the beach."

And Jean? We both gave him an inquiring stare.

"I have Paris. What more could I want?"

§§§

The summer of 2025 was even hotter than usual in Washington. I met individually with members of Congress whose support for the Dignity Deal was shaky. Gwyneth was stepping up her work for Dignity Now!, and when she was abroad, Marisol often shared dinner with me in the White House. She had taken an apartment walking distance from her office in the West Wing. As she was a key political advisor, I saw her during working hours, often several times a day.

Evenings with Marisol in the living quarters were the best part of my day. After a late supper we'd talk about the politics and our hopes for the future. It was in these talks that the strategy for bringing the Dignity Council into the world took shape.

Usually by midnight, we'd end our evenings with talk of family and friends. Marisol kept in close touch with Ellie, often visiting her in the official residence of the vice president. Although Ellie participated in arts-related activities, she saw her primary responsibility as maintaining a refuge for Ben. Since their daughter Galia had moved out on her own, Ellie, for whom family was everything, was, for the first time in her life, looking for something meaningful to do with her time. Marisol said she'd suggested that Ellie join forces with Gwyneth on Dignity Now!, but she'd rejected the idea. When I tried to find out why, Marisol didn't care to pass on any specifics regarding Ellie's reservations.

My sister and my wife had never been close and, without having discussed the reason, both Marisol and I knew why. The fact that we had begun our relationship as lovers had left a mark on all of us.

Though I'd never discussed it with Gwyneth, I was sure that when Marisol and I had gone to Philadelphia to work in Ben's first campaign, he had filled Gwyn in on this bit of ancient history. There was a tacit agreement between the two of us to let the past be the past.

I realized that under the guise of informing me of Ellie's feelings about Gwyneth, Marisol was also conveying her own. I knew that both my sister and Ellie felt that there was something detached about Gwyneth. On occasion, I'd countered that her reserve was a mask she wore until you got to know her; but in truth, I don't know that she ever took it completely off with me.

§§§

Raj Redux: The Subcontinent, October 2025

The philosophical perspective I'd absorbed from Lahiri had been incubated in India. Before Confucius, before the Christian Era, India's holy men developed a philosophy known as *advaita*—which teaches that, appearances notwithstanding, you and apparent "otherness" are "not two." Or, put the other way round, if you look hard enough, there's always a oneness to be found in multiplicity. This assumption had shaped my life and my politics, and was the bedrock of the dignitarian perspective. In politics, as in science, the advaita philosophy calls for synthesis.

This line of thought took me back to the formative days I'd spent with Malika Kapoor in Banaras three decades earlier. Malika and I had seen each other once or twice during the intervening years, most recently on a stopover I made in Bangalore en route to the Maldives.

During cool spells in my marriage to Gwyneth, I'd sometimes wondered how things had turned out for Malika, who held a professorship in geology at the Indian Institute of Science. When I inquired about her arranged marriage, she held out her hand to show me that she'd shed her wedding band when she divorced her husband. On what turned out to be my last full day as Speaker of the House, we spent a nostalgic afternoon reminiscing about Professor Lahiri, the philosophically-minded geologist who had supervised Malika's doctorate and changed my life with his teachings.

In July, 2025, I invited Malika to come to the States to brainstorm with me and my team on how to gain India's support for the Dignity Council. The challenge would be to get India, Pakistan, and Bangladesh to consider forming a supranational organization that would qualify for a seat alongside the EU, the CIS, and the North and South American Unions as they took shape. Recent progress in India and Pakistan's long-standing dispute over Kashmir, and India's constructive response to the most recent flooding and refugee crisis in Bangladesh gave us grounds for hope.

I asked Malika to search the subcontinent for the best thinking on how to nudge the three successors to the British Raj to further pursue rapprochement. In the back of my mind was this thought: If the three occupants of the subcontinent realized that together they could match China's power and influence, they might be willing to begin work on constructing a single *transnational* identity that would be a match for China's.

Malika proposed something I would never have thought of: a week-long trip during which I would join with the leaders of each of the three nations to pay respect to the subcontinent's culture and history. In what she characterized as political performance art, she proposed that I first go to Islamabad and present the proposal for a Dignity Council to the president of Pakistan. Then, by prearrangement, he and I would proceed together to Pakistan's cultural capital, the ancient city of Lahore, where the president would introduce me to the cultural and religious history of his country.

From there I would go to Delhi where, after discussing plans for the Council with the prime minister, together we would pay our respects to Mahatma Gandhi at the museum built on the site of his assassination.

Then on to Dhaka to make the case to the prime minister of Bangladesh. As one of the first nations to make dignity an explicit constitutional right—at its birth in 1971—Bangladesh could be expected to assume a leading role in championing dignity worldwide.

After political talks in Dhaka, I'd ask the Bangladeshi leader to accompany me to Sylhet, Bangladesh's City of Saints and the site of the mausoleum of Hazrat Shah Jalal, who brought Islam to Bengal during the fourteenth century.

Capping these three visits, each of which paid its respects to culture, history, and politics, we would all rendezvous in the holy city of Varanasi, where the Indian prime minister would receive the three of us and we would announce the establishment of bilateral and multilateral task forces to explore participation in the Council.

The purpose of this whirlwind tour was to suggest to them that they could be more than a study group. The goal was to set in motion a process in each country, and stimulate joint consideration of the subcontinent's future role in global governance.

§§§

The plan that Malika had proposed was carried out, step by step. The three presidents were cordial in public and conciliatory in private. Meeting outside the political capitals in traditional cultural capitals had the effect of sacralizing the mission. A certain solemnity imbued the talks, which, by putting current political problems in historical perspective, inclined the leaders to look beyond old quarrels.

Given that none of the three nations of the subcontinent had a seat on the Security Council, they had nothing to lose and much to gain by playing a founding role in the modernization of the United Nations.

But I suspect that what really made the difference was the knowledge that, after these meetings on the subcontinent, I would be going to Beijing to enlist the Chinese.

My thinking was that if some version of the Dignity Council took hold—even if that were not to occur till long after I'd left office—nations would no longer be the principal players on the world stage. As they were folded into regional organizations, national interests would be supplanted by regional ones.

I doubt that anyone who understood this was unaware that a day would come when regional interests would give way to the global interest. I didn't expect to see that day myself, but I believed that a Dignity Council based on a half-dozen supranational organizations, and gradually doubling in size to a dozen Guardians of Dignity, to use the Russian president's phrase, would, within a few score years, mark the end of tyranny and war. It was a grand scheme, if not grandiose, but I thought that even if the final reset were to bear little resemblance to the initial vision, it would accomplish the one imperative: It would give the world not just a forum for discussing global issues, but the agency to address them.

Now, for China, the Council's sine qua non. If America was the catalyst, China was the lynchpin.

§§§

China's Toe in the Water, November 2025

I left India with great expectations. Not only had things gone as well as I dared to hope—given the enmity the three sub-continental countries had shown for one another since their independence—but the private correspondence I'd been conducting with President Zheng of China had been encouraging. After seventy years of one-party rule, and mounting calls for political liberalization, President Zheng had been hand-picked to preside over a number of "toe-in-the-water" reformist experiments. His elevation to the top leadership position had been widely seen as similar to Gorbachev's in the mid-eighties—a desperate move to modernize an autocratic system that had lost the support of the people. Though President Zheng's appointment was welcomed by reformers, the parallel with Gorbachev who, after all, had presided over the breakup of the Soviet Union, was alarming to the hardliners. The future of China would pivot on Zheng's success or failure, and I felt that the twenty-first century's fate hung in the balance.

Zheng had made it clear in our correspondence that while China was adamantly opposed to the Western practice of one person, one vote, its leaders were open to experimenting with corporate and academic governance, and he was looking forward to discussing some possible experiments in the political realm.

We knew from many sources, including their own public declarations, that China's collective leadership was afraid that if one-party rule were suddenly to be replaced by popular elections, the country might descend into chaos, in which case fifty years of economic gains would be lost. Above all, they feared that unrest among Tibetans and Uighur minorities, or protests by the rural masses against the corruption of local party officials, would spread to the urban middle class, which was now clamoring for more political freedom.

But, in the reasons they gave for eschewing traditional democratic governance, and their willingness to consider participatory governance in other realms, I thought I saw a sliver of hope for a dignitarian outcome.

After several days of private talks, during which I refrained from making any specific suggestions, the Chinese president agreed to expand our private conversations into a series of annual summit meetings to be held alternately in the two capitals, beginning in Washington, in December, 2026. That left a year for the Chinese to try out some of their ideas, and it gave us time to prepare for the first summit. I knew I'd painted myself into a corner. For the Dignity Council to succeed it needed Chinese participation, yet for it to be accepted as a legitimate global arbiter of dignity, all its members, including China, would have to practice what its leaders preached. There was no doubt that if President Zheng failed to persuade his comrades to participate in the Dignity Council, it would not get off the ground.

From Air Force One I put in a call to Secretary Fisher and briefed him on developments. Though the secretary's name had not been on the calendar I'd received the previous evening, on my first morning back in the White House I found him waiting for me just outside the Oval Office.

§§§

Deploying Family Assets, December 2025

"Would you consider asking your father to spend some time in Beijing as your personal emissary?" Secretary Fisher asked me before we'd even sat down. "He could work directly with Chinese officials to prepare the Washington summit."

I knew Fisher was referring to Rowan, but I was shocked into silence for a full ten seconds. Although I'd often asked Rowan for political advice I'd never have thought of asking him to undertake a foreign posting. In the coming year he'd be ninety.

Fisher forged ahead. "Every diplomat knows how important Harry Hopkins was to the Soviet-American Alliance during World War II. I can think of no one better suited to play that role with the Chinese than your father. His reputation as one of the architects of nuclear disarmament will give him credibility with their strategic thinkers. His behind-the-scenes role in ending the cold war will endear him to professional diplomats. And the fact that he is the father of the sitting president of the United States will give him access to China's highest-ranking leaders."

As I tried to picture Rowan in China, Fisher continued.

"When the going gets tough, a back channel can make the difference between failure and success. They won't just say yes to your father," Fisher cautioned, "but neither are they apt to say no."

"Wouldn't his presence undercut our ambassador?"

"If that's how she sees it, we'll get a new one," Fisher replied. "Deploying Dr. Ellway is a unique opportunity. If the ambassador cares about American national interests, she'll welcome his presence. Do I have your permission to raise the possibility with her?"

"First, let me talk to my father," I said. "No point if he doesn't feel up to it. How's the smog in Beijing these days?"

"Getting better, and we can put him up at the Embassy where our filtration system keeps the air pretty clean."

I told Fisher I'd get back to him shortly, and asked the switchboard to put in a call to my parents' apartment. My god, I thought, how lucky I am to have such a brilliant, selfless man at State.

My mother answered the phone and I asked her if I could stop by that afternoon for tea. She tried to wheedle the reason out of me but I managed to get off the phone without tipping my hand.

At eighty-nine and seventy-five my parents, whose careers had often forced them to live apart, had become inseparable. And to be nearer me they'd sublet Rowan's apartment in New York and rented an apartment in Washington.

That it would be both of them in Beijing was a given. As I suspected, Rowan immediately grasped that he might be of service and was eager to take on the mission. That would leave the decision to Easter, which was why I'd wanted to see them in person.

She listened carefully and asked several practical questions, but I knew that her only real consideration was whether Rowan could handle the strain of living abroad. He'd given up jogging in his early eighties, but he still took vigorous daily walks, and twice a week he went to a fitness club where he worked out and swam. He believed his physical workouts helped stave off mental decline and, although Marisol and I had noticed that he no longer worked into the evening, what he produced before noon still bore the stamp of a questing, rigorous mind.

From Easter's line of questioning I knew that she could be persuaded. I could tell, and knew she could too, that Rowan wanted to go, and she was not wont to oppose his desires. But at the last minute, she introduced a condition.

"Okay, I think we can manage it, but you'll have to provide us with an assistant. We'll go if you'll give us Galia as our interpreter and amanuensis."

Galia's fluency in spoken and written Chinese would be a huge asset, and she'd already had some diplomatic experience as part of our delegation to the G-20 Summit in March, 2024, when she'd befriended the son of the Chinese president.

Easter's "condition" made good sense; I should have thought of it myself. As I left my parents' apartment I realized that the Council was now in the care of the oldest and the youngest of my personal advisors.

On my schedule for that same day was the lighting of the national Christmas tree on the Mall. Gwyn and I enjoyed this tradition, and she met me there. With her were several dozen girls drawn from a middle school in Washington that had taken the lead in pairing American schools with sister schools worldwide. The smell of spruce, the colored lights, and hundreds of happy, excited kids who, after the ceremony, came back to the White House with us for hot cider and cookies, made Gwyn light up too. Watching that joyful scene made me wonder if our marriage might have been a happier one if we'd had children of our own.

§§§

Confucius Redux, Spring, 2026

At least once a week when we were both in town, Ben and I managed to find time in the late afternoon to work out on the Obama Court near the White House. When we went one-on-one, his height and strength gave him an advantage I rarely overcame. But when we matched each other in a shooting contest like HORSE, my losing wasn't a foregone conclusion.

In this first talk after my lengthy trip to France, Russia, India, and China, Ben told me what he thought about my travels.

"You need to show the flag in America. Voters are beginning to see you as caring more about the Chinese than about them."

"Our national and personal destinies are inseparable," I said.

"I know that, but a lot of Americans do not. And the Republicans have taken to calling you 'the president of the world'."

"That can't be a compliment," I admitted.

"You and I don't have to face the voters yet, but in six months both the House and Senate are up for grabs. Early polling says we could lose our majority in both houses."

"All right, I understand. But you've been out there. They still love *you*, right?"

"You're the leader, Ad. I can't win the midterm for us, let alone a second term. Only you can do that."

"I'll ask Karen to set up a speaking tour."

"Even our base needs attention. And, by the way, so does your jump shot."

With that, Ben put a thirty-footer cleanly through the hoop, retrieved the ball, and bounce-passed it to me. "You're on," he said.

§§§

Two weeks after Rowan's move to Beijing he sent me the first of what would be a series of weekly cables and, per my request, copied Vice President Steinsaltz and Secretary of State Fisher.

From Easter, I knew that she and Rowan were settled into a comfortable apartment in the US Embassy—quarters normally reserved for visits of the president or secretary of state, but at Fisher's directive and with my blessing, assigned to Rowan and Easter for the duration of their stay.

Adjacent to it was a studio apartment given over to Galia Liang Steinsaltz.

Easter cooked about half the time, and the rest of their meals they took in the Embassy dining room or had sent up to their suite. Everything was done to make life in the foreign capital as much like home as possible, including Rowan's workouts. He continued them as usual in the Embassy gym, and Easter joined him every other day. Galia passed on their invitation to work out with them; she said she got all the exercise she needed dancing and partying into the night with the Chinese friends she'd made in Paris.

Rowan didn't need a great deal of preparation for his talks with President Zheng. He saw Confucius as an early advocate of dignitarian governance. The Chinese sage, 2500 years before, had imagined a Mandate of Heaven in which rulers chosen on the basis of merit, not entitlement, would bring peace and prosperity to the people through the power of exemplary behavior. Confucius's idea, new at the time, was that the governing class is not above the law, but rather, honor-bound to serve the people's interests.

Interpreted in today's language, this criterion of good governance boils down to honoring rank, but abjuring rankism. Dignitarian governance, regardless of the purview and purpose of the governing body in question, rests on precisely that distinction. Rankism, not rank, is the source of indignity, so by disallowing rankism, dignity is secured.

I'd always wondered if the Chinese actually deferred to age or, like Westerners, made a show of honoring the elderly while discounting their ideas. Rowan's role as special emissary would shed light on this question.

§§§

By early summer, if you knew where to look you could find modest dignitarian initiatives under way in many sectors of Chinese society. Supported by President Zheng, change had become fashionable.

Within a few months, Rowan had developed quite a friendship with Zheng, whom he saw as a genuine modernizer. The president opened doors for him at every level of the political establishment, and Rowan reported that, in private, the Chinese had taken to referring to the array of reforms under consideration collectively as Confucius Redux. True to its name, the common element in the reforms was a commitment to merit-based determinations of rank. In the spirit of Confucianism, leaders were being chosen who manifestly served "society, not self," and were therefore modeling dignitarian values.

All this was well and good, but it failed to provide an answer to the question famously posed by the Romans: "Quis custodiet ipsos custodes?" (Who guards the guardians?) Again and again, Rowan pressed the senior leadership to address this issue.

In practice, it boiled down to the problem of how to hold those same party leaders accountable. But to whom would they be willing to make themselves accountable? And by what mechanism?

During the early decades of China's spectacular economic development, in the late twentieth century, popular demand for a role in governance had been passively stifled or actively repressed. But by the end of the second decade of the twenty-first century, China's leaders no longer found it possible to ignore the demands of a burgeoning, educated middle class for an end to paternalism.

Since the early days of Communist Party rule, the issue of accountability to the citizenry had been the sore point of Chinese-American relations. I knew that, until the Chinese could find their answer, and implement it, China's membership in the Dignity Council—if it were to qualify for and choose to participate in it—would be seen as belying the Council's raison d'être.

I asked Rowan for his own answer to the question he had put to the Chinese. His response came in the form of a memorandum.

> To: Adam Blue, President of the United States
> Subject: Governance in China (and in the US)
> CCs: Vice President Benjamin Steinsaltz, Secretary of State Timothy Fisher
>
> Date: May 2, 2026
>
> The Chinese believe that today's issues are too complex to entrust to an ill-informed, capricious electorate. "One person, one vote" democracy may have been up to the tasks of governance in an agrarian age, perhaps even in an industrial age, but that formula is inadequate in the age of technology. The issues have become too complex for all but specialists.
>
> The Chinese argue that humankind survived the vagaries of elections only because science was in its infancy and humans lacked the means to destroy life on Earth. But now, avoiding irreversible damage to the planet is too important to risk opening decisions of great consequence to either the whims of dictators or the prejudices of voters.
>
> China cites Germany's election of Hitler as evidence of democracy's vulnerability to demagoguery. Society pays a cost when citizens learn politics "on the job" (just as there's a cost to on-the-job training in business or medicine).

The Chinese mock our one-person, one-vote formula as hypocritical because it gives no electoral weight to the interests of people under eighteen. That means one third of the population has no voice in politics. They're not proposing to give minors the vote, but rather to introduce a mechanism that gives weight to the interests of the young commensurate with their numbers. If we don't do likewise, we'll soon have a sclerotic society that takes care of its elders at the expense of its youth.

I'm suggesting to President Zheng and the senior leadership that they present their reform as leapfrogging democracy, and moving directly to dignitarian rule. The principal difference lies in how officialdom is held accountable. We hold our rulers accountable through periodic popular elections in which all adults have the franchise, though many decline to exercise it. The Chinese are trying to design a mechanism in which accountability is achieved through a hierarchy of committees comprised of professionals. They're borrowing from both the parliamentary model and our system of checks and balances—all infused with a healthy dose of Confucianism.

Any move in the direction of Plato's "philosopher kings" brings to mind William Buckley's wisecrack that he'd rather be governed by the first two thousand people in the Cambridge phonebook than by the Harvard faculty.

Coming to grips with this age-old conundrum has finally reached the top of China's agenda. My guess is that it's going to take the Chinese a few years to design a system they're willing to put into practice, and a few years beyond that to get the bugs out.

I'll keep you posted.

§§§

I kept Ben Steinsaltz in the loop by discussing Rowan's cables with him, and Ben kept me in the loop by sharing the news that he and Ellie received from their daughter, Galia. She was taking classes at Beijing University, and her e-mails, full of criticism of the generation in power, reminded me of a slogan that expressed a widespread sentiment on American campuses in the sixties: Don't trust anyone over 30. It made me wonder if Chinese society was on the verge of a generational transformation like the one wrought by our own baby boomers.

Galia wrote to her parents:

> Dear Mom and Dad,
>
> I see Rowan and Easter every day. He shows me the cables he sends you and the president, and I try out the same ideas on my friends here. One of them is Xiao, President Zheng's son, who discusses everything with his dad. I'm often invited to their family dinners, and most of the talk is politics. They remind me of discussions with you and President Blue— opinions flying, no hard feelings.
>
> What I'm saying is that the Chinese are serious about overhauling governance. They know that what they've got isn't working, and they're not just talking, they're testing new ideas.
>
> For example, a top university in Beijing has adopted a system of academic governance in which everyone—students, staff, faculty, and administrators—has a voice. Votes regarding distinct areas of academic life are apportioned according to responsibility for those areas, e.g., professors hold a majority of votes on educational policy, students hold the majority on issues of student life, and administrators hold a

499

majority, but don't have a monopoly, on budgetary issues.

Also, the government has set up a Chinese version of the Truth and Reconciliation Commission in Xinjiang. If it's successful, President Zheng wants to use it in Tibet. When I asked about Taiwan, all he would say was "let's wait and see."

These experiments are all people talk about. They're seen as the Party's response to popular unrest and, so long as there's a sense of progress, most people seem willing to give the current leadership a chance. China's leaders are increasingly identified with these reforms, and if they fail, Party rule will not survive.

Already, though, I've noticed a difference in the public mood. I'd characterize it as patient optimism. No one wants to risk bringing the house down. It's like there's an unspoken agreement, on all sides, to keep modernizing, bit by bit, until a new workable system is put in place.

Sometimes, when I get back to the Embassy after an evening with Xiao and our friends, I go up on the roof and listen to the hum of the city. It sounds like the hum of the planet. Usually, city lights and smog block the stars, but last night a full moon shone overhead. Gazing upward, I had a vision of pockets of poverty shrinking like puddles in the sun. My two countries, America and China, on the same side of history.

Please don't think I'm looking only through rose-colored glasses. I know clouds sometimes hide the light. But they're not the black clouds of war and poverty. They're new ones—green, yellow, and blue. I don't know what the colors mean, but whatever the challenges, my generation wants to face them together, as one family, moved by a love our ancestors could only dream of.

Perhaps it's Mo Zi's vision of universal love. Rowan mentions Mo Zi as often as he does Confucius, Mencius, and Huang Zongxi. I only hope that Mo Zi's attacks on music and dancing are ignored because, when we're not talking politics, that's how my friends and I spend our time. I like to tease Rowan that he can go ahead and try to reason his way to a new world, but my generation intends to dance our way there.

I miss you. Can't you find an excuse to visit Beijing?

Love, Galia

In the person of this young Chinese American there was a human link between our two nations. I couldn't think of a better representative—of either country! But that was just it. Galia wasn't representing "us" or "them." She was already living in a world without borders.

§§§

Damsels in Distress, December, 2026

While Rowan was in Beijing, he had worked on the agenda for the summit to be held in Washington at year's end. Galia sweetened an invitation she'd made earlier to the president's son: She offered to show him the "real America" the only way it could be seen—in a coast-to-coast road trip.

In planning for the summit, the Chinese delegation decided that en route to Washington, it would stop in California for a briefing on the joint American-Chinese project to devise a safe, reversible way to reflect just enough of the sun's rays back into space to offset global warming.

When the Chinese leader got to Washington, his focus would be politics; oddly, problems *between* our two nations were not much of an issue. As we prepared for the summit it became clear that the real threats we faced came from our own dysfunctional systems of governance.

In our first meeting, when I asked President Zheng how they intended to increase accountability of the ruling party itself, he didn't duck the issue. He told me he had tasked a national commission consisting of leading professionals in five areas—political science, economic policy, international relations, sociology, and law—to propose solutions.

"Won't they just talk forever?" I asked. (Rowan's skepticism toward academic commissions had infected me.)

"We gave the professors an ultimatum: 'No new ideas, no more funding.' There are certain advantages to centralized power."

After we'd both had a laugh, President Zheng spelled out his position.

"If your example has shown us one thing, it's that the complexities of modern life cannot be entrusted to voters who stop learning at twenty." To make his point, he added, "I myself have a doctorate in engineering, and I do not really understand the science of climate change. But I *can* tell the difference between professional judgment and ideological bias. Leaving the choice of your political leaders up to voters who take their cues from paid lobbyists and media demagogues is irresponsible. We're committed to designing a better system."

I couldn't argue with that. China had a half-billion people still living off the land. Many had completed only a primary-school education. As for his critique of our system, I'd been making the same one for years.

"Most of the issues we face today require analytic, technical solutions," Zheng continued, "not political, let alone ideological, ones. The real problem is making sure that the people in charge of designing those solutions serve the national good."

"Yes, but if they do not?" I persisted. "If they put themselves above the law, award themselves privileges, or serve special interests, then what?"

I stopped myself, fearful that my frustration and impatience were showing. It wasn't fair to criticize China when we ourselves had no answer to these same problems.

"We don't have a complete answer to that yet," President Zheng replied, "but we're planning some experiments to see what works."

"For example?"

"Using Internet polling to track public opinion, not just every two or four years, but in real time. Also, we're looking for a way to revitalize the impeachment process. I know that impeachment is allowed for in your system, but it is rarely used, and when it is, it seems to us that partisanship often trumps common sense."

I pressed him on how they proposed to shield decision-makers from interference or retaliation; he responded by offering a trenchant critique of our system.

"While we accept the Western idea of an independent judiciary, we believe that the way you elect your legislators, and especially your president, is obsolete. Permitting businesses and special interests to fund political campaigns encourages demagoguery and invites corruption. That is not government of the people, by the people, and for the people. It's government of, by, and for money."

I chuckled quietly, wondering if the Chinese weren't perhaps catching on a bit too fast. Either they were humoring us, or we'd grown so accustomed to Chinese intransigence in the realm of political reform, we hadn't noticed that they were acutely aware of the need for it and, if anything, more serious about it than we were.

I was heartened by our talk, and proposed that we announce our joint exploration of new models of governance in reciprocal toasts at the dinner later in the week.

§§§

The state dinner with the Chinese got off to a great start. White House staff knocked themselves out, and the Chinese delegation seemed pleased with the honors accorded them. Dessert was being served when I saw an aide whispering in the vice president's ear. When Ben got to his feet and hurried toward me I knew that something had happened. Instead of waiting for him to reach me, I excused myself and motioned to him that we should meet off to one side of the room.

"Pirates have kidnapped twenty girls and two Americans from the school named for Gwyneth in Banda Aceh," he said. "They're holding them for ransom."

My heart contracted. "Where's Gwyn? She's in Jakarta, right?"

"Yes, she's safe, but the two Americans work for Dignity Now!. The school was to be dedicated tomorrow with Gwyn doing the honors. The pirates didn't want to tangle with the Secret Service, but figured that they could exchange the girls and Gwyneth's staffers for something just shy of a queen's ransom."

I was momentarily relieved. The annual conference of Dignity Now! had been on the calendar long before the summit with the Chinese, and with my approval, and apologies to the Chinese, Gwyn had kept her prior commitment to attend the dedication of a school in Banda Aceh, Indonesia.

"How much are they asking for?" I asked Ben.

"Twenty million in U.S. currency."

We both glanced at President Zheng and saw an aide talking to him.

"The whole world will know by the time this banquet is over," Ben said.

I told Ben that I intended to ask the Chinese to help us with this, and charged him with seeing to it that the ransom money would be available in Indonesia if and when it was needed.

"I'll take it to Jakarta myself," he said and, thanking me for my trust, he headed for the exit.

I returned to the head table where Marisol yielded her seat to me so I could confer confidentially with the Chinese president.

What happened in the next twenty-four hours would, in unforeseeable ways, affect the rest of my presidency—and my life forever after.

President Zheng and I immediately excused ourselves and, with our senior military aides, left for the Situation Room. I put in a call to the Indonesian president, and informed him that President Zheng and I were speaking to him from the White House. I asked him to quietly meet the kidnappers' ransom demands with the money the vice president was bringing, then get out of the way.

When the Indonesian president hesitated, Zheng spoke up.

"Let the kidnappers know that if a single person is hurt, our warships will hunt down and sink every last pirate vessel." He paused for effect, then added: "After you've gained the release of the hostages, our navy will coordinate with yours to eliminate this scourge once and for all."

By working with the Chinese, and through the Indonesian authorities, we secured the hostages' release in just over twenty-four hours. Vice President Steinsaltz arranged for Indonesian intermediaries to transfer the ransom to representatives of the pirates at the same moment that the schoolchildren and Gwyneth's aides were released to Indian authorities in the port city of Tenlaa on the isle of Great Nicobar.

In small planes and helicopters provided by the Indonesian military, Ben and Gwyneth had flown from Jakarta to Tenlaa, where the world got its first pictures of the hostages as the first lady and vice president led them onto the portico of the municipal headquarters.

Watching from the White House, I waited until Gwyn had finished with the media and then asked the switchboard to connect us.

"So glad everyone's safe, Gwyn. I hate to think what might have happened if the pirates had done this during the dedication."

"I was never in any danger, Adam. Whatever you did worked perfectly!"

"Ben can fill you in on the details. When are you coming home?"

"Ben thinks I should skip the meeting in Jakarta, but I disagree. It's important to show people that we aren't intimidated, so I'm going to give the keynote as planned."

"The show must go on."

"Exactly. It'll be grand, don't you think?"

"They're going to love you."

"You made it possible."

"China's support was invaluable," I added. "I've been holding my breath since this happened, Gwyn, and I won't relax till you're back."

Then Gwyn asked me if I was upset with her for skipping the summit. How could I be? I'd often wondered if my work had a fraction of the impact hers did. When I told her this, she thanked me for the opportunity to do something worthy of the privilege she was born into. Until that moment, I hadn't understood what a mixed blessing wealth can be. Growing up, Gwyn could never be sure that people weren't more interested in her money than in her. Moved by her grit, all I could manage was the old show biz, "Break a leg!"

"I'll do my best, then I'll come home, I really will." Gwyneth ended by suggesting that we spend a quiet weekend at Camp David, and I readily agreed.

How fitting that one of the most intimate conversations of our White House years occurred when we were on opposite sides of the globe.

§§§

After delivering her keynote, Gwyn flew straight home. I was at Andrews Air Force Base as the door to the plane opened and she descended the stairs to the tarmac. Network TV covered our embrace.

As we approached the White House we were informed that a crowd had gathered in nearby Lafayette Park. On an impulse, Gwyneth asked the driver to swing by and let her out. I expected her to wade into the crowd, but instead she just stood near the curb. No one moved toward her, but thunderous applause, punctuated with whistles and bravos, washed over her. Gwyneth smiled and waved appreciatively, and then, taking my extended hand, she stepped back into the limo. This was the happiest I had ever seen my indomitable wife in her role as first lady.

§§§

Secretary Fisher felt the hostage incident had given the world a preview of the Dignity Council in action. When I asked if he realized that the CIA had staged the whole thing, it took him a moment to realize I was kidding.

Later, when I called President Zheng to thank him for his support, he said that it was a privilege to cooperate with us to combat lawlessness, and that he knew we'd have done the same for China if the situation had been reversed. He told me that Chinese helicopter gunships had waited until the hostage transfer was complete, then descended on the vessels in which the pirates had left Great Nicobar and sent them all to the bottom of the Andaman Sea. He expressed his regrets over the forfeiture of our twenty million dollars.

It seemed only right to let Zheng know that the bank notes were sophisticated forgeries, stockpiled for just this kind of emergency. We hoped that any spending by accomplices would leave a trail of marked bills that would lead to their capture.

As we ended the call, Zheng thanked me for sending my father to Beijing. He told me that Rowan's ability to establish an atmosphere of dignity and respect had more than once helped overcome opposition from hardliners. Zheng also let me know that he expected to have significant progress to report at our summit in Beijing that coming fall.

We agreed that, in addition to the three nations of North America, China would invite representatives from the EU, the CIS, and the Indian Subcontinent to Beijing to participate in the second summit, set for October, 2027. Chinese media reported that China was developing a modern synthesis of Eastern and Western models.

§§§

I arrived for the Beijing summit confident that nothing could stop dignity's march across the planet. Gwyn would be leaving Beijing a day before me to preside over the annual meeting of Dignity Now! in Kabul. The location of the meeting was in itself a statement of her organization's growing success, and an indication of the profound change that had come over Afghanistan since Élodie and I had encountered the Taliban there three decades before.

At the suggestion of President Zheng, we were to make a joint visit to the Confucius Temple where, for centuries, Chinese emperors and their ministers had paid homage to Confucian ideals. In front of the Hall of Great Accomplishment stands a 700-year old cypress, known as "Distinguish Evil Cypress," that, according to legend, can tell the difference between good and evil people. Detecting an evil-doer in its presence, the ancient tree lowers one of its branches and knocks his hat off. My staff let me know that President Zheng would be wearing a hat, thus exposing himself to the tree's judgment, and he expected me to do no less.

That evening Chinese TV showed us standing beneath the Cypress with our hats resting securely on our heads.

At the end of our first full day, Gwyneth asked about the prospects for Senate ratification of United States participation in the Dignity Council. President Wilson's League of Nations had died in Congress, and we didn't want the Dignity Council to suffer a similar fate. When I said that the vote on ratification would be the defining event of our second full term, Gwyneth suggested that Ben's role as president of the Senate would surely be a plus.

"If Ben were president of the country, our chances would be even better," I replied.

"What do you mean?"

"The polls are saying he's more popular than I am."

"You're not thinking of stepping aside are you?"

"No, of course not. Ben and I are going to announce our bid for reelection as soon as we return to Washington."

"You'll get even more of the women's vote this time."

"Thanks to you."

"Not really, Ad, it's your vision that holds things together. You have to see this through."

Gwyneth's acknowledgement came as a surprise. It had never been her way to offer much praise. At times, she'd seemed to suggest that Dignity for All was too grand and vague a goal, and it would be more effective to narrow the focus to women's dignity.

I'd resisted this because I believed that dignity for women is inseparable from dignity for men. It wasn't grandiosity that predisposed me to the more inclusive goal; it was practicality: No one's dignity would be secure until everyone's was.

§§§

The banquet on the last day of the conference was held in the Great Hall of the People on Tiananmen Square. In Gwyneth's absence, Marisol was serving as my consort.

As the evening went on, the mood became festive. The prospect of success—even though it lay in the indefinite future—was sweet. Add to that a half-dozen champagne toasts—and my habitual inhibitions dissolved.

During my years in Congress, Marisol had taught me how to dance well enough not to embarrass myself at events like these. When the orchestra struck up a familiar tune, she surprised me by getting to her feet and leading me onto the floor.

Although we knew we were being watched, it was as if we were protected by the innocence we'd known in Paris. When the music stopped, we didn't return to our seats but drifted to the side of the room. Until I saw my Secret Service detail trailing us, I was unaware that I was still holding Marisol's hand.

"Don't let go," Marisol said.

"Tipsy?"

"A little, aren't you?"

"Enough not to care what the bodyguards think."

"Did you recognize that song?"

"The tune is familiar."

"It's 'Somewhere'," from *West Side Story*." Marisol, keeping a polite distance, spoke the words just loudly enough for me to hear. *"There's a place for us. A time and place for us. Hold my hand and we're halfway there. Hold my hand and I'll take you there. Somehow, Someday, Somewhere."*

When I didn't respond, she took my free hand and spun me around to face her. Looking upwards, she said, "That's all I've ever wanted, Ad. A time and place for us."

"I can't let myself think about that. I've got to finish this. It's all we've got to show for ourselves. If I stop now, my life will count for nothing. I'd be of no good to anyone."

"But when you leave office, when your work is done. Will you think about it then?"

I'd given up on ever picking up where we'd left off in Paris. I knew that's what Marisol wanted, and I didn't have the heart to disappoint her.

"If you'll help me not think about it now, I promise to think about it later."

§§§

Broken Bonds, Spring and Summer, 2028

Had Ben and I been opposed in the primaries and had to campaign, we might have sensed the national mood sooner, and taken the Republican threat more seriously.

Ben assured me that a post-convention bounce would close the gap the Republican nominees had over us in the polls, and that we'd pull ahead well before election day. The truth is, Ben was always more popular with the public than I was. That had been true during our playing days at Princeton and through our partnership in presidential politics. People gravitated to Ben. They liked about him what they'd liked about President Reagan—buoyancy, imperturbability, and optimism. On top of that, they identified him with the Dignity Deal, which had benefited many Americans; and they identified me with the Dignity Council, which some saw as infringing on American sovereignty. Political cartoonists and late-night comedians depicted Ben as putting a chicken in every pot, and me as pulling a dove out of every hat.

Ben and I saw our roles as complementary; we each played our part in public, and as a team we'd been successful. On the home front, Congress had enacted the Dignity Deal into law.

Abroad, there was every reason to believe that the EU, the CIS, the Indian Subcontinent, and China would support a shift from the Security Council to the Dignity Council as the preeminent institution of global governance. Bringing that to pass so the world would have a compass to guide it through the twenty-first century was the paramount goal of my presidency—and my life.

But at home, the Council was the subject of intense and mounting controversy in both Senate hearings and the media. As the Dignity Council inched its way toward global acceptance I came to regard my neglect of the home front as the biggest failure of my presidency. Ben, Karen, and Marisol had tried to warn me, but I was too focused on overcoming the obstacles abroad to sense the discontent at home. If we were reelected, winning Senate ratification of the Dignity Council would be at the top of our agenda—but if we lost, it would die with our one full term in office.

All summer long our campaign director, Brad Alvarez, had been urging me to spend more time in swing states, and after the Republican Convention, which nominated Governor Charles Arden of Missouri for the presidency, Brad and Karen asked for a meeting in the Oval Office.

"We were anticipating an uptick in Governor Arden's poll numbers," Brad began, "but not a surge. He's up ten points and his lead is growing. It's my professional judgment that a lead of that size this late in the day cannot be overcome."

"Don't you expect a bounce from our convention?" I asked. It was two weeks away.

"Yes, but not ten points, and by then he'll have an even bigger lead."

"The bounce may cut into that," Karen put in hopefully, but I knew from the resignation in her voice that she also felt defeat was inevitable.

"What's the problem?" I asked.

"You are, Mr. President," Karen said. "We've had a few private polls taken that suggest we'd do better with Ben at the head of the ticket. The public sees him as a knight in shining armor for championing the Dignity Deal."

"And me?"

"Out of touch," Brad said. "Preoccupied with foreign affairs. Our opponents have revived the old slogan—'America First.' They're running an ad that aims to pin 'America Last' on you."

"This is the twenty-first century. No one's 'first.' Either we all make it, or none of us will. I thought the public had made their peace with that."

"Some of them have," Brad said, "but more of them have not."

§§§

I told Karen to cancel my appointments and went upstairs to the living quarters. Gwyneth was out for the afternoon. Marisol was visiting her mother in Boston. I thought of calling Rowan, but decided I didn't want his advice on this problem.

Like Woodrow Wilson, I'd sold the idea to the world, but not to America. Ironic, humiliating, dumb.

I imagined trying to turn things around, campaigning nonstop from that day forward till election eve, but I couldn't convince myself that it would work. You just can't dig yourself out of a hole that deep with talk. We couldn't have done it last time around, either. No speech would have beaten General Harris in 2024. It was Operation AmerRuss, with its perfect timing and fortunate outcome, that had won that election for us.

A deed—that's what I needed. Action, not talk. Nothing else could reverse our fortune.

The solution came to me in a flash. I'd been given the answer before, had even imagined it myself, but I hadn't recognized it till that moment. It was obvious.

I couldn't save the Dignity Council, but Ben could.

All I had to do was get out of the way. Step down in his favor. Do it at the convention with America watching. Pass the torch to Ben and leave the stage.

That had been my job as Ben's teammate at Princeton; it had been my role as he pushed the Dignity Deal through Congress.

This is what I'd do so he could fight for ratification of the Dignity Council.

Karen had even told me that the ticket would have a better chance with Ben at the top. I knew she was right.

I heard Gwyneth come in, and asked her to join me in the sitting room. She'd always been able to read me, and she knew immediately that something was up.

"What's the matter?" she asked.

"Remember I told you Ben would run stronger than me? Governor Arden is ten points ahead and his lead is growing. Karen and Brad are telling me the election's lost."

"You haven't begun to fight."

"That's just the problem, Gwyn. I've been fighting another battle. Voters don't see me as their champion."

"Surely they don't want Governor Arden. They can't!"

"They seem to want him more than me. But I think they still see Ben as a winner. He's always been more popular, and I think he can beat Arden."

"This is a bad idea, Adam. You can turn this thing around if we all just go out there and fight."

"It's too late, Gwyn. I've decided. I'm going to ask Ben to take over."

"No!" Gwyn shouted. "No! This is not right. You've earned another term. I want to finish the work I'm doing as first lady. You can't just walk away."

When I got up to go, Gwyneth tried to stop me. I'd never seen her so distraught. At the time, I attributed it to the loss of status she would suffer if I were no longer president.

§§§

I went back to the Oval Office and asked the switchboard to get the vice president on the line.

"What can I do for you, Mr. President?" Ben still called me by my title sometimes, and although he did it in jest, his invocation of my rank expressed a mysterious deference that had long been an aspect of our relationship.

"Come on over. I have something I want to ask you."

Ten minutes later Ben walked into the Oval Office. Like Gwyneth, he could read me. When our eyes met I knew he saw that this would be no ordinary conversation.

I got up when he came in, and we met in the center of the room.

"I can't win this race, Ben. You may be able to. If you'll serve, I'll withdraw my name and put yours in nomination for president. I'm sure the convention will do as I ask."

What happened next I count as one of the biggest shocks of my life. Ben sat down, put his head in his hands, and wept. When he spoke, I could hardly make out his words.

"I'll do anything for you, Adam. You know I'd rather be your number two, but if you want me to serve you as president, then I'll do that."

"I think you can beat Governor Arden, and then you can push the Dignity Council through Congress. That's what I want. That's how you can serve me."

"I don't deserve your trust."

I took his hand and pulled him to his feet.

"No one knows except Gwyneth. Apart from her, and Marisol and Karen, no one must know until I speak to the convention."

"I understand. I'll say nothing to anyone until you make it public knowledge."

Our conversation was concluded, but Ben hovered for a moment, as if there were more to say, before he took his leave. When I returned to the living quarters I found Gwyneth in despair.

§§§

The next morning I had an appointment with my campaign staff. Karen had asked me to review a video they were planning to use at the convention and in campaign ads to highlight the achievements of my administration.

I watched the video in my private office with bittersweet feelings, revisiting the high points of our five years in office—Operation AmerRuss, signing the Dignity Deal into law, meetings with foreign leaders, and cooperating with China to free the hostages. There was no video of sinking their ships, but there was footage of Gwyneth with the freed captives on Great Nicobar Island.

Though I'd seen it on live TV at the time and not noticed anything unusual, when I watched it again, something caught my eye. I replayed it several times until I finally zeroed in on the few seconds I'd been looking for: Gwyn looking up at Ben, and him returning her gaze.

In our twenty years together I'd learned to read what was behind the smiles, scowls, and shadows that crossed Gwyneth's face. I stared at the frame I'd paused, and a tiny voice inside me whispered, They're not just friends, they're lovers.

The image—with the words sounding in my head—cleaved my world into a before and after. Memories I'd brushed aside returned: While I was in Paris for the G-20 and Gwyneth was speaking at the UN, Ben had unaccountably left Washington for New York; I'd meant to find out why, but had never followed up.

My wife and best friend had often traveled together to faraway places in support of dignity; now I suspected there had been an additional reason. Then, when I'd asked Ben to replace me on the ballot, he'd broken down. He'd always been respectful, but on that occasion he'd crossed the line that separates humility from self-abasement. Could it be that when he said he didn't deserve my trust his shame was speaking?

I sat with all this for a while and began to doubt my senses. After all, there was no proof. It was just a look, possibly distorted by the camera, and it had occurred at a moment of euphoria. Ben and Gwyn had every right to be pleased. I'd had hunches before that had proved wrong. My gut instincts were certainly not infallible.

Yet I *knew* that look from Gwyneth. It was the gaze of love, and I had seen it at the beginning of our relationship when she looked at me. But for many years now, I'd known it only by its absence.

When I first met Gwyneth, she was working in Ben's senatorial campaign. She always glowed in his presence, but then so did everyone. I'd counted myself lucky that Ben was already married, because that opened the way to Gwyn for me. Though she'd seemed to welcome my attention, I'd never quite shaken the feeling that she was holding something back. I blamed myself, thinking it was because, deep down, I knew I'd already met the love of my life in Marisol, and Gwyn sensed it. Then, the more I thought about it, the clearer it became that Gwyneth also had met the love of hers.

§§§

I had a basketball date with Ben that afternoon, and decided to keep it. When we'd warmed up I challenged him to a game of one-on-one. The score went back and forth, my anger at his betrayal mounting each time we made physical contact. Ben didn't like to lose, and as the game went on and I stayed even with him, he got more aggressive. Not a word was spoken, but two men who've played together for decades know when a certain line has been crossed. In an attempted steal, Ben elbowed me and, catching him off balance I drove right through him, knocking him down, then slammed the ball through the hoop.

When he called "foul," I walked back to his prone body, stood over him, and put it to him: "Are you having an affair, Ben?"

He raised himself on one arm. His mouth was open as if to protest, but nothing came out.

"With my wife?" I persisted.

Ben closed his eyes and lowered his head.

I walked out, and the Secret Service drove me to the White House. Gwyneth was in the family quarters, and without changing out of my gym clothes I confronted her with what I knew—the truth.

She blanched.

As if things were being orchestrated by an omnipotent master of ceremonies, Gwyn's mobile rang. We both knew it was Ben. Before he could speak, Gwyn said, "Adam is with me."

"Ask him to come over," I said. "We have some decisions to make."

§§§

Sitting there with my wife of more than twenty years, waiting for Ben to join us, I realized I wasn't angry with her. Gwyn's infidelity didn't break my heart because of what it said about her. It broke my heart because of what it said about Ben. How could my oldest, closest friend, my ally in so many battles, have betrayed me with my wife?

Nor was Gwyneth angry with me. We were allies, partners, friends. We had been for years, and our relationship had served our common cause. I think we knew that neither of us was to blame. We were, both of us, married to someone we could not love, and in love with someone we could not marry. Passion is what it is. You have to take it when it comes and face it when it goes.

As if she were reading my thoughts, Gwyneth said, "We're not so different, you know. I've always known of your love for Marisol."

"But I've never been unfaithful to you," I said.

"Not physically, no, but emotionally?" It was a question I didn't want to face. Gwyneth answered it for both of us. "The real difference between my relationship with Ben and yours with Marisol is that we followed our hearts and you didn't."

When Ben joined me and Gwyneth, he looked broken. He couldn't raise his head to look me in the eye. I was embarrassed, and also inexplicably moved, by his obeisance. For her part, Gwyneth seemed more embarrassed by Ben's shame than by their infidelity.

Ben was shaking, as if he expected me to take up a sword and strike off his head.

Finally, he spoke, choking on the words. "Forgive me, Adam. I needed her … to carry on."

"How could you put our life's work in danger? Risk everything?"

"It's you I love, Adam, but it's Gwyneth I need. Without her I would have failed you. Now I have anyway."

I was dumbstruck. I felt my anger turn to pity.

The three of us sat in silence for a minute. Ben was the first to speak. "You can't still want me to carry on. No one need ever know about this. I'll drop off the ticket and disappear into private life."

"On the contrary, Ben. The only way to keep our dream alive is for you to run and win. You can restore your honor by being a good president."

§§§

I never quite figured out exactly why Gwyn had protested my stepping down so vehemently. Yes, it meant that her days as first lady were numbered. But would losing that title really slow her down? I believed that her role as president of Dignity Now! was all she needed to carry on. Her power no longer depended on being consort to a president. Gwyneth Lionel had become an independent force.

And Ben? Would he be able to finish what we'd started? While he was not without ambition, I'd never felt he was envious—not at Princeton, not of my speakership, and not in the White House. Ben was the perfect Number Two. He was actually more able than anyone he'd ever served—in all but one respect.

Ben was a doer, not a dreamer. He needed someone else to supply the vision. But he had no peer when it came to making dreams come true. He'd demonstrated it in winning support for the Dignity Deal. If anyone could persuade the Senate to ratify our participation in the Dignity Council, it would be Ben. He'd do it, not to bring glory to himself but to make amends to me.

In the days that followed, without going into the details, I let Marisol know what had happened. The empathy in her face told me that she understood, and would never say I told you so. As Marisol and I went over my speech declining the nomination and endorsing Ben, the reality sank in. We would both be leaving the White House. Where would we go? What did this mean for us?

For the first time since Paris, I had an answer. We were on the sofa in my private office. I put my arm around her shoulder and drew her to my side. Sobbing softly, she leaned into my embrace.

§§§

It has long been the custom for the president-elect and his wife to come to the White House and join the president and first lady for the ride down Pennsylvania Avenue to the Capitol. There, on the western rotunda, at noon on January 20th, power passes from the outgoing to the incoming president.

Ellie waited in the limousine while Ben was ushered into the White House to fetch Gwyn and me. It was the first time the three of us had been together since the infidelity had been disclosed, and it would mark the end of the partnerships that had given meaning to our lives.

Ben promised me to finish what we'd started. On my suggestion, he'd taken Defense Secretary Chilton as his running mate, and her popularity with women voters may well have provided the ticket with the margin of victory. We both knew that the battle Ben and Hazel were taking on would be titanic, and that it might well run beyond four years.

To those who knew Ben and Gwyneth, it soon became obvious that their relationship had changed. Gone was their easy familiarity; in its place was professional formality. Whether the reason was a change of heart, or the knowledge that their secret was no longer theirs, could not be determined.

In the months since the day of reckoning, my anger and disappointment had morphed into a fond regard for my two fellow warriors. I would not know their like again. Partnerships like ours are even rarer than love.

At noon, Ben would take over. At precisely the same moment, Gwyneth would lose her role as first lady, and Ellie would assume it. I wondered how it would go for the new first couple. There's a rhythm to history, and we had ridden a wave. Would the quest retain its savor until the dragons were slain? For everyone's sake, I hoped so.

As the limousine reached the Capitol and we prepared to get out, Ben surprised me.

"You're still eligible for a second term, Mr. President. If you should ever feel called to return, I'd be honored to serve you."

§§§

After Ben's Inaugural address we went our separate ways. Ben, Ellie, and Galia rode together to the White House in the presidential limousine. Gwyneth left for her new home on Fifth Avenue in Manhattan. I was flown in Air Force One to the Hartford-Springfield airport, then driven to the Ellway family cabin in the Berkshires.

We made no public announcement of Gwyneth's and my separation. Better, we agreed, to let it gradually dawn on the public that we were living apart.

Although Inauguration Day brought a kind of deliverance, it was the saddest day of my life. Ben, Gwyn, and I had worked together for a quarter-century. My history with Ben went back to our teens. A man never had a more stalwart ally, yet this same man had betrayed me. I wondered if, in some mysterious way, the affair with Gwyneth had been the price of his devotion to me.

Like my mother and father, Ben and Gwyneth had defied a taboo and followed their hearts. Marisol would have too. What had stopped me?

There'd been something I had to do first. Before I could allow myself to love, I had to find dignity. And, having found it, I had to share it. Now that my work was done, I was free.

EPILOGUE

April 28, 2029

It was late. Almost dark. Adam turned the last page of the manuscript.

Swiveling in place to return his feet to the floor, he cleared some space beside him on the sofa.

"I think I'd better toss this in the fire," he called out.

Marisol came into the room carrying a tray with a teapot and two cups. She sat down beside him, the tray on her lap.

"Couldn't you just keep it under wraps till we're all gone?"

"I can't imagine a time when the back story would serve the front story. But working it out, writing it down, has served me."

"How so?"

"I know now what Easter meant by the holiness of the heart's affections, what you've been saying all along."

Adam stood up, took the tray from Marisol's lap, and set it down on the end table. Then he drew his sister to her feet and together they went to the window to look out upon Lake Baikal from their cottage on its western shore.

CODA: ROWANBERRIES

Adam and Marisol had spent their first winter in the cabin in the Berkshires that Rowan called Nobodyland. But tourists at their gate, and the stares of strangers in town, made them want to withdraw even further from the world. A word to Vice President Hazel Chilton was all it took. True to his word, Anatoly Kostikov put a cottage on Lake Baikal at Adam's disposal for as long as he wanted it. There, Adam and his sister spent their first free summer under the brightest stars on Earth.

Walking along the shore, sailing on the lake, gathering mushrooms and berries, and shopping in the village nearby, they felt a happiness they hadn't known since their blissful Parisian holiday. Marisol's Russian gained the respect of the locals, enough so that they shielded their famous guests from the few journalists who came in search of a story.

It was in their Siberian hideaway that Adam finished his journal. Apart from Marisol and Karen, he showed it to no one. Karen put her response in the form of a quote from the Roman poet Horace. Two thousand years ago, Horace advised writers to put their "parchments in the cupboard, and let them be quiet till the ninth year. What you have not published you will be able to destroy. The word once uncaged never comes home again."

This advice had the paradoxical effect of staying Adam's impulse to toss the journal on the fire. Let it sit in the cupboard for nine years where it could do no harm and, who knows, maybe, decades hence, he would find a use for some of it.

That fall, just as the snows began and Adam and Marisol were wondering if they could endure the hardships of a Siberian winter, Easter called to say that the flu Rowan had been fighting had taken a turn for the worse. Being almost ninety-three, the doctor had warned her, his situation was precarious.

They left immediately and reached Washington on the twenty-sixth of October. Rowan died two days later, but not before he smiled upon his children.

In what was to be their last conversation, he shared a concern and a vision with the two of them.

"There will be setbacks. Democracy took centuries to develop, and so will dignitarian governance. But in time it will become obvious that peace and justice cannot endure apart from dignity for all."

During his stint in Beijing, Rowan had gotten to know Galia.

"She has all the virtues of her father, and none of his vices," he said of her. "She's getting an insider's knowledge of politics that will complement the vision she carries in her heart. Don't be surprised if it falls to Galia to realize what you and her father have begun."

"What *you* began," Adam said, but Rowan would have none of it. "Philosophy is easy," he countered. "Politics is hard. In you, Adam, the two were mixed in just the right proportions."

Rowan was a man of second acts, and Adam asked if he saw one for him and Marisol. Rowan reminded them that he'd had his best ideas late in life, and suggested that it might be like that for them. "If you take your dreams seriously, they will bring you a second life as full as your first. But you must be willing to be a nobody."

"That's what I am now," Adam said.

"Me too," added Marisol.

"Then, there's a pair of you, don't tell. In Nobodyland, rules are made to be broken. It's the only place I ever came up with anything new. I'll be heading that way myself, any day now."

When Adam reported Rowan's remark to Easter she said that Rowan had never been able to resist a mordant quip. That day was his last.

In the forest near their Siberian hideaway were trees with hard crimson berries that the natives identified as rowan trees. Marisol had brought a handful of rowanberries home with her, and a few days after Rowan died, Easter, Adam, and Marisol planted them in the fertile soil of Nobodyland.

ACKNOWLEDGEMENTS

We are all products of the assistance we can accept.
– I. A. Richards

Among the many who left their mark on this work are Chuck Blitz, Jennifer Bloomfield, Noah Brand, Robert Cabot, Napier Collyns, Elisa Cooper, Ina Cooper, Doris Cross, Lisa Davis, Emma Edwards, Jacob Freeze, Adam Fuller, John Fuller, Willmine Fuller, Peter Funkhouser, Pamela Gerloff, Lizbeth Hasse, Charlotte Hill, John Hobbs, David Hoffman, Janet Hooker-Haring, Antonella Iannarino, Lou Judson, Coleen Judson, Shaun Kadlec, Janet Kastelic, David Landau, Evelyn Messinger, David Nelson, John O'Neil, Jennifer Prost, Thomas Purvis, Peter Putnam, Catherine de Saint Phalle, Joan Stepp Smith, John Steiner, Rosemary Sutcliffe, Justine Toms, Philip Turner, Catherine Webb, John A. Wheeler, Mary Willis, and Mike Wollenberg.

It's time to give up the myth of the solitary author. Rather, authors are scavengers, working with a far-flung group of largely unrecognized "co-authors." The better we understand creativity, the clearer it becomes that every work of art, no matter how unassisted it may seem, is in fact a co-creation. It is in recognition of its inherently collaborative nature that I acknowledge my fellow co-creators, named and unnamed, for their indispensable contributions to this work.

For her unflagging moral and editorial support throughout the long gestation period of this book, and for providing its title, I dedicate *The Rowan Tree* to my wife Claire Sheridan.

ABOUT THE AUTHOR

Robert Fuller is a physicist, a former president of Oberlin College, and a leader of the dignity movement to overcome *rankism*. He has consulted with Indira Gandhi, met with Jimmy Carter regarding the president's Commission on World Hunger, worked in the USSR to defuse the Cold War, and keynoted a *Dignity for All* conference hosted by the president of Bangladesh. Fuller's books on dignity and rankism have been published in India, Bangladesh, Korea, and China, featured in the *New York Times*, the *Oprah Magazine*, the *Boston Globe*, in TED talks, on *NPR* and the *BBC*. He has four children and lives in Berkeley, California, with his wife Claire Sheridan. **The Rowan Tree** is his first novel.

Other Books by Robert W. Fuller

Mathematics of Classical and Quantum Physics
(with Frederick W. Byron, Jr.)

Somebodies and Nobodies: Overcoming the Abuse of Rank

All Rise: Somebodies, Nobodies, and the Politics of Dignity

Dignity for All: How to Create a World Without Rankism
(with Pamela A. Gerloff)

Religion and Science: A Beautiful Friendship?

Genomes, Menomes, Wenomes: Neuroscience and Human Dignity

Belonging: A Memoir

The Wisdom of Science

The Theory of Everybody

15866608R00297

Printed in Great Britain
by Amazon